PENGUIN BOOKS

THE MITFORD BEDSIDE COMPANION

Jan Karon is the author of nine Mitford novels, *At Home in Mitford;
A Light in the Window; These High, Green Hills; Out to Canaan; A
New Song; A Common Life; In This Mountain; Shepherds Abiding;*
and *Light From Heaven,* all available from Penguin. She is also the
author of *The Mitford Bedside Companion; Jan Karon's Mitford Cook-
book and Kitchen Reader; A Continual Feast: Words of Comfort and
Celebration, Collected by Father Tim; Patches of Godlight: Father Tim's
Favorite Quotes; The Mitford Snowmen: A Christmas Story; Esther's
Gift;* and *The Trellis and the Seed.* Her children's books include *Miss
Fannie's Hat; Jeremy: The Tale of an Honest Bunny;* and *Violet Comes
to Stay.* The first Father Tim novel, *Home to Holly Springs,* is available
from Viking.

Brenda Furman is Jan's younger sister and the perfect person to shape
a volume that contains the very cream of nine bestselling novels.

www.mitfordbooks.com

Join the Mitford community online to share news,
recipes, birthday greetings, and more, and to receive
notes from Jan and special offers.

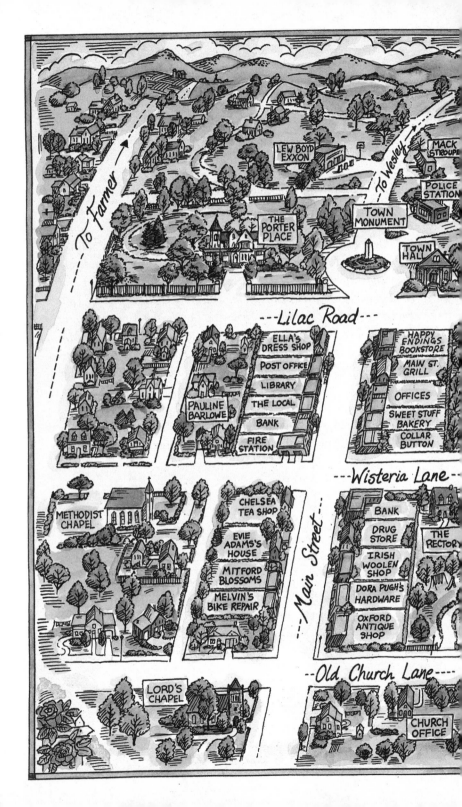

The
Mitford
Bedside Companion

JAN KARON

New Essays, Family Photographs,
Favorite Mitford Scenes,
and Much More

Edited by Brenda Furman

PENGUIN BOOKS

PENGUIN BOOKS
Published by the Penguin Group
Penguin Group (USA) Inc., 375 Hudson Street, New York, New York 10014, U.S.A.
Penguin Group (Canada), 90 Eglinton Avenue East, Suite 700, Toronto,
Ontario, Canada M4P 2Y3 (a division of Pearson Penguin Canada Inc.)
Penguin Books Ltd, 80 Strand, London WC2R 0RL, England
Penguin Ireland, 25 St Stephen's Green, Dublin 2, Ireland (a division of Penguin Books Ltd)
Penguin Group (Australia), 250 Camberwell Road, Camberwell,
Victoria 3124, Australia (a division of Pearson Australia Group Pty Ltd)
Penguin Books India Pvt Ltd, 11 Community Centre,
Panchsheel Park, New Delhi – 110 017, India
Penguin Group (NZ), 67 Apollo Drive, Rosedale, North Shore 0632,
New Zealand (a division of Pearson New Zealand Ltd)
Penguin Books (South Africa) (Pty) Ltd, 24 Sturdee Avenue,
Rosebank, Johannesburg 2196, South Africa

Penguin Books Ltd, Registered Offices: 80 Strand, London WC2R 0RL, England

First published in the United States of America by Viking Penguin,
a member of Penguin Group (USA) Inc. 2006
Published in Penguin Books 2007

1   3   5   7   9   10   8   6   4   2

PUBLISHER'S NOTE
Some of the selections in this book are works of fiction. Names, characters, places, and incidents
either are the product of the author's imagination or are used fictitiously, and any resemblance to
actual persons, living or dead, business establishments, events, or locales is entirely coincidental.

ISBN 0-670-03785-0 (hc.)
ISBN 978-0-14-311241-9 (pbk.)
CIP data available

Printed in the United States of America
Set in Adobe Garamond   Designed by Francesca Belanger

Dedicated to my
Gentle Readers

—

May you spend
happy hours
in
Mitford

—

Jan Karon

Acknowledgments

Hats off to my sister, Brenda Furman, the dedicated, hardworking editor of this book, and creator of the entertaining crossword puzzle in these pages.

Your editor, left; your author, right.
From my family to yours.

About My Sister, the Editor

When my sister, Brenda, was born at home in an upstairs bedroom, I remember hearing her first cry.

Who knew that a wonderful editor had just made her entrance into the world?

As I neared the end of the Mitford series, I noodled my noggin, as Uncle Billy would say, about finding someone to tackle the absolutely whopping job of pulling together a bedside companion that would give you, I hoped, the very cream of the Mitford novels.

It would require, first of all, a reader who relished the printed word, and who knew the Mitford novels intimately. Someone who knew Esther Bolick from Esther Cunningham, and Bill Watson from Bill Sprouse. It needed someone with a sense of humor, and the common sense to know when a scene out of context should begin—and end. It also needed something more than text and a few drawings, it needed . . . maybe lots of trivia? Maybe even a crossword puzzle? *Yes!*

In the end, it would be a mammoth task, to be undertaken only by one who'd do far more than methodically excerpt text, and one who would care about the story lines, the characters, and the spirit of the work. That person would also need a great work ethic, as plowing through a million-and-a half words is no day at the beach.

I made a few inquiries. All led nowhere.

Then here's what happened.

As I had spoken to God about this, He did what He so often does: He spoke back. To my heart, of course, and in a way I couldn't dismiss.

The one for the job was my sister.

Hallelujah!

Brenda and I worked together on the book you now hold in your hands for more than two years. Or was it three?

I found her sensitivity in choosing the excerpts to be absolutely . . . well, divine. And her amazing skill at constructing a crossword puzzle simply floored me.

So, here it is, gentle readers.

From my family to yours.

May you laugh. May you cry. May your noggin be noodled. May your memory of favorite scenes and characters be refreshed. And most of all, may your spirits be lifted.

And next time you need a big task accomplished, who knows? The one for the job might be right in your own family.

> *Children of the same family, the same blood, with the same first associations and habits, have some means of enjoyment in their power, which no subsequent connections can supply. . . .*
>
> —Jane Austen, *Mansfield Park*

About My Sister, the Author

You keep your past by having sisters. As you get older, they're the only ones who don't get bored if you talk about your memories.

—Deborah Moggach

Actually, it's not *if* Jan and I talk about our memories, it's *when*.

Nearly every time my sister and I chat, we share—and compare—our memories, which often include these:

For at least two years, Jan schooled me at home. My lessons began when she was in first grade, and continued until I went off to first grade. Perhaps because Jan had been so thorough in her teaching, I remained in first grade for just six weeks. After all, I knew my multiplication tables forward and backward, and could rattle them off faster than anyone could understand.

It's good to have a big sister who teaches you. As a matter of fact, by the time I graduated from high school, I had been a student for fourteen years!

When we were four and six, Jan came up with a get-rich-quick scheme. First, we gathered up all the old magazines (some were *really* old) in our house, and stacked them in our little red wagon. Piled in the wagon were issues of *Life, Look, Collier's,* and *Ladies' Home Journal.* Jan loved magazines and decided the entire batch was really worth something, like maybe a quarter. I never knew how she arrived at that price.

Next, we had to have a marketing strategy. After some thought, I believe it was Jan who came up with the idea that our nearest neighbor (just under half a mile) would probably *love* to have these magazines. We began our journey up the dirt road (it wasn't paved until years later), taking turns pulling the wagon. Sometimes Jan would pull and I would push and vice-versa. We made it to the neighbor's driveway, which looked awfully long to me. It was just about dusk and the house was dark. Since my sister was the CEO of our newly formed company, she decided I would be the one to take the wagon down that long driveway to the house with no lights on. At four years of age, you just don't argue with the boss.

I am excited to tell you that my first big sales job was a complete success. I came back up that driveway (which seemed a lot shorter than before) with an empty wagon and a big, fat quarter in my hand. We were very pleased with ourselves. I think Jan may have been even more pleased, as she pulled me most of the way home in the wagon.

When I was three years old, Mother presented Jan and me with a beautiful baby brother, Barry Dean. When I was six, she completed the circle with another wonderful brother, Philip Randolph, whom we call Randy. Now *I* was a big sister, reveling in the best of both worlds.

I will never forget the day Jan called and asked if I would edit *The Mitford Bedside Companion*. When she reeled off the list of things to be accomplished, I thought the driveway, if you will, looked awfully long. But now that the deed is done, I confess that the three years it took to create these pages has been a wonderful journey with my sister, and yet another way that we are "keeping our past."

May you spend many happy hours in Mitford, just as I have so gladly done.

Introduction:
Everything but the Kitchen Sink

I'm often asked if it was hard to leave Mitford when I wrote the ninth, and final, novel, *Light from Heaven*.

The truth is, not really. I had told the story of that small mountain town as completely as I knew how, and there was absolutely nothing more to say. Nor did I have any inspiration to do what many readers have suggested, which was to continue the series with the lives of Dooley and Lace. (Trust me, books written without inspiration are no books at all.)

However, it's also true that I will miss the characters now and then.

For more than a decade, they were like family to me. Indeed, I carried an entire township around in my head, some of them speaking simultaneously (think about *that*) as they told me their stories. It was enough to make your author forget her own name on occasion, or, when out and about, the name of an old friend or acquaintance. A handful of characters assembled in a story is one thing; more than seven hundred characters assembled in nine novels—and one head—is quite another.

Of course, I reasoned, if I really needed a visit to Mitford, I could always sit down and thumb through the books. But wouldn't it be nice to have the thumbing, as it were, done *for* me—and for my readers?

Miss Sadie, whom I still miss, would be quite alive at the wonderful wedding reception at Fernbank, and Uncle Billy would be telling the joke about the census taker. We could be a fly on the wall all over again as Father Tim tells Dooley about sex, and we could revisit the most fun I ever had in Mitford, which was at the big town festival, with the llamas batting their long eyelashes and the children sitting on the knee of the statue of Willard Porter and the little ragwing airplanes dipping and rolling above the crowd on the lawn. . . .

Thus, this book.

Here you'll find what I hope are some of your favorite scenes, all the Uncle Billy jokes, all the major town events, Father Tim's prayers and table blessings, loads of Scripture verses, which, themselves, have played important parts in the books, the (nearly) full cast of characters, varieties of mountain weather, a bushel of essays by yours truly, a peck of my family photographs, the recipe for that darned Orange Marmalade Cake, trivia for the whole family, an original Mitford crossword puzzle— indeed, everything but the kitchen sink. (In a few places we've edited some of the longer scenes a bit—otherwise the book might take a crane to lift it!)

Archibald Rutledge said this:

"I am absolutely unshaken in my faith that God created us, loves us, and wants us not only to be good but to be happy."

In these pages, I pray you will find a portion of happiness, however infinitesimal. And speaking of happiness, I would leave us with this thought, penned by a wise, albeit unknown writer:

"In daily life we must see that it is not happiness that makes us grateful, but gratefulness that makes us happy."

Contents

"I Know the Plans I Have for You"

❧

If you think of life as a journey, then in 1988, one might say I stood at a great crossroads. Though yearning to be an author since the age of ten, I had instead mired myself quite deeply in advertising, where I worked as a writer for more (much more, actually) than three decades.

Though I desperately wanted out of a notoriously unkind business and into the gentler realm of book writing, I couldn't find the courage to walk away from certain income. What if I failed at writing a book? What if a leap into the unknown ended with dashing myself on the rocks below? And how did one write a book, anyway? I simply couldn't find what Sir Walter Scott called "the soul to dare."

I began to pray about all this, not randomly or when I happened to think of it, but persistently. What do you want me to do, Lord? And how am I to accomplish it?

After two years of focused prayer, and using my journal as a sounding board, God spoke to my heart and said, *Go. And I will go with you.*

I was nearly fifty years old when this long-awaited but oddly terrifying answer came. It was springtime, and every azalea and dogwood was abloom in my lovely old neighborhood. I put a For Sale sign in the yard of my small cottage, and a day and a half later, I was signing a contract for an amount that pleased me very much.

I bought a little house near my brother and his family in the mountain village of Blowing Rock, North Carolina. I traded my Mercedes sedan for a Jeep. I cut my living expenses by roughly half, and having never used anything more complicated than a typewriter, bought a secondhand computer, which, by the grace of God, I learned to use.

All this accomplished, I sat down with breathless expectation to write my first book.

That's when I found I had nothing to say.

Nothing.

Writer's Dream Turns to Nightmare.

Soon, God spoke to my heart again. *Don't look back* was the message I strongly perceived. *I am with you.*

If God is with us, who or what can be against us?

I continued to pray and hope and believe. I clung to quite a few promises of Scripture, not the least of which is found in Jeremiah 29:11.

"I know the plans I have for you," says the Lord. "They are plans for good and not for disaster, to give you a future and a hope."

God had plans for me.

They were plans for good.

And, I had a future and a hope.

If taken seriously, as I took this Scripture passage then, and take it today, this is thrilling news.

I soldiered on.

Though I was freelancing with national ad agencies, the country had entered into a deep recession, and sometimes I earned no money at all. I wondered whether I might lose my little house, which had cost scarcely more than a car I recently saw in a showroom. Yet, worse than the fear of losing my house was the fear of losing face. I had come to the mountains to write books, and I had failed.

Then, lying in bed one night, I had an odd and surprising mental image.

It was of a man walking down a village street. That, and nothing more.

I examined this figment of my restless imagination.

The man, I could see by his collar, was a priest. He was short of stature, balding, and a dash overweight. He had a positive, upbeat stride. How did he live his life? What were his thoughts and aspirations? Who was this obviously ordinary man and what did he mean to me, if anything?

I got up and sat at my desk for a long time, and then began to write.

"He left the coffee-scented warmth of the Main Street Grill and stood for a moment under the green awning.

"The honest cold of an early mountain spring stung him sharply. . . ."

I wrote on for several days, though absolutely nothing of any consequence was happening with this character. Then, days turned into weeks, and soon, I had a chapter or two. But a chapter or two of what?

I took it to the editor of the *Blowing Rocket,* Jerry Burns, who is as close to literati as we have in the little town of Blowing Rock. I remember how uncomfortable I was, asking someone to read a work that even I couldn't define or categorize.

"What do you think I have here?" I asked, afraid of the answer.

"I don't know," he said.

"Ah."

"But I like it. Why don't we run it in the paper?"

Clearly, small-town newspaper editors are desperate men.

Once a week, my story occupied a half-page of the little newspaper that, at the time, sold for ten cents a copy. Without meaning to at all, I became a bona fide columnist with a weekly deadline and the sole compensation of a newspaper, hot off the press, every Thursday.

As I wrote the installments, I continued to keep a journal. Unfortunately, someone posing as a computer expert lost it, along with an entire fiction file, but that's another story.

Often, I wanted to give up writing what I called "The Mitford Years." But I couldn't give up. I had an agreement to help fill space in our local newspaper! Better still, I was eager to know what was happening in the life of a character who was the bookish, unmarried, sixtysomething Episcopal priest Father Tim.

In truth, a lot was happening. A dog the size of a sofa, a thrown-away boy, and a good-looking neighbor moved into this earnest man's quiet life, and suddenly, as they say in the film business, "the story had legs." (So did his neighbor, by the way.)

When I finished writing this story, I was amazed to find I had written far more than two years' worth of "columns." I had, in fact, written a book.

Two more years, great anguish, and considerable privation passed before *At Home in Mitford* was sold. And you know the rest.

I tell you all that in order to assure you of this:

God has plans for you.

His plans are for good.

And, if you trust Him, you have both a future and a hope.

How do I know this to be utterly and absolutely true?

Because I have lived it.

And I am living it still.

To God be the glory, great things He hath done. And will continue to do, if only we trust Him.

"For I know the plans I have for you," says the Lord. "They are plans for good and not for disaster, to give you a future and a hope. In those days when you pray, I will listen. If you look for me in earnest, you will find me when you seek me."

—Jeremiah 29:11-13, New Living Translation,
Tyndale House Publishers

A Little World
of Our Own:
The Town of Mitford

*L*ong *after the* fictitious small town of Mitford was conceived, and a couple of the novels were written, I came upon a lovely little book called *Our Village*.

Written by Mary Russell Mitford, an Englishwoman, and published in 1839 by Cassell and Company, Ltd., it was a tender tribute to the English village and its people. Indeed, it was an attempt to preserve something precious; to so document a way of life that it might remain forever our own.

In the opening pages, Miss Russell pens much of my thinking when I created Mitford, North Carolina.

Of all situations for a constant residence, that which appears to me most delightful is a little village . . . with inhabitants whose faces are as familiar to us as the flowers in our garden; a little world of our own, close-packed and insulated like ants in an ant-hill, or bees in a hive, or sheep in a fold, or nuns in a convent, or sailors in a ship; where we know every one, are known to every one, interested in every one and authorized to hope that every one feels an interest in us.

How pleasant it is to slide into these true-hearted feelings from the kindly and unconscious influence of habit and to learn to know and to love the people about us, with all their peculiarities, just as we learn to know and to love the nooks and turns of the shady lanes and sunny commons that we pass every day.

. . . nothing is so delightful as to sit down in a country village in one of Miss Austen's delicious novels, quite sure before we leave it to become intimate with every spot and every person it contains.*

Over the years, you've become intimate with nearly every spot and person contained in Mitford. In your lively imagination, the faces of Uncle Billy and Miss Rose, George Gaynor, Hope Winchester, Miss Sadie and Louella, Mule Skinner, Dooley, Lace, Esther Bolick are all as familiar to you as the flowers in your garden.

In truth, Mitford has done what I hoped it might do. According to your many letters, it has become a little world, and an extended family, all your own.

As I go on to write of other worlds, my fondest wish is that Mitford won't be allowed to collect dust on your shelves. Just as we visit loved ones again and again, so you may go again and again to Mitford.

Sometimes for refreshment. Often for peace. And always for hope.

THE PAUSE THAT REFRESHES

THE VILLAGE OF MITFORD was set snugly into what would be called, in the west, a hanging valley. That is, the mountains rose steeply on either side, and then sloped into a hollow between the ridges, rather like a cake that falls in the middle from too much opening of the oven door.

According to a walking parishioner of Lord's Chapel, Mitford's business district was precisely 342 paces from one end to the other.

At the north end, Main Street climbed a slight incline, and circled a town green that was bordered by a hedge of hemlocks and anchored in the center by a World War II memorial. The green also contained four benches facing the memorial and, in the spring, a showy bed of pansies, which one faction claimed was the official town flower.

*Here's the information from inside my book: Mary Russell Mitford, *Our Village,* published by Cassell and Company, Ltd., London, 1839. I don't think it's currently in print, but I know it's available from used-book booksellers.

Directly to the left of the green was the town hall, and next to that, the First Baptist Church. Set into the center of its own display of shrubs and flowers on the front bank was a wayside pulpit permanently bearing the Scripture verse John 3:16, which the members long ago had agreed was the pivotal message of their faith.

To the right of the green, facing Lilac Road, was the once-imposing home of Miss Rose and Uncle Billy Watson, whose overgrown yard currently contained two chrome dinette chairs that they used while watching traffic circle the monument.

Visitors who walked the two-block stretch of the main business district were always surprised to find the shops spaced so far apart, owing to garden plots that flourished between the buildings. In the loamy, neatly edged beds were wooden signs:

Garden Courtesy of Joe's Barber Shop, Upstairs to Right

Take Time to Smell the Roses, Courtesy Oxford Antiques

A Reader's Garden, Courtesy Happy Endings Bookstore

"Mitford," observed a travel feature by a prominent newspaper, "is a village delightfully out of step with contemporary America. Here, where streets are named for flowers, and villagers can seek the shade of a dozen fragrant rose arbors, spring finds most of the citizenry, including merchants, making gardens.

". . . and while Mitford's turn-of-the-century charm and beauty attract visitors like bees to honeysuckle, the town makes a conscious effort to discourage serious tourism.

"'We want people to come and visit,' says Mayor Esther Cunningham, 'but we're not real interested in having them stick around. The college town of Wesley, just fifteen miles away, is perfect for that. They've got the inns and guesthouses and all. Mitford would simply like to be the pause that refreshes.'"

Going south on Main Street to Wisteria Lane were the post office, the library, a bank, the bookstore, Winnie Ivey's Sweet Stuff Bakery, and a new shop for men's furnishings.

There was also a grocery store, so well-known for its fresh poultry and produce from local sources that most people simply called it The Local. For thirty-six years, The Local had provided chickens, rabbits, sausage, hams, butter, cakes, pies, free-range eggs, jams, and jellies from a farming community in the valley, along with vegetables and berries in season. In summer, produce bins on the sidewalk under the green awnings were filled each day with Silver Queen corn in the shuck. And in July, pails of fat blackberries were displayed in the cooler case.

To the left of Main Street, Wisteria Lane meandered past the Episcopal rectory, whose back door looked upon the green seclusion of Baxter Park, and then climbed the hill to the Presbyterians.

To the right of Main, Wisteria led only to Wesley Chapel, a tiny Methodist church that stood along the creek bank in a grove of pink laurel and was known for the sweetness of its pealing bells.

The second and only other business block of Main Street was lined with a hardware store, a tea shop, a florist, an Irish woolen shop, and an antique shop, with gardens in between.

Next, Main was crossed by Old Church Lane, rising steeply on the left to Church Hill Drive, where the ruined foundation of Mitford's first Episcopal church stood in the tall grass of the upland meadows near Miss Sadie Baxter's Fernbank.

At the opposite end of the lane was Lord's Chapel, which stood between two vacant lots. After passing the church, which was noted for its fine Norman tower and showy gardens, the lane narrowed to a few comfortable houses on the bank of a rushing stream, where Indian pipes were said to grow in profusion.

As the streets and lanes gave way to countryside and sloped toward the deeper valley, the rolling farmland began. Here, pastures were stocked with Herefords and Guernseys; lakes were filled with trout and brim; barnyards succored chattering guineas. And everywhere, in town or out, was the rich, black loam that made the earthworm's toil one of unending satisfaction.

At Home in Mitford, Ch. 1

THE TOWN MERCHANTS

It occurs to me that a town isn't a town without its merchants. Indeed they, as much as anyone or anything, give a community its unique persona.

If you're new to the series, here's a small handful of Main Street businesses that will help you feel more at home in Mitford.

The Local
AVIS PACKARD, PROPRIETOR

IN THE LITTLE village of less than a thousand, everyone's dinner—party or otherwise—began at The Local, unless they wanted to make the fifteen-mile drive to Food Value. Of course, they could go out on the highway to Cloer's Market, but Hattie Cloer was so well-known for telling customers her aches and pains that hardly anyone ever did that.

Avis Packard once said that Hattie Cloer had sent more business to The Local than any advertising he'd ever run in the paper.

One thing Father Tim liked about Avis Packard was the way he got excited about his groceries. He could rhapsodize about the first fresh strawberries from the valley in a way that made him a veritable Wordsworth of garden fare. "We got a special today on tenderloin that's so true to the meanin' of th' name, you can cut it with a fork."

At Home in Mitford, Ch. 4

Main Street Grill
PERCY AND VELMA MOSELY, PROPRIETORS

AS MULE SKINNER puts it, "Percy's daddy opened it fifty-two years ago. It's a dadgum historic landmark."
A Light in the Window, Ch. 12

"DID YOU SEE IT?" asked Percy.

"See what?"

"Th' banner."

"Aha! Got it up, did you?"

Percy looked grim. "Went up this mornin' at ten o'clock. Caused a stir."

"It's hard to see a banner when it's on an awning over your head. I'll step across the street and take a look."

"They left a letter out of th' dadgum thing."

"You don't mean it."

"But they knocked fifty bucks off th' price."

"The least they could do."

"I started to tell 'em to jus' shove th' whole business, but . . ." Percy shrugged, despondent.

"Go ahead and make me a tuna melt. I've got some leeway in my diet today. Be right back."

He jaywalked toward the other side of the street, barely dodging Esther Bolick in her husband's pickup truck. Esther screeched to a halt and leaned out the window. "I hear th' mayor leaked the news to Miss Sadie."

"We're forging ahead."

"I'm not doing orange marmalade," said Esther. "I'm doing peanut butter. Three layers, with jelly in between. Apple or grape?"

"Grape!"

"For gosh sake, get out of the street before somebody nails you," she said, roaring off.

Safely on the other side, he turned and peered at the banner over Percy's awning.

Eat Here Once, And You'll Be Regular

He guffawed, slapping his leg.

But whoa. He couldn't stand here laughing. What if Percy looked out the window and saw him?

He turned his back to the Grill as if he were examining the brickwork in the post office, and hooted. The postmaster stuck his head out the door and pointed to the banner, grinning. "I've also known it to be otherwise," he reported.

He trotted across the street. "Percy," he said, soberly, "I'd give the banner company their fifty dollars back."

"What do you mean?"

"I mean that banner is going to be the talk of the town."

Percy brightened. "You think so?"

"That's what advertising is all about, isn't it?"

"Well . . ." said Percy.

"Trust me on this," said the rector.

These High, Green Hills, Ch. 13

"I GOT TO do somethin' to rake in business."

Percy slid into the booth, looking. . . . Father Tim pondered what Percy was looking. . . . Percy was looking old, that's what; about like the rest of the crowd in the rear booth. He sucked up his double chin.

"Maybe I ought t' mess around with th' menu," said Percy, "an' come up with a special I could run th' same day ever' week."

"Gizzards!" said Mule.

"What about gizzards?"

"I've told you for years that gizzards is th' answer to linin' your pockets."

"Don't talk to me about gizzards, dadgummit! They're in th' same category as what goes over th' fence last. You'll never see me sellin' gizzards."

"To make it in th' restaurant business," said Mule, "you got to set your personal preferences aside. Gizzards are a big draw."

"He's right," said J.C. "You can sell gizzards in this town. This is a gizzard kind of town."

"*Oddly, it is not real cooks who insist that the finest ingredients are necessary to produce a delicious something. . . . Real cooks take stale bread and aging onions and make you happy.*"

—Susan Wiegand, *Cooking as Courtship*

"*Cooking is like love. It should be entered into with abandon or not at all.*"

—Harriet Van Horne

Mule swigged his coffee. "All you got to do is put out a sign and see what happens."

Percy looked skeptical. "What kind of sign?"

"Just a plain, ordinary sign. Write it up yourself an' put it in th' window, no big deal."

"When me an' Velma retire at th' end of th' year, I want to go out in th' black, maybe send 'er to Washington to see th' cherry blossoms, she's never seen th' cherry blossoms."

"That's what gizzards are about," said Mule.

"What d'you mean?"

"Gizzards'll get some cash flow in this place."

"Seem like chicken livers would draw a better crowd," said Percy.

"Livers tie up too much capital." J.C. was hammering down on country ham, eggs over easy, and a side of yogurt. "Too much cost involved with livers. You want to go where the investment's low and the profit's high."

Mule looked at J.C. with some admiration. "You been readin' th' *Wall Street Journal* again."

"What would I put on th' sign?" asked Percy.

"Here's what I'd put," said Mule. "*Gizzards Today.*"

"That's it? *Gizzards Today?*"

"That says it all right there. Like you say, run your gizzard special once a week, maybe on . . ." Mule drummed his fingers on the table, thinking. "Let's see . . ."

"Tuesday!" said J.C. "Tuesday would be good for gizzards. You wouldn't want to start out on Monday with gizzards, that'd be too early in th' week. And Wednesday you'd want something . . ."

"More upbeat," said Mule.

Father Tim buttered the last of his toast. "Right!"

"Wednesday could be your lasagna day," said J.C. "I'd pay good money for some lasagna in this town."

There was a long, pondering silence, broken only by a belch. Everyone looked at Mule. "'Scuse me," he said.

"Do y'all eat gizzards?" Percy inquired of the table.

"Not in this lifetime," said J.C.

"No way," said Mule.

"I pass," said Father Tim. "I ate a gizzard in first grade, that was enough for me."

Percy frowned. "I don't get it. You're some of my best reg'lars—why should I go to sellin' somethin' y'all won't eat?"

"We're a different demographic," said J.C.

"Oh," said Percy. "So how many gizzards would go in a servin,' do you think?"

"How many chicken tenders d'you put in a serving?"

"Six," said Percy. "Which is one too many for th' price."

"So, OK, as gizzards are way less meat than tenders, I'd offer fifteen, sixteen gizzards, minimum."

J.C. sopped his egg yolk with a microwave biscuit. "Be sure you batter 'em good, fry 'em crisp, an' serve with a side of dippin' sauce."

Percy looked sober for a moment, then suddenly brightened. "Fifteen gizzards, two bucks. What d'you think?"

"I think Velma's going to D.C.," said Father Tim.

A brief silence was filled with the sound of the dishwasher running full throttle behind the rear booth. Accustomed to its gyrations, the occupants of the booth no longer noticed that the wash cycle occasioned a rhythmic tremor in the floorboards.

"So how do you think your jewel thief will go over?" asked J.C.

"He's not *my* jewel thief," snapped Father Tim.

"It was your church attic he hid out in," said Percy.

"I think he'll go over just fine. He's paid his debt to society in full, but better than that, he's a redeemed man with a strong faith."

Silence.

Chewing.

Slurping.

"I hope," said Father Tim, "that you'll extend the hand of fellowship to him." There. That's all he had to say about it.

Mule nodded. "No problem. It's th' right thing to do."

More chewing.

"So how come you're not goin' to Rwanda or someplace like that?" asked Percy.

"Hoppy wouldn't allow it." Hoppy would never have considered such a thing. Father Tim knew his limitations and they were numerous.

"What about th' kids in your own backyard? You ever thought of doin' somethin' for them?"

The fact that he'd supported the Children's Hospital in Wesley for twenty years was his own business; he never talked about it. "Tennessee *is* our own backyard." How he ever ended up with this bunch of turkeys was more than he could fathom.

"We'll miss you," said Mule, clapping him on the shoulder. "I won't hardly know what to order around here."

Father Tim laughed, suddenly forgiving. He thought he might miss them, too, though the possibility seemed a tad on the remote side.

"Here comes Hamp Floyd," said J.C. "Hide your wallet."

"What for?"

"Th' town needs a new fire truck."

"Seems like a good cause," said Father Tim. He took out his billfold and removed a ten.

"Th' town's got th' money for a standard truck, but Hamp wants a few bells an' whistles."

"Aha."

"Plus, he won't have anything to do with a red truck," said J.C.

"Seems like a fire chief would like red. Besides, what other color is there?"

"Yellow. He's holdin' out for yellow."

A *yellow* fire truck? Father Tim put the ten back in his billfold and pulled out a five.

In This Mountain, Ch. 3

Happy Endings Bookstore
HELEN HUFFMAN, PROPRIETOR
HOPE WINCHESTER, MANAGER

HOPE WINCHESTER CLIMBED the wooden stepladder and, poised on the third rung, cleaned the topmost interior of the bookstore display window with a solution of vinegar and water.

She had considered asking George Gaynor to do the job, since he was so much taller and wouldn't have to stand on tiptoe as she was doing. But she couldn't ask a Ph.D. to perform a menial task like washing windows.

She was careful not to splash any of the smelly solution onto the display below, which featured stacks of *Foggy Mountain Breakdown* by Sharyn McCrumb, and other books set in the southern highlands. So far, the third annual Mountain Month at Happy Endings had enjoyed only mild success, even in view of the ten percent discount for every book containing the word *mountain* in its title. People could get ten percent off anything, anywhere, she concluded. She proposed that next year they offer fifteen percent. In her opinion, fifteen percent was when people started to pay attention.

She raised the squirt bottle with her right hand and fired the solution toward the window, then turned slightly to wipe it down with the paper towel in her left hand.

It seemed as if she were falling in slow motion, like a feather, or perhaps some great hand held her gently, guiding her down and breaking her fall to the floor of the display window, where she landed on an arrangement of Charles Frazier's *Cold Mountain* in paperback.

"I declare!" said the Woolen Shop's Minnie Lomax, who was on her way to the post office. "That is the most *interesting* window display. Very modern. A mannequin lying on books." She knew Hope Winchester liked to try different things; she had once put a fake cat on a footstool, which caused half the population to stand in front of the window waiting for the cat to move. Though impressively lifelike, it never did, of course, which made some people feel foolish.

Adjusting her bifocals and walking on, Minnie deemed the current display "too New York for this town!"—a criticism she proclaimed aloud, albeit to herself, as she waited for the light to change.

In This Mountain, Ch. 17

AT SIX-THIRTY, Hope Winchester dashed along Main Street under a red umbrella. Rain gurgled from the downspouts of the buildings she fled past and flowed along the curb in a bold and lively stream.

To the driver of a station wagon heading down the mountain, the figure hurrying past the Main Street Grill was but a splash of red on the canvas of a sullen, gray morning. Nonetheless, it was a splash that momentarily cheered the driver.

Hope dodged a billow of water from the wheels of the station wagon and clutched even tighter the pocketbook containing three envelopes whose contents could change her life forever. She would line them up on her desk in the back room of the bookstore and prayerfully examine each of these wonders again and again. Then she would put them in her purse at the end of the day and take them home and line them up on her kitchen table so she might do the same thing once more.

UPS had come hours late yesterday with the books to be used in this month's promotion, which meant she'd lost precious time finishing the front window and must get at it this morning before the bookstore opened at ten. It was, after all, October first—time for a whole new window display, and the annual Big O sale.

All titles beginning with the letter *O* would be twenty percent off, which would get Wesley's students and faculty hopping! Indeed, September's Big S sale had increased their bottom line by twelve percent over last year, and all because she, the usually reticent Hope Winchester, had urged the owner to give a percentage off that really "counted for something." It was a Books-A-Million, B&N, Sam's Club kind of world, Hope insisted, and a five percent dribble here and there wouldn't work anymore, not even in Mitford, which wasn't as sleepy and innocuous as some people liked to think.

She dashed under the awning, set her streaming umbrella down, and jiggled the key in the door of Willard Porter's old pharmacy, now known as Happy Endings Books.

The lock had the cunning possessed only by a lock manufactured in 1927. Helen, the owner, had refused to replace it, insisting that a burglar couldn't possibly outwit its boundless vagaries.

Jiggling diligently, Hope realized her feet were cold and soaking wet. She supposed that's what she deserved by wearing sandals past Labor Day, something her mother had often scolded her for doing.

Once inside, and against the heartfelt wishes of Helen, who lived in Florida and preferred to delay heating the shop until the first snow, Hope squished to the thermostat and looked at the temperature: fifty degrees. Who would read a book, much less buy one, at fifty degrees?

As Margaret Ann, the bookstore cat, wound around her ankles, Hope turned the dial to "on."

The worn hardwood floor trembled slightly, and she heard at once the great boiler in the basement give its thunderous annual greeting to autumn in Mitford.

Shepherds Abiding, Ch. 1

Joe's Barber Shop
JOE IVEY, PROPRIETOR

JOE IVEY WHIPPED open a folded cape, draped it over Father Tim's front section, and tied it at the back of his neck.

"I hear you got a convict comin'."

"He won't be a convict when he gets here; he'll be a free man, re-pentant and eager to join society."

"That don't always work."

"What don't, ah, doesn't?"

"That repentance business."

"It worked for you. How long have you been dry?"

"Four years goin' on five."

"See there?"

Father Tim was dead sure he heard

Fancy Skinner's high-heel shoes pecking on the floor above their heads, but he wouldn't introduce that sore subject for all the tea in China.

Joe picked up his scissors and comb.

"Just take a little off the sides," said Father Tim.

"It's fannin' out over your collar, I'm gettin' rid of this mess on your neck first."

"Cynthia said don't scalp me."

"If I had a' Indian-head nickel for every time a woman sent me that message, I'd be rich as cream an' livin' in Los Angelees."

"Why on earth would you want to live there?"

"I wouldn't, it's just th' first big town that popped to mind."

"Aha." Father Tim saw a veritable bale of hair falling to the floor.

"Where's he goin' to work at?"

"I don't know. We have a couple of possibilities."

"You wouldn't want him to be out of work."

"Of course not."

"That'd be too big a temptation."

"You're going to like this man. Remember, he made a public confession and turned himself in; he was willing to admit his mistake and spend eight years paying for it. Give him a chance."

"I don't know . . ."

"Ours is the God of the second chance, Joe."

Joe stood back and squinted at his handiwork, then handed Father Tim a mirror. "Well, there they are."

"There what are?"

"Your ears. How long has it been since you seen 'em?"

In This Mountain, Ch. 4

The Hair House
FANCY SKINNER, PROPRIETOR

"LORD!" SAID FANCY, who had worked him in between her eleven-thirty trim and twelve o'clock perm. "Look at this mess, it's cut in three different lengths. I hate to say it, but I hear Joe Ivey gets in th' brandy, and if your hair's any proof, his liver's not long for this world.

"How's your wife? I'm glad you married her, she's cute as anything and really young. How much younger is she than you, anyway? Lord, I know I shouldn't ask that, but ten years is my guess.

"So, what are you givin' Cynthia for Christmas? Mule's givin' me a fur coat, I have always wanted a fur coat, I said, 'Honey, if you buy me a fur coat at a yard sale, do not come home, you can sleep at your office 'til kingdom come.' I know it's not right to wear fur, think of the animals and how they feel about it, but it gets so dern *cold* up here in th' winter. Of course, it's not been cold *this* winter, they say th' fleas will be killer this summer.

"D'you want some gum, have some gum, it's sugarless.

"Speakin' of sugar, I hear you're diabetic, how does that affect you? I hear it makes some people's legs swell or is it their feet? Lord, your scalp is tight as a drum, as usual—you ought to be more relaxed now that you're married, but of course, some people get more uptight when they tie th' knot. I bet married people come bawlin' to you all th' time, I don't know how you have a minute to yourself, bein' clergy.

"My great-uncle is clergy, they handle snakes at his church. Mule says for God's sake, Fancy, don't tell that your uncle handles snakes, so don't say I mentioned it. Have you seen anybody handle snakes, it's in th' Bible about handlin' snakes, but if you have to do that to prove you love th' Lord, I'm goin' to hell in a handbasket.

"Oops, I like to poked a hole in you with that fingernail, it's acrylic.

"How's Dooley, I hope he don't get th' big head in that fancy school. I've never been to Virginia, I hear seven presidents were born in that state, I think we had one president from our state, maybe two, but I can't remember who it was, maybe Hoover, do you think he had anything to do with th' vacuum cleaner, I've always wondered that. Speakin' of school, they asked me to come to Mitford School and talk about bein' a hairdresser for Occupation Day, I think I'll do a make-over, wouldn't that be somethin'? I'd like to make over th' principal, that is the meanest school principal in the world! I'd dye her hair blue in a heartbeat, then swing her around in this chair and say, 'Look at that, Miss Hayes, honey, don't you just love it, it's *you*!'

"See there? Aren't you some kind of handsome with all that glop cut from over your ears? You looked like you were wearing earmuffs. Oooh, yes! Cute! I'll just swivel you around so you can look at the back, your wife'll eat you with a spoon . . ."

He paid Fancy and reeled out of her shop, his ears ringing. By dodging the Skinners' driveway and taking the footpath, he was able to avoid the next customer, who merely glimpsed his back as he fled the premises.

These High, Green Hills, Ch. 6

As FANCY DRAPED him with the pink shawl, he sighed resignedly and closed his eyes.

"Prayin', are you? You ought to know by now I won't cut your ear off. Law, I've had too much coffee this mornin', you know I can't drink but two cups or I'm over the moon, how about you, can you still drink caffeine, or are you too old? Course, your wife is young, she probably can do it, I used to drink five or six cups a day . . . and smoke, oh, law, I smoked like a stack! But not anymore, did you know it makes you wrinkle faster? I hate those little lines around my mouth worse than anything, but that wadn't coffee, that was sun, honey, I used to lay out and bake like a chicken.

"Look at this trim! Who did this? I thought Joe Ivey was workin' at Graceland. Mama, come and look at this, this is what I have to put up with. Father, this is Mama, Mama, he's a friend of Mule's, he got married a while back for the first time.

"He preaches at that rock church down the street where they use incense, I declare, Mule and I passed by your church one Sunday, you could smell it comin' out of th' chimney! Lord, my allergies flare up somethin' awful when I smell that stuff, I thought incense was Catholic, anyway, do y'all talk Latin? I had a girlfriend one time, I went to church with her, I couldn't understand a word they said.

"Your hair's growin' like a weed. I hear if you eat a lot of grease, it'll make your hair grow, you shouldn't eat grease, anyway, you've got diabetes.

"Mama! Did you know th' Father has diabetes? My daddy had diabetes. Is that what killed him, Mama, or was it smokin'? Maybe both.

"Look at that! Whoever trimmed your hair, you tell 'em to leave your hair alone. You can call me anytime, I'll work you in. I'm sorry I couldn't take you—when was it?—I think your pope was here, I guess he don't always stay at the Vatican, have you ever been to the Vatican? Law, I haven't even been to Israel, everybody's been to Israel, our preacher is takin' a whole group next year, but I'd rather go on a cruise, do you think that's sacrilegious?"

Out to Canaan, Ch. 7

Mitford Blossoms
JENNA IVEY, PROPRIETOR

AT MITFORD BLOSSOMS, he asked Jenna Ivey for a dozen roses; long-stemmed, without wires, ferns, or gypsophila, please, in a box lined with green paper and tied with a pink satin ribbon.

"Oh, I remember how she likes her roses!" Jenna looked him in the eye, smiling. "And it's been ages since you've done this."

He blushed. He was still smarting from the dark recognition that he desperately feared being separated from his wife. It had made him feel suddenly weak and frail, like a child. All those years alone, a bachelor who seldom yearned for the hearthstone of a wife's love, and now . . . he was a man beset with a dreadful mixture of anxiety and humiliation over the depth of his attachment.

"Make that . . ." The words lodged in his throat. "Make that two dozen!"

Jenna blinked, unbelieving. She had never known but one other man in Mitford to buy two dozen roses at a whack, and that was Andrew Gregory, the mayor. Every time he and his Italian wife had an anniversary, Mr. Gregory hotfooted it to Mitford Blossoms and laid out cash money, no matter what the going rate.

"Why, Father! Cynthia will think . . . she'll think you've gone 'round the bend!"

He forced a grin. "And she would be right," he said.

In This Mountain, Ch. 2

Sweet Stuff Bakery
WINNIE IVEY, PROPRIETOR

HE INHALED DEEPLY as he went in. The very gates of heaven! "Winnie!" he bellowed.

She came through the curtains. Or was that Winnie?

"Winnie?" he said, taking off his glasses. He fogged them and wiped them with his handkerchief. "Is that you?"

"Course it's me!" she said. Winnie was looking ten years younger, maybe twenty, and tanned to the gills.

"Velma said you brought something back."

"Come on," she said, laughing. "I'll show you."

He passed through the curtains and there, standing beside the ovens, was a tall, very large fellow with full, dark hair and twinkling eyes, wearing an apron dusted with flour.

"This is *him!*" crowed Winnie, looking radiant.

"Him?"

"You know, the one I always dreamed about standin' beside me in th' kitchen. Father Kavanagh, this is Thomas Kendall from Topeka, Kansas."

"What . . . where . . . ?"

"I met him on th' ship!"

"In the kitchen, actually," said Thomas, extending a large hand and grinning from ear to ear. "I'm a pastry chef, Father."

"You stole the ship's pastry chef? Winnie!"

They all laughed. "No," said Winnie, "it was his last week on the job, he was going back to Kansas and decided he'd come home with me first. He's stayin' with Velma and Percy."

No doubt about it, he was dumbfounded. First Andrew, now Winnie . . .

"He likes my cream horns," she said, suddenly shy.

"Who doesn't?"

Thomas put his arm around Winnie and looked down at her, obviously proud. "I'm mighty glad to be in Mitford," he said simply.

"By jing, we're mighty glad to have you," replied the rector, meaning it.

Out to Canaan, Ch. 19

Collar Button

PROPRIETOR KNOWN ONLY AS "THE COLLAR BUTTON MAN"

HE HAD A hurried lunch of Percy's soup of the day, with a salad, and went home to say a word to Barnabas. This took him past the new men's store, which he had failed to stop and inspect since it opened with some fanfare before Easter. The Collar Button, it was called.

It had been a long time, indeed, since he'd gone into a clothing store. In the first place, he didn't like to shop. In the second place, the prices for clothes these days were absolutely—yes, he thought he could honestly say it—sinful. And in the third place, what was the going fashion for a rector who didn't wish to appear conspicuously well-dressed?

He slipped his hand into his jacket pocket, and felt his mended gloves, which he still needed from time to time on cold mornings. He must not get carried away in this place, he thought. He would say he was just looking.

The Collar Button was new, but it seemed old. The walls were dark, burnished panels of mahogany, a low fire burned in a grate, and a large golden retriever, lying by the hearth, opened one eye as he came in.

"Good heavens!" he said with earnest appreciation. This was like walking into a study in some far reach of Cambridge, where he had once gone to research a paper on the life and works of C. S. Lewis.

"Father Tim, I believe!" boomed a deep voice, and from behind a wall of brocade curtains stepped the new proprietor, extending his hand to the rector.

"That's right. How did you know?"

"Oh, I've seen you pass now and again, and I thought to myself, there goes a proper candidate for the Collar Button style!"

"And what, ah, style is that, exactly?"

"English gentleman, country squire, village rector, the man of thoughtful reflection and quiet taste."

"Aha."

"What can I show you? Oh, and would you care for a dash of sherry?"

His head was fairly swimming with the unexpected dazzle of the modern shopping experience.

At Home in Mitford, Ch. 3

Oxford Antiques
ANDREW GREGORY, PROPRIETOR

ON SATURDAY MORNING, he visited the Oxford Antique Shop, carrying an apple pie in a basket.

"Little Red Riding Hood!" said Andrew Gregory, coming from the back of the store to greet him.

The rector held out the basket. "Homemade apple pie," he said, with some pride.

"'The best of all physicians is apple pie and cheese'!" exclaimed Andrew, quoting a nineteenth-century poet. "What an excellent treat, my friend. Thank you and come in." He took the basket, delighted as a child. "Why don't we just polish off the whole thing right now and you can carry your basket back?"

The two men laughed.

"I'm afraid I'll have to take my basket back in any case, as there's five more to be delivered in it."

"I don't know how you find time to feed your sheep physically as well as spiritually."

"Andrew, Providence has blessed me with the finest house help a man could ever have. Puny Bradshaw is her name, and she not only baked a dozen pies yesterday, she canned fourteen quarts of tomatoes last week."

"Extraordinary!"

They sat down on the matched love seats at the shop door.

"Here's something even more extraordinary. I've discovered that Uncle Billy Watson is a splendid artist. Uneducated, grew up in the valley, never had training of any kind. 'Rough as a cob,' as he says. Yet, he draws like a Georgian gentleman."

"You always seem to have a Vermeer of one kind or another on your hands."

"The drawings are in my office, and I'd like your opinion. Perhaps you'll stop over on Monday morning. After all, I've been drinking your coffee for years, now come and have a go at mine."

"I'll look forward to it," said Andrew. "And please don't leave yet. I have something to show you."

Andrew went to the back room and returned with two books.

"Just look at this!" he said. "A first edition of the first volume of Churchill's *History of the English-Speaking Peoples.* Something I've wanted for a very long time." He turned to the opening page and read aloud: "'Our story centres in an island, not widely sundered from the Continent, and so tilted that its mountains lie all to the west and north, while south and east is a gently undulating landscape of wooded valley, open downs, and slow rivers. It is very accessible to the invader, whether he comes in peace or war, as pirate or merchant, conqueror or missionary.'

"Ah," said Andrew, unashamedly beaming. "A prize! I shall read all the volumes over again. Now, for you," he said, with a twinkle in his eyes, "a prize of your own." He handed the rector an early leather-bound volume of Wordsworth.

The rector was touched by the feeling of the softly worn covers against his palm. It was as if the book had belonged to him all along and had at last come home.

Smiling, he turned the linen-weave pages until he found a favorite passage. "Andrew, if you'll permit me, I also would covet a moment to read aloud."

It was Saturday morning in Mitford. The village was up and stirring, yet a slow, sweet peace reigned, a certain harmony of mood and feeling. In the open door of the shop the two men sat, one reading, one listening, and both, for the passing moment, were content.

At Home in Mitford, Ch. 7

Dora Pugh's Hardware
DORA PUGH, PROPRIETOR

AT THE OFFICE one morning, it occurred to him that, instead of bathing Barnabas in the guest room shower stall, he would stop by the hardware store and buy a large tin tub. That way, he could begin the practice of bathing him in the garden and avoid the cleanup in the bathroom.

After a quick lunch with Harry Nelson, who reported that the origin of the painting still hadn't been verified, he went to the hardware.

One of his favorite smells was that of an old hardware store. In fact, it was right up there with the smell of wood smoke, leather-bound books, and leaf mold after a rain. More than that, it unfailingly brought back a rush of memories from his Mississippi boyhood.

As a 4-H rabbit grower for two years, he had often traded at the local hardware for hutch materials and feed. He could even remember the time he picked out six yellow goslings from a box kept warm by a lightbulb.

He decided on a tin tub for $22.95, and took it to Dora Pugh at the cash register.

"You want to drive around for this, Father?"

"No, Dora, this is cash and carry."

"I see you walk by here every day and I still forget you don't drive a car. How in the nation do you make out?"

"Not too bad, actually. Nearly everything I could want, and some things I don't, are all right here in these two town blocks."

"I guess you're goin' to tote this tub on your head like in Africa?"

He gave her cash to the penny. "I don't know exactly how I'm going to do it till I get started."

He tried to hold the tub under his arm, but that didn't seem to work, so he took it by one of the handles and was disappointed to note that the rim of it banged against his ankle as he walked to the door.

Turning to say good-bye, he saw that Dora had ducked down behind the pocketknife display case, shaking with laughter.

"Dora, I see you back there laughing! You better quit that and show some respect to the clergy!"

He waved cheerfully and stepped out on the sidewalk, pleased with both his idea and his purchase. He just hoped that people did not think him eccentric. He would far rather be thought ingenious or practical.

By the time he turned the corner at the bank and headed home, he was willing to admit that a car provided something more valuable than convenience. It provided privacy. Otherwise, he reasoned, everyone passing by could stare into your business, which one and all seemed to be doing.

He hurried the last half block to the rectory, set the tub down in a clearing amid some laurel, and unwound the garden hose to make certain it would reach. "Perfect!" he exclaimed, warming to his task on Friday.

At Home in Mitford, Ch. 4

Irish Woolen Shop

MINNIE LOMAX, MANAGER

WHILE EVERYONE ELSE offered lamentations exceeding those of the prophet Jeremiah, the rector felt smugly indifferent to complaints that spring would never come. He had to admit, however, that last Sunday was one of the few times he'd conducted an Easter service in long johns and ski socks.

Turning up his collar, he leaned into a driving wind and headed toward the office.

Hadn't winter dumped ice, snow, sleet, hail, and rainstorms on the village since late October? Hadn't they been blanketed by fog so thick you could cut it with a dull knife, time and time again?

With all that moisture seeping into the ground for so many long months, didn't this foretell the most glorious springtime in years? And wasn't that, after all, worth the endless assault?

"Absolutely!" he proclaimed aloud, trucking past the Irish Woolen Shop. "No doubt about it!"

"See there?" said Hessie Mayhew, peering out the store window. "It's got Father Tim talking to himself, it's that bad." She sighed. "They say if sunlight doesn't get to your pineal glands for months on end, your sex drive quits."

Minnie Lomax, who was writing sale tags for boiled wool sweaters, looked up and blinked. "What do you know about pineal glands?" She was afraid to ask what Hessie might know about sex drive.

"What does anybody know about pineal glands?" asked Hessie, looking gloomy.

Out to Canaan, Ch. 1

Chelsea Tea Shop
MRS. HAVNER, PROPRIETOR

"SO WHAT DO you think?" he asked Mule Skinner over breakfast at the Grill.

"Beats me," said Mule. "I'm sure not drivin' to Wesley for some overpriced lunch deal."

"I saw him on the street yesterday. He suggested we meet him down at the tea shop."

"J.C.'s hangin' out at th' *tea shop?*" Mule's eyebrows shot skyward.

"Actually, he hasn't had the guts to go there yet—he's been packing a sandwich—but he said he'd do it if we'd go with him."

"Percy won't like us goin' down th' street."

"Right. True." The owner of the Grill thought he also owned his regulars. One underhanded meal at another eatery was grimly tolerated, but two was treason, with scant forgiveness forthcoming.

"I double dare you," said Mule.

Father Tim dipped his toast into a poached egg and considered this. Buying the crèche had made him feel slightly reckless.

"I will if you will," he said, grinning.

Shepherds Abiding, Ch. 2

"I LEFT MY glasses back at th' office," said J.C. "Somebody read me what's on this pink menu deal."

"Let's see." Mule adjusted his glasses. "Chicken salad with grapes and nuts. That comes with toast points."

"Toast points? I'm not eatin' toast points, much less anything with grapes and nuts."

"Here's a crepe," said Father Tim, pronouncing it in the French way. "It's their house specialty."

"What's a krep?" asked Mule.

"A thin pancake rolled around a filling."

"A filling of what?" J.C. wiped his forehead with a paper napkin.

"Shredded chicken, in this case."

"A pancake rolled around shredded chicken? Why shred chicken? If God wanted chicken to be *shredded* . . ."

"I could gnaw a table leg," said Mule. "Let's get on with it."

"I can't eat this stuff. It's against my religion."

"Whoa! Here you go," said Father Tim. "They've got flounder!"

"Flounder!" J.C. brightened.

"Fresh fillet of flounder rolled around a filling of Maine cranberries and baked. This is quite a menu."

"I don't trust this place. Everything's rolled around somethin' else. No way."

"Look," said Father Tim. "Aspic! With celery and onions. Hit that with a little mayo, it'd be mighty tasty."

J.C. rolled his eyes.

"I was always fond of aspic," said Father Tim.

"You would be," snapped J.C. "Let's cut to the chase. Is there a burger on there anywhere?"

"Nope. No burger. . . . Wait a minute . . . *organic turkey burger!* There you go, buddyroe." Mule looked eminently pleased.

"I'm out of here," said J.C., grabbing his briefcase.

"Wait a dadblame minute!" said Mule. "You're th' one said meet you here. It was your big idea."

"I can't eat this stuff."

"Sure you can. Just order somethin' an' we'll have th' kitchen pour a bowl of grease over it."

"This kitchen never saw a bowl of grease, but all right—just this once. I'm definitely not doin' this again."

"Fine!" said Mule. "Great! Tomorrow, we'll go back to th' Grill, and everybody'll be happy. I personally don't take kindly to change. This is upsettin' my stomach."

"I'm not goin' back and let that witch on a broom order me around."

"Hey, y'all."

They turned to see a young woman in an apron, holding an order pad. Father Tim thought her smile dazzling.

"Hey, yourself," said Father Tim.

"I'm Lucy, and I'll be your server today."

"All *right!*" said Mule.

"What will you have, sir?" she asked J.C.

"I guess th' flounder," grunted the editor. "But only if you'll scrape out th' cranberries."

"Yessir, be glad to. That comes with a nice salad and a roll. And since we're taking out the cranberries, would you like a few buttered potatoes with that?"

Father Tim thought J.C. might burst into tears.

"I *would!*" exclaimed the *Muse* editor. "And could I have a little butter with th' *roll?*"

"Oh, yessir, it comes with butter."

"Hallelujah!" exclaimed Mule. "An' I'll have th' same, but no butter with th' roll."

"Ditto," said Father Tim. "With a side of aspic."

"No, wait," said Mule. "Maybe I'll try it with th' cranberries. But only if they're sweet, like at Thanksgiving. . . ."

"Don't go there," said J.C. "Bring 'im th' same thing I ordered."

Father Tim didn't mention to his lunch partners that Hessie Mayhew and Esther Bolick were sitting on the other side of the room, staring at them with mouths agape.

Shepherds Abiding, Ch. 2

Making Mitford Real

I *grew up in Mitford.*

Actually, it was a small town named Lenoir, near our farm in the foothills of North Carolina.

Lenoir had a town clock, a town square, a monument, a popular café, a drugstore soda fountain, and plenty of people who were kind, colorful, outrageous, and memorable.

In lots of important ways, Lenoir had all the hallmarks of Mitford:

One felt safe there.

Everybody knew everybody.

And people lingered to pass the time of day, share a joke, and keep the word-of-mouth news network, so vital to the personality of a small town, up and running.

When I went to Lenoir with my grandfather on Saturdays, I visited his barbershop (four chairs, and all the baseball and politics you could talk), then set off with a dime clutched in my fist. I could go to the movies and see *Song of the South,* starring Bobby Driscoll, or buy a cherry Coke and cheese crackers at McNairy's soda fountain.

One Saturday, I asked for special permission to cross Main Street, alone, and visit the public library at the top of the hill.

"That's a mighty big place!" said my grandfather.

And it was.

My first view of a public library simply boggled my mind. As a ten-year-old girl in a rural school, I was an omnivorous reader who'd never seen so many books at once!

I tiptoed. I gaped. I pondered. I had no earthly idea how to select a book from such endless treasures, until a kind librarian recommended

Girl of the Limberlost and *Lorna Doone*. It seemed particularly impressive that she whispered, and so I whispered back.

I dashed across the side street, heart pounding, and sat on the broad steps of First Methodist, our family church, and opened the pages of *Lorna Doone*.

> If anybody cares to read a simple tale told simply, I, John Ridd, of the parish of Oare, in the county of Somerset, yeoman and churchwarden, have seen and had a share in some of the doings of this neighbourhood, which I will try to set down in order. . . .

I shall never forget that precious moment of happiness, it was one of the flagstones on my path to becoming an author.

Yet there came a time when I left this safe and secure place. In truth, I could scarcely wait to see the world. Living variously in New York, San Francisco, and other large cities, my career in advertising flourished, and my bright-spirited daughter grew up and prospered.

Years later, I don't know exactly when, I began to listen to my heart and discovered the oddest desire:

I wanted to go home.

I longed to return to the uncommon music of common speech in our foothills and mountains, to hear "ain't" for *aren't,* and "tote" for *carry.*

I wanted to eat a smashed-flat pimiento cheese sandwich from a drugstore soda fountain grill, and hear a church bell toll the hour. Most of all, I wanted to be where people stopped to pass the time of day, and really seemed to care about each other.

But living in cities can exact a high price.

It can make us skeptical that such places—and such people—still exist.

I wondered if there were any towns left where children go safely to drugstores and libraries, watched by caring eyes.

I wondered if there were still magical places where we really know our neighbors, and where a few happy dogs roam Main Street.

The answer, I found, is yes.

I know, because I live in a town like this.

Better still, I've visited such places all over America, as I tour for my Mitford books.

I've found Mitford in Milford (Michigan), in Manteo (North Carolina), in Montrose (California), and even in certain neighborhoods of Manhattan. There are Mitfords everywhere!

All of which goes to prove one thing:

Mitford isn't about place. It's about community. And community happens wherever "two or more are gathered together."

Mitford (or Milford or Montrose) is wherever people still care for each other, and are willing to go out of their way to demonstrate it.

In my novels, Esther Bolick helps make Mitford real every time she bakes her legendary Orange Marmalade Cake and carries it to some deserving (or undeserving) soul.

> *"Mitford is about connecting with each other. This takes time we don't really have, but must be willing to make."*

To be on the receiving end of Esther's cake makes you feel cared about and loved. To be on the giving end of Esther's cake makes her feel she's loved back.

It's so simple, really, this thing of sharing and giving and, ultimately, *connecting*.

Besides, life is short, and why wait for surgery to open our hearts?

It's also simple enough to give away a hug once in a while, for Pete's sake.

In *A Light in the Window*, Father Tim phoned Miss Sadie and found his elderly parishioner sounding a bit weary.

> "It seems to me you could use a hug," he said.
> "A hug?"
> "Have you had one since Sunday?"
> "Not that I can think of, but the man doing the plasterwork shook my hand."
> "I'll be right up," he said.

"Mush and double mush!" Dooley might say about the suspect business of hugging.

That Dooley. Not only has he changed Father Tim's life, he's changed mine.

For example, I might once have said, "What a perfectly glorious sunset, it's like watercolors run wild in the heavens!" Now, I might simply say, with feeling, *"Man!"* Dooley Barlowe is possibly the first character in fiction to rob its author of civilized speech.

Which reminds me. Many of the people in Mitford are easily delighted—by sunsets, cakes, or hugs. In fact, a sunset once emptied Lord's Chapel of its cleanup crew in *These High, Green Hills*. They dropped their mops and brooms and hurried up Old Church Lane to see banners of crimson unfurling above blue mountains, which caused them to gasp with wonder.

I, too, am easily delighted.

In fact, my sister-in-law says I can make more out of nothing than anyone she knows, meaning, perhaps, the way I can be perfectly enthralled by a pattern of light upon a pond, or a ladybug crawling in the grass.

Something out of nothing! Isn't that the very crux of the creative process? Isn't that, in the end, one of the great keys to living?

I love the way Uncle Billy takes a long-term, difficult marriage to the fierce Miss Rose, and molds it into a good life, no matter what.

One of the ways he takes the edge off hard times is by telling jokes.

Now, Uncle Billy is careful about his jokes; he doesn't tell just any old joke that comes along. For example, he's known for having a new joke every spring, which he carefully sifts from those heard at the Grill, or found in the pages of the venerable *Farmer's Almanac*.

To prepare, he tells it over and over to himself, so he fully understands the meaning and doesn't, as I recently did before six hundred people, forget the part that makes the punch line work.

Thus, just as I've learned a new vocabulary from Dooley, I've learned joke-telling from Uncle Billy. Shy all my life about telling jokes, I've started telling his to anyone who'll listen, and I can now recommend this as the most *delicious* therapy!

I do hope you'll try it yourself, though we can't be certain whether you'll attract new friends or, possibly, lose one or two!

Speaking of friends, I knew very few people when I moved to the village of Blowing Rock, which sits atop the mountain above Lenoir.

The first thing I did was look for a church, for I'm convinced that one mustn't wait for people to reach out—we must reach in.

I became a lay reader, I volunteered to help in the kitchen, I worked hard on special fund-raisers.

Joining "a family of faith" in a church or synagogue can give us just that: a *family*. And the best way to get started being family is to jump in with both feet.

Next week, I'll be reading my children's book *Miss Fannie's Hat* to the children at our volunteer library.

"Goodness!" said a friend. "I don't see how you have time to read a book to children!"

If I can't find such precious time, then I'd better stop writing Mitford books. After all, if Mitford isn't real in my own life, how can I make it real for my readers?

Bottom line, this is what I believe:

If Mitford is to become real, *we* must become real.

And being real has everything to do with being whole.

Being whole, I've learned, greatly depends upon acknowledging the spiritual part of our natures. We can ignore this crucial part of our being until it withers and dies, or we can nurture it until it flourishes and shines.

I keep a quote book, as does Father Tim. In it, I've recorded something the brilliant young French mathematician Blaise Pascal said:

"There is a God-shaped vacuum in the heart of every person, and it can never be filled by any created thing. It can only be filled by God. . . ."

Father Tim knows God loves us and that we really matter to Him.

However, Buck Leeper, Pauline Barlowe, and the man in the attic couldn't possibly believe that God loves us even when we aren't lovable. Then, one day, on faith alone, they began to believe, to allow their God vacuum to be filled, and their hearts and lives were transformed.

You'll notice that Father Tim is a "praying priest." Because he believes God is real and living, he prays often. That's how he *connects* with Him— about the big things, about the very smallest things. And he doesn't always pray from the prayer book, he prays straight from the heart.

In my first novel, *At Home in Mitford,* he utters daily a prayer taught him by his grandmother:

"Lord, make me a blessing to someone today."

Frail and human though he is, I believe this prayer may be part of what helps Father Tim stay open to everyone he meets—from the down-and-out, toothless Harley Welch to an often ill-tempered secretary, not to mention a man who owns but one pair of britches and lives in the woods.

Another way of becoming whole is through forgiveness.

In *These High, Green Hills,* Father Tim and Cynthia were desperately lost in a wild cave.

As you may know, I'm not one for making fancy literary metaphors. Yet, as I wrote these scenes, it became clear to me and to my main character that this impenetrably dark labyrinth illustrated Father Tim's terrible helplessness in the relationship with his long-deceased father.

At the age of sixty-four, the village priest who had helped so many find the grace to forgive was finally able to forgive his embittered, controlling father—who had damaged his view of a divine Father.

After Father Tim and Cynthia's rescue, she marveled at finding something lighter, something freer in her husband.

In Father Tim's act of forgiveness, his heart was melted; an old wall had crumbled.

Faith, prayer, and forgiveness, then, can free us to do something that is characteristic of Mitford:

We become able, at last, to care more deeply about each other.

There's one last thing I'd like to say about Esther Bolick, who shows her care for others by baking cakes.

For the first year or two, Esther was asked to bake fourteen two-layers for the annual Bane and Blessing sale at Mitford's Lord's Chapel.

Then, in ensuing years, she was *expected* to bake fourteen two-layers.

Have you ever baked fourteen two-layer cakes? I haven't and I hope I never do! But Esther, you see, was willing to stand on her feet over a hot oven for the many hours it takes to accomplish such a task.

That is how Esther loves. That is how Esther gives. What would Mitford be without Esther Bolick?

As most of you already know, Mitford doesn't come cheap. It doesn't come easy. And it doesn't come free.

Because Mitford is about doing and giving and feeling and stretching ourselves to be all God made us to be.

One of the quotes in my ever-expanding quote book great John Wesley (1703–1791), who said:

"Do all the good you can, in all the places you can, at all the times you can, to all the people you can, as long as you ever can."

Wherever even part of this challenging philosophy is lived out, I faithfully promise you this:

Mitford will be real.

Tending to the Needs:
Blessings at Mealtime

In A New Song, Father Tim does what retired clergy do—he goes to supply a pulpit as an interim priest.

After a long night of being hopelessly lost, caught in a storm, occupying the wrong beach house, and generally suffering the indignities of moving to a strange place, he and Cynthia sit down to breakfast with Marion and Sam Fieldwalker.

These dear, long-time parishioners of St. John's in the Grove have just introduced the Kavanaghs to the charming small house where they'll live for a year near the ocean. And as if this sparkling cottage weren't enough, Marion has prepared a celebratory breakfast.

He'd faced it time and again in his years as a priest—how do you pour out a heart full of thanksgiving in a way that even dimly expresses your joy?

He reached for the hands of the Fieldwalkers and bowed his head.

"'Father, you're so good,'" he begins. And he begins aright. When we pray, let us first acknowledge the One Who gives us life and breath.

"'So good to bring us out of the storm into the light of this blessed new day, and into the company of these new friends.'" If you or someone else at the table has recently received a blessing—and who hasn't, if you think about it—why not thank Him for it, right up front?

"'Touch, Lord, the hands and heart and spirit of Marion, who prepared this food for us when she might have done something more important.'"

What a blessing it confers on the cook to be remembered!

Father Tim moves along quickly, now, as the fragrance rises off the platter of crisply fried perch and the pot of strong coffee, hard by a bowl of sliced cantaloupe and a pan of homemade biscuits, already buttered.

"'Lord, we could be here all morning only thanking You, but we intend to press forward and enjoy the pleasures of this glorious feast which You have, by Your grace, put before us.'"

By Your grace, says Father Tim. That is precisely how food shows up on our table, no matter how hard we've worked for it, shopped for it, or sacrificed for it.

"'We thank You . . . for Your goodness and mercy, and for tending to the needs of those less fortunate, in Jesus' name.'"

This prayer spanned roughly thirty-five seconds. Yet it accomplished so much, and took so little time from the twenty-four hours He gives us daily.

While our priest specifically thanked God for tending to the needs of those less fortunate, the prayer also tended to other important needs.

For example, giving thanks makes us feel good. It helps keep us in balance. It connects us to God, no matter how simple the thanks may be.

And, I notice that when thanks are given, some new feeling, quite subtle but real, infuses us all, making the meal more special and our time together more precious.

Amount.

Amen.

ເຂົ້ອ

S HE HAD PUT the glass plates on a green wicker table, with a sprinkle of white lace cloth. There were old-fashioned roses in a vase, and a tall pitcher of sweetened tea. They sat down to lunch, and Miss Sadie held her hands out to the rector.

"At Fernbank," she said, "we always hold hands when we say the blessing."

He prayed with a contented heart. "Accept, O Lord, our thanks and praise for all that You've done for us. We thank You for the blessing of family and friends, and for the loving care which surrounds us on every side. Above all, we give You thanks for the great mercies and promises given to us in Christ Jesus our Lord, in whose name we pray."

At Home in Mitford, Ch. 5

THERE WAS A quickening in the air of the mayor's office. Ray was setting out his home-cooked supper on the vast desktop, overlooked by pictures of their twenty-three grandchildren at the far end.

"Mayor," said Leonard Bostick, "it's a cryin' shame you cain't cook as good as Ray."

"I've got better things to do," she snapped. "I did the cookin' for forty years. Now it's his turn."

"Whooee!" said Paul Hartley. "Baby backs! Get over here, Father, and give us a blessin'."

"Come on!" shouted the mayor to the group lingering in the hall. "It's blessin' time!"

Esther Cunningham held out her hands, and the group eagerly formed a circle.

"Our Lord," said the rector, "we're grateful for the gift of friends and neighbors and those willing to lend their hand to the welfare of this place. We thank You for the peace of this village and for Your grace to do the work that lies ahead. We thank You, too, for this food and ask a special blessing on the one who prepared it. In Jesus' name."

"Amen!" said the assembly.

A Light in the Window, Ch. 1

ESTHER BOLICK RANG the bell for silence in the parish hall.

"I'm glad," said Stuart Cullen, "that Lord's Chapel hasn't grown too big for us to hold hands around the table."

The excited throng formed a circle, as someone fetched Rebecca Jane Owen from under a folding chair and rescued five-year-old Amy Larkin from the hot pursuit of a mechanical toy run amok from the nursery.

"Give us grateful hearts, our Father, for all Thy mercies, and make us mindful of the needs of others; through Jesus Christ our Lord."

A Light in the Window, Ch. 20

MISS SADIE WAS wearing a blue dress with an ecru lace collar and one of her mother's hand-painted brooches. He didn't think he'd ever seen her looking finer. Her wrist appeared almost normal, and the car key was hanging on a hook in the kitchen, untouched in recent months, thanks be to God!

They sat down to green beans and corn bread, with glasses of cold milk all around, and held hands as he asked the blessing.

"Lord, we thank You for the richness of this life and our friendship, and for this hot, golden-crusted corn bread. Please bless the hands that prepared it, and make us ever mindful of the needs of others."

These High, Green Hills, Ch. 13

"Low-fat meat loaf, hot from the oven!" he announced, setting the sizzling platter on the table.

Louella wrinkled her nose. "Low-fat? Pass it on by, honey, you can *skip* this chile!"

"Don't skip this 'un," said Harley.

"He was only kidding," Cynthia declared. "In truth, it contains everything our doctors ever warned us about."

He saw the light in Pauline's face, the softness of expression as she looked upon her scrubbed and freckled children. Thanks be to God! Three out of five . . .

He sat down, feeling expansive, and shook out one of the linen napkins left behind, he was amused to recall, by an old bishop who once lived here.

He waited until all hands were clasped, linking them together in a circle.

"Our God and our Father, we thank You!" he began.

"Thank you, Jesus!" boomed Louella in happy accord.

"We thank You with full hearts for this family gathered here tonight, and ask Your mercy and blessings upon all those who hunger, not only for sustenance, but for the joy, the peace, and the one true salvation which You, through Your Son, freely offer. . . ."

They had just said "Amen!" when the doorbell rang.

Out to Canaan, Ch. 11

If last night had been a nightmare, this was a dream come true. The sun streamed through a sparkling bay window and splashed across the broad window seat. Bare hardwood floors shone under a fresh coat of wax.

"You see just there?" Marion pointed out the window. "That patch of blue between the dunes? That's the ocean!" She proclaimed this as if the ocean belonged to her personally, and she was thrilled to share it.

"Come and have your breakfast," said Sam, holding the chair for Cynthia.

"Dearest, do you think it possible that yesterday in that brutal storm we somehow died, and are now in heaven?"

"Not only possible, but very likely!"

He'd faced it time and again in his years as a priest—how do you pour out a heart full of thanksgiving in a way that even dimly expresses your joy?

He reached for the hands of the Fieldwalkers and bowed his head.

"Father, You're so good. So good to bring us out of the storm into the light of this blessed new day, and into the company of these new friends.

"Touch, Lord, the hands and heart and spirit of Marion, who prepared this food for us when she might have done something more important.

"Bless this good man for looking out for us, and waiting up for us, and gathering the workers who labored to make this a bright and shining home.

"Lord, we could be here all morning only thanking You, but we intend to press forward and enjoy the pleasures of this glorious feast which You have, by Your grace, put before us. We thank You again for Your goodness and mercy, and for tending to the needs of those less fortunate, in Jesus' name."

A New Song, Ch. 5

FATHER TIM DUCKED to the refrigerator and pulled out the platter of chicken and the bowls of potato salad and cranberry sauce, and displayed them proudly. "And there's fresh corn to boot. Puny cut it off the cob and creamed it, it's sweet as sugar. Let me heat you a bowlful."

"That'd be good," said the old man. "I hate t' trouble you."

"No trouble at all!" In truth, he was thrilled to do something for somebody after weeks of being as useless as moss on a stump.

He poured a hearty portion of corn into a bowl, assembled a few leftover biscuits, and zapped the whole caboodle in the microwave.

As he served two plates and got out the flatware, he eyed the old man from the corner of his eye. Something was wrong. "Uncle Billy, you're not your old self. I'm going to ask a blessing on our supper, then I'd like you to tell me what's what.

"Father, thank You for sending this dear friend to our table, it's an honor to have his company. Lord, we ask You for Bill Watson's strength: strength of spirit, strength of mind, strength of purpose, strength of body. May You shower him with Your mighty, yet tender grace, and give him hope and health all the days of his long and obedient life. We pray You'd heap yet another blessing on Puny for preparing what You've faithfully provided, and ask, also, that You make us ever mindful of the needs of others. In Jesus' name, Amen."

"A-men!"

In This Mountain, Ch. 14

"AND IN THIS mountain the Lord of hosts will make for all people a feast of choice pieces, a feast of wines on the lees, of fat things full of marrow. . . ."

In his blessing of the meal, Father Talbot quoted from the prophet Isaiah, then invited all to break bread together.

"Did you bring your brownies?" Amy Larkin asked Harley, who was ahead of her in the queue to the food table.

"Yes, ma'am," he told the eleven-year-old. "Right over yonder."

"I brought pimiento cheese sandwiches." Her eyes shone. "No crusts."

"Where're they at?"

"Right next to the potato salad in the red bowl," she said. "On the left."

He nodded, respectful. "I'll make sure to have one."

Amy Larkin reminded him of Lace when she was still a little squirt, running to his trailer with a book under her arm. He hated she had grown up and gone off to school, but he knew it was for the best.

He fixed his gaze on Cynthia's lemon squares on the dessert table. He had set his mouth for a lemon square, and hoped he could get to the familiar blue and white platter before it was too late.

In This Mountain, Ch. 22

Hometown Appetites:
Gathering Around
the Table

"*I gain ten pounds* just reading a Mitford book!" someone writes to say.

Why is there so much food in the Mitford books?

First, food is a great way of communicating. When I write about Dooley loving fried baloney sandwiches, you can connect with that. When I write about Puny baking corn bread and Louella frying chicken, most of you can connect with that. (Hardly anyone, of course, connects with Percy Mosely's gizzard special in *In This Mountain*, but that's another story.)

Food is something we all understand; it's a common language. And it's one more way readers are encouraged to feel at home in Mitford.

There's a deeper reason, however, why food is endlessly referenced in the Mitford books.

When I began writing the series, I had stepped out on faith and left a successful writing career in advertising. In order to put food on the table, I freelanced in my old profession while trying to learn how to write a book.

Indeed, my first novel is loaded with food references largely because my cupboards were bare, and I was writing hungry. No self-pity here, however. I could wear my size tens!

This is when I learned to make soup from chicken bones, which is explained as follows. It has a sort of World War II spirit, which some of you will recognize from personal experience.

After you've enjoyed several meals from what was originally roasted chicken, sauté some chopped onion in a little olive oil, add the remains of the chicken, bones and all (that's where much of the flavor still resides), pour in two or three cups of water, and start simmering. Add salt and pepper, a handful of rice or pasta, some leftover canned peas, a carrot if you have it, a few garlic cloves. As it simmers some more, it will begin to smell marvelous. You will feel happy. You will feel expectant. *You will feel rich!*

I learned a lot of other things about making "something out of nothing" as I wrote the first three books, including how to cut open a presumably empty toothpaste tube and find that *it isn't empty at all.* And trust me, in the absence of Chanel's costly Serum Extreme, Vaseline works just fine as a night cream.

What I learned mostly, however, is that God is faithful. He really does love us. And here's what some may have trouble believing:

He really does want the best for His children.

If you're on a painful journey through the valley, ask Him to walk through it with you. Make some chicken soup from chicken bones, and give thanks. And when you finally get to the mountaintop, give thanks for the valley you've just been through. Because you will almost certainly go there again. And again, it will be hard.

But it will be good.

I N THE LITTLE village of less than a thousand, everyone's dinner—party or otherwise—began at The Local, unless they wanted to make the fifteen-mile drive to Food Value. Of course, they could go out on the highway to Cloer's Market, but Hattie Cloer was so well-known for telling customers her aches and pains that hardly anyone ever did that.

"See this right here?" she might say, pointing to her shoulder. "Last night somethin' come up there big as a grapefruit. I said, 'Clyde, put your hand right here and feel that. What do you think it is?'

"And Clyde said, 'Why, law, that feels like some kind of a golf ball or somethin' in there,' and don't you know, Darlene took to barkin', and that thing took to hurtin', and I never laid my head on th' pillow 'til way up in the mornin'. Wouldn't you like a pound or two of these nice snap beans?"

Worse than that, according to some, was Darlene, Hattie's Chihuahua, who lay on a sack by the cash register. Every time Hattie rang up a sale, the dog growled and snapped at the customer.

Avis Packard once said that Hattie Cloer had sent more business to The Local than any advertising he'd ever run in the paper.

Two weeks after his first jog up to Church Hill, Father Tim made an early Saturday call at The Local.

Since Barnabas was running with him these days, he found it convenient that The Local had an old bike rack near the front door, where his dog could be tied on a short leash.

He was still out of breath, and Barnabas was panting with some exhaustion himself. The route had by now fallen into place. They ran through Baxter Park and up to Church Hill, then along the quiet road by Miss Sadie's apple orchards, past the Presbyterian church, three times around the parking lot, down Lilac Road to Main Street, and then to Wisteria Lane, where they turned toward home.

"Two miles, right on the money," he discovered with immense satisfaction.

"Mornin', Father," said Avis, who was sitting at the cash register. "How does joggin' compare to workin' up a sermon?"

"Well, Avis, I can't see as there's much difference. I dread both, but once I get started, there's nothing I'd rather be doing."

"We got those fine-lookin' brown eggs you like. And Luther Lovell's boys delivered the nicest bunch of broilers you ever seen. You ought to look at those, and check that pretty batch of calf liver while you're at it."

> *"We all have hometown appetites. Every other person is a bundle of longing for the simplicities of good taste once enjoyed on the farm or in the hometown left behind."*
>
> —Clementine Paddleford

One thing Father Tim liked about Avis Packard was the way he got excited about his groceries. He could rhapsodize about the first fresh strawberries from the valley in a way that made him a veritable Wordsworth of garden fare. "We got a special today on tenderloin that's so true to the meanin' of th' name, you can cut it with a fork."

"Well, now, I'm not shopping, Avis. I'm looking."

"What're you lookin' for?" Avis cocked his head to one side like he always did when he asked a question.

"Ideas. You see, I've decided to give a dinner party."

"You don't mean it!"

"Oh, I do. But the thing is, I don't know what to cook."

"Well, sir, that's a problem, all right. I'll be thinkin' about it while you look around," Avis assured him.

A little line was forming at the cash register, so the rector moved away, greeting shoppers as he went.

At the produce bins, he admitted he was feeling slightly nervous over his idea. First of all, he didn't even have a guest list.

Of course, he was going to ask Emma, and yes, Miss Sadie. He thought she would make a splendid contribution. Besides, he had heard she once went to school in Paris, and he wanted to know more about it.

Hal and Marge, of course. No doubt about that.

Hoppy Harper, now there was a thought, his wife gone and no one to look after him but that old housekeeper. That made six, including himself.

Six. For the life of him, he couldn't think of another soul that would fit in just right with that particular group.

Perhaps he should invite Winnie Ivey, since she was always feeding everybody else. Maybe he would do that.

Avis came down the aisle with a gleam in his eye. "I turned the register over to my boy. I want to help you get your party goin'. What do you think about beef stroganoff, a salad with bibb lettuce, chickory, slices of navel orange and spring onions, and new potatoes roasted with fresh rosemary? 'Course, I'd put a nice bottle of cabernet behind that. 1982."

* * *

He sat with Barnabas one evening with a lapful of cookbooks. As much as he appreciated Avis Packard's menu planning, beef stroganoff seemed too ordinary. He wanted something that spoke of spring, that made people feel there was a celebration going on, and that would fill them up without being too heavy.

"This is a lot of work," he confided to Barnabas, who appeared to understand, "and I haven't even started yet."

He wondered why he had waited so long to entertain. It was clear to him that he had gotten completely out of the notion, although once he had loved doing it. He'd had the bishop and his wife for tea three times and twice for dinner, the vestry had come for a light supper on at least four occasions, and, once, he had the courage to give a luncheon for the members of the Altar Guild, who had such a good time they didn't leave until four o'clock.

Not that he was a great cook, of course. Still, he wasn't half bad at barbecued short ribs, an occasional sirloin tip roast that would melt in your mouth, if he did say so himself, and, in the summer, Silver Queen corn, cooked in milk for precisely sixty seconds. Of course, there was always the economical Rector's Meat Loaf, as he'd come to call it, which he usually made at least once a week.

He'd even been known to bake his own bread, but the interest these days somehow eluded him. Gardening had taken over. And where once he had sat and read cookbooks, he now read catalogs from Wayside Gardens and White Flower Farm, not to mention Jackson and Perkins.

"And another thing," he said to Barnabas, who raised one ear in response, "is the cost. Do you realize what entertaining costs these days?"

Barnabas yawned.

"Lamb, I think it should be lamb," he mused to himself after going to bed. And he didn't think it should take the form of anything *nouvelle.*

The thought came to him as he laid his head on the pillow. Company Stew! It was an old recipe, nearly forgotten, but one that had always brought raves.

He got out of bed and put on his faded burgundy dressing gown. Noticing that the clock said eleven, he slipped his feet into the chewed leather slippers and went downstairs to look for the recipe.

The search revealed how vagrant his closets had become, so he began rearranging the one in the hall, which, very likely, his guests might see.

When he finished, he was surprised to find that it was two o'clock in the morning, and he'd collected a boxful of odds and ends for the "Bane and Blessing" sale.

It was rather a free feeling, he noticed, prowling about the house at such an odd hour. To explore this strange freedom even further, he went into the kitchen, made himself a meat loaf sandwich with no mayonnaise, and sat at the table reading *Bon Appétit,* which he had bought for ideas and inspiration.

"No wonder I haven't done this sort of thing in years," he muttered. "It's too demanding."

* * *

On Friday, he left the office early, stopped by The Local, and went home to change into an old T-shirt and khaki pants.

He would get the bath out of the way straight off, he thought, then begin the stew around three, open the wine to breathe at six, and have everything in good order for his guests at seven.

When he opened the door to the garage, Barnabas leaped into the hallway, skidded nearly the length of it on a small Oriental rug, then dashed into the kitchen and hurled himself onto the bar stool, where he began to lick a vinyl place mat on the counter.

The rector put Barnabas on his longest leash. Not only would this give him freedom to thrash about in the bath, it would keep him from bounding into the street if the new setup alarmed him.

Unfortunately, this would prove to be the worst idea he'd had in a very long time.

* * *

He was pleased with his location of the tub. The little clearing was shielded from the street by the laurels, and afforded him plenty of elbow room. As soon as Barnabas was bathed, he thought, he'd rub him down with a towel, then lead him into the garage, where he could finish drying off and make himself presentable.

Attaching the looped end of the leash to a laurel branch high over his head, he encouraged Barnabas to get into the water, which he'd liberally sudsed with Joy.

Instead, Barnabas hurled himself into the tub with a mighty leap.

Just as quickly as he went in, he came out, diving between the rector's legs. He circled his right leg and plunged back into the water, soaking his master from head to foot.

Then, he leaped out of the tub, raced again between Father Tim's legs, joyfully dashed around his left ankle, and headed for a laurel bush.

It seemed to the rector that it all happened within a matter of seconds. And while his memory searched wildly for a Scripture, nothing came forth.

Barnabas circled the bush at a dead heat, catching the leash in the crotch of a lower limb, and was brought to an abrupt halt.

The tautly drawn leash had run out. Barnabas was trapped on the bush. And each of the rector's ankles was tightly bound.

Shaken, Father Tim observed this set of circumstances from a sitting position, and in the most complete state of shock he could remember.

Miraculously, he was still wearing his glasses.

Barnabas was now lying down, though the leash was caught so tightly in the tree that he could not lower his head. He stared at Father Tim, obviously suffering the misery of remorse. Then, his contrition being so deep that he could not bear to look his master in the eye, he appeared to fall into a deep sleep.

The rector began spontaneously to preach one of the most electrifying sermons of his career.

His deep memory bank of holy Scripture came flooding back, and the power of his impassioned exhortation made the hair fairly bristle on the black dog's neck. In fact, Barnabas opened his eyes and listened intently to every word.

When his oration ended, the rector felt sufficiently relieved to try and figure out what to do.

He could see it now. His guests ringing the doorbell, finally coming inside, searching the house, calling out the back door, and then spying him in this miserable condition, while the stew pot sat cold on the stove.

No wonder so many people these days had heart fibrillations, high blood pressure, and a thousand other stress-related diseases. No doubt all these people were dog owners.

Lord, be Thou my helper, he prayed.

"Father Tim! Is that you back there?"

Avis Packard came crashing through the laurel hedge, looked down at his good customer, and said, without blinking, "I let you get away without your butter. Do you want me to put it in the refrigerator or just leave it right here?"

* * *

The Company Stew, which had simmered with the peel of an orange and a red onion stuck with cloves, was a rousing success. In fact, he was so delighted with the whole affair that he relented and let Barnabas into the study after dinner.

Marge helped serve coffee and triple-layer cake from the old highboy, as the scent of roses drifted through the open windows.

Barnabas, meanwhile, was a model of decorum and lay next to his master's wing chair, occasionally wagging his tail.

"You must have quoted this dog the whole book of Deuteronomy," said Emma, who still refused to call him by name.

"This dog," he said crisply, "is grounded."

"Uh-oh," said Hal. "I guess that means no TV for a week?"

"No TV, no pizza, no talking on the phone."

"Ogre!" said Marge.

"What did the big guy do, anyway?" Hoppy wondered, leaning over to scratch Barnabas behind the ears.

"I'm afraid it's unspeakable, actually."

"Oh, good!" exclaimed Miss Sadie. "Then tell us everything."

Miss Sadie enjoyed the bath story so much, she brought out a lace handkerchief to wipe her eyes.

Miss Rose, however, was not amused. "I leave dogs alone."

"Nope, dogs leave you alone," said her husband.

"Whatever," said Miss Rose, with a wave of her hand.

Hoppy set his dessert plate on the hearth, then leaned back and stretched his long legs. He looked fondly at his elderly patient of nearly a decade. "Uncle Billy, I'd sure like to hear a joke, if you've got one."

Uncle Billy grinned. "Did you hear the one about the skydivin' lessons?"

"I hope you didn't get this from Harry Nelson," said Emma, who didn't like Harry Nelson jokes, not even secondhand.

"Nossir. I got this joke off a feller at the Grill. He was drivin' through from Texas."

Everyone settled back happily, and Miss Rose gave Uncle Billy the go-ahead by jabbing him in the side with her elbow.

"Well, this feller he wanted to learn to skydive, don't you know. And so he goes to this school and he takes all kind of trainin' and all, and one day comes the time he has to jump out of this airplane, and out he goes, like a ton of bricks, and he gets on down there a little ways and commences to pull th' cord and they don't nothin' happen, don't you know, and so he keeps on droppin' and he switches over and starts pullin' on his emergency cord, and they still don't nothin' happen, an' th' first thing you know, here comes this other feller, a shootin' up from the ground, and the feller goin' down says, 'Hey, buddy, do you know anything about parachutes?' And the one a comin' up says, 'Nope, do you know anything about gas stoves?'"

Uncle Billy looked around proudly. He would have considered it an understatement to say that everyone roared with laughter.

"I've heard that bloomin' tale forty times," Miss Rose said, removing a slice of cheese from her pocket and having it with her coffee.

At Home in Mitford, Ch. 4

WHEN HE ARRIVED home that afternoon at five-thirty, he found a steaming, but spotless, kitchen and a red-cheeked Puny.

"That bushel of tomatoes like to killed me!" she declared. "After I froze that big load of squash, I found some jars in your garage, sterilized 'em in your soup pot, and canned ever' one in th' bushel. Looky here," she said, proudly, pointing to fourteen mason jars containing vermilion tomatoes.

"Puny," he exclaimed with joyful amazement, "this is a sight for sore eyes."

"Not only that, but I scrubbed your bathroom 'til it shines, and I want to tell you right now, Father, if I'm goin' to stay here—and I dearly need th' work—you're goin' to have to put your toilet seat up when you relieve yourself."

He felt his face burn. A little Emma, her employer thought, darkly. Now I've got one at the office and one at home, a matched set.

He could not, however, dismiss the joy of seeing fourteen jars of tomatoes lined up on his kitchen counter.

* * *

On Friday afternoon, he arrived at the rectory to find the house filled with ravishing aromas.

Baked chicken. Squash casserole. Steamed broccoli. Corn on the cob. And frozen yogurt topped with cooked Baxter apples. Oh, ye of little faith, why didst thou doubt? he quoted to himself.

"I know about that old diabetes stuff, my granpaw had it worse'n you," Puny told him with satisfaction. "An' not only can I cook for diabetes, I can cook for high blood pressure, heart trouble, nervous stomach, and constipation."

During the past twelve years, he had sometimes asked in a fit of frustration, "Lord, what have I done to deserve Emma Garrett?" Now, he found himself asking with a full heart, "Lord, what have I done to deserve Puny Bradshaw?"

At Home in Mitford, Ch. 7

"I WISH I could make you some corn bread," Puny said, wistfully. "I just crave to do that."

"And you don't know how I appreciate it, and thank you for the thought," he said, eating a tuna sandwich made with whole wheat, and no mayonnaise. "But I can't eat corn bread because of this aggravating diabetes."

"I could leave out th' bacon drippin's, and use vegetable oil. But it wouldn't be no good."

"That's right!"

"If my granpaw didn't git corn bread once a day, he said he couldn't live. I'd bake him a cake at night, he'd eat half of it hot. Then he'd git up in the night and eat what was left, crumbled up in milk."

"Really?"

"Stayed a string bean all his life, too. He said preachin' the word of God kept the fat wore off."

"It has never served me in that particular way, I regret to say."

Puny filled the scrub bucket and went to work with her brush.

At Home in Mitford, Ch. 10

HE SET TWO places at the counter and took the bubbling sausage casserole from the oven. There would be no diet this day. Then, he turned on the record player and heard the familiar, if scratchy, strains of the *Messiah*.

Dooley appeared at the kitchen door, dressed in the burgundy robe. "Sounds like a' army's moved in down here."

"My friend, you have hit the nail on the head. It is an army of the most glorious voices in recent history, singing one of the most majestic musical works ever written!"

Dooley rolled his eyes.

At Home in Mitford, Ch. 12

IN THE FADING afternoon light, Absalom Greer's slim frame might have been that of a twenty-year-old as he hurried down the steps of the old general store.

"Welcome to God's country!" he said, opening the door of the Buick. "Get out and come in, Father!"

The rector was astonished to see that the face of his eighty-six-year-old host was remarkably unlined, and, what was more astounding, he had a full head of hair.

"I was looking for an elderly gentleman to greet me. Pastor Greer must have sent his son!"

The old man laughed heartily. "I can still hear an ant crawling in the grass," he said with satisfaction, "but there's not a tooth in my head I can call my own."

The country preacher led the village rector up the steps and into the dim interior of the oldest store in several counties.

Father Tim felt as if he'd walked into a Rembrandt painting, for the last of the sunlight had turned the color of churned butter, casting a golden glow upon the chestnut walls and heart-of-pine floors.

"My daddy built this store when I was six years old. It's got the first nails I ever drove. It sold out of the family in 1974, but I bought it back and intend to keep it, though it don't do much toward keeping me.

"Let me give you a little country cocktail," said his host, who was dressed in a neat gray suit and starched shirt. He selected a cold drink from an icebox behind the cash register, opened it, and handed it to the rector.

"You're looking at where I do my best preaching," he said, slapping the worn wood of the old counter. "Right here is where the rubber hits the road.

"Like the Greeks said to Philip, 'Sir, we would see Christ.' If they don't see him behind this counter six days a week, we might as well throw my Sunday preaching out the window. Where is your weekday pulpit, my friend?"

"Main Street."

"That's a good place. Some soldiers set around and smell the coffee and watch the bacon frying, but the battle is waged on your feet."

"Absalom," said a quiet voice from the back of the store, "supper's ready. You can come anytime."

A door closed softly.

"My sister, Lottie," the old man said with evident pride. "She lives with me and does the cooking and housekeeping. I can assure you that I never did anything to deserve her ministry to me. She is an angel of the Lord!"

His host turned the sign on the front door to read Closed, and they walked the length of the narrow store on creaking floorboards, passing bins of seeds and nails, rows of canned goods, sacks of feed, thread, buttons, iron skillets, and aluminum washtubs.

Absalom Greer pushed open a door and the rector stood on the threshold in happy amazement. Before him was a room with ancient, leaded windows gleaming with the last rays of sunlight. In the center of the room stood a large table laid with a white cloth and a variety of steaming dishes, and on it burned an oil lamp.

In the corner of the room, a fire crackled in the grate, and books lined the walls behind a pair of comfortable reading chairs. A worn black Bible lay on the table next to one of the chairs, and an orange cat curled peacefully on the deep windowsill.

He thought he'd never entered a home so peaceable in spirit.

A tall, slender woman moved into the room from the kitchen, wearing an apron. Her blue dress became her graying hair, which was pulled back simply and tied with a ribbon. She smiled shyly and extended her hand. "Father Tim," said Absalom Greer, "Lottie Miller! My joy and my crown, my earthly shield and buckler, and my widowed sister."

"It's my great pleasure," said the rector, feeling as if he had gone to another country to visit.

"My sister is shy as a deer, Father. We don't get much company here, as I do all my pastoring at church or in the store. Why don't you set where you can see the little fire on the hearth, it's always a consolation."

After washing up in a tidy bathroom, Father Tim sat down at the table, finding that even the hard-back chair seemed comforting.

* * *

"I left school when I was twelve," said Absalom Greer over dinner, "to help my daddy in the store, and I got along pretty good teaching myself at night. One evenin', along about the age of fourteen—I was back here in this very room, studyin' a book—the wind got to howling and blowing as bad as you ever heard.

"Lottie was a baby in my mother's arms. I can see them now, my mother sitting by the fire, rocking Lottie, and humming a tune, and I was settin' right there on a little bed.

"My eyes were as wide open as they are now, when suddenly I saw a great band of angels. This room was filled with the brightness of angels!

"They were pure white, with color only in their wings, color like a prism casts when the sun shines through it. I never saw anything so beautiful in my life, before or since. I couldn't speak a word, and my mother went on rocking and humming, with her eyes closed, and there were angels standing over her, and all around us was this shining, heavenly host.

"Then, it seemed as if a golden stair let down there by the door, and the angels turned and swarmed up that staircase, and were gone. I remember I went to sobbing, but my mother didn't hear it. And I reached up to wipe my tears, but there weren't any there.

"I've thought about it many a time over the years, and I think it was my spirit that was weeping with joy."

Lottie Miller had not spoken, but had passed each dish and platter, it seemed to the rector, at just the right time. He had a second helping of potatoes that had been sliced and fried with rock salt and chives, and another helping of roasted lamb, which was as fine as any lamb he'd tasted in a very long time.

"It's a mystery how I could have done it, but I completely forgot that heavenly vision," said the preacher, who was buttering a biscuit.

"Along about sixteen, I got to feeling I had no soul at all. They'd take me to hear a preaching, and I couldn't hear. They'd take me to see a healing and I couldn't see. My daddy said it was the name they'd put on me—Absalom! A wicked, rebellious, ungodly character if there ever was one, but my mother was young when I was born, and heedless, and she liked the sound of it, and I was stuck with it. Later on, when I got to reading the Word, I got to understanding Absalom and his daddy, and that pitiful relationship, and the name got to be a blessing to me instead of a curse, and, praise God, some of my best preaching has come out of my name.

"Well, along about twenty, I kissed my mother and daddy good-bye, and my baby sister, and I walked to Wesley and took the train and I went out west carrying a cardboard box tied with twine.

"Times were so hard, I couldn't get a job. I ended up putting the cardboard from that box in the bottoms of my shoes. A fella told me the bottom of one foot said Cream of Wheat, and the other said This Side Up.

"I walked on that box for three months 'til I got work in a silver mine. Way down in that mine, in that deep, dark pit, I heard the Lord call me. 'Absalom, my son,' He said as clear as day, 'go home. Go home and preach my Word to your people.'

"Well sir, I didn't know his Word to preach it. But I up and started home, took the train back across this great land, got off at Wesley, walked twelve miles to Farmer in the middle of the night with a full moon shining, and I got to my mother's and daddy's door right out there, and I laid down with the dogs and went to sleep on a flour sack.

"I remember I told myself I'd never heard the Lord call me in that mine, that I'd just been lonesome and was looking for an excuse to come home.

"I went on like that for a year or two, went to church to look at the girls, helped my daddy in the store. But that wasn't enough, something was sorely missing. One day, I commenced to read everything theological I could get my hands on.

"I drenched myself in Spurgeon, and plowed through Calvin, I soaked up Whitefield and gorged on Matthew Henry, as hard as I could go. But I was fightin' my calling, and my heart was like a stone.

"One day I was settin' in the orchard I planted as a boy, and the Lord spoke again. 'Absalom, my son,' He said, clear as day, 'spread my Word to your people.'

"It made the hair stand up on my head. But in five minutes, I had laid down in the sunshine and gone to sleep like a lizard.

"I went on that way for about three years, not listening to God, 'til one night He woke me up, I thought I'd been hit a blow on the head with a two-by-four.

"It was like a bolt of lightning knocked me out of bed and threw me to the floor. Blam! 'Absalom, my son,' said the Lord, 'go preach my Word to your people, and be quick about it.'

"I got up off that floor, I ran in here where it was cold enough to preserve a corpse, I wrapped up in a blanket and lit an oil lamp, and I got to reading the Good Book and for two years I did not stop.

"Everybody who knew me thought I'd gone soft.

"'Absalom Greer has got religion,' they said, but they were only partly right. It was religion that had got me, it was God Himself who had me at last, and it was the most thrilling time of my life.

"The words would jump off the page, I would understand things I had never understood before. I could take a verse my tongue had glibbed over in church, and see in it wondrous and thrilling meanings that kept the hair standing up on my head.

"I would go out to work at the lumber company and take it with me. I would set on the toilet and read it. I would walk to town reading, and I'd be so transported I would fall in the ditch and get up and go again, turning the page.

"I felt God spoke to me continuously for two transcendent years. Glory, glory, glory!" said the old preacher, with shining eyes.

"One Sunday morning, I was settin' in that little church about three miles down the road there and Joshua Hoover was pastoring then. I remember I was settin' there in that sweet little church, and Pastor Hoover come down the aisle and he was white as a ghost.

"He said, 'Absalom, God has asked me to let you preach the service this morning.'

"I like to dropped down dead at his feet.

"He said, 'I don't know about this, it makes me uneasy, but it's what the Lord told me to do.'

"When I stood up, my legs gave out under me, I like to fainted like a girl."

Lottie laughed softly.

"I recalled something Billy Sunday said. He said if you want milk and honey on your bread, you have to go into the land of giants. So, I went into that pulpit and I prayed, and the congregation, they prayed, and the first thing you know, the Holy Ghost got to moving in that place, and I got to preaching the Word of God, and pretty soon, it was just like a mill wheel got to turning, and we all went to grinding corn!"

"Bliss!" said the rector, filled with understanding.

"Bliss, my friend, indeed! There is nothing like it on earth when the spirit of God comes pouring through, and He has poured through me in fair weather and foul, for sixty-four years."

"Have there been dry spells?"

The preacher pushed his plate away and Lottie rose to clear the table. Father Tim smelled the kind of coffee he remembered from Mississippi—strong and black and brewed on the stove.

"My brother, dry is not the word. There was a time I went down like a stone in a pond and sank clear to the bottom. I lay on the bottom of that pond for two miserable years, and I thought I'd never see the light of day in my soul again."

"I can't say my current tribulation is anything like that. But in an odd way, it's something almost worse."

"What's that?" Absalom Greer asked kindly.

"When it comes to feeding his sheep, I'm afraid my sermons are about as nourishing as cardboard."

"Are you resting?"

"Resting?"

"Resting. Sometimes we get so worn out with being useful that we get useless. I'll ask you what another preacher once asked: Are you too exhausted to run and too scared to rest?"

Too scared to rest! He'd never thought of it that way. "When in God's name are you going to take a vacation?" Hoppy had asked again, only the other day. He hadn't known the truth then, but he felt he knew it now—yes, he was too scared to rest.

The old preacher's eyes were as clear as gemstones. "My brother, I would urge you to search the heart of God on this matter, for it was this very thing that sank me to the bottom of the pond."

They looked at one another with grave understanding. "I'll covet your prayers," said Father Tim.

* * *

As the two men sat by the fire and discussed the Newland wedding, Lottie Miller shyly drew up an armchair and joined them. She sat with her eyes lowered to the knitting in her lap.

"Miss Lottie," said Father Tim, "that was as fine a meal as I've enjoyed in a very long time. I thank you for the beauty and the goodness of it."

"Thank you for being here," she said with obvious effort. "Absalom and I don't have supper company often, and I'm proud for my brother to have an educated man to talk with. It's a blessing to him."

An educated man! thought Father Tim. It is Absalom Greer who is educating me!

* * *

"Take home a peck of our apples." Lottie handed him a basket of what appeared to be Rome Beauties.

"If you like 'em," said her brother, "we'll give you a bushel when you come again!"

"I'm deeply obliged. We have quite an orchard in Mitford, as you may know. Miss Sadie Baxter is the grower of what we've come to call the Baxter apple."

A strange look crossed Lottie Miller's face.

"Miss Sadie Baxter," Absalom said quietly. "I once made a proposal of marriage to that fine lady."

At Home in Mitford, Ch. 14

A BREEZE STIRRED through the open windows of the bedroom, with its high ceiling and cool, hardwood floor. On Miss Sadie's dressing table, Father Tim saw again the old photos in the silver frames. There was the face of the woman so eerily identical to Olivia Davenport. And the brooding, intense gaze of the young man named Willard Porter, whose grand house had been brought to ruin in full view of the whole village.

Miss Sadie took a deep breath.

"Father," she said, "what I'm about to tell you has never been spoken to another soul. I trust you will carry it to your grave."

"Consider it done," he said, solemnly, sitting back in the slipcovered chair, and finding it exceedingly comfortable.

"I've thought many times about where to begin," she said, folding her small hands and looking toward the open windows. "And while it doesn't have much to do with the rest of the story, my mind keeps going back to when I was a little girl playing in these apple orchards.

"You'll never know how I loved the orchards then, and the way the apples would fall on the grass and burst open in the sun. Then the bees would come, and butterflies by the hundreds, and the fragrance that rose from the orchard floor was one of the sweetest thrills of my life."

She lay back against the pillows and closed her eyes, smiling. "Do you mind if I ramble a bit?"

"I'd be disappointed if you didn't."

"I used to carry my dolls out under the trees. If you walk down the back steps and go straight past the gate and the old washhouse and then turn right—that was my favorite place. Louella's mother, China Mae, loved to go with me! Why, she played with dolls as if she were a little girl, herself. She was the most fun, so full of life. I was nine when we moved here from Wesley, into the new house Papa built, and China Mae was twenty. She was my very best friend on earth.

"She was so black, Father! I liked to turn her head in my hands to see the light play on her face, to see the blue in the black!

"She used to call me Little Toad. I have no idea why, I'd love to know. But I'll just have to find that out when I see her in heaven."

"I hope you're not planning to find that out anytime soon."

"Of course not! I'm going to live for ages and ages. I have things to do, you know."

The clock ticked on the dresser.

"Back then, there was a big house in Mitford, right where the Baptist church stands today. It's long gone, now, but it was named Boxwood, and oh, it was a pretty place. Miss Lureen Thompson owned that house, she was like me, an only child; her parents both died in a fall from a rock when they were out on a picnic. Their chauffeur was waiting in the car for them to come back, and they didn't come and didn't come, and when he went to look . . ." Miss Sadie shivered. "It was an awful thing, they say, Miss Lureen was so stricken. You know how she tried to get over it?"

He didn't know.

"Parties! There was always something fine and big going on at Miss Lureen's. And China Mae and I were always invited to come by and sample the sweets before a party. Her cook was as big as the stove, and her cream puffs were the best you ever tasted, not to mention her ambrosia. I have dreamed about that ambrosia several times. She used to make enough to fill a dishpan, because people took such a fit over it.

"Miss Lureen liked to say, 'The firefly only shines when on the wing. So it is with us—when we stop, we darken.' I never forgot that.

"Oh, we all loved Boxwood! It had so many servants hurrying about, and they all seemed so happy in their work. Miss Lureen was good to her people. Why, when her Packard wore out, do you know who she gave it to? Her chauffeur! He fixed it up good as new and drove it back to Charleston when she died.

"His name was Soot Tobin. Black as soot, they said. He was a big, strapping man with a stutter so bad he scarcely ever spoke, but when he did, people listened, colored and white, for his voice was as deep as the bass on a church organ. He made China Mae fairly giddy. 'Most everything he'd say, she'd just giggle and go on, to beat the band. You know, China Mae was not all . . . well, she never grew up, exactly, which is one reason I loved her so. She was just like me!

"One day I came home from school and I could not believe my eyes what had happened.

"China Mae would never have to play with my baby dolls again, for she had one of her own, just her color. It was lying asleep in the bed with her, and had on a little white gown. My mama was standing by the bed looking at that baby, with tears just streaming down her face.

"'Sadie,' she said to me, 'this is Louella. God has sent her to live with us.'"

Miss Sadie shook her head and smiled at the rector. "Isn't that a surprise? To come home from school one day, and there's your second-best friend of life, sent down from heaven?"

He laughed happily. If there was anything more amazing and wonderful than almost anyone's life story, he couldn't think what it was.

"Well, I took after that baby somethin' awful. I rocked her, I bathed her, I pulled her around in a little wagon, I sewed dresses for her, I was as happy as anything to have her to play with and love, and Mama was, too.

"When she got weaned, I started taking her to town. I'd dress her up myself, and they'd say, 'Here comes Sadie Baxter with that little nigger.'

"I never did like to hear that, even as a child. I wanted Louella to be my sister, I played like she was my sister, and then when I'd go to town, they'd say that. So, I stopped going.

"We stayed home and played and I never did miss going to town. Mama hired a tutor for me, anyway. Mr. Kingsley. I declare, he had the worst bad breath in the world, but he taught the prettiest cursive you ever saw, and was real good at history. Mama ordered off for all my clothes and shoes, and China Mae cut my hair, and we went to the doctor and dentist at Papa's lumberyard down in the valley. Or, sometimes, the doctors would drive up the mountain to give us our checkups, and Mama would put on a big spread like the president was coming.

"We called it 'Doctor Day,' and I didn't take to it one bit. I would grab Louella and we would run off and hide in the orchard."

Miss Sadie laughed to herself, with her eyes closed. Father Tim could see that she was watching a movie in which she was both the star and the director. He closed his eyes, too, and quietly slipped his feet out of his loafers.

"When Louella was about three, Mama said she was tired of going off and leaving her and China Mae at home when we marched off to Lord's Chapel. There were only a dozen or so colored people in Mitford, not enough for a church, I suppose. So, Mama said that from now on, we were all going together, that was what God gave us churches for.

"Papa didn't like this one bit, but Mama would not let up on him. She got down the Bible and the prayer book and without a shadow of a doubt, she showed him what was what.

"So, China Mae and Louella and Papa and Mama and me would walk down the road to the old Lord's Chapel that stood on the hill. And we would all sit in the same pew.

"If anybody ever once said 'nigger,' I don't know who it was, for they were scared of Papa. I mean, they respected him, not to mention that he gave a lot of money.

"In a little while, it seemed like nobody noticed anymore, it was just the most natural thing on earth. What they said outside the lych-gates, I don't know, but if China Mae missed a Sunday from being sick, lots of ladies would ask about her.

"Life was better in those days, Father, it really was. When China Mae did the wash in the washhouse, and we put the fire under that big iron pot, why, it was an exciting event. China Mae had joy over making the clothes come clean, while people today would think it was drudgery. We kind of celebrated on wash day. Mama would make a pineapple upside-down cake, and Louella and I would make stickies out of biscuit dough and cinnamon and sugar, and after that big load of work was done, we all sat down and had a tea party."

A bird called outside the open windows, and a breeze filled the fragile marquisette curtains. Father Tim caught himself nodding off and sat upright with a start.

At Home in Mitford, Ch. 19

HE SPIED THE THING on his counter at once. It was Edith Mallory's signature blue casserole dish.

He was afraid of that.

Emma had written to Sligo to say that Pat Mallory had died soon after he left for Ireland. Heart attack. No warning. Pat, she said, had felt a wrenching chest pain, had sat down on the top step outside his bedroom, and after dropping dead sitting up, had toppled to the foot of the stairs, where the Mallorys' maid of thirty years had found him just before dinner.

"Oh, Mr. Mallory," she was reported to have said, "you shouldn't have gone and done that. We're havin' lasagna."

Sitting there on the farmhouse window seat, reading Emma's five-page letter, he had known that Edith Mallory would not waste any time when he returned.

Long before Pat's death, he'd been profoundly unsteadied when she had slipped her hand into his or let her fingers run along his arm. At one point, she began winking at him during sermons, which distracted him to such a degree that he resumed his old habit of preaching over the heads of the congregation, literally.

So far, he had escaped her random snares but had once dreamed he was locked with her in the parish-hall coat closet, pounding desperately on the door and pleading with the sexton to let him out.

Now Pat, good soul, was cold in the grave, and Edith's casserole was hot on his counter.

Casseroles! Their seduction had long been used on men of the cloth, often with rewarding results for the cook.

Casseroles, after all, were a gesture that on the surface could not be mistaken for anything other than righteous goodwill. And, once one had consumed and exclaimed over the initial offering, along would come another on its very heels, until the bachelor curate ended up a married curate or the divorced deacon a fellow so skillfully ensnared that he never knew what hit him.

In the language of food, there were casseroles, and there were casseroles. Most were used to comfort the sick or inspire the downhearted. But certain others, in his long experience, were so filled with allure and innuendo that they ceased to be Broccoli Cheese Delight intended for the stomach and became arrows aimed straight for the heart.

In any case, there was always the problem of what to do with the dish. Decent people returned it full of something else. Which meant that the person to whom you returned it would be required, at some point, to give you another food item, all of which produced a cycle that was unimaginably tedious.

Clergy, of course, were never required to fill the dish before returning it, but either way, it had to be returned. And there, clearly, was the rub.

He approached the unwelcome surprise as if a snake might have been coiled inside. His note of thanks, which he would send over tomorrow by Puny, would be short and to the point:

Dear Edith: Suffice it to say that you remain one of the finest cooks in the county. That was no lie; it was undeniably true.

Your way with (blank, blank) is exceeded only by your graciousness. A thousand thanks. In His peace, Fr Tim.

There.

He lifted the lid. Instantly, his mouth began to water, and his heart gave a small leap of joy.

Crab cobbler! One of his favorites. He stared with wonder at the dozen flaky homemade biscuits poised on the bed of fresh crabmeat and fragrant sauce.

Perhaps, he thought with sudden abandon, he should give Edith Mallory a ring this very moment and express his thanks.

As he reached for the phone, he realized what he was doing—he was placing his foot squarely in a bear trap.

He hastily clamped the lid on the steaming dish. "You see?" he muttered darkly. "That's the way it happens."

Where casseroles were concerned, one must constantly be on guard.

A Light in the Window, Ch. 1

THE FIRE WAS fairly crackling, and he closed his mind to the fact that its cheer would be short-lived.

"This is neat."

"Bologna to die for," he said, picking two thick, browned slices out of the skillet with a fork and putting them on Dooley's toast. "Eat up, my friend, and don't hold back on the mustard." As for himself, he hadn't tasted such bacon since he was a Scout. He looked at their camp mess spread around the hearth. Not a bad way to live, after all.

The wind had cast torrents of snow against the study windows, where it froze solid, shutting out the light. They might have been swaddled in a cocoon, filled with an eerie glow.

He took a swallow of the coffee that he'd brewed over the fire in a saucepan. "Whose name did you draw at school? I've been meaning to ask."

"I drawed ol' Buster's name, but I didn't git 'im nothin'."

"Why not?"

"I traded for somebody else's name."

"Really?"

"Yeah. Jenny's."

"Aha."

"Had t' give ol' Peehead Wilson a dollar and a half to swap."

"Not a bad deal, considering."

"I got 'er a book."

"A book! Terrific. Best gift out there, if you ask me."

"About horses."

"She likes horses?"

"She hates horses."

"I see."

"So I got 'er this book so she can git t' know 'em and like 'em."

"Good thinking, pal."

They drew closer to the brightness of the fire.

"You like ol' Cynthia?"

"Yes. Very much."

"You love 'er?"

"I . . . don't know. I think so."

"How come you don't know?"

He really did dislike feeling that he had to have all the answers. "I don't know why I don't know! Do you love Jenny?"

Dooley looked forlorn. "I don't know."

"One thing's for sure," said the rector, "this is the dumbest conversation I've heard since the vestry made its new ruling on toilet paper."

A Light in the Window, Ch. 6

HE WENT UP the hill at Miss Sadie's request, for an impromptu lunch of collards, navy beans, hot rolls, and fried chicken.

"Miss Sadie," Louella had said over their early breakfast, "we've crackered and san'wiched that poor preacher half to death. Let's give 'im somethin' can stick to 'is ribs."

Miss Sadie sniffed. "Fried chicken in the daytime is too heavy if you've got work to do. Why not chicken salad?"

"Too much trouble—skinnin', stewin', cuttin' off th' bone. Besides, I feel a cookin' spell comin' on."

"Oh, dear." Miss Sadie drew a deep breath. If Louella was too long discouraged from what she called "real" cooking, she would suddenly take a fit of meal preparation that cost a fortune, the results of which they couldn't possibly eat at one or two sittings. This meant all the leftovers had to be frozen in a veritable stack of containers. She knew for a fact that loading up the freezer made the refrigerator motor work harder, which reflected on the electric bill.

She tried, however, to be reasonable. She didn't mind losing a battle or two if, in the larger issues, she might win the war.

A Light in the Window, Ch. 8

A Partial List of Covered Dishes
Brought to the Annual All-Church Thanksgiving Feast

Presbyterians . . . three turkeys ("whoppers")

Esther Bolick . . . two towering orange marmalade cakes

Ray Cunningham . . . ham (smoked with hickory chips)

Esther Cunningham . . . bag of Winesaps

Cynthia Kavanagh . . . two pumpkin chiffon pies

Dooley Barlowe . . . tray of yeast rolls (still hot from the oven)

Father Tim . . . pan of sausage dressing and a bowl of cranberry salad

Sophia and Liza . . . platter of cinnamon stickies

Evie Adams . . . gallon jar of green beans

Mule and Fancy Skinner . . . sheet cake from Sweet Stuff Bakery

Dora Pugh . . . pot of stewed apples (from her own tree)

Plus a spinach casserole somebody forgot to set out

These High, Green Hills, Ch. 3

"LEG OF LAMB!" exclaimed Cynthia.

"Man!" Sometimes there was nothing else to do but quote Dooley Barlowe.

"And glazed carrots, and roasted potatoes with rosemary."

"The very gates of heaven."

"Dearest," she said, putting her arms around his neck, "there's something different about you. . . ."

"What? Exhaustion, maybe, from only four hours of sleep."

She kissed his chin. "No. Something deeper. I don't know what it is."

"Something good, I fondly hope."

"Yes. Very good. I can't put my finger on it, exactly. Oh. I forgot—and a salad with oranges and scallions, and your favorite dressing."

"But why all this?"

"Because you were so brave when we were lost in that horrible cave."

The payoff was definitely improving. He brushed her hair back and kissed her forehead. "It wasn't so horrible."

"Timothy . . ."

"OK," he said, "I was scared out of my wits."

She laughed. "I knew that!"

"You did not."

"Did so."

"Did not."

"Are y'uns havin' a fuss?" Uncle Billy peered through the screen door.

"Not yet," said the rector. "Come in and sit!"

These High, Green Hills, Ch. 11

MARGE OWEN'S FRENCH grandmother's chicken pie recipe was a study in contrasts. Its forthright and honest filling, which combined large chunks of white and dark meat, coarsely cut carrots, green peas, celery, and whole shallots, was laced with a dollop of sauterne and crowned by a pastry so light and flaky, it might have won the favor of Louis XIV.

"Bravo!" exclaimed the rector.

"Man!" said Dooley.

"I unashamedly beg you for this recipe," crowed Cynthia.

The new assistant, Blake Eddistoe, scraped his plate with his spoon. "Wonderful, ma'am!"

Hardly anyone ever cooked for diabetes, thought the rector as they trooped out to eat cake in the shade of the pin oak. Apparently it was a disease so innocuous, so bland, and so boring to anyone other than its unwilling victims that it was blithely dismissed by the cooks of the land.

He eyed the chocolate mocha cake that Marge was slicing at the table under the tree. Wasn't that her well-known raspberry filling? From here, it certainly looked like it. . . .

Ah, well. The whole awful business of saying no, which he roundly despised, was left to him. Maybe just a thin slice, however . . . something you could see through. . . .

"He can't have any," said Cynthia.

"I can't believe I forgot!" said Marge, looking stricken. "I'm sorry, Tim! Of course, we have homemade gingersnaps, I know you like those. Rebecca Jane, please fetch the gingersnaps for Father Tim, they're on the bottom shelf."

The four-year-old toddled off, happy with her mission.

Chocolate mocha cake with raspberry filling versus gingersnaps from the bottom shelf . . .

Clearly, the much-discussed and controversial affliction from which Saint Paul had prayed thrice to be delivered had been diabetes.

Out to Canaan, Ch. 4

WHEN HE WALKED into Esther's hospital room on Thursday morning, her bed was surrounded by Bane volunteers. One of them held a notepad at the ready, and he felt a definite tension in the air.

They didn't even look up as he came in.

Hessie leaned over Esther, speaking as if the patient's hearing had been severely impaired by the fall.

"Esther!" she shouted. "You've got to cooperate! The doctor said he'd give us twenty minutes and not a second more!"

"Ummaummhhhh," said Esther, desperately trying to speak through clamped jaws.

"Why couldn't she write something?" asked Vanita Bentley. "I see two fingers sticking out of her cast."

"Uhnuhhh," said Esther.

"You can't write with two fingers. Have you ever tried writing with two fingers?"

"Oh, Lord," said Vanita. "Then *you* think of something! We've got to hurry!"

"We need an alphabet board!" Hessie declared.

"Who has time to go lookin' for an alphabet board? Where would we find one, anyway?"

"Make one!" instructed the co-chair. "Write down the alphabet on your notepad and let her point 'til she spells it out."

"Ummuhuhnuh," said Esther.

"She can't move her arm to point!"

"So? We can move the notepad!"

Esther raised the forefinger of her right hand.

"One finger. *One!* Right, Esther? If it's yes, blink once, if it's no, blink twice."

"She blinked once, so it's yes. *One!* One what, Esther? Cup? Teaspoon? Vanita, are you writin' this down?"

"Two blinks," said Marge Crowder. "So, it's not a cup and it's not a teaspoon."

"Butter!" said somebody. "Is it one stick of butter?"

"She blinked twice, that's no. Try again. One *teaspoon?* Oh, thank God! Vanita, one teaspoon."

"Right. But one teaspoon of what? Salt?"

"Oh, please, you wouldn't use a teaspoon of *salt* in a *cake!*"

"Excuse me for living," said Vanita.

"Maybe cinnamon? Look! One blink. One teaspoon of cinnamon!"

"Hallelujah!" they chorused.

Esther wagged her finger.

"One, two, three, four, five . . ." someone counted.

"Five what?" asked Vanita. "Cups? No. Teaspoons? No. *Tablespoons?*"

"One blink, it's tablespoons! *Five tablespoons!*"

"Oh, mercy, I'm glad I took my heart pill this morning," said Hessie. "Is it of butter? I just have a feelin' it's butter. Look! One blink!"

"*Five tablespoons of butter!*" shouted the crowd, in unison.

"OK, in cakes, you'd have to have baking powder. How much baking powder, Esther?"

Esther held up one finger.

"One teaspoon?"

"Uhnuhhh," said Esther, looking desperate.

"One *tablespoon?*" asked Vanita.

"You wouldn't use a *tablespoon* of baking powder in a cake!" sniffed Marge Crowder.

"Look," said Vanita, "I'm helpin' y'all just to be nice. My husband personally thinks I am a great cook, but I don't do cakes, OK, so if you'd like somebody else to take these notes, just step right up and help yourself, thank you!"

"You're doin' great, honey, keep goin'," said Hessie.

"Look at that!" exclaimed Vanita. "She's got one finger out straight and the other one bent back! Is that one and a half? It *is,* she blinked once! I declare, that is the cleverest thing I ever saw. OK, one and a half teaspoons of bakin' powder!"

Everyone applauded.

"This is a killer," said Vanita, fanning herself with the notebook. "Don't you think we could sell two-layer triple chocolates just as easy?"

"Ummunnuhhh," said Esther, her eyes burning with disapproval.

Hessie snorted. "This could take 'til kingdom come. How much time have we got left?"

"Ten minutes, maybe eleven!"

"Eleven minutes? Are you kidding me? We'll never finish this in eleven minutes."

"I think she told me she uses buttermilk in this recipe," said Marge Crowder. "Esther," she shouted, "how much buttermilk?"

Esther made the finger-and-a-half gesture.

"One and a half cups, right? Great! Now we're cookin'!"

More applause.

"OK," commanded the co-chair, "what have we got so far?"

Vanita, being excessively nearsighted, held the notepad up for close inspection. "One teaspoon of cinnamon, five tablespoons of butter, one and a half teaspoons of baking powder, and one and a half cups of buttermilk."

"I've got to sit down," said the head of the Food Committee, pressing her temples.

"It looks like Esther's droppin' off to sleep, oh, Lord, Esther, honey, don't go to sleep, you can sleep tonight!"

"Could somebody ask th' nurse for a stress tab?" wondered Vanita. "Do you think they'd mind, I've written checks to th' hospital fund for nine years, goin' on ten!"

"By the way," asked Marge Crowder, "is this recipe for one layer or two?"

He decided to step into the hall for a breath of fresh air.

Out to Canaan, Ch. 18

THEY HAD GONE to Mona's and eaten fried perch, hard-shelled crabs, broiled shrimp, yellowfin tuna fresh off the boat, hush puppies, french fries, and buckets of coleslaw. They had slathered on tartar sauce and downed quarts of tea as sweet as syrup, then staggered home in the heat with Jonathan drugged and half asleep on Father Tim's back.

As they walked, Cynthia did her part to deliver after-dinner entertainment, loudly reciting a poem by someone named Rachel Field.

If once you have slept on an island
You'll never be quite the same;
You may look as you looked the day before
And go by the same old name.
You may bustle about the street or shop;
You may sit at home and sew,
But you'll see blue water and wheeling gulls
Wherever your feet may go.

"I declare!" said Earlene. "You're clever as anything to remember all that. I wonder if it's the truth."

"What?"

"That part about never being quite the same."

"I don't know," said Cynthia. "We'll have to wait and see."

They sat on the porch and watched the gathering sunset through the trellis, where the Marion Climber had put forth several new blooms.

A New Song, Ch. 10

UNCLE BILLY WATSON slogged to the Grill with his pant legs stuffed into his galoshes and his wife's felt hat jammed onto his head. He also wore gloves with both thumbs missing; under an ancient coat of his own, Rose's deceased brother's military jacket displayed a variety of tarnished war medals.

"I was hopin' you'd have a loaf of bread a feller could take home," the old man told Percy. Uncle Billy's arthritic fingers clutched three dimes, a nickel, and two pennies, which he thought was a fair price. "I'll pay cash money, don't you know."

"Go on in an' take it offa th' shelf," said Percy. To tell the truth, he was tired of Bill Watson gouging a loaf of bread out of him every week for the last hundred years, but he wouldn't fret over it now, being the time of year it was.

"What y'uns doin'?" asked Uncle Billy.

Father Tim scooped another shovelful of snow. "There's a snowman contest on Main Street, and Percy wants to nab the prize for the Grill." He was huffing like a steam engine and had lost feeling in most of his fingers and toes.

Uncle Billy surveyed the creation in front of him. "Only thing is, hit's naked as a jaybird."

"Right," said Father Tim. "Needs two eyes, a nose—you know, the basics."

"Needs a hat is more like it," said Uncle Billy. "What's th' prize?"

"Doughnuts. Maybe a snow shovel, but definitely doughnuts."

"Doughnuts!" said Uncle Billy. "Would that be plain or glazed?"

The Mitford Snowmen

SWADDLED IN A pink chenille robe and wearing a mesh hairnet, Esther Bolick lay sprawled in her recliner, staring at the ceiling.

The view of the brass chandelier from Home Depot vanished; in her mind's eye she saw an imaginary row of two-layer orange marmalade cakes standing proud on her countertop.

By tomorrow afternoon, the whole caboodle would be baked, filled, frosted, and ready to roll out of her kitchen as gifts coveted from one end of Mitford to the other. She and Gene would trot to the five o'clock Christmas Eve service at Lord's Chapel, then strike out in their van to make deliveries.

Though she'd never been much on frills, she had for years longed to use paper doilies to set off her marmalades, and for a fleeting moment imagined a circular, scalloped doily with machine-made cutwork under each of her creations. However, a package of such doilies was four dollars, and that was four dollars she wasn't willing to part with. No, ma'am, she would never be using doilies, so why even think about it?

In her imagination, the doilies disappeared and the cakes sat directly on cardboard rounds, which she'd cut from packing boxes found at The Local.

While she was minding costs, she wondered what it was costing her to bake an orange marmalade these days. Though she'd formed a vague notion over the years, she was inspired to ask Gene to compute the actual figure. It seemed to her that a two-layer had once come to around four or five dollars. She didn't mind giving away a cake that cost five dollars, not at all, she'd been doing it for years, especially at Christmas, when the flat broke and lonesome seemed to have a particularly rough go of things.

"Forty-three dollars a pop!" said Gene. The color drained from his face as he made this announcement.

"What?" She clutched her heart with one hand and held on to the countertop with the other. "Am I hearin' you right?

"Well, then." Esther caught her breath. "I'll have to go to my short list."

Eager to forget the particulars of the cake deal, Gene picked up the remote and aimed it at the TV; on came a full choir of children, singing their hearts out beneath a large star of Bethlehem. Esther cranked back in her recliner and sighed deeply. She would wait awhile before she started baking those two cakes for Hessie and Louella . . . or maybe she would leave Hessie out and just give one cake this year. . . .

How silently, how silently
The wondrous gift is given!
So God imparts to human hearts
The blessings of his heaven.

* * *

At four-thirty, Gene came in from his rounds about town, stomping snow onto the kitchen mat. "One, two, three, four, five, six, *seven?*" He grinned from ear to ear. "That don't look like a short list."

She put her hands on her hips. "Do like me an' don't think about th' cost."

* * *

One by one, she set a cake on the scalloped paper doily she'd proudly placed in the bottom of each box, and closed the lid. What difference did a piddling four dollars make in the scheme of things? After all, it was Christmas.

Esther's Gift

"FATHER!"

Hélène Pringle darted from the side of the house and hastened up the steps to his front stoop—apparently she'd popped through the hedge—wearing blue striped oven mitts and bearing a dish covered by a tea towel.

"For you!" She thrust her offering at him with seeming joy, but how could he take it from her if oven mitts were required to handle it?

He stepped back.

Miss Pringle stepped in.

"Roast *poulet!*" she exclaimed. "With olive oil and garlic, and stuffed with currants. I so hope you—you and Cynthia—like it."

"Hélène!" His wife sailed down the hall. "What have you *done?* What smells so heavenly?"

"Roast *poulet!*" Miss Pringle exclaimed again, as if announcing royalty.

"Oh, my!" said Cynthia. "Let me just get a towel." She trotted to the bathroom at the end of the hall and was back in a flash. "Thank you very much, Hélène, I'll take it. Lovely! Won't you come in?"

"Oh, no, no indeed, I don't wish to interfere. I hope . . . that is, I heard about . . ." She paused, turning quite red. "*Merci*, Father, Cynthia, *bon appétit, au revoir!*"

She was gone down the walk, quick as a hare.

"I like her mitts," said Cynthia.

* * *

"Delicious!" He spooned the thick currant sauce over a slice of tender breast meat and nudged aside the carrots Cynthia had cooked.

"Outstanding!" He ate heartily, as if starved.

He glanced up to see his wife looking at him.

"What?" he asked.

"I haven't seen you eat like this in . . . quite a while."

"Excellent flavor! I suppose it's the currants."

"I suppose," she said.

In This Mountain, Ch. 9

"FRESH SALMON!" he told Avis Packard. "That's what I was hoping. But of course your seafood comes in on Thursday, and if I buy it on Thursday, I'd have to freeze it 'til Monday."

"For ten bucks I can have a couple pounds flown in fresh on Monday, right off th' boat. Should get here late afternoon."

No one in the whole of Mitford would pay hard-earned money to have salmon shipped in. But his wife loved fresh salmon, and this was no time to compromise. Not for ten bucks, anyway.

"Book it!" he said, grinning.

"You understand th' ten bucks is just for shippin'. Salmon's extra."

"Right."

"OK!" Avis rubbed his hands together with undisguised enthusiasm. "I've got just the recipe!"

Some were born to preach, others born to shop, and not a few, it seemed, born to meddle. Avis was born to advocate the culinary arts. Father Tim took a notepad and pen from his jacket pocket. "Shoot!"

"Salmon roulade!" announced Avis. "Tasty, low-fat, and good for diabetes."

"Just what the doctor ordered!" said Father Tim, feeling good about life in general.

In This Mountain, Ch. 17

His travel-worn wife was devouring the salmon roulade as if she hadn't eaten in weeks.

"Heavenly!" she murmured. "Divine!"

"Thank you." His cheeks grew warm with pleasure. "I got the recipe from Avis."

"Perfection!"

He'd nearly forgotten her boundless enthusiasm, it was wondrous to have it again, he'd been barren without her. . . .

She peered at him over the vase of late-blooming roses. "It's no wonder women chase after you, Timothy."

"Now, Kavanagh . . ."

"It's true. You're handsome, charming, thoughtful, sensitive—and you can *cook!* The very combination every woman dreams of. However . . ." She patted her mouth with her starched napkin and went after another forkful of wild rice. "Do remember this . . . ."

"Yes?"

"You're mine."

He laughed.

"All mine."

"Amen," he said.

"Totally, completely, absolutely mine, just like it says in the marriage service."

"I vowed so once, I vow so again."

"So watch it, buster."

"Consider it done," he said, grinning like an idiot. He loved it when she talked like that.

In This Mountain, Ch. 21

"I love you madly," she said.

"I love you madlier."

"Do not!"

"Do, too!"

"Prove it!"

"I shall. I'm serving you dinner tonight, Puny made chicken and dumplings."

"Chicken and dumplings!" she crowed.

"With fresh lima beans."

"I'm your slave!"

"I'll remember that," he said.

A Common Life, Ch. 4

IN HER HOME a half mile from town, Puny Guthrie crumbled two dozen strips of crisp, center-cut bacon into the potato salad and gave it one last, heaving stir. Everybody would be plenty hungry by six or six-thirty, and she'd made enough to feed a corn shuckin', as her granpaw used to say. She had decided to leave out the onions, since it was a wedding reception and very dressy. She'd never thought dressing up and eating onions were compatible; onions were for picnics and eating at home in the privacy of your own family.

Because Cynthia and the father didn't want people to turn out for the reception and go home hungry, finger foods were banned. They wanted to give everybody a decent supper, even if they would have to eat it sitting on folding chairs from Sunday school. What with the father's ham, Miss Louella's yeast rolls, Miss Olivia's raw vegetables and dip, her potato salad, and Esther Bolick's three-layer orange marmalade, she didn't think they'd have any complaints. Plus, there would be ten gallons of tea, not to mention decaf, and sherry if anybody wanted any, but she couldn't imagine why anybody would. She'd once taken a sip from the father's decanter, and thought it tasted exactly like aluminum foil, though she'd never personally tasted aluminum foil except when it got stuck to a baked potato.

A Common Life, Ch. 8

"MIZ KAVANAGH, IS it all right t' give Timothy some of this candy fruit?"

"Two cherries!" he said, extending both hands. Why did Peggy have to ask his mother everything? If it was up to Peggy, he could have almost anything he wanted.

"Please," he remembered to say.

"Very well," said his mother, "but only two."

He also wanted raisins and a Brazil nut, but he would ask later. He liked a lot of things that went into the fruitcake his mother and Peggy made every year, but he didn't like them *in* the cake, he liked them *out* of the cake.

Coffee perked on the electric range, a lid rattled on a boiling pot, he smelled cinnamon and vanilla. . . .

At the kitchen table, his mother wrote thoughtfully on a sheet of blue paper. "There'll be the Andersons, of course," she said to Peggy, "and the Adamses."

"What about th' Judge?"

"The Judge goes without saying. We always have the Judge."

"An' Rev'ren' Simon."

"Yes, I think his influence is good for Timothy."

"Ain't you havin' th' Nelsons?"

"Oh, yes, and the Nelsons. Definitely!"

"Them Nelson boys'll be slidin' down yo' banister an' crawlin' up yo' curtains," Peggy muttered.

He dreaded the Nelson boys; when they came, it was always two against one.

"Can Tommy come?" His father had never allowed Tommy to come in the house, but since this would be Christmas . . .

"No, dear. I'm sorry. Perhaps another time."

His mother furrowed her brow and looked at the rain lashing the windows. Peggy stirred batter in a bowl, shaking her head.

"What shall we serve, Peggy? Certainly, we want your wonderful yeast rolls!"

"Yes, ma'am, an' Mr. Kavanagh will want his ambrosia and oyster pie."

His mother smiled, her face alight. "Always!"

"An' yo' famous *bûche de Noël!*" said Peggy. "That always get a big hand clap."

"What is boose noel?" he asked, sitting on the floor with his wooden truck.

"*Buoosh,*" said Peggy. "*Bu* like *bu*-reau. *Buoosh.*"

"Boosh."

"No, honey." Peggy bent down and stuck her face close to his. He liked Peggy's skin, it was exactly the color of gingerbread. "Look here at my lips . . . *bu* . . ."

"*Bu* . . ."

"Now . . . law, how I goin' t' say this? Say shhhh, like a baby's sleepin'."

"Shhhh."

"That's right! Now, *bu*-shhh."

"*Bu* . . . shhh."

"Run it all together, now. *Bu*shhh."

"*Bu*shhh!"

"Ain't that good, Miz Kavanagh?"

"Very good!"

Peggy stood up and began to stir again. "Listen now, honey lamb, learn t' say th' whole thing—*bûche de Noël.*"

"*Bûche de Noël!*"

"He be talkin' French, Miz Kavanagh!"

He was thrilled with their happiness; with no trouble at all, he'd gotten raisins and a Brazil nut for talking French.

"What does it mean, Mama?"

"Log of Christmas. Christmas log. A few days before Christmas, you may help us put the icing on. It's a very special job."

"Icin' on a log?"

"A log made from cake. We had it last year, but you probably don't remember—you were little then." His mother smiled at him; he saw lights dancing in her eyes.

"Yes, ma'am, and now I'm big."

"You ain't big," crowed Peggy, "you my *baby!*"

He hated it when Peggy said that.

Shepherds Abiding, Ch. 4

ALOUD, HE COUNTED heads for dinner on Christmas Day.

"Dooley, Sammy, Lon Burtie, Poo, Jessie, Harley, Hélène, Louella, Scott Murphy, the two Kavanaghs . . . eleven!" Who else?

"Lord, we have room for one more!"
Oysters . . .

But how many? Chances are, his favorite thing on the menu wouldn't be so popular with this assembly.

Two pints, he wrote.

Heavy cream
10-lb ham, bone in

. . . He would bake the ham; Cynthia would trot out her unbeatable oyster pie, a vast bowl of ambrosia, and a sweet potato casserole; Hélène would bring the haricots verts, and Harley had promised a pan of his famous fudge brownies. What's more, Puny was baking a cheesecake and making cranberry relish; Louella was contributing yeast rolls from the Hope House kitchen; and rumor suggested that Esther Bolick was dropping off a two-layer orange marmalade . . .

. . . altogether a veritable minefield for the family diabetic, but he'd gotten handy at negotiating minefields.

Shepherds Abiding, Ch. 7

STEAK, OVEN FRIES, and arugula dressed with a hint of orange and walnuts. He had checked his sugar, and not only would he have some of everything, he would also have a hot roll. What's more, he would butter it, hallelujah.

As the steak platter passed from Lace to Dooley, he felt Dooley's mood brighten. His own spirits brightened, as well.

"Man!" said Dooley, forking the steak he'd earlier chosen as it came from the butcher's paper.

Cynthia passed the potatoes, arrayed on a blue and white platter. "I've slaved over these fries," she confessed, "and I think, I hope, I pray I got it."

"I think you got it," said Dooley, hammering down on the fries.

"Crispier on the outside?" asked Cynthia.

"Yep."

"Softer on the inside? More golden in color?"

"Yes, ma'am."

"Dooley Barlowe! I can't believe you called me ma'am."

Lace laughed. "That's really good."

"I know I'm a Yankee, and such things aren't supposed to matter, but would you continue to call me ma'am? I love the sound of it."

Dooley laughed the cackling laugh that Father Tim loved to hear.

"How did you do it?" Lace asked the cook.

"Bottom line, it's the pan. I've been using a lightweight pan, which caused the fries to look very pale and boring. So Avis suggested I use a heavy pan, and there you have it—the heavier pan conducts heat more evenly, and gives this lovely golden crust into the bargain."

"Well done!" exclaimed Father Tim.

Light from Heaven, Ch. 4

GOOD FRIDAY WAS a fast day, and though Cynthia later vowed she'd asked for something "very simple," Lily-who-cooks-for-parties had done herself proud.

Cheese grits, bacon, fried apples, scrambled eggs, drop biscuits, and cream gravy sat in bowls and platters on the pine table. She had also fried up half the sausage she'd toted as a gift from the sausage-making operation, and set out two jars of jam from the farm coffers.

His wife trotted in from the laundry room and gasped. "Is this a *dream?*"

"Hallelujah and three amens!" said the vicar. He'd better call the Mitford Hospital and reserve a room.

Light from Heaven, Ch. 9

THE CONTRIBUTIONS OF early arrivals had been placed on the rose-colored cloth.

In the center of the table, Miss Martha's German chocolate cake was displayed on a footed stand next to Lily's three-layer triumph. Also present were Lloyd's foil-covered baked beans, Cynthia's potato salad made from Puny's recipe, Father Tim's scandal to the Baptists—a baked ham with bourbon sauce, Agnes's macaroni and cheese, and Granny's stuffed eggs.

"Granny," said the vicar, "how are stuffed eggs different from deviled?"

"Th' diff'rence is, I don't *call* 'em deviled," Granny declared. "They's enough devilment in this world."

"Amen!" he said.

At the far end of the folding table, the vicar's surprise gift stood tall and gleaming, perking into the air an aroma fondly cherished in church halls everywhere.

"French roast," he told Lloyd, tapping the percolator. "Freshly ground. Full bore."

"Hallelujah!" said Lloyd, who didn't think much of church coffee, generally speaking.

Sammy had cut an armload of budding branches from the surrounding woods, and delivered them to Cynthia for a table arrangement. Removing himself from the fray, the vicar trooped into the churchyard to greet new arrivals and contemplate the view with Granny. A chill wind had followed the long rain; the ocean of mountains shone clear, bright, and greening.

"Robert! Good morning to you!"

Robert wiped his right hand on his pant leg before shaking.

"Thank y' f'r th' eggs, I didn' bring nothin' f'r th' dinner."

"No need, we have plenty. Can you sing, Robert?"

"Ain't never tried."

"Try today! We've got to crank up the singing around here, to help keep us warm. Just get in behind me and go for it. I'm not much to listen to, but I can keep us on key at any rate.

"Sparkle! You're the very breath of spring."

"Yeller, blue, green, purple, an' pink, topped off by a fleece jacket! If anybody's havin' a tacky party today, I want to be th' winner!"

"Where's Wayne?"

"Down on his back, rollin' around under a piece of junk he calls a car."

"Tell him to get up here, we need his fine baritone."

"If Wayne Foster ever shows 'is face up here ag'in, I'll drop over. He didn't know doodley-squat about what was goin' on last Sunday. He thought your kneelers was somethin' to prop his feet up on."

"A good many Episcopalians think the same! What is that heavenly aroma?"

Sparkle held forth her foil-covered contribution "Meat loaf!" she declared. "My mama's recipe. You will flat out *die* when you taste it."

"A terrible price to pay, but count me in."

Light from Heaven, Ch. 12

The Quintessential
Mitford Menu:
Digging In

The Quintessential Mitford Menu

❧

LOUELLA'S FRIED CHICKEN

PUNY'S POTATO SALAD

LOUELLA'S DEVILED EGGS

CYNTHIA'S CRISPY GREEN BEANS
WITH CANADIAN BACON

LOUELLA'S YEAST ROLLS

LOUELLA'S CINNAMON ROLLS

CYNTHIA'S RASPBERRY TEA

ESTHER'S ORANGE MARMALADE CAKE

T ruth be told, not everyone in Mitford is a great cook. And lots of people don't cook at all. That's because most people in Mitford live like we live—after working all day, they lack even the slightest desire to chop, dice, sauté, bake, or fry.

So they get takeout in Wesley, or fast food on the bypass, or maybe they come home and microwave a mac and cheese, or eat leftover pizza and a half-quart of Ben & Jerry's. But that's *most* people, not *all* people in Mitford.

Puny still cooks (but only after the diapers are washed and folded). Marge Owen still cooks. Cynthia and Father Tim still cook. Andrew Gregory's gorgeous Italian third cousin and second wife, Anna, cooks every day. Avis Packard most certainly cooks. Louella would if she could. And Hope Winchester Murphy is learning.

By the way, Percy Mosely, who cooked for the public for nearly four decades and is now retired, makes breakfast every Saturday morning but that is absolutely, positively IT. In short, he is totally over cooking and so, incidentally, is his wife, Velma. Except for their big Saturday cook-off, they're currently subsisting on grape Jell-O, pimiento cheese, buffalo wings from the bypass, Snickers bars, cheese popcorn, canned chili, canned tuna, loaf bread, ice cream sandwiches, vacuum-packed Southwestern-style chicken pieces, and Cheerwine (which, by the way, has nothing to do with wine).

Their children argue that they are ruining their health, and are trying to talk them into a sensible diet of tofu, whole grains, and fresh fruit—a ridiculous idea that is met with derision, to say the least.

Anyway, *some* people still cook and in case you do, I wanted to create a menu that would make you feel, so to speak, at home in Mitford.

Indeed, this menu represents the quintessential Mitford.

For example, it's what Esther Bolick will soon be making for her three cousins, Edna, Grace, and Mamie, who occasionally visit each other's homes now that they're all widowed.

It's what Puny is thinking of making for Joe Joe's grandma and grandpa, Esther and Ray Cunningham, if Esther and Ray ever come home from their trip in the RV.

It's what Marge Owen made after her year in France, as soon as she got over jet lag.

And it's definitely what Louella would make for Miss Sadie if Miss Sadie were still alive and things were like they used to be.

If you're the kind of cook who'd prefer things to be like they used to be, you will especially enjoy this menu. There is nothing to sear in triple-virgin olive oil, nothing to marinate in white wine, and certainly nothing to brine or deglaze.

In fact, to begin this meal, you don't even have to say *bon appétit* or anything in a foreign language.

You just say *Dig in.*

After you say the blessing, of course.

Louella's Fried Chicken

1 (2½- to 3-pound) broiler chicken, cut up and soaked in brine
1 quart buttermilk
2 cups White Lily self-rising flour
1½ teaspoons salt
1 teaspoon freshly ground black pepper
½ cup bacon drippings
¾ to 1 cup lard

Place the chicken pieces in a large bowl, pour in the buttermilk, and place in the refrigerator to soak for 2 to 4 hours.

Combine the flour, 1½ teaspoons salt, and pepper in a shallow dish such as a pie plate. Drain the chicken and dredge in the flour mixture. Shake off excess flour.

Heat the bacon drippings and lard in a black iron skillet over medium-high heat until a small bit of flour pops when dropped in the fat. Add the chicken, a few pieces at a time, skin side down. Cover and cook the chicken for 15 to 20 minutes. Remove the cover and turn the chicken over. Cook for another 15 to 20 minutes. The chicken is done when it is a light golden brown color.

Drain the chicken on paper towels before serving.

4 to 6 servings

Puny's Potato Salad

7 medium russet potatoes
1 tablespoon plus 1¼ teaspoons salt
2 tablespoons bacon drippings
4 medium hard-cooked eggs (see p. 97), mashed
2 tablespoons red onion, chopped
½ cup thinly sliced celery
1¾ cups Hellmann's mayonnaise
2 teaspoons prepared mustard
2 tablespoons sour cream

2½ teaspoons apple cider vinegar
½ teaspoon freshly ground black pepper
6 slices cooked bacon, crumbled
    Parsley flakes, for garnish
    Paprika, for garnish

Peel and cube the potatoes. Place the potatoes in a large saucepan, and add water to cover along with 1 tablespoon salt. Bring to a boil over high heat, reduce the heat, cover, and simmer until the potatoes are just tender. Drain the potatoes in a colander. Add the bacon drippings and shake the colander to coat. Cover loosely and let the potatoes cool completely.

In a large bowl, combine the potatoes, mashed eggs, red onion, and celery. In a separate bowl, combine the mayonnaise, mustard, sour cream, and vinegar and stir it into the potatoes. Add 1¼ teaspoons salt and ½ teaspoon pepper. Just before serving, adjust the seasonings with salt and pepper. Garnish the salad with the crumbled bacon, parsley flakes, and paprika.

6 servings

LOUELLA'S DEVILED EGGS

6 large hard-cooked eggs (see p. 97), peeled
2 tablespoons Hellmann's mayonnaise
2 tablespoons sour cream
1 teaspoon apple cider vinegar
1 teaspoon prepared mustard
⅛ teaspoon salt
⅛ teaspoon freshly ground black pepper
    Paprika, for garnish

Slice the eggs in half lengthwise and carefully remove the yolks. In a small bowl, use a fork to mash the egg yolks with the mayonnaise, sour cream, vinegar, mustard, salt, and pepper.

Spoon the filling back into the egg white halves. You can also spoon the filling into a sandwich size zip-top bag, cut a small opening in one corner of the bag, and pipe the filling into the egg white halves.

Refrigerate until ready to serve, garnish with a sprinkle of paprika, and serve on a deviled egg plate.

12 deviled egg halves

PERFECT HARD-COOKED EGGS

Place eggs in a single layer in a large saucepan. Add enough cold water to cover the eggs. Bring the water to a rolling boil. Remove the saucepan from the heat, cover, and allow the eggs and water to stand for 17 minutes. Drain the water immediately after 17 minutes and add cold water and ice cubes. After the eggs have cooled, peel under cold running water.

CYNTHIA'S CRISPY GREEN BEANS WITH CANADIAN BACON

- 1 pound fresh green beans
- 1 teaspoon salt
- 1 tablespoon unsalted butter
- 4 pieces Canadian bacon, chopped
- 1 bunch green onions, sliced
   Freshly ground black pepper

Remove the ends and string the green beans. Bring 2½ quarts of water to a rolling boil. Add the green beans and salt. Reduce the heat a little, cover, and cook until the green beans are crisp-tender, about 5 minutes. Drain and set aside.

Place the butter, bacon, and green onions in a large skillet over medium heat and sauté for 5 to 7 minutes, or until the bacon is crispy. Add the green beans to the skillet and toss to heat them through. Adjust the seasonings with salt and pepper and serve immediately.

1 to 6 servings

Louella's Yeast Rolls

  2½ cups milk
  ½   cup granulated sugar
  2   packages dry yeast
  ½   cup vegetable shortening
  5   cups bread flour, plus more for rolling out the dough
  2   large eggs, lightly beaten
  ¼   cup unsalted butter, at room temperature, plus more for greasing the bowl and baking sheet
  ½   teaspoon baking soda
  1   teaspoon baking powder
  2   teaspoons salt
      Melted butter for dipping the dough

In a medium saucepan over low heat, heat the milk until bubbles just start to form around the edges. Pour ½ cup of the heated milk into a 2-cup measuring cup, stir in 1 teaspoon of the sugar, and let the mixture cool to 115°F. Stir in the yeast. Allow the yeast to proof (bubble). Add the remaining sugar and the shortening to the saucepan of milk and stir until the shortening is melted. Let this mixture cool to 115°F as well.

In a large mixing bowl, combine 2 cups of the flour, the yeast mixture, and the milk mixture. Mix well until thoroughly combined. Cover with a kitchen towel and let the dough rise for 1 hour, until doubled in bulk. Punch down the dough and add the eggs, butter, and 1 cup of the flour, and mix well. Combine and add the baking soda, baking powder, salt, and the remaining 2 cups of the flour, and mix well. Coat the inside of a large bowl with butter and transfer the dough to the greased bowl. Cover and place in a warm spot free of drafts and let rise for another hour. Punch the dough down, cover with plastic wrap, and refrigerate overnight.

Bring the dough to room temperature before working with it. Grease a cookie sheet. Roll the dough out on a lightly floured surface until it is about ⅛ inch thick. Cut the dough out with a 2-inch cookie cutter and dip the pieces in the melted butter. Place the rolls on the cookie sheet, fold over, and pinch the edges of the dough to form a pocketbook roll. Cover with a kitchen towel and let rise for 1½ hours, until doubled in bulk, before baking.

Preheat the oven to 450°F. Just before placing the rolls in the oven, turn the temperature down to 375°F. Bake for 15 to 20 minutes, until the rolls are lightly browned or sound hollow when tapped on the bottom. Set on a rack to cool or serve right out of the oven.

About 4 dozen rolls

LOUELLA'S CINNAMON ROLLS

- 1 cup brown sugar
- ½ cup granulated sugar
- ½ cup unsalted butter, softened
- 1 tablespoon ground cinnamon
- ½ teaspoon salt
- 1 recipe dough for Louella's Yeast Rolls (above)

Prepare the filling by combining the brown sugar, granulated sugar, butter, cinnamon, and salt in a large bowl. Bring the dough to room temperature and roll it out on a lightly floured surface into a 24 x 12-inch rectangle that is about ⅛ inch thick. Spread filling on the lower half of one of the 24-inch sides of the dough. Fold the other half over the filling and pinch the edges to seal. Cut crosswise into 1-inch strips and twist each strip into a circle, tucking under the ends to shape a pinwheel. Cover with a kitchen towel and let the rolls rise until doubled in bulk, about 1 hour.

Preheat the oven to 375°F. Bake the rolls for 15 to 20 minutes, or until lightly browned.

About 4 dozen rolls

Cynthia's Raspberry Tea

      3 Lipton family-size tea bags, tags removed
      1 cup granulated sugar
      1 (12-ounce) can frozen raspberry lemonade, thawed
         Maraschino cherries

Place the tea bags in a pottery or glass pitcher, and pour 2 cups of cold water over them. Bring a kettle with 4 cups of water to a rolling boil. Pour over the tea bags and cover the pitcher with a small plate. Steep for 10 to 15 minutes, then remove the tea bags, add the sugar, and stir until dissolved. Add 3 cups of cold water to the tea and stir in the lemonade until dissolved. Add the cherries before serving. Serve over ice.

About 10 cups

Esther's Orange Marmalade Cake

For the cake
      1 cup unsalted butter, softened, plus more for greasing the
         pans
    3¼ cups cake flour, plus more for dusting the pans
      1 tablespoon baking powder
      1 teaspoon salt
    2⅔ cups granulated sugar
      5 large eggs, at room temperature
      4 large egg yolks, at room temperature
    ⅔ cup vegetable oil
      1 tablespoon grated orange zest
      2 teaspoons vanilla extract
      1 cup buttermilk, at room temperature

For the orange syrup
> 1 cup freshly squeezed orange juice
> ¼ cup sugar

For the filling
> 1 (12-ounce) jar orange marmalade

For the frosting
> 1 cup heavy cream, chilled
> 4 tablespoons granulated sugar
> 1 cup sour cream, chilled

The cake Preheat the oven to 350°F. Lightly butter three 9-inch round cake pans, line them with parchment paper, then lightly butter and flour the paper, shaking out any excess.

Sift the flour, baking powder, and salt into a large bowl. Sift a second time into another bowl. In the bowl of an electric mixer, beat the butter on medium speed until light in color, about 4 minutes. Add the 2⅔ cups sugar in a steady stream with the mixer running. Beat until light and fluffy, about 4 minutes. Add the eggs and yolks, one at a time, beating well after each addition. Be sure to stop at least once to scrape down the batter from the sides of the bowl. After all the eggs have been added, continue to beat on medium speed for 2 more minutes. With the mixer on low speed, add the oil and beat for 1 minute. Using a rubber spatula, fold in half the dry ingredients. In a small bowl combine the orange zest, vanilla, and buttermilk. Scrape the batter down the sides of the bowl and add half the buttermilk mixture. Fold in the remaining dry ingredients, scrape down the sides, and add the remaining buttermilk.

Divide the batter among the prepared pans, smooth the surface, rap each pan on the counter to expel any air pockets or bubbles, then place in the oven. Bake for 30 to 35 minutes, or until a toothpick inserted into the center comes out clean. Let the cakes cool in the pans on racks for 20 minutes.

The orange syrup In a small bowl stir together the orange juice and the ¼ cup sugar until the sugar is dissolved. While the baked cakes are still in the cake pans, use a toothpick or skewer to poke holes at ½-inch intervals in the cake layers. Spoon the syrup slowly over each layer, allowing the syrup to be completely absorbed before adding the remainder. Let the layers cool completely in the pans.

The filling   Heat the marmalade in a small saucepan over medium heat until just melted. Let cool for 5 minutes.

The frosting   In a chilled mixing bowl using the wire whisk attachment, whip the heavy cream with the 4 tablespoons sugar until stiff peaks form. Add the sour cream, a little at a time, and whisk until the mixture is a spreadable consistency.

To assemble the cake   Invert one of the cake layers on a cake plate and carefully peel off the parchment. Spread one third of the marmalade over the top, smoothing it into an even layer. Invert the second layer on top of the first, peel off the parchment, and spoon another third of the marmalade on top. Place the third cake layer on top, remove the parchment, and spoon the remaining marmalade onto the center of it, leaving a 1¼-inch border around the edges. Frost the sides and the top border with the frosting, leaving the marmalade on top of the cake exposed. Or, if you prefer, frost the entire cake first, adding the marmalade as a garnish on top. Chill for at least 2 hours before serving.

   10 to 12 servings

Jan Karon's Mitford Cookbook and Kitchen Reader

The Right Ingredients

❧

*U*ncle *Billy Watson* could hardly read the *Mitford Muse* these days. It seemed that a while back, maybe after the war, the print in the *Muse* had been bigger, much bigger. But now, with things costing so much, maybe they couldn't afford big print.

He held the newspaper close to his face with one hand, and gripped a magnifying glass in the other, wishing his hand wouldn't shake and cause the words to jump up and down.

Around Town

by Vanita Bentley

Uncle Billy silently formed each word with his mouth.

Is Mitford getting to be the crossroads of the world?

Not too long since Winnie Ivey, now Winnie Kendall, won a cruise with Golden Band Flour Company, here Golden Band turns up in Mitford with a baking contest, can you believe it???!!!

Next Thursday, Golden Band will arrive in Mitford to watch our good cooks strut their stuff. Golden Band is going around to the small towns of America to prove that somebody out there still actually cooks and bakes. I don't, thank goodness, but I hope you do, because . . . first prize in each category is $500.00!!!!!!

The categories are Cakes, Pies, and Bread. Bread is the only category with two divisions—Loaf Bread or Biscuits—so you get two chances to win $500.00!!!!!!

Pick up your entry forms at The Local, today! And start your ovens!

Uncle Billy laid the newspaper in his lap and closed his eyes.

The story had suddenly put him in mind of his mother's kitchen, and the baking and cooking she'd done from sunup to sundown.

Until he was old enough to hunt rabbits in the piney woods, he had hung around the door of the cabin smelling the good smells, eating sweet scraps from his mother's floured hands, stealing sips of her coffee from a cracked blue cup.

As much as he'd like five hundred dollars to jingle in his pocket, he would pay every cent of that amount, if he had it, just to taste one of her pies again.

He patted his foot, and looked out the window without seeing.

Something was throbbing in his right temple, which he knew at once was his blood pressure.

He was going to do it. He was going to enter that contest.

The first thing he wished is that he could get his wife, Rose, out of the house so he could do what he had to do in peace and quiet.

The second thing he wished is that he'd be able to find the twenty dollar bill he hid in the stack of newspapers in the dining room, so he could buy what he needed to make . . . to make what?

Sweet potato pie.

The thought came to him as naturally as breathing.

* * *

Esther Bolick refolded the *Muse* and thumped it onto the kitchen table. She rued the day she ever parted with her orange marmalade cake recipe.

It was something she had vowed she'd never do. In fact, she refused to write the recipe down, thinking that would be extra protection against it landing in the wrong hands.

Then, a couple of years ago, just days before the annual Bane and Blessing sale, she'd fallen off that blooming ladder at Lord's Chapel and ended up in the hospital with two broken arms and her jaws wired shut.

The Bane was the biggest fund-raiser in the church's entire history. And everybody and his brother had counted on her to produce the dozen two-layer orange marmalades she'd baked every year for fourteen years.

She shuddered to recall the way the Bane volunteers had descended on her hospital bed like a swarm of vultures, gouging the recipe out of her, teaspoon by teaspoon, you might say, while the pain in her jaws was so searing, the pounding in her head so blinding, that she wished to the good Lord she'd never heard of orange marmalade cake, much less gotten famous for it.

Naturally, the volunteers had scrambled home and baked off the dozen two-layers in the nick of time, which raised a total of three hundred dollars for digging wells in east Africa. This news had been wonderful medicine for Esther who, lying in the hospital bed, pictured eager children dancing around the well, drinking from dippers and feeling happy.

There was only one problem.

Since that day, half of Mitford had gotten their hands on her recipe.

Esther rose from the kitchen table and yanked open the freezer door.

If she was a betting woman, she'd bet Evie Adams would enter an orange marmalade in the Golden Band flour bake-off. Time and again, she'd been told that Evie not only liked using the orange marmalade recipe, but liked doctoring it up with Cointreau.

Cointreau? thought Esther, jabbing a knife between two cookies that had frozen together. If you couldn't bake a decent cake without resorting to liquor, you had the brains of a chicken.

And hadn't Hessie Mayhew said the hospital supervisor baked Esther's recipe all the time, and just loved adding nuts to the batter?

Nuts? She shivered.

She'd be surprised if her recipe didn't show up forty times in that bloomin' contest, since everybody in creation was walking around with it in their pockets, grinning like apes. Heaven knows, her rector's wife was the only one of the lot who'd ever called and asked permission.

Esther put the bag of cookies back in the freezer and slammed the door.

She wouldn't touch that contest with a ten-foot pole, as she'd never entered a contest less important than the State Fair and didn't expect to start now.

* * *

Hope Winchester sat on a stool behind the bookstore cash register, and watched a summer rain lash Main Street.

Through the block lettering, HAPPY ENDINGS, which was painted on the front windows, she could see people dashing along the sidewalk, some with umbrellas, some with today's *Mitford Muse* held over their heads.

She read Vanita Bentley's story for the third time and hoped nobody came in for a while, because she wanted to think.

What if she entered one of Golden Band's three contest categories? She figured if she got up the nerve to do it at all, she would enter Bread.

She'd never baked a loaf of bread in all her thirty-one years, nor anything else, for that matter, but she desperately needed five hundred dollars.

With a little practice, she could actually *see* the bread in her mind's eye, and the nice, brown crust on top. This was called "imaging." If you can image it, you can do it, she read in a self-help book, which was not a publishing genre she especially cared for.

When she was little, her father had said, "You read too many books. If I catch you reading another book, I'll throw it in the fire. Reading will rot your brain, go help your mother."

She had read in bed for years, under the covers with a flashlight, which was how she'd read every word of her second favorite book, *Jane Eyre.* She had nearly put her eyes out and ended up wearing glasses, which to this day she blamed on small print in paperbacks.

But the point was, hadn't Sir Walter Scott written about "the will to do, the soul to dare"? Just because you'd never done a thing didn't mean you shouldn't dare to do it, maybe she would just *start,* and something in her soul would show her how—she'd heard about people who had never in their lives played the piano, but one day they sat down on the piano bench and touched the keys, and the most beautiful music in the world poured forth.

She had the will to do it, but did she have the soul to dare and enter a contest to be judged at the town hall, with everybody she knew looking on, especially her customers from Happy Endings?

Then she remembered why she needed the five hundred dollars.

During lunch break at the bookstore, she went to The Local and bought everything the James Beard recipe called for.

* * *

As Lew Boyd read the story in the *Muse,* he got the shivers, thinking how he'd won that pickle-canning contest in 4-H. When he took the blue ribbon to school, Earlene Dickson had kissed him on the mouth and run. . . .

And Granmaw Minnie . . . he could see her plain as day, lying on her deathbed and transferring ownership of her recipes to the grandchildren.

"I want Wilma to have the recipe for my chicken pie," his granmaw said, speaking through a tube in her throat.

"Little Sue, I want you to have my chocolate cake recipe. . . ."

Overcome with gratitude, Little Sue burst into tears.

"Pearl, where is Pearl?"

"Over here, Big Mama."

"You get th' fried chicken recipe, and if you ever tell a soul th' secret ingredient . . ."

Pearl's eyes were the size of saucers in a doll's tea set. "Oh, no, Big Mama!"

". . . and I want Lew to have th' pickle recipe."

Everyone nodded their agreement. After all, he'd worked with her each summer as a boy, slicing cucumbers into a huge crock that, even when empty, smelled of pickles.

At this point, Lew remembered his granmaw half-sitting up in bed, and looking fierce as anything. The fact that she'd removed her dentures didn't help matters.

"Now listen to me," said Minnie. "These recipes have been in th' family since I was a young 'un. Don't *ever* give 'em out of th' family, or I'll come back and haint ever' one of you!"

"Yes, *ma'am!*" Lew gulped.

Minnie lay back on the pillow. "Now bring me a little touch of whisky and sugar," she said. . . .

Lew walked around the gas pumps at his Exxon station, located just beyond the Mitford town monument. He slapped his leg with the rolled-up copy of the *Muse,* thinking hard.

He was barely able to wait till five when the rates went down.

"Little Sue?"

There was a pause at the other end of the line. "Is that you, Lew?"

"It's me, all right."

"You haven't called me in ten years," said Little Sue.

"Well," said Lew, not knowing what else to say. Then he remembered why he hadn't called. "I've been real busy with my gas station."

"Bull. What d'you want?"

"Well . . . I was just thinkin' about Granmaw Minnie."

"Like I said, Lew, what d'you want?"

He hadn't meant to blurt it out. "I want her chocolate cake recipe!"

"What in th' dickens d'you want it for?"

"I want to enter a contest, they don't take pickles!"

"Your brain is pickled, askin' me for that recipe."

"Little Sue, dadgummit, I'm *family!!*"

* * *

It was four o'clock at the nursing home on the hill above Mitford.

In Room Number One, Louella Baxter Marshall was tired of watching *All My Children.* She wanted to sing hymns or bake a pan of biscuits or cook a pot of greens, something constructive.

She didn't want to read the *Mitford Muse* that a nurse just delivered to her room.

She didn't want to put in her order for Pokey, either. That little speckled dog would jump in her lap and sleep so long, her bladder would get full and she couldn't get up without dumping him on the floor.

She missed Miss Sadie, who had gone to heaven over two years ago. Except for the short, sweet time she'd been married to Moses Marshall, she had been Miss Sadie's lifelong companion. And never once had Miss Sadie acted like she was boss and Louella was help. Fact is, Miss Sadie had given the money for this very building and everything in it, and had written in her will that the best room in the building was to be reserved for her "sister in the Lord, Louella B. Marshall."

Louella closed her eyes and rocked in her chair, humming.

Just being *around* Miss Sadie had been fun. They used to sing to beat the band, all the hymns they'd been raised with at Lord's Chapel, and then they might have a little game of dominoes or Chinese checkers or read to each other from the Bible. Louella had read to someone from the Bible only last night, someone so old and feeble, it hurt her terribly just to look at the frail figure in the wing chair.

She had taken Violet Larkin's hand in hers, and noted how much it felt like Miss Sadie's, so small and delicate, like a child's hand.

"The Lord is my shepherd," Louella read aloud, "I shall not want. He maketh me to lie down in green pastures, he leadeth me beside still waters, he *restoreth* my soul. . . ."

Don't give her any of that modern stuff that leaves out the leadeth and restoreth and the thee and thou, no sir, the language of the old King James was beautiful to her ears, like music.

Speaking of music, that's how she'd read the rest of that psalm— she'd sung it. Something just came over her and she'd started singing the words.

"Surely goodness and mercy
Will *follow* me
All the *days* of my *life*
And I will dwell in the
House of the *Lord*
For*ev*———er-r-r-r!"

She'd really held on to that last note, and the word that contained all of eternity in it.

Miss Larkin had closed her eyes and repeated the last line in a warbly voice, her face beaming like an angel's. Then she looked at the chocolate-colored woman who lived down the hall and was so good to her.

Without meaning to, Violet Larkin told Louella Baxter Marshall her heart's desire—she wanted more than anything on earth to see her grandson again, but he lived so far away, somewhere in Canada, and it would cost nearly five hundred dollars to get him here.

Sitting alone in Room Number One at Hope House, Louella said aloud, "Miss Sadie, I got t' do this thing, an' you an' Jesus got t' help me."

* * *

On the high hill above Mitford, Louella Baxter Marshall rang for a nurse to come to Room Number One.

"I want t' go t' th' kitchen," said Louella, easing her heavy frame into the wheelchair.

"The *kitchen*, Miss Louella?"

"That's right, honey."

"How's your knee today, Miss Louella? Is it hurtin' you bad?"

"Not too bad 'less I stand on it," said Louella. When they arrived at the double doors behind the Hope House dining room, the nurse helped Louella out of the chair. "You go on, now," she told the bewildered young woman, "and come back at ten o'clock."

The Hope House cook didn't know who was blowing through his kitchen door on a walking cane; he never saw the residents, he only got wind of their complaints. It was true he sometimes heard praise, as well—usually when he gave them lasagna, but only if it wasn't too spicy.

"I'm lookin' for th' boss," Louella said, in a mezzo voice that bounced off the saucepans and made the large kitchen seem smaller.

"That's me," said the cook, who actually preferred to be called a chef. He had an odd compulsion to bow, though he had no idea why.

"I need to bake a pan of biscuits," said Louella, looking him in the eye.

"You need to . . . what?"

"Bake a pan of biscuits," she said as if speaking to the deaf. "I need flour, shortenin', buttermilk, an' the whole caboodle. You can set me up right over there, honey." She waved her cane at a surface he'd just floured down to work croissants for lunch.

"She's Room Number One," whispered his sous chef. "Miz Louella Baxter Marshall."

Room Number One! When he came to work here, he was told that Room Number One could have anything she wanted—at anytime, from anybody—and he wasn't to forget it.

"Yes *ma'am*," he said, stepping out of her way before she mowed him down.

* * *

Esther Bolick was not accustomed to having teenagers call her on the phone.

Her grandson used to call at Christmas and Easter, but stopped when he turned twelve and now communicated solely by letters written on his computer in a font called Spiderman.

"Miz Bolick? This is Dooley Barlowe."

Dooley Barlowe was the red-headed mountain boy Father Kavanagh had taken to raise a few years ago; he worked summers at The Local, bagging groceries, and had come a mighty long way, in Esther's opinion.

"Excuse me for calling, but I know . . ." She heard him gulp and swallow. ". . . I know you're the best cake baker in town."

Esther's face flushed.

"Cynthia says so, and my dad does, too."

"Mercy! Really?" She was touched.

"Plus a lot of people who're enterin' the contest talk about your cake when I'm baggin' their groceries."

Thieves, thought Esther.

"That's why I'm callin', because I'm workin' to save money for a car, and my dad says he'll match everything I make."

"My, my," she said, having forgotten entirely what it felt like to be a teenager.

"I also mow yards and clean out attics and basements, and . . ."

She heard him gulp again.

". . . and I've been thinking—would you, I mean, could you tell me how to bake that cake you're famous for? If I could enter that contest and win, that would really help a lot, I mean, if you could maybe give me a few tips on how to do it, I'd really appreciate it."

She heard him breathing as if he'd run a race. She liked Dooley and thought he was made of the right stuff. But more than that, she cared about Father Kavanagh—hadn't he pastored them for years, loving them like his own and never demanding anything back?

As for herself, she had no intention of entering that jackleg contest where half the town was using her recipe without permission.

"Let me think about it," she said, not wanting to think about it at all. On the other hand, here was an innocent boy trying to make a dollar and willing to work for it, unlike some people she knew.

She went in the den and told Gene about the odd request.

"I don't want to enter that bloomin' contest," she said.

"You wouldn't be enterin' it, Dooley would."

She patted her foot, frowning. Why couldn't people let her alone about that cake?

Gene grinned. "I think you should do it."

"You really think so, cross your heart?"

He crossed his heart. "Y'all could blow th' competition out of th' water."

She went back to the kitchen and walked around the cooking island three times before she dialed the number at The Local, which she had memorized years ago.

When Dooley came to the phone, she said, "If you ever breathe to a *soul* that I helped you . . ."

"No, *ma'am!* I *won't.*"

"I wish you'd asked me a couple of days ago, that cake's better if it sets awhile before you eat it."

"Oh," Dooley said, sounding stricken.

"But no use to cry over spilled milk. What d'you want to do, two layers or three?"

"Umm," said Dooley, who didn't have a clue.

"I'd do three-layer for a contest. Showier."

"Great! Thank you, Miz Bolick. I appreciate it a whole lot. I'll do somethin' for you anytime you say, like clean out your basement or your attic, or I could do your yard . . ."

Esther walked around with the cordless, opening cabinets and looking in the refrigerator. "I'm a little low on ingredients. How soon can you get up here with six oranges, a pound of butter, and a dozen eggs?"

* * *

Since his wife passed four years ago, Lew Boyd had used nothing in his kitchen but a toaster oven and a stove-top percolator. He did not believe in microwaves, in case anybody came to see him who had a pacemaker.

For this reason, he didn't have a clue what might be stored in his kitchen cabinets, and spent four hours on the eve of the contest trying to make sense of the clutter.

He called his sister Little Sue three times, and nearly had a stroke when he realized he forgot to grease the cake pans. He poured the batter back into the bowl and washed the pans and started over, speaking aloud to his departed Granmaw Minnie.

Why in the world he'd ever gotten into this mess was more than he could fathom. Little Sue had nearly laughed her head off about the whole thing and told him to get a life. He thought she said Get a wife, and replied that it was very hard to find one that didn't drink and run around.

He freely admitted he was lonesome, how much time could a man spend at his gas station, anyway? He had to eventually come home to an empty house.

He had developed a ritual for evenings. He walked in the back door, passed through the kitchen where he heated his supper, watched TV in the den, and ended up in the bedroom, all on the back side of the house. In truth, he hadn't seen his living room for months, it seemed as remote as Mesopotamia. And he had no idea what to do, if anything, about the dining room, which had become a year-round storage bin for Christmas ornaments, odd boxes, and a nonflammable tree.

Setting the oven to preheat at 325, he thought again about Earlene Dickson kissing him when he won the pickle contest years and years ago. That had been on his mind a lot lately.

He surveyed what he had done and felt pleased. He might be a pickle man, but he knew a creamy, velvety batter when he saw one.

He could hardly wait to get the brimming cake pans in the oven, so he could go sit in his recliner with the mixing spoon and batter bowl.

* * *

Louella felt the sharp, shooting pain in her knee as she rolled out the dough, but she had better things to think about than hurting.

She was thinking about healing, about sending the prize money to Canada so Miss Violet Larkin's grandson could buy a plane ticket and come to Hope House where he would kneel down and kiss his granmaw's hand. Louella didn't know where she got such an image, but she thought it was a good one, Miss Violet being the only granmaw the boy had.

Louella's head and heart seemed suddenly full of images, as if rolling out biscuit dough was returning something to her that was lost.

She closed her eyes and saw her husband-to-be walking into the kitchen of the Atlanta boarding house. She was fifteen years old, with her hair in corn rows, and the sense that something wonderful was about to happen.

Moses Marshall flashed a smile that nearly knocked her winding. She had never seen anybody who looked like this when she was growing up in Mitford, the only people of color they had in Mitford were old and white-headed.

"Who's th' one baked them good biscuits for supper?"

Louella could hardly speak. "What you want to know for?"

"Because th' one baked them good biscuits, that's th' one I'm goin' to marry."

Louella looked at old Miss Sally Lou, who had to stand on tiptoe to peer into a pot on the stove. She was so little and dried up, some said she was a hundred, but Louella knew she was only eighty-two and still the boss cook of three meals a day at the boarding house.

Louella pointed at old Miss Sally Lou, afraid to say the plain truth that she, Louella Baxter, had baked the biscuits herself, three pans full and not one left begging.

Moses Marshall looked his bright, happy look at Miss Sally Lou and walked over and picked her up and swung her around twice before he set her down. "Fine biscuits, ma'am. Will you jump th' broom with me?"

"Git out of my way 'fore I knock you in th' head," said Miss Sally Lou. "Marry that 'un yonder, she th' one do biscuits." The old woman threw back her head, looking imperious. "*I* does yeast rolls."

* * *

Hope Winchester didn't know if she believed in God. She was thinking this as she searched the James Beard bread book, making sure she had picked the right recipe.

She had thought all along that raisin bread would be perfect. Then, she had second thoughts and was convinced that salt-rising might cut through the clutter of entries and stand out more.

She sat at the table, feeling scared. She couldn't keep going back and forth, she had to decide right now and start baking.

She knew that if she believed in God, she would pray about which recipe, even if God wouldn't be interested in such petty, self-serving issues. The priest at Lord's Chapel, Father Kavanagh, had once said God wanted people to pray about everything, he told her one of the saints had said "Pray all the time," or maybe it was "Pray without ceasing."

That was all right for saints who had nothing else to do, who did not work in retail and do inventory and try to keep everyone happy, even grouchy, mean-spirited, tight-fisted people who thought they should get a discount just for living.

She pulled two straws from the broom behind the refrigerator, then shut her eyes and switched the straws around and held them in her hand. The short straw would be raisin, the long would be salt.

It was raisin.

She didn't understand why she burst into tears, as if a terrible weight had been lifted. Then she remembered, all at once and for the first time, that raisin was her mother's favorite bread.

She turned the oven on preheat, which is what the book said to do, feeling a tingle of excitement as if she'd set the stove dial while standing in a tub of water.

Whether she won or lost, she would take the bread to her mother at the hospital and show it to her through the oxygen tent, she only hoped they would let her have her bread back from the contest.

She set a jar of grape jelly on the open cookbook, to hold her place, and hurriedly pulled the ingredients from the cabinets and the refrigerator, because more than anything on earth, she wanted to start baking the bread right now, this minute, so that her mother who was dying a little every day, would be able to see it and perhaps even smell it, and find it wonderful.

* * *

Uncle Billy Watson was quiet as a mouse as he stirred about the kitchen. He had hunkered under the covers, sleeping fitfully until three a.m., then crept out of the bedroom and closed the door behind him.

He didn't know if he could do this, even with the Lord's help. What he was trying to do was re-create the sweet potato pie his mother had made in their little cabin in the valley.

Oh, they'd been a poor and ragged lot, the Watsons, but hadn't they had a fine time hunting in the woods and eating deer meat and wild turkey and even bear when they could get it?

He remembered grubbing in the sweet-smelling earth to pull those taters out, and rubbing them off on his britches and carrying them to the house by the peck and bushel.

He hadn't been able to read or write a word in those days, but he could draw. By joe, he could spot a squirrel on a log and before it could dash away, he had drawed it with his pencil, log and all.

That's when the sweet potato pies had started. Before, his mama had roasted the yams in the ashes, or sliced them up and fried them in bacon grease in a black skillet. But when he started drawing pictures of dogs and geese and partridges and all, she took to rewarding him with sweet potato pies. "Because you're special, William," she once said.

In all his seventy-eight years, or was it seventy-nine, he could not remember anything ever tasting so good. All good-tasting things had fallen short next to the faded memory of her pies.

Intoxicated by the smell of freshly ground cinnamon and cloves, he had eagerly observed how much butter she used, and the careful way she sprinkled sugar into the orange-brown mash. But mostly, he'd watched her making the pie dough and rolling it out, her fingers working like magic to hand the soft, perfect circle off the dough board and into the old pie pans.

Through the closed door at the end of the hall came the sound of his wife snoring. He was glad his hearing hadn't gone; he could still hear a chigger in the leaves.

Everything was set out, now; he had everything he needed— everything but a recipe.

Uncle Billy closed his eyes and turned his heart back across the years to the sound of a fresh, crackling cook fire, and his mother's bare feet whispering across the wooden floor.

"Lord," he prayed in a low voice, "you're a mighty God and I'm a speck tryin' to do a foolish thing. Please help me."

* * *

Uncle Billy Watson was thankful to hear the horn blow at the back steps.

It was Coot Hendrick in his old red truck, come to carry him to Town Hall for the judging.

"A man cain't go trottin' down th' street with a cane in one hand and a pie in th' other," said Coot.

Uncle Billy left his wife ranting and raving over the mess on the sink, the table, the countertop, and the stove. "I'll clean it up soon as I git back!" he shouted above the din.

"I don't know why I done it," he said, as the truck eased onto Main Street. "Hit's th' hardest dadjing thing I ever tried t' do."

"Let me see it," said Coot, who had some expertise when it came to eating, if not baking, pies.

Uncle Billy pulled back the tea towel to reveal the pie, encased in Saran Wrap.

"That's a beauty, all right!" said Coot, who fervently hoped he'd get a piece for doing the driving.

* * *

Lew Boyd arrived early at Town Hall, and found the place already packed. People milled around like ants on a hill observing the cake, pie, loaf bread, and biscuit entries displayed on several long tables.

"How many in th' cake division?" Lew asked the Golden Band official as he filled out the entry form. As accustomed as he was to dealing with the public, he felt suddenly shy and realized he was blushing.

"Forty-seven in cake, thirty-three in pie, fourteen in loaf bread, and twenty-six in biscuits!" recited the official, looking pleased with herself.

He claimed a chair toward the back and sat nervously through the slide show about making flour. As the award ceremonies began, he hammered down on biting his cuticles.

The sound system wasn't exactly borrowed from Radio City Music Hall, and during the awards part, Lew knew he misunderstood several things the judges said.

Like, when they announced the winner in the biscuit division, he could have sworn they said *Use yellow batter marshmallow.* He soon realized they said *Louella Baxter Marshall.*

Once again, he wondered why in the dickens he'd done all this, anyway. Sure, he could use the money, who couldn't, yet it seemed like the part he liked best was the baking, itself, and thinking about the good feeling he had when he won that pickle contest back in 4-H, and afterward, how Earlene Dickson had puckered up her lips and shut her eyes before she kissed him on the mouth and run off, laughing.

When the judges announced the winning cake, Lew was positive he heard wrong.

"What'd they say?" he asked Percy Mosely, who sat next to him.

"They said Dooley Barlowe."

"What about Dooley Barlowe?" asked Lew.

"Dooley won th' cake contest with a three-layer orange marmalade."

Lew felt like somebody had punched him in the stomach. He couldn't believe Granmaw Minnie's chocolate cake hadn't won; it had never occurred to him, even for a moment, that it wouldn't win. Everybody in his family, everybody in his hometown of Siler's Creek, and even the lieutenant governor who once judged it at the fair, knew her cake to be an unfailing winner.

Afraid he'd bust out crying, he got up and headed at a trot to the men's room.

* * *

Hope Winchester didn't want anyone to see how jittery she was, nor did she want anyone to think it really mattered whether she won or lost.

To further this intent, she brought a book with her and sat in the very back row of the town hall, reading Emily Eden.

"The library at St. Mary's was of a high, old-fashioned form, and within it was a small flight of steps which led to a light gallery built round . . ."

The announcement crackled over the microphone. "And now, the winning entry in the loaf bread division . . ."

". . . three sides of the room, giving thus an easy access to the . . ."

". . . let's see, here's the card right here . . ."

". . . higher shelves of books. The room itself was full of odd, deep recesses. . . ."

". . . the very savory and delicious Beard's Raisin Bread, baked by Hope Winchester!"

Hope dropped the book on the floor and bent to pick it up, her face flaming.

"Where are you, Miss Winchester? Ah, there she is! Come right up, and we hope you have a big pocket to put all this money in!"

Hope's heart was pounding furiously as she mounted the steps to the podium. She felt an uncharacteristically large smile freeze on her face, and was concerned that it might never go away.

"Congratulations, Miss Winchester! Now, tell us, what are you going to do with your five hundred dollars?"

She hadn't expected to be asked anything at all, and was utterly stunned by the question. Without meaning to, she blurted into the microphone what she had desperately wanted to keep to herself.

"I'm going to buy my mother a wedding and engagement ring," she said. "She never had either one, really, because my father . . . because their money . . ."

She noticed that her voice was getting louder. "I mean, she had a band, but it got lost in the washing, and she never got another one because our money had to go for other things . . . and then my father was killed, and it took all she had to send me to college and buy my books and . . ."

She stopped and looked at the check handed to her and was suddenly, to her great humiliation and confusion, blinded by tears.

* * *

After filling out the form and entering his pie with thirty-two others at Town Hall, Uncle Billy realized he felt as tuckered as if he'd plowed a cornfield.

He had never seen the place so crowded, even for a town meeting. In fact, he didn't see an empty seat anywhere.

"Uncle Billy!" Winnie Ivey, who owned the Sweet Stuff Bakery, jumped up to give him her chair on the front row.

"As a professional, I can't enter th' dern contest!" she said. "So I sure don't need to sit down front! Good luck, and I hope you win."

He was mighty glad to take a load off his feet, and visit with everyone around him. And it was a treat to see Louella win the biscuit division; the whole crowd stood and cheered at the announcement. When asked what secret she had for making such fine biscuits, Louella said, "Short-'nin' is th' trick, honey, make 'em plenty short and don't hold back."

As far as the prize money was concerned, Uncle Billy figured there were lots of people who needed it more than he did. Even the oil in his tank, thanks to the good heart of the mayor, was taken care of.

Of course, winning wasn't the point, anyway, the point was to see if he could search back across the faded years and unlock the mysterious secret of his mother's pies. And in his heart, he knew he'd done it.

When he tasted the pie filling before sunrise this morning, he recognized that a wondrous thing had happened—something outside his own ken and ability, maybe a miracle.

Even the crust, which had cracked down the middle the first time, had come around to his way of thinking and slipped into the pan as perfect as you please. He had cut away the dough overhanging the pan and ate every bite of the trimmings, considering it breakfast.

* * *

"And now, ladies and gentlemen," said the Golden Band Flour spokesman, "we're going to do something we haven't done in any other of the fine towns we've visited . . .

"Our judges were so impressed by an entry called Granmaw Minnie's Chocolate Cake that we're prepared to award a very special consolation prize.

"Will Mister Lew Boyd please come forward?"

"Where is Lew?" Gene Bolick asked Percy Mosely.

"I don't know, I seen 'im go in yonder a little bit ago." Percy pointed toward the men's room.

"I'll check," said Gene.

Gene found Lew just coming out of the stall, his eyes as red as if he'd stayed up all night playing gin rummy.

"Congratulations!" said Gene, dragging him out the door and into the hall.

"On what?" asked Lew.

"The consolation prize!"

The microphone honked and squeaked. "Mr. Lew Boyd—is he *here?*"

The editor of the *Mitford Muse* pushed through the crowd with his Nikon and grabbed Lew's arm. "That's you, buddyroe. Get on up there so I can crank off a shot for Monday's front page."

* * *

As the crowd poured out of Town Hall, Gene Bolick hurried home and gave his wife a bear hug. He was proud of her and no two ways about it.

"Well, Doll, you've done it again! There were nine marmalades runnin' against you, but th' one *you* baked was . . ."

Esther ignored the joyous fibrillation of her heart. "I didn't bake it, Dooley baked it."

"It looked to me like you did most of the work."

"I didn't," said Esther. "I set it all out and told him what to do and he did it. He earned his prize, and Hessie Mayhew called and said he gave me credit. Did you hear his speech?"

"He stood right up there and said, I baked my cake from the best cake recipe in the whole nation, compliments of Miz Esther Bolick!"

"Did he say nation? Hessie thought he said state."

"*Nation* is exactly what he said."

"Well," said Esther. A smile crept onto her face. "I declare!"

* * *

Louella Baxter Marshall asked the nurse to dial the number, and when it was busy, the nurse showed her how to push re-dial. Louella pushed re-dial two times before Miss Violet's grandson answered. He was so happy he was coming to see his granmaw that he shouted a happy shout right into the phone. "But I wouldn't wait 'til Thanksgivin'," Louella said, keeping her voice low.

Louella didn't know when she had moved so fast in a wheelchair.

She turned right into Miss Violet's room, where the crocheted ballerina slippers hung on the door. "Miss Vi'let?"

Miss Violet's paper-thin eyelids fluttered.

"Who you think is comin' t' see you nex' week?"

"I don't know. You, I guess."

"No, Miss Vi'let, this goin' t' be somebody special." Louella's large, strong hand stroked the small, frail hand.

"You're special," said Miss Violet, meaning it.

"Yes, ma'am, but this be somebody han'some an' young."

"I don't know anybody handsome and young." Her chaplain at Hope House was handsome and young, but he was on vacation.

"Yes, ma'am, you do," said Louella. "You try an' think, now."

Miss Violet thought hard. "Bobby Darin!" she exclaimed, lacking any earthly idea why he'd want to come all the way to Mitford from Hollywood.

* * *

"Mother?" Hope Winchester stood by the oxygen tent, the ring box in her pocket, holding the raisin bread aloft.

Her mother looked up and, for the first time in what seemed a long time, smiled at her daughter.

Hope became aware that she was saying something over and over in her mind, as the words of a song or a jingle sometimes repeat themselves and won't go away. She was saying, *Thank you, God.*

* * *

Uncle Billy asked Coot Hendrick to ride him down to the Preacher's office at the other end of Main Street.

"I'd be beholden to you for a piece of that pie," said Coot, when it appeared he wouldn't be offered any.

"I'll be bakin' another'n next day or two, I'll see to it you git a piece," said the old man.

At the church office, he put his cane over his arm and carried his pie to the door and walked in without knocking. Nobody ever knocked at the Preacher's office.

"Well, sir," he said to Father Tim, "I didn't win that fool contest up th' street." He put the pie, which was missing the judges' slice, on the rector's desk, then peeled back the tea towel to reveal his handiwork.

"Smells good!" said Father Tim, as the aroma of cinnamon and nutmeg floated out into the small room.

"I want t' give you and Miss Cynthia half of it. You'uns have been awful good to me an' Rose." Uncle Billy grinned broadly, displaying his gold tooth.

"Let's see," said Father Tim, scratching his head. "What will I carry half of it in?"

Uncle Billy pondered this. In the meantime, he thought it looked mighty tasty sitting there on the desk with the tea towel rolled back.

"Tell you what," said the old man, "let's you and me jis' set down right here and eat th' whole thing."

* * *

When Lew Boyd arrived at Golden Band Flour Company in Bishopville, just over the state line from Mitford, three people came out to the lobby to greet him, one being the vice president of the whole shebang. A secretary aimed a point-and-shoot camera in his direction and took a picture to go in the company newsletter.

The consolation prize, which he had come to collect, was a plant tour, a night in Bishopville's finest and only hotel, a steak dinner with the marketing department, and a five-pound bag of Golden Band self-rising.

As soon as the plant tour was over, he asked what he'd wanted to ask since he hit the front door.

"Is there a phone I could use? It's a local call."

He sat in an office with his bag of flour, and carefully combed his hair. Then he looked up the number of the library where he heard she was working since her husband died.

He dialed the number with a ballpoint pen, his hand shaking.

"Earlene?" he said when she came to the phone. His throat was dry as a crumb.

"This is Lew Boyd. Remember me?"

Calling Home:
Prayer

Imagine this:

Your children are grown and gone, and you miss them terribly. Much to your sorrow, they call home only once in a blue moon—or not at all.

This is loosely akin to the relationship that many of us have with God. There are some who check in with Him regularly, and some who never bother to call Home.

We know how we feel when our children don't call, and I believe it matters deeply to God when we fail to connect with Him in prayer.

As Father Tim says in *A New Song,* "God wishes us to be as near to us as our very breath." There's simply no way to have a relationship with Him unless we talk to Him—and also listen.

St. James said, "Draw nigh to God and He will draw nigh to you."

King David said, "The Lord is nigh unto all them that call upon Him, to all that call upon Him in truth."

Oswald Chambers said this: "Prayer doesn't fit us for the greater work, prayer is the greater work."

I hope you'll call Home right now. And whether we tell Him everything or merely utter His name, God is longing to hear the prayer that's in our hearts.

HE LEFT the coffee-scented warmth of the Main Street Grill and stood for a moment under the green awning.

The honest cold of an early mountain spring stung him sharply.

He often noted the minor miracle of passing through a door into a completely different world, with different smells and attractions. It helped to be aware of the little things in life, he told himself, and he often exhorted his congregation to do the same.

> *"Nothing is worth more than this day."*
>
> —Goethe

As he headed toward the church office two blocks away, he was delighted to discover that he wasn't walking, at all. He was ambling.

It was a pleasure he seldom allowed himself. After all, it might appear that he had nothing else to do, when in truth he always had something to do.

He decided to surrender himself to the stolen joy of it, as some might eat half a box of chocolates at one sitting, without remorse.

He arrived at the office, uttering the prayer he had offered at its door every morning for twelve years: "Father, make me a blessing to someone today, through Christ our Lord. Amen."

At Home in Mitford, Ch. 1

AT THE CHURCH, he found the door unlocked and, coming inside in his snow-encrusted boots, was greeted by the lush, alluring fragrance of flowers. Their fresh scent spoke at once to his heart and lightened his sober thoughts.

He looped the red leash around a chair leg and took off his boots as Barnabas lay down contentedly. Apparently, the Altar Guild had been in to arrange the flowers and had forgotten to lock the side door. He must speak to them about it, of course.

Not that he didn't like an unlocked church. No, indeed; he preferred it. If there was anything disheartening, it was to seek out a church for prayer and refreshment and find its doors barred.

But the Mortlake tapestry, woven in 1675 and now hanging behind the altar, was of such extraordinary rarity that the insurance company not only demanded a darkened room and locked doors, it stipulated the type of locks.

It was unusual for him to visit Lord's Chapel on Saturday, but today he was seeking special refreshment of his own. Who was there, after all, to counsel the counselor? He crossed himself. "Revive me, O Lord," he prayed, "according to Thy word."

At Home in Mitford, Ch. 11

> *"What lies behind us and what lies before us are tiny matters compared to what lies within us."*
>
> —Ralph Waldo Emerson

AS HE PAUSED TO let his eyes adjust to the dimness of the nave, he heard a strange sound. Then, toward the front, on the gospel side, he saw a man kneeling in a pew. Suddenly, he leaned back and uttered such a desperate cry that the rector's heart fairly thundered.

> *"Mercy has converted more souls than zeal, or eloquence, or learning, or all of them together."*
>
> —Søren Kierkegaard

Give me wisdom, he prayed for the second time that morning. Then he stood waiting. He didn't know for what.

"If you're up there, prove it! Show me! If you're God, you can prove it!" In the visitor's voice was a combination of anger, despair, and odd hope.

"I'll never ask you this again," the man said coldly, and then, with a fury that chilled his listener, he shouted again, "Are . . . you . . . up . . . there?"

With what appeared to be utter exhaustion, he put his head in his hands as the question reverberated in the nave.

Father Tim slid into the pew across the aisle and knelt on the worn cushion. "You may be asking the wrong question," he said, quietly.

Startled, the man raised his head.

"I believe the question you may want to ask is not 'Are you up there?' but 'Are you down here?' "

"What kind of joke is that?"

"It isn't a joke."

The man took a handkerchief from his suit pocket and wiped his face. He was neatly dressed, the rector observed, and his suit and tie appeared to be expensive. A businessman, obviously. Successful, quite likely. Not from Mitford, certainly.

"God wouldn't be God if He were only up there. In fact, another

r Him is Immanuel, which means 'God with us.'" He was
at the casual tone of his voice, as if they'd met here to chat for
a while. "He's with us right now, in this room."

The man looked at him. "I'd like to believe that, but I can't. I can't
feel Him at all."

"There's a reason . . ."

"The things I've done," the man said flatly.

"Have you asked Him to forgive the things you've done?"

"I assure you that God would not want to do that."

"Believe it or not, I can promise that He would. In fact, He
promises that He will."

The man looked at his watch. "I've got a meeting," he said, yet he
made no move to leave. He remained on his knees.

"What business are you in?" It was one of those questions from a
cocktail party or Rotary meeting, but out it came.

"Shoes. We make men's shoes. I was on my way to a sales meeting
in Wesley when I saw this place and I came in. I didn't mean to do it,
I just couldn't help it. I had to come in. And now I don't know what
I'm doing here. I need to get on the road."

Still, he made no move to rise from his knees.

> *Do not look forward to what may happen tomorrow;
> the same everlasting Father who cares for you today will take
> care of you tomorrow and every day. Either He will shield
> you from suffering, or He will give you unfailing strength to
> bear it. Be at peace, then, put aside all anxious thoughts and
> imaginations, and say continually:*
>
> *"The Lord is my strength and my shield; my heart has
> trusted in Him and I am helped. He is not only with me . . .
> but in me . . . and I in Him."*
>
> —St. Francis de Sales, from *A Continual Feast:*
> *Words of comfort and celebration,*
> *collected by Father Tim*

It was an odd thought, but the rector pursued it. "Let's say you need to move into another factory building. Trouble is, it's crowded with useless, out-of-date equipment. Until you clear out the rubbish and get the right equipment installed, you're paralyzed, you can't produce."

"How did you know we're looking for a new factory?"

"I didn't know. A divine coincidence."

There was a long silence. A squirrel ran across the attic floor.

"You can keep the factory shut down and unproductive, or you can clear it out and get to work. Is your life working?"

"Not in years."

Somewhere in the dark church, the floor creaked. "There's no other way I can think of to put it—but when you let Him move into your life, the garbage moves out. The anger starts to go, and the resentment, and the fear. That's when He can help get your equipment up and running, you might say."

"Look, I don't want to wallow around in this God stuff like a pig in slop. I just want some answers, that's all."

"What are the questions you want answered?"

"Bottom line, is He up there, is He real?"

"Bottom line, He's down here, He's with us right now."

"Prove it."

"I can't. I don't even want to try."

"Jesus," the man said, shaking his head.

This was like flying blind, the rector thought, with the windshield iced over. "I get the feeling you really want God to be real, perhaps you even want to be close to Him, but . . . but you're holding on to something, holding on to one of those sins you don't think God can forgive, and you don't want to let it go."

The man's voice was cold. "I'd like to kill someone, I think of killing him all the time. I would never do it, but he deserves it and thinking about it helps me. I like thinking about it."

The rector felt suddenly weakened, as if the anger had seeped into his own bones, his own spirit. He wanted the windshield to defrost; where was this going?

"Do you like the fall of the year?"

The man gave an odd laugh. "Why?"

"One of the things that makes a dead leaf fall to the ground is the bud of the new leaf that pushes it off the limb. When you let God fill you with His love and forgiveness, the things you think you desperately want to hold on to start falling away . . . and we hardly notice their passing."

The man looked at his watch and made a move to rise from his knees. His agitation was palpable.

"Let me ask you something," said the rector. "Would you like to ask Christ into your life?"

The stranger stared into the darkened sanctuary. "I can't do it, I've tried."

"It isn't a test you have to pass. It doesn't require discipline and intelligence . . . not even strength and perseverance. It only requires faith."

"I don't think I've got that." There was a long silence. "But I'd be willing to try it . . . one more time."

"Will you pray a simple prayer with me . . . on faith?"

He looked up. "What do I have to lose?"

"Nothing, actually." Father Tim rose stiffly from the kneeler and took the short step across the aisle, where he laid his hands on the man's head.

"If you could repeat this," he said. "Thank You, God, for loving me, and for sending Your Son to die for my sins. I sincerely repent of my sins, and receive Christ as my personal savior. Now, as Your child, I turn my entire life over to You. Amen."

The man repeated the prayer, and they were silent.

"Is that all?" he asked finally.

"That's all."

"I don't know . . . what I'm supposed to feel."

"Whatever you feel is exactly what you're supposed to feel."

The man was suddenly embarrassed, awkward. "I've got to get out of here. I was on my way to a meeting in Wesley, and I saw this old church and I . . . things have been, I've been . . . I've got to get out of here. Look, thanks. Thank you," he said, shaking the rector's hand.

"Please . . . stay in touch."

He stood at the door for a moment and watched him go. There was so much he hadn't said, so much he'd left out. But the Holy Spirit would fill in the blanks.

As they were leaving the church, Barnabas looked up, sniffed the air, and began to bark wildly at the ceiling. His booming voice filled the small nave like the bass of an organ.

With some difficulty, he unglued his charge from the narthex floor, and pulled him along on the leash.

It seemed years ago that he'd come in this door, he thought. Yet his watch told him he'd been at Lord's Chapel only a little more than two hours.

He felt strangely at peace, following the man's footprints along the snowy path to the street.

At Home in Mitford, Ch. 11

"WHAT ARE YOU grinnin' all over yourself about?" Dooley asked, his eyes bleary with approaching sleep.

"I am not grinning all over myself." He sat on the side of the bed. "Did your studying go well? Did you need me to help?"

"Naw, I got 'at ol' mess figgered out."

"I'll be praying for you tomorrow at one o'clock when your test begins."

"Prayin' ain't goin' t' knock 'at ol' test in th' head."

"You're right about that, my friend. However, praying will help *you* knock it in the head."

Dooley yawned and turned over. "'Night," he said.

"'Night," said the rector, putting his hand on the boy's shoulder.

Father, he prayed silently, thank you for sending this boy into my life. Thank you for the joy and the sorrow he brings. Be with him always, to surround him with right influences, and when tests of any kind must come, give him wisdom and strength to act according to your will. Look over his mother, also, and the other children, wherever they are. Feed and clothe them, keep them from harm, and bring them one day into a full relationship with your Son.

He sat for a long time with his hand on the sleeping boy's shoulder, feeling his heart moved with tenderness.

At Home in Mitford, Ch. 17

It was J. C. Hogan who was ringing his office phone at eight-thirty on Monday morning. "I got a letter to the editor I need to answer," said J.C.

"How can I help you, my friend?"

"This kid read my story about the man in the attic, about the prayer you prayed with the guy in the pew, and how you got two birds with one stone, you might say. Wrote me this letter."

J.C. cleared his throat. "'Dear Editor, What exactly was the prayer the preacher prayed when the man in the attic got saved? My daddy wants to know, and I do too. Thank you.'"

"Do you want me to write it down and drop it by, or just tell you on the phone?"

"Phone's fine," said J.C., breathing heavily into the receiver.

"Well, then. Here it is. 'Thank You, God, for loving me, and for sending Your Son to die for my sins' . . ."

"Got it," said J.C.

"'I repent of my sins and receive Jesus Christ as my personal savior.'"

"Got it."

"'And now, as Your child' . . ."

"As your what?"

"'As Your child.'"

"Got it."

"'I turn my entire life over to You. Amen.'"

"What's the big deal with this prayer? It looks like some little ol' Sunday school thing to me. It's too simple."

"It's the very soul of simplicity. Yet, it can transform a life completely when it's prayed with the right spirit."

"I was lookin' for something with a little more pizzazz."

"My friend, the one who prays that prayer and means it will get all the pizzazz he can handle."

At Home in Mitford, Ch. 18

"When Papa and Mama died, I did perhaps the only independent thing I had ever done in my life." She looked at him and smiled weakly. "I moved across the aisle and started sitting on the gospel side."

She slumped a little in the chair. He leaned forward and reached for her hand, which felt small and cold.

"That's my love story, Father. I'm sorry it did not have a happier ending. The nursing home will give it a happy ending. The building will be given in honor of Mama and Papa. The beautiful fountain out front will be in memory of Captain Willard James Porter. It will be a place of solace and peace, a place for healing."

Father Tim got up from his chair and placed a hand on her fragile shoulder. "Father," he prayed, "I ask you to heal any vestige of bitter hurt in your child, Sadie, and by the power of your Holy Spirit, bring to her mind and heart, now and forever, only those memories which serve to restore, refresh, and delight. Through Jesus Christ, your Son our Lord, amen."

"Amen!" she said, reaching up to put her hand on his.

At Home in Mitford, Ch. 19

"I HAD ONE of them dreams th' other night at th' farm. I was dreamin' m' little brother Kenny had fell in th' creek and turned into a fish an' I was runnin' after 'im along th' bank, hollerin', 'Kenny, Kenny, come back, don't be a fish, don't leave me!' an' Miz Owen said I woke up Rebecca Jane, but that was all right, she come in and talked t' me."

"Do you miss your brother?"

"Yeah. He was my best friend."

Dear God! Five children wrenched apart like a litter of cats or dogs.

"Tell me about your brothers and sisters."

"There's Jessie, she's th' baby, still poopin' in 'er britches, and Sammy, he's five, he stutters. Then, there's ol' Poobaw . . ."

"What does *Poobaw* mean?"

"Means he took after a pool ball my mama brought home, had a eight on it, she said it was a keepsake. Poobaw hauled 'at ol' thing around, went t' sleepin' with it, an' that's where 'is name come from, it used t' be Henry."

"What's Henry like?"

"Wets 'is bed, 'e's seven."

He dreaded this. "Do you know where they are?"

"Mama said she'd never tell nobody, or th' state would come git 'em. I was th' last'n t' go." There was a long silence.

If it wrenched his own heart to hear this, how must Dooley's heart be faring? "Have you ever prayed for your brothers and your baby sister?"

"Nope."

"Prayer is a way to stay close to them. You can't see them, but you can pray for them, and God will hear that prayer. It's the best thing you can do for them right now."

"How d'you do it?"

"You just jump in and do it. Something like this. You can say it with me. Our Father . . ."

"Our Father . . ."

"Be with my brother Kenny and help him . . ."

"Be 'ith m' brother, Kenny, an' he'p him . . ."

"To be strong, to be brave, to love you and love me . . ."

"T' be strong, t' be brave, t' love you an' love me . . ."

"No matter what the circumstances . . ."

"No matter what th' circumstances."

"And please, God . . ."

"An' please, God . . ."

"Be with those whose names Dooley will bring you right now . . ."

He heard something hard and determined in the boy's voice. "Mama. Granpaw. Jessie an' Sammy an' Poobaw. Miz Ivey at church, an' Tommy . . . 'at ol' dog . . . m' rabbit . . . Miz Coppersmith an' ol' Vi'let an' all." He buried his face in the pillow and pulled it around his ears.

The clock ticked. Somewhere, through the open alcove window, he heard the rooster crow, the rooster whose whereabouts he couldn't identify, but whose call often gave him a certain

poignant joy. Dooley moved closer to him, and in minutes, he heard a light, whiffling snore. He sat up and pulled the blanket over the boy's sleeping form.

He didn't know why he felt this would be a splendid summer for Dooley Barlowe.

At Home in Mitford, Ch. 20

THE BELL JINGLED, and a customer walked in. "Brother Greer, I need a box of oatmeal!"

"Comin' up," said Absalom, leaving his guest.

The rector noted the slowness of the old man's gait as he walked toward the shelves. He hadn't seen that last year and felt troubled by it. Deep down, he expected the people he loved to live forever, no matter how many funerals he had performed during his years as a priest.

Absalom rejoined the rector and sat again.

"My brother, I was in deep prayer as I preached, that the Holy Ghost would knock through the crust on every heart along that creek—but I have to tell you, my own heart was sinking, for it looked like the vineyard wasn't givin' off a single grape."

"I hear you."

"That's the way it was goin' when I noticed a young girl sitting on a limb of that big tree by the water.

"Usually, a good many young 'uns would sit up there for the preaching, but somebody had put a board across some rocks that evenin', and all the young 'uns but her was sitting on the board. I pay a good bit of attention to young 'uns, having been one myself, but I'd never spotted Lacey Turner before.

"You talk about listening! Her eyes like to bored a hole in me. If a preacher had a congregation to sit up and take notice like that, he'd be a happy man. It seemed like every word the Holy Ghost put in my mouth was something she craved to hear. I got the feeling my words were like arrows, shooting straight at that long-legged, barefooted girl, but still missing the souls on the ground.

"Wellsir, that young 'un slid off that limb and landed on her feet right in front of me, blam!

"Strikin' the ground like that kicked the dust up around her feet. I looked at that dust and looked at that girl, and I knew the Lord was about to do a work.

"She said, 'I'm sorry for th' bad I've done, and I want to git saved.' It was as matter-of-fact a thing as you'd ever want to hear.

"Well, the young 'uns on the board, they started in laughing, but that girl, she stood there like a rock, you should have seen her face! She was meaning business.

"I said, 'What would you be repenting of?' And she said, 'Bein' generally mean and hatin' ever'body.'

"My brother, that's as strong an answer as you're likely to get from anybody, anywhere.

"I said, 'Do you want to be forgiven of meanness and hatred?' and she squared back her shoulders and said, 'That's what I jumped down here for.'

"I said, 'Well, jump in here and say a prayer with me and turn your heart over to Jesus.' And we both went down on our knees right there by the water, saying those words that's changed the lives of so many lost and hurting souls.

" 'Lord Jesus,' she prayed in behind me, 'I know I'm a sinner. I believe You died for my sins. Right now, I turn from my sins and receive You as my personal Lord and Savior. Amen.'

"Wellsir, I looked up and half the crowd had moved over to that big tree and was going down on their knees, one by one, and oh, law, the Holy Ghost got to working like you never saw, softening hearts and convicting souls 'til it nearly snatched the hair off my head.

"We stayed kneeling right there, and I led first one and then another in that little prayer, and before you know it, brand-new people were getting up off their knees and leaping for joy!

"Oh, you know the lightness that comes with having your sins forgiven! It's a lightness that fills you from one end to the other and runs through your soul like healing balm."

The rector could feel the smile stretching across his face.

"My brother, I scrambled down the bank to that creek, and that little handful swarmed down over rocks and roots, some crying, some whooping for joy, and we baptized in the name of the Father and the Son and the Holy Ghost 'til I was sopping wet from head to toe."

The old preacher was silent, then he smiled. "I've never seen anything to top it."

"Nor I," said the rector.

Absalom got up and set his empty bottle in a crate.

"You can baptize anywhere you've got water," he said, "but to my way of thinking, you can't beat a creek. It's the way ol' John did it— out in the open, plain and simple.

"Only one thing nags me," he told the rector. "Who's goin' to disciple those children of God?

"What's goin' to become of Lacey Turner, as pert and smart a young 'un as you'll ever see, with a daddy that's beat her all her life, and a mama sick to death with a blood ailment?

"I can't keep goin' back in there. My arthritis won't hardly let me get down the bank from the main road."

The old man shook his head. "It grieves me, brother, it grieves me."

The knot in the rector's throat was sizable. "I don't know right now what we can do," he said, "but we'll do something. You can count on it."

They walked out to the porch and looked across the pasture and up to the hills. The sun was disappearing behind a ridge.

"How's Sadie?" asked Absalom.

"Never better, I think. She has a heart like yours."

"Well . . ." said the old preacher, gazing at the hills. They stood on the porch for a moment, silent.

Absalom Greer had passed a torch, and Father Tim had taken it. The only problem was, he had no idea what to do with it.

These High, Green Hills, Ch. 4

"WHAT?" HE SAID, his heart thundering.

"Something fell on my head, oh, please, oh, no, it's running down my neck, oh, get it off. . . . !"

"Water," he said stoically, feeling a large drop crash onto his own head and roll down his back.

"Are you sure? Run your hand down my back."

It had hit with such force, it must have come from a great distance. "Water," he said again, smoothing her damp shirt.

"Timothy, we've got to get out of here. We can't just stand around talking about the seventh grade!"

"Did you say you have candy bars in your day pack?"

"Snickers. Two." She turned her back to him and he reached into the pack and felt around among the colored pencils and the sketchbook and the dead flashlight and socks, and found them rolled up in her underwear.

He didn't know why it swam to the surface at just that moment, but he remembered Miss Sadie's story of falling in the well, of the darkness and her terrible fear, and the long night when no one seemed destined to find her because of the rain. The rain had destroyed the scent for the bloodhounds. What if it were raining out there again, erasing their scent?

But he was making mountains out of molehills. Good Lord, they'd been fumbling around in here for only ten or fifteen minutes, and already he was calling in the bloodhounds.

His adrenaline had stopped pumping, and he felt exhausted, as if he wanted nothing more than to lie down and sleep. He ate two bites of the candy, wondering at its astonishing sweetness, its texture and form, the intricate crackle of the paper, and the way the smell of chocolate intensified in the darkness.

"Please don't eat the whole thing." She had seen him in a diabetic coma once, which had been once too often.

He put the rest of the bar in her day pack, realizing he felt completely befuddled. He didn't want to press on until the sugar hit his bloodstream.

"I'm going to start walking," she said impatiently.

"Which way?"

"To my right. That's the way we were going when we stopped to reflect on our early love interests."

"We were going to your left. I was ahead of you, remember?"

"I thought I was ahead of you. No, wait. That was before."

"Trust me. We go this way. Grab my belt and hold on."

"I think it's time to scream. In fact, I think we should scream now and walk ten paces and scream again, and so on until someone comes or we see the light."

"Have at it," he said tersely.

She swallowed the last bite of her Snickers, then bellowed out a sound that would have shattered the crystal in their own cabinets, forty miles distant.

"How was that?" she wanted to know.

"You definitely get the job of screaming, if further screaming is required."

"Every ten paces," she said, feeling encouraged. "You pray and I'll scream."

"A fair division of labor." He was feeling the numbing cold, now, and the dampness of his clothes. Didn't the French keep wine in caves because of a mean temperature in the fifties? This felt like thirty degrees and dropping.

"Five, six, seven . . ." said Cynthia.

* * *

Her voice seemed to come from somewhere above him. He reached up, feeling nothing but air, then touched a flat rock. He inched his hand along the edge, and found the tip of her shoe. "You're standing on some kind of ledge. Back up a little, and take it easy."

"Timothy . . ."

"Don't panic. I'm fine. I'm telling you, we've got to be right at the entrance. We'll be out of here in no time. Stay calm."

"Let me give you a hand."

"Back up and stay put."

He grabbed the ledge and hauled himself up. He had fallen only a couple of feet, thanks be to God.

Lord, You know I'm completely in the dark, in more ways than one. I don't have a clue where we are or what to do. I know You're there, I know You'll answer, give me some supernatural understanding here. . . .

He stood up and leaned against the wall, and reached for her, and found her sleeve and took her hand. He had lost all sense of time. *A thousand years in Thy sight are but as yesterday when it is past, and as a watch in the night. . . .* Was he being introduced to something like God's own sense of time?

"I'm going to scream again."

"Don't," he said, meaning it.

"Why not, Timothy? People will be looking for us. We'll never get out of here."

"Turn around."

"Turn around? Again? We're so turned around now we can't think straight. We've turned around and turned around, 'til we're fairly churned to butter!"

"Clearly, this is not the way. It vanishes into thin air."

He stepped around Cynthia, and she tucked her hands into his belt.

The sugar was beginning to work. He felt suddenly victorious as he moved along the wall, his wife attached to his belt like a boxcar to an engine.

These High, Green Hills, Ch. 10

HE HAD LOVED the smell of his churches over the years, perhaps especially the little mission church by the sea. With the windows cranked open to the fresh salt breezes, and the incense wafting about on high holy days, it was enough to send a man to the moon. The Protestants didn't think much of incense, and the culture of the sixties hadn't done anything for its reputation, either, but he was all for it.

When the Lord was laying out the plan for the Tent of Meeting to Moses, He was pretty clear about it. He asked that Aaron "burn sweet spices every morning" when he trimmed and filled the lamps, and to burn them again in the evening. Bottom line, there was to be "a perpetual incense before the Lord, throughout the generations."

Ah, well, it wasn't worth wrangling over, incense. In the end, it was just one more snare of church politics.

Why are church politics so bitter? someone recently asked. Because the stakes are so small, was the answer.

He chuckled.

Lord's Chapel had had its share of political squabbles, but thanks be to God, not in the last three or four years. No, things had gone smoothly enough, and he was grateful.

But why was he musing on politics, when the church was so sweetly hushed and somehow expectant? The light poured through the stained-glass depiction of the boy preaching in the temple, through purple and scarlet and gold, and the azure of the boy's robe as He stood before the elders. That was one smart, courageous kid, he thought. I'm glad I know Him.

"Rest. Rest. Rest in God's love," Madame Guyon had written. "The only work you are required now to do is to give your most intense attention to His still, small voice within."

He sighed and moved forward in the worn pew, and fell to his knees on the cushion.

"Lord," he said aloud, "I'm not going to pray, I only want to listen. Why does Dooley turn away from us?

"And what was the lesson of the cave?"

These High, Green Hills, Ch. 13

HE WOKE UP with it on his mind, and went downstairs to his study, padding as quietly as he could through the bedroom.

Five o'clock.

He had been getting up at five a.m. for years. It had become his appointed hour, even if he'd gone to sleep wretchedly late.

He leaned against the mantel and stretched, breathing the prayer he learned from his grandmother: *Lord, make me a blessing to someone today.*

Good. So good to stretch, to come alive, he thought, pushing up on the balls of his feet.

He would make coffee, he would read the Morning Office and pray, he would sit quietly for twenty minutes; then he'd go to the hospital, a round he made every morning, with rare exceptions.

Visiting the sick continued to be good medicine, as far as he was concerned. If he was having a rough go of it, all he had to do was pop up the hill to the hospital and self-concern went out the window.

When he retired, he intended to keep at that very thing. . . .

When he retired?

He let the tension go from his arms and stood holding the mantel.

When he *retired.* Where had that come from?

He went to the kitchen and ground the beans and brewed the coffee, feeling an odd blessing in this simple daily ritual. A ritual of well-being, of safekeeping, in the still and slumbering house.

He took the steaming cup and set it next to his wing chair, then turned on the lamp and picked up his worn prayer book.

This was the time to fill the tank for the day's ride. He could put in a quarter of a tank and, later, get stranded on the road, or he could pump in a full measure now and go the distance.

But something was pushing ahead of the Morning Office.

Why haven't You answered those questions? he asked silently.

He had received nothing in that hour at the church but a sense of calm. That in itself *was* an answer, but not the one he was looking for.

Forgiveness.

He felt the word slowly inscribe itself on his heart, and knew at once. This simple thing was the answer.

"Forgiveness," he said aloud. "Forgiveness is the lesson of the cave. . . ."

He sat still, and waited.

"And what about Dooley, Lord? Why does Dooley pull away from us?"

Again, a kind of inscription.

Ditto.

He shook his head. Ditto? God didn't talk like that; God didn't say ditto. He laughed out loud. Ditto?

He felt his spirit lifting.

Ditto! Of course God talks like that, if He wants to.

He got up and walked to the window and looked out at the new dawn.

He would have to forgive Dooley Barlowe and Marge and Hal Owen, whether he liked it or not.

These High, Green Hills, Ch. 13

ESTHER BOLICK BANGED on a dishpan with a wooden spoon. "Quiet, get ready, here she comes!" Esther threw down the dishpan and took her place at the piano.

"I hope I don't break your camera!" said Miss Sadie, arriving with Louella and Ron Malcolm, and her best silver-tipped cane.

"Hit it!" shouted Esther.

> *Happy Birthday to you!*
> *Happy Birthday to you!*
> *Happy Birthday, Miss Sadie,*
> *Happy birthday to you!*
> *And many mo-oh-ore!*

"Happy Birthday, Miss Sadie!" chorused the children, holding up posters they had made for the occasion.

The entire room burst into hoots, cheers, and applause as he offered his arm and led the guest of honor to a chair in front of the fireplace.

"I'd better sit down before I fall down!" she warbled.

Laughter all around.

"Please come and pay your respects to our precious friend on the occasion of her ninetieth birthday," said the rector. "Help yourself to the refreshments, and save room for cake and ice cream after the mayor's speech. But first, let's pray!"

Much shuffling around and grabbing of loose toddlers.

"Our Father, we thank You profoundly for this day, that we might gather to celebrate ninety years of a life well-lived, of time well-spent in Your service.

"We thank You for the roof on this house which was given by Your child, Sadie Baxter, and for all the gifts she freely shares from what You graciously provide.

"We thank You for her good health, her strong spirits, her bright hope, and her laughter. We thank You for Louella, who brings the zestful seasoning of love into our lives. And we thank You, Lord, for the food You've bestowed on this celebration, and regard with thanksgiving how blessed we are in all things. Continue to go with Sadie, we pray, and keep her as the apple of Your eye. We ask this in Jesus' name."

"Amen!" chorused the assembly, who either broke into a stampede to the food table or queued up to deliver felicitations to the honored guest.

These High, Green Hills, Ch. 15

HE STOOD BY her bed and held the rail, and watched the random flickering of the lid over her closed eye. Sleeping, perhaps, or lost in the mist produced by morphine. The air in the tube that formed her breath sounded harsh against the constant hiss and gurgle of the IV drips.

He prayed aloud, but kept his voice quiet. "Our Father, thank You for being with us, for we can't bear this alone. Cool and soothe, heal and restore, love and protect. Comfort and unite those who're concerned for her, and keep them in Your care. We're asking for Your best here, Lord, we're expecting it. In Jesus' name."

She opened her eye after a moment and he looked into the deep well of it, feeling a strangely familiar connection.

"Hey, there," he said, smiling foolishly.

These High, Green Hills, Ch. 17

BACK AND FORTH, back and forth—always the same questions, and never any answers. At least, not as far as he was concerned.

He couldn't deal with this any longer.

He got up from the sofa and knelt by his desk in the quiet study.

"Lord, Miss Sadie's house belongs to You, she told me that several times. You know I've got a real problem here."

He paused. "Actually, You've got it, because I'm giving it to You right now, free and clear. I'll do my part, just show me what it is. In Jesus' name, amen."

Out to Canaan, Ch. 13

THE NAVE OF Lord's Chapel became a deep chiaroscuro shadow as dusk settled over Mitford. Candles burned on the sills of the stained-glass windows to light the way of the remnant who came for the evening worship on Thursday, scheduled unexpectedly by the rector.

Winnie Ivey had donated tarts and cookies for a bit of refreshment afterward, and the rector's wife had made pitchers of lemonade from scratch, not frozen. Hearing of this, Uncle Billy and Miss Rose Watson, not much used to being out after dark, arrived in good spirits.

Esther Bolick, weary in every bone, trudged down the aisle with Gene to what had long ago become their pew on the gospel side. Several Bane volunteers, already feeling the numbing effects of pulling together the largest fund-raiser in the diocese, slipped in quietly, glad for the peace, for the sweetness of every shadow, and for the familiar, mingled smells of incense and flowers, lemon wax and burning wick.

Most of the vestry turned out, some with the lingering apprehension that they'd robbed Mitford of a thriving new business, others completely satisfied with a job well done.

Hope Winchester, invited by the rector and deeply relieved that the A sale was successful, stood inside the door and looked around awkwardly. She found it daunting to be here, since she hadn't been raised in church, but Father Tim was one of their good customers and never pushy about God, so she figured she had nothing to lose.

She slid into the rear pew, in case she needed to make a quick exit, and lowered her head at once. It was a perfect time to think about the S sale, coming in September, and how they ought to feature *Sea of Grass* by Conrad Richter, which nobody ever seemed to know about, but certainly should.

The *Muse* editor and his wife, Adele, slid into the rear pew across the aisle, and wondered what they would do when everybody got down on their knees. They both had Baptist backgrounds and felt deeply that kneeling in public, even if it was in church, was too in-your-face, like those people who prayed loud enough for everybody in the temple to hear.

Sophia Burton, who had seen the rector on the street that morning, had been glad to come and bring Liza, glad to get away from the little house with the TV set she knew she should turn off sometimes, but couldn't, glad to get away from thinking about her job at the canning plant, and the supervisor who made her do things nobody else had to do. Not wanting her own church, which was First Baptist, to think she was defecting, she had invited a member of her Sunday school class so it would look more like a social outing than something religious.

Farther forward on the gospel side, Lace Turner sat with Olivia and Hoppy Harper, and Nurse Kennedy, who had been at the hospital long before Dr. Harper arrived and was known to be the glue that held the place together.

And there, noted the rector, as he stood waiting at the rear of the nave, were his own, Cynthia and Dooley, and next to them, Pauline and Jessie and Poo and . . . amazing! Buck Leeper.

The rector might have come to the church alone and given thanks on his knees in the empty nave. But he'd delighted in inviting one and all to a service that would express his own private thanksgiving—for the outcome of Fernbank, for Jessie, for this life, for so much.

He came briskly down the aisle in his robe, and, in front of the steps to the altar, turned eagerly to face his people.

"Grace to you and peace from God our Father and from the Lord Jesus Christ!" he quoted from Philippians.

"I will bless the Lord who gives me counsel," he said with the psalmist, "my heart teaches me, night after night. I have set the Lord always before me; because He is at my right hand, I shall not fall."

He spoke the ancient words of the sheep farmer Amos: "Seek Him who made the Pleiades and Orion, and turns deep darkness into the morning, and darkens the day into night; who calls for the waters of the sea and pours them out upon the surface of the earth: the Lord is His name!"

There it was, the smile he was seeking from his wife. And lo, not one but two, because Dooley was giving him a grin into the bargain.

"Dear friends in Christ, here in the presence of Almighty God, let us kneel in silence, and with patient and obedient hearts confess our sins, so that we may obtain forgiveness by His infinite goodness and mercy."

Here it comes, thought Adele Hogan, who, astonishing herself, slid off the worn oak pew onto the kneeler.

Hope Winchester couldn't do it; she was as frozen as a mullet, and felt her heart pounding like she'd drunk a gallon of coffee. Her mouth felt dry, too. Maybe she'd leave, who would notice anyway, with their heads bowed, but the thing was, there was always somebody who probably wasn't keeping his eyes closed, and would see her dart away like a convict. . . .

"Most merciful God," Esther Bolick prayed aloud and in unison with the others from the Book of Common Prayer, "we confess that we have sinned against You in thought, word, and deed . . ."

She felt the words enter her aching bones like balm.

". . . by what we have done," prayed Gene, "and by what we have left undone."

"We have not loved You with our whole heart," intoned Uncle Billy Watson, squinting through a magnifying glass to see the words in the prayer book, "we have not loved our neighbors as ourselves."

He found the words of the prayer beautiful. They made him feel hopeful and closer to the Lord, and maybe it was true that he hadn't always done right by his neighbors, but he would try to do better, he would start before he hit the street this very night. He quickly offered a silent thanks that somebody would be driving them home afterward, since it was pitch-dark out there, and still hot as a depot stove into the bargain.

"We are truly sorry and we humbly repent," prayed Pauline Barlowe, unable to keep the tears back, not wanting to look at the big, powerful man beside her. Though plainly reluctant to be there, he nonetheless held the hand of her daughter, who was sucking her thumb and gazing at the motion of the ceiling fans.

"For the sake of Your Son Jesus Christ, have mercy on us and forgive us," prayed Cynthia Kavanagh, amazed all over again at how she'd come to be kneeling in this place, and hoping that the stress she'd recently seen in her husband was past, and that this service would mark the beginning of renewal and refreshment.

". . . that we may delight in Your will, and walk in Your ways," prayed Sophia Burton, wishing with all her heart that she could do that very thing every day of her life, really do it and not just pray it—but then, maybe she could, she was beginning to feel like she could . . . maybe.

". . . to the glory of Your Name!" prayed the rector, feeling his spirit moved toward all who had gathered in this place.

"Amen!" they said in unison.

Out to Canaan, Ch. 15

THE SOUND CAME through the open bedroom windows—a terrible screeching noise, a loud thud, the high-pitched yelping of a dog. Dooley was shouting.

He bolted to the front window and looked down on Wisteria Lane.

Good God! Barnabas lay in the street with Dooley bending over him.

He didn't remember racing down the stairs, but seemed to be instantly in the street with Dooley, crouching over Barnabas, hearing the horrific sound that welled up from his own gut like a long moan.

Blood ran from his dog's chest, staining the asphalt, and he reached out. . . .

"Don't touch 'im!" shouted Dooley. "He'll bite. We got t' muzzle 'im! Git Lace! Git Lace!"

The rector was on his feet and running for the house, calling, shouting. "And git me some towels!" yelled Dooley. "He's got a flail chest, I got t' have towels!"

His heart was pounding into his throat. Dear God, don't take my dog, don't take this good creature, have mercy!

Lace flew through the door. "Help Dooley!" he said, running toward the guest bathroom, where he picked up an armload of towels, then turned and sprinted up the hall and down the steps and into the street in a nightmarish eternity of slow motion.

"Give me that thing on your head," Dooley told Lace, "and help me hold 'im! We got to muzzle 'im or he'll bite, look, do it this way, hold 'im right here."

Father Tim could hardly bear the look of his dog, suffering, whimpering, thrashing on the asphalt, as fresh blood poured from the wound in his chest.

Dooley tied the bandanna around the dog's nose and mouth, and knotted it. "Okay," he said, taking off his T-shirt. "Don't look, you can see 'is lungs workin' in there." He pressed the balled-up shirt partially into the gaping wound; immediately, the dark stain of blood seeped into the white cotton.

"Give me a towel," Dooley said, clenching his jaw. He took the towel and wrapped the heaving chest, making a bandage. "Another one," said Dooley, working quickly. "And git me a blanket, we got t' git 'im to Doc Owen. He could die."

The rector ran into the house, praying, sweat streaming from him, and opened the storage closet in the hall. No blankets. The armoire! *He could die.*

Christ, have mercy. He dashed up the stairs and flung open the door of the armoire and grabbed two blankets and ran down again, breathless, swept out of himself with fear.

Cynthia, come home . . . *he could die.*

"Spread 'em down right there," Dooley told the rector. "Help 'im," he said to Lace.

They spread the blankets, one on top of the other, next to Barnabas, as a car slowed down and stopped. "Can we help?" someone called.

"You can pray!" shouted Lace, waving the car around them.

Together, they managed to move Barnabas onto the blankets. "Careful," said Dooley, "careful. He's in awful pain, and his leg's broke, too, but they ain't nothin' I can do about it now, we got to hurry. Where's Harley?"

"He walked t' town," said Lace, her face white.

"Git his keys, they're hangin' on th' nail. Back 'is truck out here, we'll put Barnabas in th' back, an' you'n me'll ride with 'im."

She raced to the house as Dooley, naked to the waist, crouched over Barnabas and put his hand on the dog's head. "It's OK, boy, it's OK, you're goin' t' be fine."

"Thank You, Jesus, for Your presence in this," the rector prayed. "Give us your healing hands. . . ."

They heard Lace gun the truck motor and back out of the driveway. She hauled up beside them and screeched to a stop, the motor running.

"Let down th' tailgate," said Dooley. Lace jumped out of the truck and let it down.

"Grab this corner of th' blanket with me," he said to Lace. "Dad, you haul up that end. Take it easy. Easy!"

The dog's weight seemed enormous as they lifted him into the truck bed. "OK, boy, we're layin' you down, now."

Lace and Dooley climbed up with Barnabas and gently positioned the whimpering dog in the center of the bed. Then Dooley slammed the tailgate and looked at the rector.

"Hurry," he said.

Out to Canaan, Ch. 17

BUCK WAS SHAKING as they went into the study. Though the rector knew it wasn't from the cold, he asked him to sit by the fire.

There was a long silence as Buck waited for the trembling to pass; he sat with his head down, looking at the floor. The rector remembered the times of his own trembling, when his very teeth chattered as from ague.

"Does Pauline know you're back in Mitford?"

"No. I came for . . . I came for this." He looked up. "I didn't want to come back."

"I know."

"It was sucking the life out of me all the way. I was driving into Huntsville when I knew I couldn't keep going. . . ."

He was shaking again, and closed his eyes. Father Tim could see a muscle flexing in his jaw.

"God a'mighty," said Buck.

Father Tim looked at him, praying. The man who had controlled some of the biggest construction jobs in the Southeast and some of the most powerful machinery in the business couldn't, at this moment, control the shaking.

"I pulled into an Arby's parkin' lot and sat in the car and tried to pray. The only thing that came was somethin' I'd heard all those years in my granddaddy's church." Buck looked into the fire. "I said, Thy will be done."

"That's the prayer that never fails."

The clock ticked.

"He can be for your life what the foundation is for a building."

Buck met his gaze. "I want to do whatever it takes, Father."

"In the beginning, it takes only a simple prayer. Some think it's too simple, but if you pray it with your heart, it can change everything. Will you pray it with me?"

"I don't know if I can live up to . . . whatever."

"You can't, of course. No one can be completely good. The point is to surrender it all to Him, all the garbage, all the possibilities. All."

"What will happen when . . . I pray this prayer?"

"You mean what will happen now, tonight, in this room?"

"Yes."

"Something extraordinary could happen. Or it could be so subtle, so gradual, you'll never know the exact moment He comes in."

"Right," said Buck, whispering.

The rector held out his hand to a man he'd come to love, and they stood before the fire and bowed their heads.

"Thank You, God, for loving me . . ."

"Thank You, God . . ." Buck hesitated and went on, "for loving me."

". . . and for sending Your Son to die for my sins. I sincerely repent of my sins, and receive Christ as my personal savior."

The superintendent repeated the words slowly, carefully.

"Now, as Your child, I turn my entire life over to You."

". . . as Your child," said Buck, weeping quietly, "I turn my entire life over to You."

"Amen."

"Amen."

He didn't know how long they stood before the fire, embracing as brothers—two men from Mississippi; two men who had never known the kindness of earthly fathers; two men who had determined to put their lives into the hands of yet another Father, one believing—and one hoping—that He was kindness, Itself.

Out to Canaan, Ch. 21

HE LOVED CYNTHIA KAVANAGH; she'd become the very life of his heart, and no, he would never turn back from her laughter and tears and winsome ways. But tonight, looking at the chimneys against the glow of the streetlight, he mourned that time of utter freedom, when nobody expected him home or cared whether he arrived, when he could sit with a book in his lap, snoring in the wing chair, a fire turning to embers on the hearth. . . .

He raised his hand to the rectory in a type of salute, and nodded to himself and closed his eyes, as the bells of Lord's Chapel began their last peal of the day.

Bong . . .

"Lord," he said aloud, as if He were there beneath the tree, "Your will be done in our lives."

Bong . . .

"Guard me from self-righteousness, and from any looking to myself in this journey."

Bong . . .

"I believe Whitecap is where You want us, and we know that You have riches for us there."

Bong . . .

"Prepare our hearts for this parish, and theirs to receive us."

Bong . . .

"Thank You for the blessing of my wife, and Dooley; for this place and this time, and yes, Lord, even for this change. . . ."

Bong . . .

Bong . . .

The bells pealed twice before he acknowledged and named the fear in his heart.

"Forgive this fear in me which I haven't confessed to You until now."

Bong . . .

"You tell us that You do not give us the spirit of fear, but of power, and of love, and of a sound mind."

Bong . . .

"Gracious God . . ." He paused.

"I surrender myself to You completely . . . again."

Bong . . .

He took a deep breath and held it, then let it out slowly, and realized he felt the peace, the peace that didn't always come, but came now.

Bong . . .

A New Song, Ch. 3

HE LOVED IT at once.

St. John's in the Grove sat on a hummock in a bosk of live oaks that cast a cool, impenetrable shade over the churchyard and dappled the green front doors.

The original St. John's had been destroyed by fire during the Revolutionary War, and rebuilt in the late nineteenth century in Carpenter Gothic style. Sam Fieldwalker said the Love family purchased the contiguous property in the forties and gave it to St. John's, so the small building sat on a tract of thirty-five acres of virgin maritime forest, bordered on the cemetery side by the Atlantic.

Father Tim stood at the foot of the steps inhaling the new smells of his new church, set like a gem into the heart of his new parish. St. John's winsome charm and grace made him feel right at home, expectant as a child.

He crossed himself and prayed, aloud, spontaneous in his thanks-giving.

"Thank You, Lord! What a blessing . . . and what a challenge. Give me patience, Father, for all that lies ahead, and especially I ask for Your healing grace in the body of St. John's."

He walked up the steps and inserted the key into the lock. It turned smoothly, which was a credit to the junior warden. Then he put his hand on the knob and opened the door.

Though heavy, it swung open easily. He liked a well-oiled church door—no creaking and groaning for him, thank you.

The fragrance of St. John's spoke to him at once. Old wood and lemon oil . . . the living breath of last Sunday's flowers still sitting on the altar . . . years of incense and beeswax. . . .

To his right, a flight of narrow, uncovered stairs to the choir loft and organ. To his left, an open registry on a stand with a ballpoint pen attached by a string. He turned to the first entry in the thick book, its pages rustling like dry leaves. *Myra and Lewis Phillips, Bluefield, Kentucky, July 20, 1975 . . . we love your little church!!*

He looked above the stand to the framed sign, patiently hand-lettered and illuminated with fading watercolors.

Let the peace of this place surround you as you sit or kneel quietly. Let the hurry and worry of your life fall away. You are God's child. He loves you and cares for you, and is here with you now and always. Speak to Him thoughtfully, give yourself time for Him to bring things to mind.

A New Song, Ch. 5

HE LAY CURLED in the fetal position, his back to his wife and Jonathan, feeling a kind of numb pain he couldn't explain or understand. Life was a roller coaster, that simple. Joy and healing here, desperation and demolition there.

With all his heart, he'd desired healing for Morris Love's broken-ness, and who was he to think he might give a leg up to such a miracle?

There were times when he didn't like being a priest, always on the front line for justice and mercy and forgiveness and redemption; trying to figure out the mind of God; giving the Lord his personal agenda, then standing around waiting for it to be fulfilled. He didn't have an agenda for Morris Love, anymore; he was giving up the entire self-seeking, willful notion. His desperate neighbor belonged to God; it was His responsibility to get the job done. He had schlepped in a paltry sack of victuals when what the man needed was the awesome, thunderstriking power of the Almighty to move in his heart and soul and spirit like a great and consuming fire. . . .

He wiped his eyes on his pajama sleeve.

"So, Lord," he whispered, "just do it."

A New Song, Ch. 20

HE DIDN'T WANT to see Mamie or anyone else this morning. He put his head down and walked quickly, focusing his mind and spirit entirely upon Morris Love and the look on Morris's face as he was ordered from Nouvelle Chanson for what may have been the final time.

He would not exhort God this morning to heal, to bind up, or to transform. He would exhort Him only to bless.

He prayed silently.

Bless the gift You have given him, Lord, to be used to Your glory, bless his spirit which craves You and yet bids You not enter, bless the laughter that is surely there, laughter that has dwelled in him all these years, yearning to be released, longing to spring forth and be a blessing to others. . . .

The laughter of Morris Love—that would be a miracle, he thought, and remembered how he had prayed to hear Dooley Barlowe laugh. That prayer had been answered; he smiled to think of Dooley's riotous cackle.

Thank You for blessing Morris with a quick and lively mind, an inquisitive intellect, and a soul able to form majestic music which ardently glorifies the Giver. Thank You for blessing Morris with Mamie, who, out of all those offered the glad opportunity of loving him, was the only one who came forth to love and serve on Your behalf.

The tears were cold on his face.

Lord, bless him today as he sits at his keyboards, as he breaks bread with Mamie, as he looks out his window onto a world which betrayed him, and which he now betrays. As he lies down to sleep, bless him with Your holy peace. As he rises, bless him with hope. As he thinks, bless him with Your own high thoughts.

Now, Father, I bless You—and praise You and thank You for hearing my prayer, through Christ our Lord who was given to us that we might have new life, Amen.

He walked on.

A New Song, Ch. 21

SHE LOVED THE way he sat with her, not saying anything in particular, not probing, not pushing her, just sitting on her love seat. Perhaps what she liked best was that he always looked comfortable wherever he was, appearing glad to live within his skin and not always jumping out of it like some men, like James, her editor, who was everlastingly clever and eloquent and ablaze with wild ideas that succeeded greatly for him, while with Timothy the thing that succeeded was quietude, something rich and deep and . . . nourishing, a kind of spiritual chicken soup simmering in some far reach of the soul.

"Tell me," he said at last. "Tell me everything. I'm your priest, after all." She thought his smile dazzling, a dazzling thing to come out of quietude. She had pulled a footstool to the love seat and sat close to him.

"I'm terribly afraid I can't make you happy," she said.

"But that was my fear! I finally kicked it out the back door and now it's run over here."

"It's not funny, Timothy."

"I'm not laughing."

He took her hands in his and lightly kissed the tips of her fingers and she caught the scent of him, the innocence of him, and her spirit mounted up again.

"Why don't we pray together?" he said. "Just let our hearts speak to His. . . ."

Sitting at his feet, she bowed her head and closed her eyes and he stroked her shoulder. Though the clock ticked in the hallway, she supposed that time was standing still, and that she might sit with him in this holy reverie, forever.

"Lord," he said, simply, "here we are."

"Yes, Lord, here we are."

They drew in their breath as one, and let it out in a long sigh, and she realized for a moment how the very act of breathing in His presence was balm.

"Dear God," he said, "deliver Your cherished one from feeling helpless to receive the love You give so freely, so kindly, from the depths of Your being. Help us to be as large as the love You've given us, sometimes it's too great for us, Lord, even painful in its power. Tear away the old fears, the old boundaries that no longer contain anything of worth or importance, and by Your grace, make Cynthia able to seize this bold, fresh freedom. . . ."

"Yes, Lord," she prayed, "the freedom I've never really known before, but which You've faithfully shown me in glimmers, in epiphanies, in wisps as fragile as . . . light from Your new moon!"

He pressed her hand, feeling in it the beating of her pulse.

"Father, deliver me from the fear to love wholly and completely, I who chided this good man for his own fears, his own weakness, while posing, without knowing it a pose, as confident and bold. You've seen through that, Lord, You've . . . You've found me out for what I am . . ."

There was a long silence, filled by the ticking of the clock.

". . . a frightened seven-year-old who stands at the door looking for a father and mother who . . . do not come home."

Give them wisdom and devotion in the ordering of their common life, that each may be to the other a strength in need, a counselor in perplexity, a comfort in sorrow, and a companion in joy.

Amen.

—The Book of Common Prayer

"Even after years of knowing You as a Father who is always home, I sometimes feel—I feel a prisoner of old and wrenching fears, and I'm ashamed of my fear, and the darkness that prevents me from stepping into the light. . . ."

"You tell us in Your Word," he prayed, "that You do not give us the spirit of fear—"

"But of power and of love and a sound mind!" she whispered, completing the verse from the second letter to Timothy.

"And so, Lord, I rebuke the Enemy who would employ every strategy to deny Your children the blessing of Your grace."

"Yes, Lord!"

"Help us to receive Your peace and courage, Your confidence and power," he said.

"Yes, Lord!"

"Thank you for being with us now, and in the coming weeks and coming years."

"And Father," she said, "please give me the grace to love Dooley as You love him, and the patience to encourage and support and understand him, for I wish with all my heart that we might grow together in harmony, as a true family." She took a deep and satisfying breath. "And now, Lord . . ."

As the prayer neared its end, they spoke in unison as they had recently begun to do in their evening prayers.

". . . create in us a clean heart . . . renew a right spirit within us . . . and fill us with Your Holy Spirit . . . through Christ our Lord . . . amen."

He helped her from the footstool and she sat beside him on the love seat and breathed the peace that settled over them like a shawl.

"There will be many times when fear breaks in," he said, holding her close. "We can never be taken prisoner if we greet it with prayer."

"Yes!" she whispered, feeling a weight rolled away like the stone from the sepulcher.

"I smelled the chicken as I came through the hedge."

"Dinner in twenty minutes?" she murmured.

"I thought you'd never ask," he said.

A Common Life, Ch. 7

IN HIS ROOM across the hall, Dooley sat on the side of his bed and felt the creeping, lopsided nausea that came with the aroma of baking ham as it rose from the kitchen. He said three four-letter words in a row, and was disappointed when his stomach still felt sick.

He hoped his voice wouldn't crack during the hymn. Though he'd agreed to sing a cappella, he didn't trust a cappella. If you hit a wrong note, there was nothing to cover you. He wished there were trumpets or something really loud behind him, but no, Cynthia wanted "Dooley's pure voice." Gag.

"God," he said aloud, "don't let me sound weird. Amen." He had no idea that God would really hear him or prevent him from sounding weird, but he thought it was a good idea to ask.

He guessed he was feeling better about stuff. Yesterday, Father Tim spent the whole day taking him places, plus they'd run two miles with Barnabas and gone to Sweet Stuff after. Then, Cynthia had given him a hug that nearly squeezed his guts out. "Dooley," she said, "I really care about you."

When he heard that, he felt his face getting hard. He didn't want it to, but it was trained that way. He could tell she really meant it, but she'd have to prove she meant it before he would smile at her; he knew she wanted him to smile. Maybe he would someday, but not now. Now he was trying to keep from puking up his gizzard because he had to sing a song he didn't even like, at a wedding he still wasn't sure of.

A Common Life, Ch. 8

A VOICE MURMURED at his right ear; he felt a warm breath that cosseted his hearing and made it acute.

**Searching for Something
You're Afraid You Can't Find?**

Read page 83 of In This Mountain.
I hope it will encourage you, as it encourages yours truly.

—Jan

"O God, Light of lights, Keep us from inward darkness. Grant us so to sleep in peace, that we may arise to work according to Your will."

The voice ceased, and he waited to hear it again, desperately wished to hear it again. *Is that all?* There came a kind of whirring in his head, as if of planets turning, and then the voice warmed his ear again. "Goodnight, dearest. I love you more than life. . . ."

He could not open his mouth, it was as if he had no mouth, only ears to catch this lovely sound, this breath as warm as the tropical isles he would never visit. Nor had he eyes to see; he discovered this when he tried to open them. No mouth to speak, no eyes to see; all he could locate was his right and waiting ear.

He tried to remember what the voice had just said to him, but could not. Speak to me again! he cried from his heart. *Please!* But he heard nothing more.

* * *

The water poured in through the top of his head, as loud as a waterfall, and rushed into his neck and arms and hands and belly and legs and streamed into his feet. Immediately the wave came in again at the top of his head and flowed through him once more.

The water's journey was warm and consoling, familiar; it was as if he'd waited for this moment all his life, and now that it had come, he was at peace.

Then he was floating somewhere, weightless, emptied of all doubt or fear, but not emptied of longing. More than anything, he longed for the sound of the voice at his ear, and the warm zephyr that came with it.

* * *

The birdsong was sharp and clear, the sky cloudless. He was walking along a woodland trail, carrying something on his back. He supposed it might be a pack, but he didn't check to see. In trying to balance the thing between the blades of his aching shoulders, he felt the weight shift wildly so that he lost his balance. He stumbled; the edge of the woodland path crumbled under his right foot and he fell to his knees, hard, and woke shouting.

Lord! Where are You?

He knew he had shouted, yet he hadn't heard his voice.

The room—was it a room?—was black, not even a streetlamp shone, and the dream—was it a dream?—had been so powerful, so convincing, that he dared not let it go. Where are You? he repeated, whispering, urgent.

Here I am, Timothy.

He lifted his hand and reached out to Jesus, whom he couldn't see but now strongly sensed to be near him, all around him.

The tears were hot on his face. He had found the Lord from whom he'd thought himself lost, and lay back, gasping, as if he'd walked a long section of the Appalachian Trail.

Thank you! he said into the silence. Had he spoken?

"'And yea, though I walk through the valley of the shadow of death . . .'"

There was the voice at his ear, and the soft, warm breath. *Stay! Don't go, don't leave me.*

"'I will fear no evil, for Thou art with me, Thy rod and Thy staff, they comfort me. . . .'"

He listened, but couldn't contain the words; he forgot them the moment they were spoken.

"I love you, my darling, my dearest, my Timothy."

A fragrance suffused the air around his pillow, and he entered into it as if into a garden. It possessed a living and deeply familiar presence, and was something like . . .

. . . Home. But what was Home? He couldn't remember. His heart repeated the word, *Home, Home,* but his head couldn't fathom the meaning.

In This Mountain, Ch. 6

"Do you feel like telling me everything?" asked the bishop.

He didn't want to talk about it. Surely someone had given Stuart the details; everybody knew what had happened. He plunged ahead, however, dutiful.

"I blacked out at the wheel of my car and hit Bill Sprouse, who pastors First Baptist. He was walking his dog. His dog was killed instantly. Bill had several fractures and a mild concussion." He took a deep breath. "He's going to be all right."

That was the first time he'd given anyone a synopsis, and he had made it through. His headache was blinding.

"Yes, I heard all that, and God knows, I'm sorry. What I'd really like to hear is how you are—in your soul."

"Ah. My soul." He put his hand to his forehead, speechless.

"The Eucharist, then," said Stuart. He bolted from the chair, took his home communion kit from the kitchen island, and brought it to the coffee table.

Father Tim watched his bishop open the mahogany box to reveal the small water and wine cruets, a silver chalice and paten, a Host box, and a crisply starched fair linen.

"I was reminded the other day," said Stuart, "that when Saint John baptized Christ, he was touching God. An awesome and extraordinary thing to consider. When we receive the bread and blood, we, also, are touching God." Stuart poured the wine and drizzled a small amount of water into each glass. "I know you recognize that wondrous fact, dear brother, but sometimes it's good to be reminded."

* * *

". . . Heavenly Father, Giver of life and health, comfort and hope; please visit us with such a strong sense of Your Presence that we may trust faithfully in Your mighty strength and power, in Your wisdom vastly beyond our understanding, and in Your love which surrounds us for all eternity. At this time, we ask Your grace especially upon Timothy, that he may know Your gift of a heart made joyous and strong by faith. Bless Cynthia, too, we pray, whose eager hands and heart care for him. . . ."

As Father Tim knelt by the coffee table next to his wife, the tears began and he didn't try to check them.

In This Mountain, Ch. 9

AT THE FOOT of the bed, Barnabas scratched furiously, causing the mattress to throb like a great, arrhythmic heartbeat.

Still awake at three in the morning, Father Tim lay in the dark room and looked out the window to darkness. The heavens were overcast, obscuring a nearly full moon, and the streetlamp had been knocked winding two weeks ago by a careless driver.

Who was to say that Cynthia wouldn't give up on him? In truth, he was wearing down while she was gearing up. How long could a bright, successful, beautiful woman be patient with a man who had no passion in him anywhere? His wife was all about passion, passion for whatever she was doing, for whatever lay ahead. At the beginning, she'd declared him charming and romantic—perhaps now she was changing her mind. But he couldn't bear such thoughts, it was blasphemy to think these vile things.

"Are you there, Lord? Sometimes I can't sense Your Presence, I have to go on faith alone. You want us to walk by faith, You tell us so . . . don't we go on faith that the sun will set, the moon will rise, our breath will come in and go out again, our hearts will beat? Give me faith, Lord, to know Your Presence as surely as I know the beating of my own heart. I've felt so far from You. . . ."

He remembered Miss Sadie's story of falling into the abandoned well, of her terror as she cried out, unheard, in the dark summer night, unable to move—she said she'd known for the first time the deep meaning of the prayers she had learned by rote. "It was the darkness," Miss Sadie had told him, "that was the worst."

The tears were hot on his face. His own life seemed overwhelmed by darkness these last weeks; there had been the bright and shining possibility, then had come the crushing darkness. Something flickered in his memory. "Songbirds," he whispered. "Songbirds, yes . . . are taught to sing in the dark."

That was a line from Oswald Chambers, from the book he'd kept by his bedside for many years. But he couldn't bear switching on the lamp to read it; his eyes had been feeling weak and even painful. He turned on his side and opened the drawer of the nightstand and took out the flashlight. Then he pulled Cynthia's pillow atop his own and shone the flashlight on the open book.

He thumbed through the worn and familiar pages. There! Page forty-five, the reading for February fourteenth. . . .

At times God puts us through the discipline of darkness to teach us to heed Him. Songbirds are taught to sing in the dark, and we are put into the shadow of God's hand until we learn to hear Him. . . . Watch

where God puts you into darkness, and when you are there keep your
mouth shut. Are you in the dark just now in your circumstances, or in
your life with God? Then remain quiet. . . . When you are in the dark,
listen, and God will give you a very precious message for someone else
when you get into the light.

The flashlight slid onto the bed beside him as he fell asleep, but his
hand resolutely gripped the book until dawn.

In This Mountain, Ch. 11

HE'D JUST WRITTEN and delivered a sermon and now it was time to
write another. A priest whose name he couldn't remember had nailed
it: "It's like having a baby on Sunday and waking up pregnant on
Monday."

He ran along the road toward Farmer, with Barnabas loping
behind.

He wanted Sunday's message to count for something. Otherwise,
why bother?

"Your words for Your people," he huffed aloud.

In This Mountain, Ch. 16

AT TWO O'CLOCK in the morning, he realized he'd fallen asleep in his
chair in the study, and found his notebook on the floor. He regretted
waking. There seemed a film over the lamplit room, as if he were wearing sunglasses. It had nothing to do with his eyes and everything to do
with his spirit. He felt at the end of himself.

Perhaps he should have gone forward with the medication for depression. The film, the darkness seemed always hovering nearby; if it
disappeared for a time, it came back. He felt again a moment of panic—
what if he were succumbing, as his father did, to the thing that brought
down his marriage, brought down his business, ruined his health?

But he mustn't dwell on that. He must dwell on the message, for
the message still hadn't come right.

He'd be forced to drum up something from days of yore, some

antiquity that might be dredged from sermon notes stored in the study cabinet.

But he didn't have what it might take even to dredge.

"Lord," he said, "speak to me, please. I can't go on like this. Speak to me in a way I can understand clearly. I've read Your word, I've sought Your counsel, I've whined, I've groveled, I've despaired, I've pled—and I've waited. And through it all, Lord, You've been so strangely silent."

He sat for a time, in a kind of misery he couldn't define; wordless, trying to listen, his mind drifting. Then at last he drew a deep breath and sat up straighter, determined.

"I will not let You go until You bless me!" he said, startled by his voice in the silent room.

He took his Bible from beside his chair and opened it at random.

Stop seeking what you want to hear, Timothy, and listen to what I have to tell you.

He felt no supernatural jolt; it happened simply. God had just spoken to his heart with great tenderness, as He'd done only a few times in his life before; it produced in him an utter calm.

"Yes," he said. "Thank you. Thank you."

Where the book had fallen open in his lap, he began to read with expectation and certainty.

He found the passage only moments later. Instantly, he knew: He'd discovered at last what God had held in reserve—expressly for him, expressly for now, and expressly for tomorrow morning.

The peace flowed in like a river.

In This Mountain, Ch. 19

IT WAS ONE of those rare days when he sensed that all the world lay before him; that it was, indeed, his oyster.

Upon leaving the Grill, he stood beneath the green awning, scarcely knowing which way to turn. Though the chilling rain continued to fall and the uproar between Velma and J.C. had definitely been unpleasant, he felt light; his feet barely touched the ground. How could someone his age feel so expectant and complete? How, indeed? It was the grace of God.

"Lord, make me a blessing to someone today!"

He uttered aloud his grandmother's prayer, raised his umbrella and, beneath the sound of rain thudding onto black nylon, turned left and headed to Lord's Chapel to borrow a volume of Jonathan Edwards from the church library.

Shepherds Abiding, Ch. 1

"I'M A SINNER saved by grace, Lew, not by works. It doesn't matter a whit that I'm a priest. What matters is that we surrender our hearts to God and receive His forgiveness, and come into personal relationship with His Son."

"Earlene, she's got that kind of thing with, you know . . ." He pointed up.

"Would you like to have it?"

Lew gazed out the driver's window, then turned and looked at Father Tim. Tears streamed down his roughly shaven face. "I don't know, I guess I ain't ready t' do nothin' like that."

"When you are, there's a simple prayer that will usher you into His presence and change your life for all time—if you pray it with a true heart."

Lew wiped his eyes on his jacket sleeve.

"How simple is it?"

"This simple: Dear God, thank You for loving me and for sending Your Son to die for my sins. I sincerely repent of my sins and receive Christ as my personal savior. Now, as Your child, I turn my entire life over to You."

"That's it?"

"That's it."

"I don't know about turnin' my entire life over."

"An entire life is a pretty hard thing to manage alone."

"Yessir."

There was a thoughtful silence as the heater blasted full throttle.

"Meanwhile," said Father Tim, "why don't we pray about what you've just told me?"

"Yessir. I 'preciate it." Lew bowed his head.

"Lord, thank You for Your mercy and grace. You know the circumstances, and You've heard Lew's heart on this hard thing.

"All we ask, Father, is that Your will be done.

"In the mighty name of Jesus, Your Son and our Savior, amen."

"Beggin' your pardon, Father, but that don't seem like much t' ask."

"It's the prayer that never fails, Lew."

"Never fails?"

"Never. I hope you'll pray it in the days and weeks to come."

Lew considered this. "Exactly what was it again?"

"Thy will be done."

Lew nodded, thoughtful. "OK. All right. I can do that. I don't see as there's anything to lose."

"Good thinking, my friend!"

Shepherds Abiding, Ch. 8

BETWEEN HIS NAP and the trek to the church, more than an inch of snow had fallen, which would undoubtedly inspire the merry greening party in their labors.

But, alas, he found no greening party, merry or otherwise. He found instead that he must unlock the double front doors and let himself in. As the key turned, the bells began to toll.

Bong . . .

The moment he stepped into the narthex, he smelled the perfume of fresh pine and cedar, and the beeswax newly rubbed into the venerable oak pews.

Bong . . .

And there was the nave, lovely in the shadowed winter twilight, every nuance familiar to him, a kind of home; he bowed before the cross above the altar, his heart full. . . .

Bong . . .

The greening of the church was among his favorite traditions in Christendom; someone had worked hard and long this day!

Bong . . .

Every windowsill contained fresh greenery, and a candle to be lighted before the service . . . the nave would be packed with congregants, eager to hear once more the old love story. . . .

Bong . . .

Families would come together from near and far, to savor this holy hour. And afterward, they would exclaim the glad greeting that, in earlier times, was never spoken until Advent ended and Christmas morning had at last arrived.

Call him a stick-in-the-mud, a dinosaur, a fusty throwback, but indeed, jumping into the fray the day after Halloween was akin to hitting, and holding, high C for a couple of months, while a bit of patience saved Christmas for Christmas morning and kept the holy days fresh and new.

He knelt and closed his eyes, inexpressibly thankful for quietude, and found his heart moved toward Dooley and Poo, Jessie and Kenny . . . indeed, toward all families who would be drawn together during this time.

"Almighty God, our heavenly Father . . ." He prayed aloud the words he had learned as a young curate, and never forgotten. ". . . who settest the solitary in families: We commend to Thy continual care the homes in which Thy people dwell. Put far from them, we beseech Thee, every root of bitterness, the desire of vainglory, and the pride of life. Fill them with faith, virtue, knowledge, temperance, patience, godliness. Knit together in constant affection those who, in holy wedlock, have been made one flesh. Turn the hearts of the parents to the children, and the hearts of the children to the parents;

and so enkindle fervent charity among us all, that we may evermore be kindly affectioned one to another; through Jesus Christ our Lord."

In the deep and expectant silence, he heard only the sound of his own breathing.

Shepherds Abiding, Ch. 9

THEY RECITED THE Lenten devotion in unison.

". . . Now as we come to the setting of the sun, and our eyes behold the vesper light, we sing Your praises, O God: Father, Son, and Holy Spirit. . . ."

He asked the blessing then, and they looked at each other for a moment across the pine table.

"I'm thankful for you," he said, "beyond words."

The dogs snored, the fire crackled, the clock struck seven.

She leaned her head to one side and smiled at him. "Here we sit, under the dome of a winter sky, two people facing the unknown, holding hands across the table in a room lighted by a single candle and a fire on the hearth. I find it all too wondrous, Timothy, and I feel the greatest peace about your new calling; He has called you to come up higher."

He knew she was right. No matter about mice and squirrels, or even, God forbid, snakes; he knew she was right.

He breathed easily, then did something he couldn't remember doing for a while. He leaned back in the chair and felt the tension release. "Ahhh," he said.

"Amen!" she replied with feeling.

Light from Heaven, Ch. 3

HE TURNED TO the communion rail, and ran his hand along the wood. Oak. Golden and deeply grained. He rubbed the wood with his thumb, musing and solemn, then dropped to his knees on the bare floor and lowered his head against the rail. Barnabas sat down beside him.

Lord, thank You for preparing me in every way to be all that You desire for this mission, and for making good Your purpose for this call. Show

me how to discern the needs here, and how to fulfill them to Your glory and honor.

He continued aloud. "Bless the memory of all those who have gathered in these pews, and the lives of those who will gather here again."

Barnabas leaned against the vicar's shoulder.

"I am Thine, O Lord. Show me Thy ways, teach me Thy paths, lead me in Thy truth and teach me.

"In the name of the Father, and of the Son, and of the Holy Spirit. Amen."

Light from Heaven, Ch. 3

AGNES MET HIM at the wall, where they stood looking down at clouds collected in the hollows after last night's rain. Then, carrying the tea basket, and the folder under his arm, he walked with her to the nave.

He saw it at once and drew in his breath.

"Beautiful!" he exclaimed, hurrying ahead of her to the pulpit placed on the gospel side of the aisle.

He smelled the familiar scent he associated only with churches and his mother's parlor; the pungent wax that had been rubbed so carefully into the oak would long after release its sweet savor upon the air.

She came behind him on her cane. "Clarence made it four years ago, when God renewed our conviction that He would send someone.

It sat here only a short time, and then we took it to the schoolhouse where it would be safe."

The polished oak glowed in the light from the window above the altar. "Exquisite!" he said.

"He brought it over on Sunday evening, and with great joy, we installed it. Do you like where it's placed?"

"Couldn't like it better! What became of the original?"

"It was stolen many years ago. The vandals who did this were not thieves, but desecrators of another stripe."

She pointed to the initials rudely carved into the left side of the pulpit. "Just there . . . 'JC loves CM.' We were at first greatly distressed, then I realized that we might take it to signify: Jesus Christ loves Clarence Merton."

He laughed. "Lemons into lemonade, and gospel truth into the bargain! And look here! Such elaborate detailing. He did this, as well?"

"Yes, with his old carving tools given him long ago."

He ran his fingers over the tooled oak, tracing the path the knife had taken before him.

A crown of thorns. A heart. A dove. A dogwood blossom. And in the center of these, a cross.

"Agnes . . ." That's all he could find to say.

She was moved, proud. "Yes."

"Let's thank God!" Indeed, it was pray—or bust wide open.

He took her hand in both of his, and they bowed their heads.

"We praise You, Lord, we thank You, Lord, we bless You, Lord!

"Thank You for the marvel and mystery of this place, for these thirty remarkable years of devotion, for Your unceasing encouragement to the hearts and spirits of Your servants, Agnes and Clarence, for Your marvelous gifts to Clarence of resourcefulness and creativity, and for Your gift to them both of a mighty perseverance in faith and prayer.

"We thank You for this nave above the clouds in which Your holy name has been, and will continue to be, honored, praised, and glorified. Thank You for going ahead of us as we visit our neighbors, and cutting for each and every one a wide path to Holy Trinity. Draw whom You will to the tenderness of Your unconditional love, the sweetness of Your everlasting mercy, and the balm of Your unbounded forgiveness.

"In the name of the Father and of the Son and of the Holy Spirit."

Light from Heaven, Ch. 6

HE BENT OVER where Dovey lay, and looked into another pair of brown and solemn eyes. "Dovey." He took her hand and instinctively held it in both of his.

"Dovey," he said again; the name seemed an odd comfort to him. "May I pray for you?" he knew nothing about her except what he saw in her eyes.

"Yes," she whispered.

He sat in the chair beside her. "Dear God and loving Father, Creator of all that is, seen and unseen, we thank You for Your Presence in this home, at this bedside, and in the heart of your child, Dovey. Give us eyes to see Your goodness in her suffering, give us faith to thank You for her healing, give us love to strengthen us as we wait. In the name of the Father, and of the Son, and of the Holy Spirit, Amen."

"Amen," said Agnes.

"Amen," whispered Dovey.

Light from Heaven, Ch. 7

EARLY AFTERNOON SUN filtered through the leaves above; they were light and shadow beneath.

He lay on his back beside her. "So what are we going to do about your work space?"

"Lloyd says we haven't seen anything yet, it's really going to get messy on Monday morning—they've been tiptoeing around the inevitable. Then there's Lily, of course, who must have the kitchen if she's going to cook, so we're looking at . . . chaos, to put it plainly."

"Sammy's room gets good light. Maybe, somehow . . ."

"I can't do that."

"Can we move you into the smokehouse? It has a window."

"Ugh. Lots of creepy crawlies in there, and spiders with legs as long as mine."

"Del would have them out of there in no time flat."

"No, sweetheart. Even with a window, too dark and confining."

"Here's a crazy thought . . ." he said.

"I love your crazy thoughts."

"The barn loft. The old hay doors open straight out to the north."

"The barn?" She was quiet for a time, thoughtful. "I don't know. But He knows. Could we pray about it?"

He took her hand.

"Father," he said, observing St. Paul's exhortation to be instant in prayer, "thank You for caring where Cynthia cultivates and expresses the wondrous gift You've given her. We're stumped, but You're not. Would You make it clear to us? We thank You in advance for Your wise and gracious guidance, and for Your boundless blessings in this life . . . for the trees above us, and the good earth beneath. For the people whose lives You intermingle with ours. For Sammy, who was lost and now is found. For Dooley, who's coming home . . ."

"And I thank you, Lord," prayed his wife, "for my patient and thoughtful husband, a treasure I never dreamed I'd be given."

He crossed himself. "In the name of our Lord and Savior, Jesus Christ . . ."

"Amen!" they said together.

"That feels better."

"Thanks for the kind words to the Boss."

She patted his hand; they listened for a while to the bleating of the lambs.

Light from Heaven, Ch. 14

Going and Telling:

The Life of a Faithful Priest

ॐ

An odd thing happened during the ten-year span of the Mitford series.

When Father Tim supplied a pulpit in Whitecap (*A New Song*), some readers vociferously objected. Though supplying other pulpits as an interim priest is precisely what many retired clergy do, readers wanted him to cling, instead, to Mitford.

Yet if Father Tim hadn't gone to Whitecap, who would have walked seven times around the wall of fear and loneliness in Morris Love, and brought the wall down through prayer and faith?

In the same way, there will be readers who object to Father Tim and Cynthia's being called to Holy Trinity (*Light from Heaven*), which is also set outside Mitford.

I would ask those readers to consider this:

If Father Tim hadn't come up higher to the little church above the clouds, who would have ministered to Rooter and Jubal and Robert and Donny and Sissie and Dovey and all the rest? How would we have gained the privilege of knowing Agnes and Clarence and witnessing their very private, yet somehow universal, ministries?

Scripture doesn't exhort us to loll about on beds of familiar ease.

Indeed, the Great Commission contains, in summary, just three words—Go and tell—not the least of which is this:

Go.

This is what our faithful priest does throughout the series.

Thus, those who insist on clinging to Mitford may wish to skip books five and nine entirely, though they will, thereby, miss a great essential in the life of a true pastor.

One Small Verse:
Scripture Quotes

Many Christians have what they call a life verse. That is, a single verse from the vast lexicon of the Word of God that will serve in any situation, no matter what. That's a lot to ask of one small verse. My brother Barry claims Proverbs 3:5–6. I take this text from the King James translation:

"Trust in the Lord with all thine heart; and lean not unto thine own understanding. In all thy ways, acknowledge him, and he shall direct thy paths."

So. If we trust Him, seek His wisdom, and acknowledge Him in all our ways, look what happens, look what we're promised:

He will direct our paths.

This is very potent stuff. Indeed, I want and need Him to direct my path, for I remember what happened when I did all the directing myself. Not good.

If I had to absolutely, positively come up with a verse to live by in this tough and out-of-control age, it's one you'll find again and again in the Mitford books.

"I can do all things through Christ, who strengthens me" (Philippians 4:13).

Indeed, Olivia Davenport and Father Tim have a little "family joke," if you will. They say to each other, "Philippians four-thirteen, for Pete's sake."

Don't have a verse of your own? I hope you'll find one, for Pete's sake. You'll be amazed at how often you call upon its reassurance and tonic wisdom.

"'L ET NO CORRUPT communication proceed out of your mouth,'" he quoted in a loud voice from Ephesians, "'but that which is good to the use of edifying. . . .'" Suddenly, the dog sat down and looked at his prey with fond admiration.

"Well, now," he said irritably, wiping the notebook on his sleeve. "I hope you've got that nonsense out of your system." At this, the dog leaped up, stood on its hind legs, and put its vast paws on the rector's shoulders.

At Home in Mitford, Ch. 1 (Ephesians 4:29)

"'A ND AS JESUS passed by,'" intoned the rector, avoiding the doleful stare, "'he saw a man which was blind from birth. And his disciples asked him, saying, "Master, who did sin, this man, or his parents, that he was born blind?"'"

Barnabas sighed and lay down.

He continued, without glancing into the corner: "'Jesus answered, "Neither hath this man sinned, nor his parents: but that the works of God should be made manifest in him."'"

He read aloud through verse five. Then, he stopped and studied Barnabas with some concentration.

"Well, now," he said at last, "this is extraordinary."

"What's that?" asked Emma.

"This dog appears to be . . . ," he cleared his throat, ". . . ah, controlled by Scripture."

At Home in Mitford, Ch. 1 (John 9:2–3)

H E HAD DASHED off a note to Walter after his morning prayers, quoting the encouraging message of Hebrews 4:16: "Let us, therefore, come boldly unto the throne of grace, that we may obtain mercy, and find grace to help in the time of need."

Boldly! That was the great and powerful key. Preach boldly! Love boldly! Jog boldly! And most crucial of all, do not approach God whining or begging, but boldly—as a child of the King.

At Home in Mitford, Ch. 5 (Hebrews 4:16)

HE HAD ALREADY had morning prayer and studied the challenging message of Luke 12: "Therefore, I tell you, do not be anxious about your life, what you shall eat, nor about your body, what you shall put on. For life is more than food, and the body more than clothing.

"Consider the ravens: they neither sow nor reap, they have neither storehouse nor barn, and yet God feeds them. Of how much more value are you than the birds?"

There was not one man in a thousand who considered these words more than poetical vapor, he thought as he dressed. Don't be anxious? Most mortals considered anxiety, and plenty of it, an absolute requirement for getting the job done. Yet, over and over again, the believer was cautioned to abandon anxiety, and look only to God.

At Home in Mitford, Ch. 7 (Luke 12:22–24)

As BARNABAS CAME bounding toward her in a frenzy of delight, Puny recited in a loud voice one of the few Scriptures she'd ever committed to memory:

"'And this is his commandment, that we should believe on the name of his Son, Jesus Christ, and love one another'!"

Barnabas sprawled at her feet and sighed.

At Home in Mitford, Ch. 7 (I John 3:23)

BARNABAS SEEMED TO sail through the air, clearing the steps entirely and landing only inches from a white cat that was streaking across the yard.

"'Blessed be the Lord, who daily loads us with benefits'!" he shouted from a psalm as he raced toward the hedge.

Barnabas, however, could hear nothing above the din of an old-fashioned cat and dog fight.

Father Tim peered into the yard where the humiliated cat was racing up a hemlock tree. "Barnabas!" he yelled.

Barnabas stood at the foot of the tree, his thick fur bristling, filling the night with a bark that seemed to carry to the monument and echo back along the storefronts.

" 'Be filled with the spirit!' " he shouted. " 'Speak to one another in psalms, hymns, and spiritual songs!' " He never knew which Scripture would float to the surface in such emergencies.

At Home in Mitford, Ch. 9 (Psalm 68:19; Ephesians 5:19)

"WHY HAVEN'T YOU told me about this woman?" Hoppy wanted to know, as they stood outside Andrew's rear office and waited for the rest room.

"What was there to tell?"

"That she's lovely, new in town, goes to Lord's Chapel, I don't know. I'm walking down the hall last week, and I see this angel sitting by Pearly's bed, reading from the Psalms. I'll never forget it. 'Thou art my hiding place and my shield. I hope in thy word,' she said. It struck me to the very marrow."

And no wonder, thought the rector, whose own marrow had been struck by the depth of Olivia Davenport's feeling.

At Home in Mitford, Ch. 10 (Psalm 119:114)

HE CAUTIOUSLY OPENED the door and peered into a minuscule but inviting kitchen.

A broiling pan sat on the stove, containing a blackened roast. Next to it, a pot had boiled over, and a tray of unbaked rolls sat disconsolately on the countertop. "Hello!" he called.

A white cat leaped onto the breakfast table, looked at him curiously, and began cleaning her paws. "Violet, I presume!" He had never been fond of cats.

He heard her coming down the stairs, then she appeared at the kitchen door, her eyes red from crying.

"I've done it again," she said sniffing. "I can never get it right. I sat down at my drawing table for just one minute. One minute! An hour later, I looked up, and the rice had boiled over and the roast had burned, and well, there you have it."

" 'Whatever your hand finds to do, do it with all your might'!" he quoted cheerfully from Ecclesiastes. "You must have been doing something you liked."

She sighed. "I was drawing moles."

At Home in Mitford, Ch. 10 (Ecclesiastes 9:10)

A SCRIPTURE FROM the Psalms came to him: "I will instruct you and teach you in the way which you shall go. I will guide you with my eye."

He felt the peace of that promise, and went upstairs.

He knocked, but there was no answer. "Dooley?"

Silence. Of course, there would be silence.

He opened the door.

Dooley sat on the side of the bed, sobbing. His whole body seemed given to grief, frustration, and rage.

My heart, thought the rector, feeling it wrench with sorrow. I have never had so many sensations of the heart in one short span of time.

He sat down beside Dooley Barlowe and held him. He held him tightly, as if to say, Hang on, hang on. I won't let go.

At Home in Mitford, Ch. 16 (Psalm 32:8)

HE LOOKED AROUND her small studio. Every inch of wall space was covered with some cheerful drawing or watercolor, or picture cut from a magazine. She had lettered a Scripture from the sixteenth chapter of

Proverbs that was push-pinned over her drawing table: "Commit thy works unto the Lord and thy thoughts shall be established."

"That," he said, "is a commendable way to do it."

"For me, it's the only way. I don't work at all without committing it to God first. I've done it the other way, and giving it to Him makes all the difference."

Period! The rector smiled. He liked Cynthia's practical relationship with God. It had none of the boldness of Olivia Davenport's glorious faith. It was simple and easy. Cynthia, it appeared, was definitely down-to-earth about heavenly things.

At Home in Mitford, Ch. 17 (Proverbs 16:3)

"MY MOTHER, BRIMMING with passion, with love for God and for people—my father, remote, arrogant, handsome, disliked. I remember what my uncle Gus once said: 'A high-falutin', half-frozen Episcopalian and a hidebound, Bible-totin' Baptist. The North Pole and the South Pole, under the same roof!' Why did they marry? I believe my mother saw in him something tender and felt she could change him."

"Oh, dear," said Cynthia, with feeling.

"At the age of ten or so, I had learned one of the most crucial verses on marriage." He laughed, remembering his mother's frequent allusion to it. " 'Be not unequally yoked together with unbelievers . . . for what communion hath light with darkness?' My father did have a dark spirit, and her brightness seemed to drive him even further into the 'darkness.' "

At Home in Mitford, Ch. 17 (II Corinthians 6:14)

"WHAT ELSE DO you like about me?" she asked, unashamedly licking the sauce off her spoon.

"Now, Cynthia . . ." He felt a mild panic.

"Oh, just say! And then I'll tell you what I like about you. . . ."

" 'These are the things that ye shall do,' " he quoted from the book of Zechariah. " 'Speak every man truth to his neighbor.' "

At Home in Mitford, Ch. 17 (Zechariah 9:16)

"THE NAME OF the house, Miss Sadie, is . . . Winterpast."

She looked at him for a long moment. "Winterpast," she repeated slowly. "Why, that's a lovely name."

"Willard left a further inscription for you, which leads us to the Song of Solomon." He put his reading glasses on, turned the pages, and read:

" 'For lo, the winter is past, the rain is over and gone. The flowers appear on the earth; the time of the singing of birds has come.' "

Miss Sadie folded her hands in her lap, and looked away. The only sound was, in fact, the singing of birds. She was silent for a while, then she spoke. "It's good to have hope. I'm so glad Willard had hope."

"Many waters, Miss Sadie, cannot quench love. Neither can the floods drown it. That, too, is from the Song."

She looked at him with a small light in her eyes.

"So be it," she said.

At Home in Mitford, Ch. 21 (Song of Solomon 2:11–12; Solomon 8:7)

"NOW, I WANT to exercise my authority as your bishop and ask you to do something else. I want you to go away for two months."

"But there's the boy, and—"

"I'm not interested in the boy, or in any other condition or circumstance that presently exists in your life. That sounds cold and hard, but it's neither. You are my interest, not because you're my friend, but because you're exceedingly valuable to this diocese, and I very much want to keep it that way.

"You've always known how to take care of everybody and everything but yourself. I can say that freely because I'm afflicted with the identical weakness, and, trust me, it is a weakness. I'm blessed with a wife who monitors me, but you have no monitor. If you're going to extend your life in the body of Christ, Timothy, you must act at once to restore, to revive, to refresh your energies.

"You tell me you've gone stale, but the sound health of your parish disproves it. 'Wherefore, by their fruits ye shall know them,' Christ said. That's how I know you, my friend, by your fruits. You haven't let Him down, you haven't let me down, and you haven't let your parish down. But you've been letting yourself down— shamefully."

At Home in Mitford, Ch. 22 (Matthew 7:20)

HOMELESS SAT AT the kitchen counter while the rector brewed a pot of coffee and an exhausted Barnabas lay sleeping by his food bowl at the door.

"It's a treat to have you in my kitchen, for a change," he told his friend from the creek. "You know, you've brought me something I thought I'd never find again."

"That brings up m' own point," said Homeless. "Somethin' I lost has been found, too."

"And what's that?" asked the rector, leaning against the sink.

"My faith. It looks like it's come back. An' t' tell th' truth, it's a whole lot stronger than it was when it left."

"I'm glad to hear it. You don't know how glad."

"Well, I took down th' New Testament you brought me, an' I said, I b'lieve I'll just crack this open f'r a minute—I knew I didn't want t' go gettin' no religion out of it, nossir.

"So I baited me a hook and I put it on m' fishin' line and went 'n' sat on th' creek bank, an' done somethin' I hadn't done since I was a boy— I tied th' line on m' big toe. You know, that makes sense, you don't have t' mess with a pole. That way, when you get a bite, you know it, and all y' have t' do is just pull 'er in. Time savin'!

"So I was settin' there an' I commenced t' read, and first thing you know, I was dead into it. I'd catch me a crappie, take it off th' hook, bait up again, and go back t' readin'. I done that all day, and by th' time I'd fried me some fish and eat a good dinner, it come to me plain as day that m' faith was back. God Almighty had put his hand on me again after all these years. You know what I figure?"

"What's that?"

"I figure what can y' lose? Jesus said, 'Verily, I say unto you, he that believeth on me hath everlasting life.'"

At Home in Mitford, Ch. 23 (John 6:47)

"In the thirty-second Psalm, He says, 'I will instruct you, Dooley, and teach you in the way which you should go. I will guide you with my eye.'"

"Did he put my name in like 'at?"

"He did. Just like He put my name in, and the Owens' name, and Cynthia's name. The Bible speaks to everyone who trusts Him."

At Home in Mitford, Ch. 24 (Psalm 32:8)

The victim dodged toward his parked Buick and crashed onto the hood with his elbow. "'Sing and make music in your hearts,'" he recited loudly from a psalm, "'always giving thanks to the Father for everything'!"

Barnabas sat down at once and gazed at him, mopping the garage floor with his tail.

His dog was the only living creature he knew who was unfailingly disciplined by the hearing of the Word.

A Light in the Window, Ch. 1 (Psalm 147:7)

Was this a dream? No, it was a nightmare, for Barnabas was now licking a perfect stranger—a visitor, no less—on the right ear.

"'Let love be genuine,'" said the lay reader, carrying on with the Scripture reading, "'hate what is evil, hold fast to what is good . . .'"

How had he forgotten to close the garage door? He had never forgotten to close the garage door. He could hear laughter breaking out like measles.

"'. . . *outdo* one another in showing honor. Do not lag in zeal, be *ardent* in spirit. . . .'"

Barnabas looked toward the lectern, then gave a sigh and lay down, his head on the visitor's foot. The man wiped his glasses and his ear with a handkerchief and, smiling broadly, gave his rapt attention to the remainder of the reading from Romans.

"'Do not repay anyone evil for evil, but take thought for what is noble in the sight of all. If it is possible, so far as it depends on you, live peaceably with all. Beloved, never avenge yourselves, but leave room for the wrath of God; for it is written, "Vengeance is mine, I will repay," says the Lord.'"

That his dog stood for the Nicene Creed and again for the dismissal hymn was, he concluded, something to marvel at.

A Light in the Window, Ch. 14
(Romans 12:9–19)

> *And then came the day when I found myself praying for Buck Leeper. I said to myself, "Child, you are working way too hard."*
>
> —*Jan*

TOMMY HAD LAUGHED today. It wasn't downright hilarity, by any means, but it had been reviving to hear.

The proverb had said, "Laughter doeth good like a medicine." Clearly, that was true for the one who heard it, as well as for the one doing the laughing.

He wanted to hear Tommy laugh again and again and see Dooley Barlowe laughing with him.

If he really put his mind to it, perhaps he could think of something funny to do.

Cynthia! There was a brilliant thought. She was funny without even trying to be. He would ask her what to do.

A Light in the Window, Ch. 18 (Proverbs 22:14)

"WE INTEND TO demonstrate to each and every member present what we should all do when we hear His Word . . . which is to let it have its way with our hearts."

"Amen!" somebody said.

J.C. sank to his knees in the grass and looked through the lens of his camera. Something interesting was bound to happen with this deal.

At that moment, Cynthia Coppersmith rose from her front-row seat, holding what appeared to be a large handbag. As she held it aloft for all to see, Violet's white head emerged. Violet perched there, staring coolly at the crowd.

"That cat is in books at the library," someone said.

Keeping a safe distance, Cynthia turned around and let Barnabas have a look. Violet peered down at him with stunning disdain.

Barnabas nearly toppled the rector as he lunged toward the offending handbag, which Cynthia handed off to Dooley.

His booming bark carried beyond the monument, all the way to Lew Boyd's Esso, and the force of his indignation communicated to every expectant onlooker.

The rector spoke with his full pulpit voice. " 'For brethren, ye have been called unto liberty, only use not liberty for an occasion to the flesh . . .' "

Barnabas hesitated. His ears stood straight up. He relaxed on the leash.

" ' . . . but by love serve one another.' "

The black dog sighed and sprawled on the grass.

" 'For all the law is fulfilled in one word: Thou shalt love thy neighbor as thyself.' "

Barnabas didn't move but raised his eyes and looked dolefully at the front row. Not knowing what else to do, the rector bowed. The crowd applauded heartily.

"A fine passage from Galatians five-thirteen and fourteen!" said the jolly new preacher from First Baptist.

A Light in the Window, Ch. 21 (Galatians 5:13–14)

HE DESPISED LOSING sleep over any issue. Broad daylight was the time for fretting and wrestling—if it had to be done at all. "Don't worry about anything," Paul had written to the church at Philippi, "but in everything, by prayer and supplication with thanksgiving, make your requests known unto God. And the peace that passes all understanding will fill your hearts and minds through Christ Jesus."

These High, Green Hills, Ch. 4 (Philippians 4:6–7)

"THEN, WE PREACHED that noble verse from Revelation that makes me shiver to hear it—'Behold, I stand at the door and knock! If any man hears my voice and opens the door, I'll come in to him, and will sup with him and he with me.'

"I said the Lord Jesus will knock and keep knocking 'til you let Him come in and make you a new creature. He'll never break down the door. Nossir, the Lord is a gentleman. He waits to be *invited*."

These High, Green Hills, Ch. 4 (Revelation 4:20)

"Some people," said Scott, "ask if I prayed while she was in that coma. Once in a while, I'd say something like 'God, I'm really mad at You, but I still believe You're God and You can do anything You want to, and I want You to heal Granma. Period.'"

"What do you think happened?"

"I think He healed Granma, just like I asked Him to. I think He did it with love, and He used us to help. He could have used anybody —a nurse, an old friend, maybe—but it was us, and I'm grateful.

"I came away from that time in my life with a special sense of a couple of verses in second Corinthians:

" 'For our light affliction, which is but for a moment, works for us a far more exceeding and eternal weight of glory; while we look not at the things which are seen, but at the things which are not seen: for the things which are seen are temporal; but the things which are not seen are eternal.'

"In my ministry as a chaplain, I try to look for the things which aren't seen."

These High, Green Hills, Ch. 14 (II Corinthians 4:17–18)

"For God has not given us the spirit of fear, but of power, and of love, and of a sound mind," he read aloud from Paul's second letter to Timothy.

He remembered Katherine's passionate counsel on the phone last year before he proposed to Cynthia. He had been sorely afraid of letting go, and Katherine had reminded him in no uncertain terms where fear comes from. If, she reasoned, it doesn't come from God, there's only one other source to consider. "Teds," she said, "fear is of the Enemy." And she was right.

These High, Green Hills, Ch. 17 (II Timothy 1:7)

HE ADJUSTED HIS glasses and read toward a favorite passage, a passage that, every year, seemed to stand apart for him.

"Continue in the things which you've learned and have been assured of, knowing of whom you learned them, and that from a child you've known the holy scriptures, which are able to make you wise unto salvation through faith in Christ Jesus."

He read on, toward the end of the second letter, where the chief apostle made a request. "The cloak that I left at Troas . . ., when you come, bring it with you. . . ." Because Paul was then almost certainly ill and dying, those few lines never failed to move him.

"Do thy diligence to come before winter," the letter said in closing.

In other words, Hurry! Don't let me down. Soon, it will be bitterly cold.

In the end, would he be able to say with Paul, *I have fought a good fight! I have finished the course! I have kept the faith!*

Time, which tells everything, would tell that, also.

These High, Green Hills, Ch. 17 (II Timothy 3:14–15, 4:13, 4:21)

HE WAS MISSING HER.

How many times had he gone to the phone to call, only to realize she wasn't there to answer?

When Sadie Baxter died last year at the age of ninety, he felt the very rug yanked from under him. She'd been family to him, and a companionable friend; his sister in Christ, and favorite parishioner. In addition, she was Dooley's benefactor and, for more than half a century, the most generous donor in the parish. Not only had she given Hope House, the new five-million-dollar nursing home at the top of Old Church Lane, she had faithfully kept a roof on Lord's Chapel while her own roof went begging.

Sadie Baxter was warbling with the angels, he thought, chuckling at the image. But not because of the money she'd given, no, indeed. Good works, the Scriptures plainly stated, were no passport to heaven. "For by grace are you saved through faith," Paul wrote in his letter to the Ephesians, "and that not of yourselves, it is the gift of God—not of works, lest any man should boast."

The issue of works versus grace was about as popular as the issue of sin. Nonetheless, he was set to preach on Paul's remarks, and soon. The whole works ideology was as insidious as so many termites going after the stairs to the altar.

Out to Canaan, Ch. 2 (Ephesians 2:8–9)

"TAKE NO THOUGHT for the morrow . . ." he muttered, quoting Matthew.

"Don't worry about anything . . ." he said aloud, quoting his all-time standby verse in the fourth chapter of Philippians, "but in everything, by prayer and supplication with thanksgiving, make your requests known unto God. And the peace that passes all understanding will fill your hearts and minds through Christ Jesus."

He'd been doing it all wrong. As usual, he was trying to focus on the big picture.

He glanced at the stepping-stones he and Cynthia had laid together last year, making a path through the hedge. There! right under his nose.

Step by step. That was the answer.

Out to Canaan, Ch. 2 (Matthew 6:34; Philippians 4:6–7)

FOR YEARS, he had feared this whole retirement issue. Even Stuart confessed to dreading it, and had once called retirement "a kind of death."

For himself, however, he had made peace with his fear last year in the cave. He had been able, finally, to forgive his father, to find healing and go on.

In some way he would never fully understand, he'd thought that by preaching into infinity, he could make up for having been unable to save his father's soul. Not that he could have saved it, personally—that was God's job. But he had somehow failed to soften his father's heart or give him ears to hear, and had believed he could never make up for that failing, except to preach until he fell.

Now he knew otherwise, and felt a tremulous excitement about stepping out on faith and finding his Canaan, wherever it may be. Indeed, the fear he now wrestled with was the fear of the unfamiliar. Hadn't he been wrapped in a cocoon for the last sixteen years, the very roof over his head provided?

"By faith, Abraham went out," he often quoted to himself from Hebrews, "not knowing where. . . ."

He knew one thing—he didn't want to leave the priesthood. He was willing to supply other pulpits here, there, anywhere, as an interim. Wouldn't that be an adventure, after all? Cynthia Kavanagh certainly thought so. He suspected she had already packed a bag and stashed it in the closet.

Out to Canaan, Ch. 5 (Hebrews 11:8)

HE THOUGHT OF the old needlepoint sampler his grandmother had done, framed and hanging in the rectory kitchen. He had passed it so often over the years, he had quit seeing it. The patient stitching, embellished with faded cabbage roses, quoted a verse from the Sixty-eighth Psalm.

"Blessed be the Lord," it read, "who daily loadeth us with benefits."

"Loadeth!" he exclaimed aloud. "Daily!"

Out to Canaan, Ch. 7 (Psalm 68:19)

IN THE KITCHEN, Cynthia said, "You won't believe this! Look!"

She pointed under the kitchen table, where Barnabas and Violet were sleeping together. The white cat was curled against the black mass of the dog's coat, against his chest, against the healing wound.

Father Tim sank to his knees, astounded, peering under the table with unbelieving eyes.

"It's a miracle," Cynthia told Buck. "They've been mortal enemies for years. You can't imagine how he's chased her, and how she's despised him."

Barnabas opened one eye and peered at the rector, then closed it.

"The lion shall lie down with the lamb!" crowed Cynthia.

"Merry Christmas, one and all!" whooped the rector.

Out to Canaan, Ch. 21 (Isaiah 11:6)

"WHEN WE FOUND the bridge was out, we thought it too far to turn back for a place to sleep," Cynthia said.

"And we nearly missed the ferry!" exclaimed Father Tim, oddly enjoying the account of their travail. "We made it with two minutes to spare."

"Oh, my poor souls! That bridge goes out if you hold your mouth wrong. You know the state bigwigs don't pay attention to little specks of islands like they pay to big cities. Well, we're thrilled you're here, and I hope you like perch."

"We *love* perch!" they exclaimed in unison.

" 'Where two or more are gathered together in one accord . . . ' " quoted the senior warden, laughing. Sam liked both the looks and the spirit of this pair.

In truth, he was vastly relieved that his prayers had been answered, and, as far as he could see, St. John's hadn't been delivered two pigs in a poke.

A New Song, Ch. 5 (Matthew 18:20)

HIS EYE FOLLOWED the aisle to the sanctuary, where a cross made of ship's timbers hung beneath an impressive stained glass.

In the dimly illumined glass, the figure of Christ stood alone with His hands outstretched to whoever might walk this aisle. Behind Him, a cerulean sea. Above, an azure sky and a white gull. The simplicity and earnestness of the image took his breath away.

" 'Come unto me . . . ' " he read aloud from the familiar Scripture etched on the window in Old English script, " 'all ye that labor and are heavy laden, and I will give you rest.' "

These were his first spoken words in his new church, words that Paul Tillich had chosen from all of Scripture to best express his personal understanding of his faith.

Suddenly feeling the weariness under the joy, he slipped into a pew on the gospel side and sank to his knees, giving thanks.

A New Song, Ch. 5 (Matthew 11:28)

HE TOOK THE Book of Psalms from the bag.

"I brought you something. You may not be able to read it for a while, but keep it near. It's King David's songs—they're about joy and praise, loss and gain, about his battles with the mortal enemy, and his battles with depression.

"Let me read to you. . . ."

As a child, the most comforting thing he knew was being read to. He figured it worked for everybody.

" 'The Lord is my light and my salvation; whom shall I fear? The Lord is the strength of my life; of whom shall I be afraid?

" 'When the wicked, even mine enemies and my foes, came upon me to eat up my flesh, they stumbled and fell.

" 'Though an host should encamp against me, my heart shall not fear; though war should rise against me, in this will I be confident.' "

He sat silent for a moment.

"David had many foes, Janette, the human kind as well as the foes that have come against you; anger, bitterness, fear, maybe even resentment toward God.

"When I read the psalms, I read them as personal prayers, naming the enemies that come against my own soul.

" 'For in the time of trouble,' " David says, " 'he will hide me in his pavilion: in the secret of his tabernacle shall he hide me: he shall set me upon a rock.'

"Let Him hide you, Janette, until you gain strength. He will set you upon a rock. Please know that."

He listened to her quiet, regular breathing. Maybe she really was asleep. He prayed silently for the seeds to fall on fertile ground.

"I've marked this psalm for you, the thirtieth. Hear this with your very soul, Janette. 'Weeping may endure for a night, but joy comes in the morning.'"

Without turning in the bed, she raised her hand slightly, and he stood, and held it.

A New Song, Ch. 9 (I Corinthians 3:6) (Psalm 27:1–5; Psalm 30:5)

BUCK'S THREE MARRIAGES had all ended tragically. His first wife had died of an undiagnosed blood disease, his second wife had committed suicide, and, twelve years ago, his third wife left with his foreman and sued for divorce.

"In those three marriages, you didn't know Him, you didn't have a clue who He really is. St. Paul says that when we give our lives to Christ, we become new creatures. 'If anyone is in Christ, he is a new creation; old things have passed away; behold all things have become new.'"

There was a grateful silence at the other end.

"I'm praying for you and Pauline and the children. You'll need His grace on this side of the cross as much as you needed it on the other. Pray for His grace, Buck, to carry you and Pauline from strength to strength as you build this new life together."

He listened to static on the line as his friend in Alaska struggled to speak.

"Thanks," said Buck, standing in a phone booth in Juneau, and feeling that a D-8 Cat had just rolled off his chest.

A New Song, Ch. 11 (II Corinthians 5:17)

"BEING BORN INTO this church body confers no special distinctions or ownership. You've hurt a great many people here, Jeffrey."

"There is such a thing as forgiveness, Father."

"Are you asking forgiveness from the people of St. John's?"

Jeffrey crossed his legs and moved his left foot rapidly back and forth. "If that's what it takes."

"Then you're admitting you sinned?"

"No. I'm admitting I made a mistake."

Father Tim looked carefully at the man before him. "There's a bottom line to asking forgiveness. And it's something I don't see or sense in you in the least."

"A bottom line?"

"Repentance. Forgiveness isn't some cheap thing to be gotten on a whim. It's purchased with a deep desire to please God. It's about renouncing. . . ."

"I have renounced. We aren't living together anymore."

"You're speaking of the flesh; I'm speaking of the heart."

Jeffrey Tolson's face blanched. "As choirmaster here for fourteen years, I've heard a good deal of Scripture. You aren't the only one equipped with the so-called truth. I seem to recall that St. Paul said, 'Forgive one another as God in Christ forgave you.'"

"Do you believe Christ is the divine Son of God?"

Jeffrey Tolson shrugged. "I suppose so. Not necessarily."

"We're told that everyone who believes in and relies on Him receives forgiveness of sins through His name. It's not really about asking me or the vestry or anyone at St. John's; it's about hammering it out with Him."

A New Song, Ch. 15 (Ephesians 4:32)

HE TOOK HIS Bible from the windowsill, opened it in the low light, and closed his eyes and prayed. *Thank you, Lord. . . .*

Let's face it, he could have been fished up from the bottom of Judd's Creek. The nail in the picket could have pierced Cynthia's eye instead of her hand. If Maude Proffitt hadn't jumped when she did, her ceiling would have landed on her head instead of her recliner. The list was endless. St. John's might have been completely demolished, the whole tree could have come down. . . .

Jericho.

He jerked awake, realizing he'd dozed off. Out of the blue, a word had come upon his heart.

He saw the word in his mind as if it were inscribed on a blackboard with white chalk, J E R I C H O.

"Jericho," he whispered, puzzled. Barnabas stirred at his feet.

Lord, is this of You? Are You telling me something?

He examined his heart, and realized he felt the peace he always required in order to know whether God was in a particular circumstance.

Intrigued, he turned in his Bible to the Old Testament, to the sixth chapter of Joshua, and began to read:

"Now Jericho was securely shut up. . . ."

A New Song, Ch. 19 (Joshua 6:1)

O Lord, you are my portion and my cup; it is you who upholds my lot. My boundaries enclose a pleasant land; indeed, I have a goodly heritage. I will bless the Lord who gives me counsel; my heart teaches me, night after night. . . .

He stood before his Sunday school class in his mother's Baptist church and recited the whole of the Sixteenth Psalm, for which he would be given a coveted gold star to wear on his lapel.

I have set the Lord always before me; because he is at my right hand I shall not fall. My heart, therefore, is glad, and my spirit rejoices; my body also shall rest in hope. . . .

You will show me the path of life; in your presence there is fullness of joy, and in your right hand are pleasures for evermore.

In This Mountain, Ch. 6 (Psalm 16)

From: hisbp@aol.com

My old friend,

I write to you as St. Paul wrote to the Hebrews.

"How can we thank God enough for you in return for all the joy that we feel before our God because of you?

"Night and day we pray most earnestly that we may see you face to face and restore whatever is lacking in your faith." (If anything be lacking, dear brother)

"Now may our God and Father himself and our Lord Jesus direct our way to you and may the Lord make you increase and abound in love . . . just as (Martha and I) abound in love for you."

I plan to come through Mitford on 28th, en route to mtg in Charlotte. Will see you then unless advised to contrary. Be encouraged.

Stuart

In This Mountain, Ch. 7 (II Corinthians 12:9)

HE HAD NO tranquillity of heart; the blame that he felt from himself and imagined from others was corrosive. He regretted, in some perverse way, that Bill Sprouse would not sue him.

"I'm not a suing man," Bill had said when they spoke on the phone. " 'Dare any of you, having a matter against another, go to law before the unjust and not before the saints?' Saint Paul said it, and I trust it! Then over in Luke, we're told, 'As ye would that men should do to you, do ye also to them likewise.' The Lord himself said it, and I trust it! Besides, I wouldn't want you suing me for something *I* couldn't help. You couldn't help it, brother. Let up on yourself."

"I'll be over to see you as soon as I can," he had said, mopping his eyes.

Bill had laughed. "Whichever cripple is th' first to get up an' around calls on th' other one. How's that?"

In This Mountain, Ch. 8 (I Corinthians 6:1); (Luke 6:31)

SAVE ME, O GOD; *for the waters are come in unto my soul.*

I sink in deep mire, where there is no standing: I am come into deep waters, where the floods overflow me.

I am weary of my crying: my throat is dried: mine eyes fail while I wait for my God. . . .

O God, thou knowest my foolishness; and my sins are not hid from thee. . . .

My prayer is unto thee, O Lord, in an acceptable time: O God, in the multitude of thy mercy hear me. . . .

Hear me, O Lord; for thy lovingkindness is good: turn unto me according to the multitude of thy tender mercies.

And hide not thy face from thy servant; for I am in trouble: hear me speedily.

Draw nigh unto my soul, and redeem it: deliver me because of mine enemies.

Thou hast known my reproach, and my shame, and my dishonour: mine adversaries are all before thee.

Pour out thine indignation upon them, and let thy wrathful anger take hold of them. . . .

He sat in the pool of lamplight at three in the morning, Barnabas at his feet. He was praying the Psalms, as he'd done in times past, with the enemies of King David translated into his own enemies of fear and remorse and self-loathing, which, in their legions, had become as armies of darkness.

In This Mountain, Ch. 8 (Psalm 69)

GEORGE GAYNOR GAZED east from the Lord's Chapel bell tower to the green hills bordering Mitford.

"X marks the spot," he said. "My soul was saved as I stood in this very place."

Father Tim crossed himself, moved by the memory of George Gaynor coming down from the church attic one Sunday morning more than eight years ago. Standing barefoot in front of a stunned congregation, he confessed his theft of the jewels, the long months of hiding in the church attic, and his newfound faith in Jesus Christ.

"Sometimes I think it was the singing," said George. Tears coursed down his cheeks; he wiped his eyes with his shirtsleeve. "Still bawling, Father, when I think of it."

"It's the Holy Spirit keeping your heart soft."

"But of course it was more than the singing. I remember stealing your Bible. . . ."

Father Tim chuckled. "I turned the place upside down looking for it."

"It took several days to make the decision to open it. I was convinced that if I opened it, something powerful would happen, something . . . out of my control."

"Yes!"

"Finally, I began reading in the Gospel of John, which was the best of all places to begin. As I moved through the chapters, I was intrigued, also, by what you'd written in the margins. What had Christ done for you? What difference had He made in your life, in the part of your life that no one sees, that maybe doesn't show from the pulpit?

"I tried to find your heart in what you'd written privately, perhaps to see whether you would slip, somehow, and expose it all as a sham."

"Did you hope to find it all a sham?"

George sat on the deep stone sill of the bell tower window. "Yes, sir, I did. It would have saved me the trouble of surrendering anything to God. Wretch that I was, I was clinging to my wretchedness."

"Don't we all, at some time or other?" He'd felt the sordidness of clinging to his own wretchedness these past weeks, seemingly unable to surrender anything.

"I read all the Gospels, but kept going back to John, where I studied what Jesus had to say with deep concentration. I began memorizing verses, thinking this was nothing more than a way to pass the time. Then a verse in the fifteenth chapter began to . . ." George hesitated.

"Began to . . . ?"

"Torment me, in a way. 'If ye abide in me, and my words abide in you, ye shall ask what ye will and it shall be done unto you.' I realized that I had no idea what to ask God for. I especially had no belief that God, if He were real, would be interested in entertaining whatever request I might cobble together."

A light breeze traveled through the tower.

"It was a kind of intellectual nightmare, a wrestling match between logic and longing, if you will. I wanted to ask Him for something, but couldn't believe He was really open to being asked.

"Then one day Pete Jamison walked in downstairs and I heard someone yell, 'Are you up there?'"

George looked at Father Tim, grinning. The two men burst into laughter as if sharing a family joke.

In This Mountain, Ch. 15 (John 15:7)

GEORGE WITHDREW A small paper bag from his jacket pocket and removed a wooden cross.

"You made this?"

"Yes, sir. Harley had a few sticks of cherry wood lying around. Cherry is hard as granite, but I managed to whittle it into shape and then rubbed it with wax."

Morning light streamed onto the polished cross. A piece of twine was looped through a hole at the top.

"See this nail, Father?" George pointed to a rusted nail between two of the tower windows.

"Ah!" He'd never seen it before, but then he hadn't often dawdled around up here. . . .

"I used to study that nail as if it were a great philosophical conundrum. Why was it there? What purpose could it possibly serve? Who had put it there, taking the trouble to fix it so neatly in the mortar between the stones? I never forgot this nail."

George looped the twine around the nail, tied the cross to it, then stood back. "In this mountain," he said, "the hand of the Lord rested on me. . . ."

The wooden cross hung against the stone wall between the windows. On either side, the view of the high, green hills rolled away to summer clouds in a dome of blue sky.

George turned and placed his hands on the shoulders of his friend. "In this mountain, may the hand of the Lord rest always upon you, my brother. You remember the last thing you said to me when I left here eight years ago?"

"I do."

"They that sow in tears shall reap in joy. He that goeth forth and weepeth, bearing precious seed, shall doubtless come again with rejoicing, bringing his sheaves with him."

Father Tim smiled. "You did come again with rejoicing."

"And so will you, Father, so will you."

Before leaving, they noted with pleasure that the cross appeared to have hung there a very long time.

In This Mountain, Ch. 15 (Psalm 126:5–6)

HE LEFT THE hospital determined to make Bill Watson laugh. Uncle Billy was being stubborn as a mule simply because he was Mitford's certified Joke King. But he'd find a good one somehow, somewhere, just wait.

In the meantime, he had to race to the airport and pick up his wife. . . .

"Good morning, Father!" said Nurse Herman.

"Herman, this is the day the Lord has made . . ."

"Yes, sir!"

". . . let us rejoice and be glad in it!"

"Proverbs?"

"Psalm One hundred and eighteen!"

Nurse Herman was pleased to see that Father Tim had definitely recovered his health and good spirits.

In This Mountain, Ch. 21 (Psalm 118:24)

FATHER TIM OPENED the fifteenth door of their Advent calendar, and read aloud a brief exegesis of verses from Luke's second chapter.

" 'And Joseph went up from Nazareth to Bethlehem, to be enrolled with Mary, who was with child.' "

Cynthia thumbed the pages of her Bible to a map of the region that extended south from the Sea of Galilee. "From Galilee in the north to Judea in the south seems a long way, Timothy."

"Maybe ninety to a hundred miles. On a donkey, that's roughly a week's travel. It could have taken longer, of course, because of the pregnancy."

"I wonder what they ate."

"Whatever it was, they probably bought it from camel trains, they couldn't have carried many supplies."

"Isn't a lot of this terrain open desert?"

"It is."

"What would the weather have been like?"

"Cold. Very cold," he said. "Some say too cold for the shepherds around Bethlehem to be in the fields. They would have had their flocks under cover by October or November."

"So the birth may have occurred earlier, before they left the fields?"

"Very likely. However, the tradition of a late December nativity is eighteen centuries old, and I'm not messing with that."

"Still, if they were traveling in December, nighttime temperatures would have been freezing." His wife pondered this, shaking her head. "Just think! All that misery over *taxes!*"

"Some things," he said, "never change."

Shepherds Abiding, Ch. 6 (Luke 2:4–5)

HIS FEELINGS WERE stirred by the clear and shining voice of his wife as she read from the first Epistle to the believers at Corinth.

" 'I have received of the Lord that which also I delivered unto you, That the Lord Jesus the same night in which he was betrayed took bread; and when he had given thanks, he brake it, and said, Take, eat: this is my body, which is broken for you: this do in remembrance of me. After the same manner also he took the cup, when he had supped, saying, This cup is the new testament in my blood: this do ye, as oft as ye drink it, in remembrance of me. For as often as ye eat this bread, and drink this cup, ye do shew the Lord's death till he come.' "

He pulled the candlestick closer and read aloud from the Gospels of Luke and John in the old prayer book.

" '. . . Then said Jesus, Father, forgive them; for they know not what they do. And they parted his raiment, and cast lots. . . .

" 'Now before the feast of the passover, when Jesus knew that his hour was come that he should depart out of this world unto the Father, having loved his own which were in the world, he loved them unto the end. And supper being ended . . .' "

He thought he heard a knock somewhere but couldn't be certain. "Did you hear something?"

It came again, louder this time, at the back door. "Willie!" he said, leaving the table. "It must be important."

He switched on the light and opened the door, but saw no one. "Willie? Is that you?"

A tall, thin figure stepped into the porch light.

"It's m-me. S-S-Sammy."

Light from Heaven, Ch. 8 (I Corinthians 11:23–26)

AGNES SIPPED HER tea. "The fifty-first psalm. Do you know it well, Father?"

"Well, indeed. During a dark hour in my own life, I learned to recite it from memory."

"Could we say it now?"

Together, they spoke the words of the psalmist.

> *"Have mercy on me, O God, according to your loving kindness;*
> *In your great compassion, blot out my offenses.*
> *Wash me through and through from my wickedness*
> *And cleanse me from my sin.*
> *For I know my transgressions, and my sin is ever before me.*
> *Against you only have I sinned. . . ."*

Above the gorge, the clouds began to lift; a shaft of sunlight shone upon the ridge.

> *"For behold, you look for truth deep within me,*
> *And will make me understand wisdom secretly.*
> *Purge me from my sin, and I shall be pure;*
> *Wash me, and I shall be clean indeed.*
> *Make me hear of joy and gladness,*
> *That the body you have broken may rejoice.*
> *Hide your face from my sins*
> *And blot out my iniquities.*
> *Create in me a clean heart, O God.*
> *And renew a right spirit within me. . . ."*

Light from Heaven, Ch. 11 (Psalm 51)

Popular Questions
from Gentle Readers

No matter *where* I travel, I can count on my readers asking certain questions.

One of the most popular is *Are you Cynthia?*

I've been known to give a glib reply, but truth be told, I *am* a lot like Father Tim's former neighbor. After all, she's artistic. She's certainly had to work for a living. And getting her hair color right is very important.

Now here's where we differ. I would never, ever color my own hair. And why she does this is beyond me. She also has the patience of Job, which I lack. She makes fish stew, which I've never done and never, ever will do. And—this is important—she has better legs.

Actually, I also have traits in common with Dooley and Miss Sadie and Miss Rose and Uncle Billy and Hope Winchester and Lew Boyd . . . you get the idea. And, I genuinely love each of my characters, who are both family and friends to me.

Here's a good one:

Is Mitford real?

Darn right it is.

If it's so real, you may ask, where is it?

It's everywhere.

And here are ten surefire ways to find it.

* Bake a pie (or cookies or banana bread), and take it to someone.
* Give somebody a hug. (Don't be afraid to do this.)

* Express appreciation to someone in your family. Express appreciation to someone *outside* your family.
* Remember to savor the seemingly minor, everyday incidents of simple decency and good humor.
* Pray for someone you don't like. Come on, you can do it.
* Ask God to open your eyes to someone's unspoken need.
* Brag on your kids. To them.
* Stroll somewhere. Don't hurry, take your time. I give you permission.
* Forgive someone. And here's the hard part: let them know it. Equally important: ask someone to forgive you.
* Volunteer. Start simply, perhaps by visiting an assisted care unit. Pretend it's Hope House in Mitford, where absolutely everyone there will be *thrilled* to see you. Pat a hand, kiss a cheek, share a smile, give a compliment. Too shy to do this alone? Take a friend. The opportunities for volunteerism are as endless as God's blessings in your life and mine. Find time to give back, and you will find Mitford as real as the beating of your heart.

Where do you get your characters?

As I've said elsewhere in this companion, my characters get me.

They show up in the story and demand to be reckoned with, and, with God's help, I take it from there. Some of the most difficult characters in the series were Buck Leeper (anger, alcoholism, profanity, a bitter spirit), Morris Love (rage, a physiological handicap, loneliness, the complex responsibility of musical genius), and Edith Mallory (disdainful of God, manipulative, controlling, self-absorbed, vindictive).

I find that the same rule applies, however, to both difficult and easy characters. One must give them free will, just as God gives it to us. Indeed, one must let the characters go and work out their own salvation.

What is your writing schedule?

I don't have one. Indeed, I was on schedule in the advertising realm for so many years that I abhor most schedules altogether.

I find that living day to day is utterly demanding, and seldom affords time to simply sit and write. To carve out the time, one must be as brave as a Valkyrie, and as relentless. I'm completely amazed at how hard it is to be relentless. But that, in my experience, is the only way to write a book.

What will you do after Mitford?

Write another series, can you believe it?

Indeed, writing a series is like having a baby on Sunday and waking up pregnant on Monday! And yet, it appears to be what I was designed to do.

In the first of the Father Tim novels, coming in 2007, he'll travel to his childhood home in Holly Springs, Mississippi, and discover a gift that could cost him dearly. The subsequent novels will take him on two other unforgettable trips—or are they journeys of the soul?

What is livermush?

You would be dumbfounded to know how often I'm asked this question. Livermush, a sort of poor man's pate, is cooked pork liver mixed with often-secret spices and cornmeal, and shaped into a loaf. One slices this loaf and fries the slices in sizzling hot bacon grease until very crisp and golden. Make a sandwich, or serve as an accompaniment to eggs, grits, and biscuits.

True livermush is as rare as hen's teeth and is found only in North Carolina. Indeed, once it travels over the state line, it becomes *scrapple*—which is to livermush what the carpet bag was to the South.

There you have it—answers to the five most popular Mitford questions.

Ask and ye shall receive!

The Common Good:
Special Events

Mitford Takes Care of Its Own

A *town is* a type of family.

And the best way to keep a family—or a town—healthy and strong is for its members to come together, interact, and work toward common goals.

Typically, politics ain't the way. Too divisive.

And while the cultural arts will involve some members, they usually fail to involve all.

But give us an Independence Day parade down Main Street, and stand back. Those who aren't in it will gather along the curb, gawking, whistling, hollering, waving—which is every bit as key as being *in* the darned thing.

In truth, community events are the glue that holds history together, that holds a town together. An Independence Day parade, to continue with this helpful example, gives everyone a common memory, though individual memories of the same event will always differ wonderfully. What matters is that all of us are drawn as one into the invigorating chemistry of the common good, for always, always, we come forth a little better, a little bigger in spirit.

I confess that Mitford town events are not easy to write. They involve lots of characters, which forces the author to do a considerable amount of "said Father Tim," "said Dooley," etc., so we can keep them all from running together into a gobbet of silly putty. When Percy and Velma were feted in *Shepherds Abiding,* on the last day of the Main Street Grill's long history, everybody and his brother came pouring through the door, just as people had done for more than forty years.

Each one had to be identified in some way, including the characters we'd never before laid eyes on (in a manner of speaking). Even the *sounds* of this landmark farewell party were important.

> *If you would tell me the heart of a man, tell me not what he reads, but what he rereads*
>
> —François Mauriac

"Hand clapping, foot stomping. A spoon ringing against a coffee mug," we read as Percy is called upon to make a speech.

The camera of our sensibilities roves the small room of the Grill, picking up bits of conversation at this momentous Christmas Eve affair.

"Whose hat is this?" inquired Avis Packard. "Somebody handed me this hat. Is this your hat?"

"You're supposed to put somethin' in it."

"Like what?"

"Money. For th' cherry blossoms."

"What cherry blossoms?"

Mitford Muse editor J. C. Hogan blows into the cramped space with his Nikon, shutter clicking; Percy delivers his speech; Father Tim tries to commandeer Percy's antiquated coffeemaker, but no cigar—the coffee leaks onto the counter, and ex-mayor Cunningham pushes in to take over; long-time widower Lew Boyd stuns the crowd by introducing his 'til-now secret wife; cake is cut; coffee is drunk; and Faye Tuttle announces a relative's sad news to Esther Cunningham. "Multiple dystrophy," says Faye, shaking her head.

At the end of this mild pandemonium, I hope everyone feels they actually attended Percy and Velma's party.

This gathering, however, was small potatoes compared to the town shindig thrown by incumbent mayor Esther Cunningham and her wily opponent, Mack Stroupe. This event included a barbecue; a fly-over involving several small planes; a skywriter who inscribed the town motto upon a perfectly blue and cloudless backdrop; a brass band; an exhibition of llamas; a petting zoo; Uncle Billy's chair caning demo; dozens of people churning around on the lawn of the town museum, and heaven knows what else. It was the most fun I ever had in Mitford.

Indeed, though several years have passed since I wrote that chapter in *Out to Canaan,* the memories of the event are as real to me as if I'd actually been there.

Maybe at least one of the reasons everybody seems to know everybody in small communities is because of town events—and the shared history and pool of collective memory that they inevitably create.

The common good.

There's plenty of it in Mitford.

And it's pretty powerful stuff, whether in fiction or in truth.

Miss Sadie's Announcement to the Vestry

MISS SADIE SAT in a straight-back chair, in front of the fireplace in his study. She was wearing a cut velvet dress of emerald green, with a high neck, and a brooch hand-painted by her mother. That she made a striking figure was an understatement.

"I know you've wondered why I never gave any money to speak of, all these years."

"No, no, certainly not," someone said.

"And don't say you didn't, because I know you did."

There was a profound silence.

"The reason I haven't given as freely as you thought I should is simply this: I've been hoarding Papa's money." She looked slowly around the room, meeting every eye.

"I've earned interest on the capital and invested the interest, and I haven't spent foolishly, or given to every Tom, Dick, and Harry who held his hand out."

There was a variety of supportive murmurs.

"So, what I'm prepared to do this evening is to give Lord's Chapel a special gift, in loving memory of my mama and papa, and in appreciation for the church I've called home since I was nine years old."

She paused for a moment. "This gift is in the amount of five million dollars."

After a collective intake of breath, a cacophony broke out in the rectory study, something like what was usually heard at the Fourth of July parade when the llamas passed by.

"Shush!" said Miss Sadie, "there's more. This money is to be used for one purpose only. And that is to build a nursing home."

She looked around the room. "But I don't mean just any nursing home. This home will have big, sunny rooms, and a greenhouse, and an atrium with real, live birds.

"It will have books and music, and a good Persian rug in the common room, and the prettiest little chapel you ever saw. I want a goldfish pond, and a waterfall running over rocks in the dining room.

"And above every door, there'll be a Bible verse, and this is the verse that will be over the front door: 'Let thy mercy, O Lord, be upon us, according as we hope in thee.'"

Miss Sadie clasped her hands in her lap and leaned forward.

"There, now!" she said, as radiant as a girl. "Isn't that wonderful?"

Of course, it was wonderful. There was no denying, in any way, shape, or form, just how wonderful it was.

She appeared to sit even straighter in her chair. "You understand, of course, that this is only half the plan—but it's enough to get us started."

When the meeting broke up at nine-thirty, those assembled had drunk two pots of coffee and a pitcher of tea, and had eaten every peanut butter and jelly sandwich on the platters. And though no one had said so, the traveling senior warden had not been sorely missed.

In all, it had felt like a very grand party, with Miss Sadie Baxter the center of attention, the belle of the ball.

At Home in Mitford, Ch. 5

Father Tim's Birthday (the Big Six-0)

EMMA HAD TOLD him over and over again that at one o'clock today, no sooner and no later, a printer was coming to pick up a purchase order for the new church letterhead.

The printer, she said, told her to ask him the following:

Did he want the line drawing of Lord's Chapel printed in dark green or burgundy, or would he like purple, which was always a good religious color and, according to the story of the building of Solomon's temple, one of God's favorites?

Also, did he want the address line run under the pen-and-ink illustration of the church, or at the bottom of the page, like the Presbyterians did theirs? And did he want a Helvetica, a Baskerville, or a Bodoni like the Baptists?

He felt that, among other things this morning, he should look up the meaning of Helvetica, Baskerville, and Bodoni, and made a note to tell the printer that God also requested purple to be used in the temple Moses built.

It was unusually cool for late June, and he savored his short walk to the office, noticing that he was feeling better than he had in years. He had dashed off a note to Walter after his morning prayers, quoting the encouraging message of Hebrews 4:16: "Let us, therefore, come boldly unto the throne of grace, that we may obtain mercy, and find grace to help in time of need."

Boldly! That was the great and powerful key. Preach boldly! Love boldly! Jog boldly! And most crucial of all, do not approach God whining or begging, but boldly—as a child of the King.

"I declare," Emma said as she made coffee, "you're skinny as a rail."

"That's what I hear," he said, with obvious satisfaction.

"What do you mean?"

"They're not calling me 'that portly priest' anymore."

"I can fix that," she said, and opened her bottom desk drawer to reveal several Tupperware containers. The open drawer also contained a glorious fragrance that wafted upward and soon filled the small room.

"Pork roast with gravy, green beans, candied sweet potatoes, coleslaw, and yeast rolls."

"What in the world is this?"

"Lunch!" said Emma. "I figure if we eat early, it'll still be hot."

Just as his clothes were beginning to fit comfortably again, he saw temptation crowding in on every side. He could outrun Winnie Ivey, but in an office barely measuring ten by fourteen, it looked like it was going to be pork roast and gravy, and no turning back.

"Emma, you must not do this again."

"Well, I won't and you can count on it. You've been meek as any lamb to the slaughter, and I thought a square meal would be just what the doctor ordered."

"Not exactly," said her rector, who enjoyed it to the fullest, nonetheless.

After lunch, Emma went headfirst into the deep bottom drawer, looking for something. She came up with a large bone, wrapped in cellophane.

"For Barnabas," she said, much to his astonishment. That she had called his dog by name was a landmark event. And to have brought him a bone was nearly a miracle.

"I don't know why you're being so good to me," he said, cheerfully.

She glared at him and snapped, "I just told you, for Pete's sake. Weren't you listening?"

For at least two weeks, he'd noticed that her moods were as changeable as the weather.

"Emma, what is it?"

"What do you mean what is it? What is what?" she demanded, then burst into tears, and fled into the bathroom, slamming the door.

By the time she had mumbled an apology, and they'd decided on Baskerville type, burgundy ink, and where to put the address line, it was nearly one o'clock.

"Put your sport coat on," she said.

"What in the world for?"

"Well, just do it, if you don't mind."

"Isn't this the same printer we've been using? He doesn't wear a sport coat."

"Peedaddle! Just trust me on this, and put your sport coat on. You might comb your hair a little, too."

Suddenly, the office had become so minuscule that he wildly imagined Harry Nelson to be right—what they needed to do was knock out the walls and add a thousand square feet.

As he put on his sport coat, she looked at her watch. "One o'clock," she announced, crisply. She went to the door, threw it open, and shouted, "Here he comes!"

He stared into a veritable sea of smiling faces. And they were all singing "Happy Birthday."

J. C. Hogan jumped in front of him with a camera, as Emma led him, dazed, down the step and onto the sidewalk.

To say that he was surprised would have been totally inaccurate. He was astounded. It had slipped his mind entirely that today, June 28, was his birthday.

He saw Pearly McGee in a wheelchair, with a hospital nurse. There was Hoppy Harper towering over the crowd, grinning, Miss Sadie in a pink straw hat. Hal and Marge, with Barnabas on his red leash. Miss Rose and Uncle Billy, holding hands on the front row. And Percy Mosely, Mule Skinner, Avis Packard, and Winnie Ivey.

He saw Andrew Gregory from the Oxford Antique Shop across the lane, Mayor Esther Cunningham, and more than a dozen others. Who in the dickens was running the town?

"Look up!" said Emma, pointing above his head at the front of the stone office building. He did as he was told and saw a large banner strung above the door. HAPPY BIRTHDAY, FATHER TIM, THE BIG SIX-O was printed in bold, red letters.

"What you thought was a squirrel on the roof this morning was Avis Packard on a ladder, hangin' that thing!"

"Way to go, Avis!" The crowd gave a round of applause.

"See why I told you to wear that dern sport coat?" Emma said as Miss Sadie pinned a rosebud on his jacket. "It's got a lapel!"

J. C. Hogan was already on his second roll of TX 400, declaring that this was better than the turnout for the American Legion barbecue.

Then, Hoppy stepped forward with a handshake and a hug for the honoree. He'd come straight from the hospital and was wearing his white coat, which Emma thought looked romantic. "A young Walter Pidgeon!" she whispered to the mayor.

"According to Avis, who takes note of such things," Hoppy declared, "it's been seven years since you gave up your car for Lent."

"Exactly!" he said, able at last to say anything at all.

"Well, we feel that a man of your distinction should have himself some wheels. But unfortunately, this bunch could afford only two."

He heard a loud, explosive sound behind the hemlock hedge in the lot next door.

"Let 'er rip!" shouted Percy, and from behind the hedge roared what someone later called "a sight for sore eyes."

It was Mule Skinner in a double-knit chartreuse yard-sale outfit, weaving wildly back and forth across the lane on a red Vespa motor scooter.

Barnabas led the group in scattering to the sidewalk.

"How do you stop this thing?" Mule yelled.

Hal leaped in front of his pregnant wife. "Turn off the key!"

Mule made a wobbly U-turn, turned off the key, dragged his foot to brake the scooter, and glided smoothly to a stop in front of Father Tim, visibly shaken.

To a loud chorus of "For He's a Jolly Good Fellow," led by Esther Cunningham, the astonished rector got on the scooter, a bit pale beneath his tan, and drove with a mixture of excitement and foreboding to the first rose arbor on the lane, then back again.

By the time he parked it on the sidewalk and put the kickstand down, he noticed that he couldn't stop grinning.

"You don't have to make a speech, since you already make one twice every Sunday," said Mule, slapping him vigorously on the back.

"We know it's not new," said Hoppy, "but it's in great shape. We got it off a little old lady who only drove it on Sundays."

"Nineteen eighty-two, 125 cc, good as new," said Percy, kicking a tire.

"Looky here," Percy said, "you got your horn. . . ." He opened up on the horn and everybody clapped.

"You got your high beam and your low beam." He demonstrated, which seemed to be another crowd pleaser.

"And get a load of these turn signals. Ain't that a sight? I rode this thing all the way from Wesley, purred like a kitten."

"Wide open," said Mule. "I followed 'im in th' truck."

Emma cupped her hands to her mouth and made an announcement. "You're all invited in for cake and iced tea. But you'll have to do it in shifts, so step right in and don't tarry. We can take four at th' time."

She had produced a cake from her bottomless bottom drawer, and two gallon jugs of tea with Styrofoam cups.

Hal and Marge filled the cups with ice, and Father Tim cut the cake, as J. C. Hogan shot another roll of black and white, and Esther Cunningham played the kazoo.

The following Monday, the *Mitford Muse* ran two front-page stories on the local Episcopal church community.

A picture of Father Tim on the motor scooter was mistakenly given this bold headline: "Lord's Chapel Rector Receives Gift Worth Five Million Dollars." The story and picture of Miss Sadie giving the rector a cashier's check had no headline at all and referred to the donor as Sudie bixter.

Mule Skinner looked at the front page and sighed.

"Law, law," he said, "J.C.'s done it again."

At Home in Mitford, Ch. 5

Art Show at the Oxford Featuring Uncle Billy's Drawings

UNCLE BILLY WAS seated in a Chippendale wing chair, balancing a plate of cheese and grapes on his lap, with a paper napkin stuck into his shirt collar.

J. C. Hogan was writing in a notebook with his left hand and mopping his forehead with his right. "When did you say you started drawin'?"

"Oh, when I was about ten or twelve, m' uncle was a railroad man and ever' time he come through the valley, he'd blow th' whistle startin' up around Elk Grove, and by th' time he got over t' Isinglass, don't you know, I was standin' by the track, and he'd th'ow somethin' out t' me.

"Sometimes, it was a sack of licorice candy, or horehound, and one time it was a little ol' pack of pencils, real wide pencils with a soft lead, don't you know. My daddy said that was a foolish thing to give a boy who couldn't write, so I took to drawin'."

"Did you ever use ink?" J.C. asked.

"Well, sir, I used it some, but I eat up a jar of pickle relish Rose said was hers, and she burned th' whole stack of m' ink pictures."

"No!" exclaimed Winnie Ivey, nearly moved to tears.

"I'd a clapped 'er upside th' head," said Percy Mosely, with feeling.

Miss Rose rustled by in her taffeta gown. "Don't be tellin' that ol' tacky story, Bill Watson! I've heard it a hundred times, and it's a lie."

"No, it ain't," said Uncle Billy, grinning.

"It most certainly is. It was not pickle relish. It was chow chow." As she turned on her heel and walked away, the rector couldn't help but notice the Ritz cracker that fell out of her cummerbund and rolled under a chair.

"I hear you've quit drawin'," said J.C. "Why's that?"

"Arthur," said Uncle Billy.

"Arthur who?"

"Arthur-itis. But that ain't hurt my joke tellin' any. Let me give y' one t' go in th' papers."

"We don't print jokes in the *Muse*," J.C. snapped.

"If that ain't a lie!" said Percy Mosely, who was thoroughly dissatisfied with a recent editorial.

* * *

"Well, what do you think?"

Andrew Gregory sat on one of the Queen Anne dining chairs that someone had placed in a neat circle around Uncle Billy.

"A smashing success!" said the rector. "Undeniably! How many have we sold?"

Andrew's pleasure was visible. "Twenty-seven!"

He saw Hoppy Harper come through the door with Olivia Davenport. There was a flush in her cheeks, and her violet eyes sparkled. From what he could see, Hoppy looked more rested than he'd looked in months. Green jelly beans! he thought. That'll do it every time.

"Well, I must be off," said Andrew. "Miss Rose and the mayor have eaten all the Brie and I have to dash to The Local and replace it with cheddar!"

Cynthia Coppersmith sat down where Andrew had gotten up. "This is my first social occasion in the village. Except, of course, for visits to the rectory."

He could not think of one word to say.

"Violet ran away today," Cynthia said matter-of-factly.

"She did?"

"But she came back."

"Good! I hear you write and illustrate books about your cat.

"Yes. *Violet Comes to Stay, Violet Goes to the Country* . . . oh, and *Violet Has Kittens*, of course. To name only a few!"

"What a full life! How old is Violet, anyway?"

"Just two."

"Two! And she's done all that?"

"Well, you see, this is Violet Number Three. I have to keep replacing my Violets. The original Violet was seven when I got her, and I painted her for two years before she died of a liver infection.

"Then there was a very haughty Violet, which I found through an ad. Oh, she was lovely to look at, but unaccountably demanding. There were three books with that Violet, before she took off with a yellow tom."

"Aha."

"I was sent scurrying, as you can imagine. A contract for a seventh book, and no model!"

"Couldn't you use a cat of another color, and just, ah, paint it white in your illustrations?"

"No, no. I really must have a Violet to do the job. And not every white cat is one, of course."

"Of course."

"So, we were all looking for another Violet, and the newspaper got wind of it and the first thing you know, fifty-seven white cats turned up."

He had a vision of Barnabas set free in the midst of fifty-seven white cats.

"Then, the eighth Violet story won a book award—the Davant Medal. It's the most coveted award in children's literature, and the whole thing absolutely took my breath away! Suddenly, all the books started selling like . . ."

"Pancakes?" he asked. Blast! He'd meant to say hotcakes.

At Home in Mitford, Ch. 10

George Gaynor's Confession and Baptism

ON SUNDAY MORNING, he made entries in the loose-leaf book provided for prayers of the people. Under prayers for the sick, he wrote the names of Olivia Davenport and Russell Jacks; Miss Sadie, who had a sore throat; Rebecca Jane, who had the colic; Harold Newland, who had cut his hand on a saw blade; the Baptist kindergarten, who were having a measles epidemic; and Dooley Barlowe, who had come home from Meadowgate this morning with a fever.

Lord, he had prayed on the way to the church at seven o'clock, keep that boy in bed and out of mischief.

While he ordinarily trained his eyes on Miss Sadie's painting at the rear of the nave, he allowed himself a quick search of the congregation. Hal, with his pipe sticking out of his jacket pocket. Emma in a leopard-skin hat. Louella with Esther Bolick. And yes, there was his neighbor, sitting on the gospel side, looking happy and expectant.

As he offered the prayer before the sermon, he heard a harsh, grating noise somewhere behind him in the sanctuary. When the prayer ended, he saw the entire congregation sitting with open mouths and astonished faces, gazing toward the ceiling.

It was, perhaps, his dysfunctional sleep pattern that caused such an odd storm of feeling. He turned around with a pounding heart, to see that the attic stairs had been let down and that someone in bare feet was descending.

He heard a single intake of breath from the congregation, a communal gasp. As the man reached the floor and stood beside the altar, he turned and gazed out at them.

He was tall and very thin, with a reddish beard and shoulder-length hair. His clothing fit loosely, as if it had been bought for someone else.

Yet, the single most remarkable thing about the incident, the rector would later say, wasn't the circumstances of the man's sudden appearance, but the unmistakable radiance of his face.

Hal Owen stood frozen by his pew on the epistle side.

"I have a confession to make to you," the man said to the congregation in a voice so clear, it seemed to lift weightlessly toward the rafters. He looked at the rector. "If you'd give me the privilege, Father."

As Hal Owen looked to the pulpit, Father Tim raised his hand. Let him speak, the signal said.

The man walked in front of the communion rail and stood on the steps. "My name," he said, "is George Gaynor. For the last several months, your church has been my home—and my prison. You see, I've been living behind the death bell in your attic."

There was a perfect silence in the nave.

"Until recently, this was profoundly symbolic of my life, for it was, in fact . . . a life of death.

"When I was a kid, I went to a church like this. An Episcopal church in Vermont where my uncle was the rector. I even thought about becoming a priest, but I learned the money was terrible. And, you see, I liked money. My father and mother liked money.

"We gave a lot of it to the church. We added a wing, we put on a shake roof, we gave the rector a Cadillac.

"It took a while to figure out what my uncle and my father were doing. My father would give thousands to the church and write it off, my uncle would keep a percentage and put the remainder in my father's Swiss bank account. Six hundred thousand dollars flowed through the alms basin into my uncle's cassock.

"When I was twelve, I began carrying on the family tradition.

"The first thing I stole was a skateboard. Later, I stole a car, and I had no regrets. My father knew everybody from the police chief to the governor. I was covered, right down the line.

"I went to the university and did pretty well. For me, getting knowledge was like getting money, getting things. It made me strong, it made me powerful. I got a Ph.D. in economics, and when I was thirty-three, I had tenure at one of the best colleges in the country.

"Then, I was in a plane crash. It was a small plane that belonged to a friend. I lay in the wreckage with the pilot, who was killed instantly, and my mother and father, who would die . . . hours later. I was pinned in the cockpit in freezing temperatures for three days, unable to move."

George Gaynor paused and cleared his throat. He waited for a long moment before he continued.

"Both legs were broken, my skull was fractured, the radio was demolished. Maybe you can guess what I did—I made a deal with God.

"Get me out of here, I said, and I'll clean up my act, I'll make up for what my father, my uncle, all of us, had done.

"Last summer, a friend of mine, an antique dealer, had too much to drink. He took me to his warehouse and pulled an eighteenth-century table out of the corner, and unscrewed one of its legs."

Father Tim's heart pounded dully. He could feel it beating in his temples.

Play It Again, Jan:
Rereading the Mitford Series

It's one thing to read all nine novels in the Mitford series.

But it's quite another to reread them. Again. And again. And again.

Indeed, I've heard from someone who has read the series seven times—and claims to find something fresh and new with each reading.

Believe it or not, so do I.

Occasionally, I'll pull a Mitford novel from the shelf and scan the pages until a word, a conversation, or a story line compels me. Voilà! Though I wrote it myself, it is suddenly quite fresh and new.

Perhaps, though, what is really fresh and new when we reread a book is ourselves. Indeed, are we not a very different reader from the she or he who read *The Great Divorce* fifteen years ago? Or the Gospel of John only months ago?

In any case, to all of you who read, and read again, the Mitford novels, this is a short thank-you. Thank you for your enthusiasm and appreciation, and thanks also for your lively imagination, which helps you believe the characters to be quite real.

Which, of course, they are.

"What he pulled out of that table leg was roughly two and a half million dollars' worth of rare gems, which were stolen from a museum in England, in the Berkshires.

"I'd just gotten a divorce after two years of marriage, and I'd forgotten any deal I'd made with God in the cockpit of that Cessna.

"The bottom line was that nothing mattered to me anymore."

George Gaynor sat down on the top step leading to the communion rail. He might have been talking to a few intimate friends in his home.

"I discovered that thinking about the jewels mattered a great deal. I was consumed with the thought of having them, and more like them.

"The British authorities had gotten wind of the stuff going out of England in shipments of antiques, and my friend couldn't fence the jewels because of the FBI.

"One night, I emptied a ninety-dollar bottle of cognac into him. He told me he had hidden the jewels in one of his antique cars. I stole his keys and went to his warehouse with a hex-head wrench. I lay down under a 1937 Packard and removed the oil pan, and took the jewels home in a bag.

"I packed a few things, then I walked out on the street and stole a car. I changed the tag, and started driving. I headed south."

He paused and looked down. He looked down for a long time. A child whimpered in the back row.

He stood again, his hands in the pockets of the loose brown trousers. "I hadn't spoken to God in years. To tell the truth, I'd never really spoken to God but once in my life. Yet, I remembered some of the language from the prayer book.

" 'Bless the Lord who forgiveth all our sins. His mercy endureth forever.' That's what came to me as I drove. I pulled off the road at a rest stop and put my head down on the steering wheel and prayed for mercy and forgiveness.

"I'd like to tell you that a great peace came over me, but I can't tell you that. I just started the car and drove on.

"There was no peace, but there was direction. I began to have a sense of where I was going, like I was attached to a fishing line, and somebody at the other end was reeling me in.

"I stopped and bought a box of canned goods and crackers . . . candy bars, Gatorade, beef jerky, so I wouldn't have to stop so often to eat and risk being seen.

"One morning about two, I hit the Blue Ridge Parkway and stayed on it until I saw an exit sign that said Mitford. I took the exit, and drove straight up Main Street, and saw this church."

His voice broke.

"I felt I'd . . . come home. I had never felt that before in my life. I couldn't have resisted the pull God put on me, even if I'd tried. I broke the side door lock, Father."

The rector nodded.

George wiped his eyes with the sleeve of his shirt.

"I brought my things in . . . a change of clothes, a flashlight, a blanket, and my box from 7-Eleven. Then I parked the car several blocks away and removed the tag. No one was on the street. I walked back here and started looking for . . . a place to rest, to hide for a few days."

George Gaynor moved to the lectern and gestured toward the attic stairs. "I've got to tell you, that's a strange place to put stairs."

Welcoming the relief, the congregation laughed. The placement of the stairs had been a parish joke for years.

"That's how I came to live behind the death bell, on the platform where it's mounted. I didn't have any idea why I was in this particular place, as if I'd been ordered to come. But just before Thanksgiving, I found out.

"I kept my things behind the bell, where they couldn't be seen. But I put the jewels in an urn in your hall closet. The closet looked un-used, I figured nobody went in there, and I didn't want them on me, in case I was discovered.

"During the day, I lived in the loft over the parish hall. I exercised, sat in the sun by the windows—I even learned a few hymns, to keep my mind occupied. On Sunday, I could hear every word and every note very clearly, as if we were all sitting in the same room.

"At night, I roamed downstairs, used the toilet, looked in the re-frigerator, found the food supplies in the basement. And I always wore gloves. Just in case.

"One day in December, my shoes fell off the platform and landed at the bottom of the bell tower." Grinning, he looked at his feet, then at the congregation. "Every time a box came in for the rummage sale, I was downstairs with my flashlight. But I've yet to find a pair of size elevens."

A murmur of laughter ran through the congregation. Hal Owen continued to stand by his pew, watching, cautious.

"One afternoon, I was sitting in the loft, desperate beyond anything I'd ever known. It made no sense to be here when I could have been in France or South America. But I couldn't leave this place. I was powerless to leave.

"I heard the front door open, and in a few minutes, a man yelled, 'Are you up there?'

"I was paralyzed with fear. This is it, I thought. Then, the call came again. But this time, I knew the question wasn't directed to me. It was directed to God.

"There was something in the voice that I recognized—the same desperation of my own soul. I told you the sound from down here carries up there, and I heard you, Father, speak to that man.

"You said the question isn't whether He's up there, but whether He's down here."

Father Tim nodded.

"He told you that he couldn't believe, that he felt nothing. You said it isn't a matter of feeling, it's a matter of faith. Finally, you prayed a simple prayer together."

Remembering, the rector crossed himself. A stir ran through the congregation, a certain hum of excitement, of wonder.

"That was a real two-for-one deal, Father, because I prayed that prayer with you. You threw out the line for one, and God reeled in two."

The congregation broke into spontaneous applause. The rector noticed that Cynthia Coppersmith was letting her tears fall without shame.

George Gaynor came down the altar steps and walked into the aisle. "After I prayed that prayer with two people I had never seen, to a God I didn't know, I came down, Father, and stole your Bible."

He looked plaintively at the rector, who smiled at him, and nodded.

"As I read during the next few weeks, I began to find the most amazing peace. Even more amazing was the intimacy I was finding with God—one-on-one, moment by moment."

The man from the attic moved to the first pew on the gospel side and leaned on the armrest.

"I come to you this morning, urging you to discover that intimacy, if you have not.

"I also come to thank you for your hospitality, and to say to whoever made that orange cake—that was the finest cake I ever ate in my life."

Esther Bolick flushed beet red and put her prayer book in front of her face, as every head in the congregation turned to look where she sat in the third row from the organ.

"Father," said George Gaynor, "thank you for calling someone to take me in."

The rector looked at his senior warden. "Hal, go over to First Baptist and get Rodney Underwood." Then he looked at his congregation.

"Let us stand, and affirm our faith," he said, "with the reading of the Nicene Creed."

At Home in Mitford, Ch. 15

The Arrival of the Church Bells

How could he have considered taking Monday off? Monday was the diving board poised over the rest of the week. One walked out on the board, reviewed the situation, planned one's strategy, bounced a few times to get the feel of things, and then made a clean dive. Without Monday, one simply bombed into the water, belly first, and hoped for the best.

To his astonishment, the bell crew met him in the churchyard promptly at eight, and it didn't take long for his worst fear to be realized. The velvety lawn, which had lain under a persistent drizzle for two days, was so thoroughly mucked about with the heaving and hauling of three vast bells that it soon looked like a battlefield.

At a little after one o'clock, the bells were chiming.

"Let them ring!" he told the foreman. "Let them ring!" What a wildly tender thing it stirred in his heart to hear those glorious bells.

A small crowd gathered, staring with wonder at the Norman tower that was pealing with music. Andrew Gregory walked briskly down the lane to offer his congratulations. "I say," he told the rector, "it's been a bit dry around here without your bells."

J. C. Hogan heard the pealing and came on the run, and was given an elaborate story of their history, manufacture, and recent long sojourn in their homeland.

It was two-fifteen before he went to his office for the first time that day and picked up the mail from the box, noting that the bundle seemed uncommonly fat. The phone was ringing as he unlocked and went in.

"Timothy! How grand of you to ring the bells on your birthday!" said Cynthia.

"My what?"

"I think that's just the boldest, most unrepressed thing to do."

"You do?"

"I'd never have thought you'd have the . . . I've always thought you were so everlastingly modest! What a surprise!"

His birthday! How extraordinary that he'd forgotten. But, of course, there had been no one around to remind him, and Walter never said a word before the fact, always letting a package from Tiffany's stationery department send his greetings, which usually followed the actual date by several days.

He laughed. "Well, then, now you know the truth. It's my birthday, but you got the surprise."

"There's a surprise for you, too. But only if you come for dinner this evening."

"I'd like that very much. How did you know it was my birthday?"

"It's on the church list I picked up last Sunday in the narthex."

"Ah, well, is nothing sacred?"

He saw that the fat bundle was largely made up of birthday cards, two of which also extended dinner invitations. There was one from Jenna Ivey, which said, "Father Tim, you are dearer to us with each passing year." And one from Meadowgate, signed by Hal, Marge, Dooley, Rebecca Jane, Goosedown, and the six farm dogs, who were all, according to the message, expecting him for an early supper on Sunday.

Emma sent a card with a watercolor of roses, and a Polaroid of Harold and herself on the beach, presumably taken by some stranger she'd snared to do the job. He put it on the bathroom door with a thumbtack, noting that Emma had picked up a jot of weight, while Harold looked a bit spindly.

There was a handwritten note from Stuart, with warm best wishes for a glad heart and good health.

He sat before the stack of cards, feeling a certain comfort.

Then he turned on the answering machine and listened to a lengthy series of well-wishers. "Father," said Winnie Ivey, "I just hate to talk on this thing, but I wanted to tell you how much you mean to everyone. I don't see how in the world any of us could get along without you. . . ." He heard Winnie sniffing. "So . . . so, well . . . good-bye!"

What a pleasant lot of activity around an event he'd entirely forgotten!

At Home in Mitford, Ch. 21

Father Tim Leaves for Ireland

HE SAT LOOKING out at the runway, which was baking in a fierce summer sun. He was the one who was leaving; why did he feel rejected, somehow? Why had they all let him go? Now, here he was, forced to do this thing, to travel thousands of miles away, across an entire ocean, and have an adventure—whether he wanted one or not.

The little plane took off with a rattle and groan so ferocious, he felt the whole thing would come apart under him. If this was the so-called, much-touted technological age, how had they failed so miserably to make a plane that didn't do its job any better than this?

He held on to the leather briefcase in his lap, the one the vestry had given him years ago for Christmas. What had he forgotten, after all? He was mildly alarmed that everything seemed to be taken care of, that there were no loose ends. And why on earth should that be alarming? For the simple reason that it happened so seldom in one's life that it encouraged suspicion, that's why.

He opened his briefcase and pulled out a folder with a legal pad and a pen, and began to make notes about a sermon topic that had occurred to him only yesterday. There. That felt better. Next, he'd make a list of things to write home about, like how had the Rose Festival done? He'd forgotten to ask. And would someone make sure the new bathtub at the Porter place had a rail to hold on to? And when Cynthia heard from her agent about Uncle Billy's ink drawings, would she let him know at once? And had he put the premium increase notice on the Mortlake tapestry in his desk drawer, or given it to Ron for the next vestry meeting? He was surprised at the list he could make if he just put his mind to it.

He happened to look out the window.

They were flying over lush, rolling countryside, with his own blue mountains to the right. He thought it might be the most beautiful thing he had seen in a very long time.

There was a peaceful farm with acres of green crops laid out in neat parcels, and a tractor moving along the road. There was a lake that mirrored the clouds, and the blue sky, and the shadow of the little plane as it passed overhead.

Away toward the mountains, there was a ribbon of water flung out on the land, glittering in the sunlight, and beyond the river, a small, white church with a steeple catching the brilliance of the sun.

He closed the folder in his lap.

"Go in new life," came unbidden to his mind.

He felt as if he were emerging from a long, narrow hallway, from a cocoon, perhaps. He felt a weight lifting off his shoulders as the little plane lifted its gleaming wings over the fields.

Go in new life with Christ, he said silently, wondering at the strangely familiar thought.

Go, and be as the butterfly.

At Home in Mitford, Ch. 24

Puny Bradshaw's Wedding

HE HAD NEVER before given away a bride.

That the bride was Puny Bradshaw supplied one of the great joys of his life.

He walked down the aisle of First Baptist Church as if on air and could not take his eyes off the lovely creature at his side. Every freckle sparkled, and under the little hat she wore, every curl of red hair seemed to glow.

As he stepped away from her at the altar, he briefly took her hand and felt the shocking roughness of it. This hand had mopped his floors, scrubbed his toilets, ironed his shirts, made his beds, cooked his meals, paired his socks, and fed his dog. He might have sunk to his knees on the spot and kissed it.

* * *

"Now we're related!" Esther Cunningham said, loud enough to be heard to the monument.

"Mayor," he said, "we've always been related. Philosophically."

When Puny marched into the reception in her enchanting dress, he had to gulp down his emotions. She flew to where he was standing with the Baptist minister and hugged him warmly.

"Father!" she said.

Father! He heard the name in a way he'd never heard it before.

I may have missed the boat in that department, he thought, but not, thank God, altogether.

A Light in the Window, Ch. 20

Cynthia and Dooley Are Confirmed

HE FELT A great swelling in his heart as he watched them come toward the altar.

His thoughts flashed back to the first time he'd seen Dooley Barlowe—barefoot, unwashed, looking for a place to "take a dump."

Today, he was seeing more than a boy wearing a new blazer and an uncontrollable grin. He was seeing a miracle.

Cynthia came behind Dooley, beaming, wearing the pearl and amethyst brooch. Cynthia! Another miracle in his life.

The candidates for confirmation were presented to the bishop by Hal and Marge Owen, who stood with them throughout the ceremony.

The sight of Stuart Cullen laying his hands on their heads, and praying the centuries-old prayer for God's defense, spoke to him more deeply than he expected.

In fact, the only thing that kept him from bawling like a baby was the sudden realization that he'd forgotten to bring the platter for the ham.

A Light in the Window, Ch. 20

Olivia and Hoppy's Wedding

AS OLIVIA DAVENPORT walked down the aisle on the arm of Dr. Leo Baldwin, the wedding guests gawked as shamelessly as tourists at a scenic overlook.

No one had ever seen anything like it in Mitford—a successful heart-transplant recipient who looked like a movie star, a famous heart surgeon from Boston, Massachusetts, and a wedding gown that would be the talk of the village for months, even years, to come.

This wedding, as someone rightly said, was "big doings."

* * *

If the wedding of Dr. Walter Harper and Olivia Davenport was big doings, the doings that followed at Fernbank were bigger still.

People turned out merely to see the long procession of cars snaking along Main Street and up Old Church Lane.

"Is it a weddin' or a funeral?" Hattie Cloer, who owned Cloer's Market on the highway, was being taken for a Sunday afternoon drive by her son. Her Chihuahua, Darlene, sat on Hattie's shoulder, with her head stuck out the window.

"Looks like a funeral," said her son. "I seen a long, black deal parked in th' church driveway."

"Oh, law," said Hattie, "I hope it's not old Sadie Baxter who's keeled over. This is her church, you know."

"I hear she had a United States president at her house one time."

"President Jackson, I think it was, or maybe Roosevelt," said Hattie.

* * *

Entering Fernbank's ballroom was like entering another world.

No one stepped across the threshold who didn't gasp with amazement or joy or disbelief, so that the reception line was backed up on the porch and down the steps and across the circle drive. No one minded standing on the lawn, some with their heels sinking into the turf, for they'd heard that a marvelous spectacle awaited inside.

Quite a few had never been on the lawn at Fernbank and had only seen the rooftop over the trees. They'd heard for years the place was falling to ruin, but all they saw was some peeling paint here and there, hardly worse than what they had at home.

Not a soul was untouched by the enchantment of it, and the skirted tables on the lawn, and the young, attractive strangers in black bow ties who smiled and poured champagne and served lime-green punch and made them feel like royalty.

Enormous baskets of tuberoses and stephanotis and country roses and stock flanked the porch steps, pouring out their fragrance. And through the open windows, strains of music—Mozart, someone said—declared itself, sweetening the air all the way to the orchards.

Uncle Billy Watson stood near the end of the line and straightened his tie. "Lord have mercy!" he said, deeply moved by the occasion. He gave Miss Rose a final check and discovered he'd missed the label that was turned out of her collar. He turned it in.

Absalom Greer felt an odd beating of his heart. Where had more than sixty years gone since his feet came down those steps and he drove away with Sadie Baxter in her father's town car, believing with all his heart that she would be his bride?

Hessie Mayhew did not wait in line. She marched up the steps and across the porch and slipped in and found a chair and claimed her territory by dumping her pocketbook in it.

Then she took out her notepad and pen. After all, she was not here to have a good time; she was here to work. She had finally talked J. C. Hogan into letting her do something besides the gardening column.

* * *

The reception line alone had been an emotional experience for the rector. When he met her, Olivia Davenport had been dying, and he had, with his own eyes, witnessed her agonizing brush with death. Now, to see her beauty and to feel her joy . . . it was another miracle in a string of miracles.

Hoppy Harper clasped his hand and held it for a long moment. Working as a team, they had pitched in and prayed for Olivia, and it would bind them together for life.

But perhaps what he was feeling most deeply of all was this strange, new sense of family as he moved through the line with Cynthia and Dooley. He felt a connection that was beyond his understanding, as if the three of them were bound together like the links of a chain.

It was a new feeling, and he was intoxicated by it even before he got to the champagne.

* * *

Esther Bolick had made the wedding cake, which was displayed on a round table, skirted to the floor with ivory tulle and ornamented with calla lilies.

"A masterpiece!" he said, meaning it.

Esther was literally wringing her hands, looking at it. "I declare, I've never done anything this complicated. I was up 'til all hours. Three different cakes, three layers each—it looks like the Empire State Buildin' on that stand the caterers brought."

"What do you think of the other masterpiece in the room?"

"Law, I haven't had a minute to look around. Where?"

"Up there."

Esther looked up and gasped. "Who painted that?"

"Leonardo and Michelangelo."

"You don't mean it!"

"I do mean it!" he said.

* * *

Once again, he went to the windows that faced the circle drive and looked out. Planes were always late, weren't they?

And then he saw the taxi coming up the drive, and he went out quickly and hurried down the steps and was there to greet the tall, dark, gentle man who was Leonardo Francesca's grandson.

* * *

Sadie Baxter came off the dance floor in her emerald-green dress, on the arm of Leo Baldwin. Leo retrieved her cane and gave it to her as she turned and saw the man walking into the ballroom.

There was an astonished look on her face, and the rector went to her at once, wondering if the shock might . . .

But Miss Sadie regained her composure and held out her hand to the young man and said, wonderingly, "Leonardo?"

Roberto took her hand and kissed it. "I am Roberto, Leonardo's grandson. My grandfather salutes your beauty and grace and deeply regrets that he could not come himself. He has made me the emissary of a very special message to his childhood friend."

The rector was enthralled with the look on her face, as she waited eagerly to hear the message that had come thousands of miles, across nearly eighty years.

"My grandfather has asked me to say—*Tempo è denaro!*"

Roberto smiled and bowed.

No one had ever seen Sadie Baxter laugh like this; it was a regular fit of laughter. People drew round, feeling yet another pulse of excitement in a day of wondrous excitements.

"Does he," she said, wiping her eyes with a lace handkerchief, "still like garden peas?"

"Immensely!" said Roberto.

Miss Sadie reached again for Roberto's hand. "Let's sit down before we fall down. I want to hear everything!"

"Miss Sadie," said the rector, "before you go . . . what does *tempo è denaro* mean, anyway?"

"Didn't I tell you? It means 'time is money'!"

* * *

"Is this heaven?" asked Cynthia as they danced.

"Heaven's gates, at the very least."

"Everyone loves you so."

"Everyone?"

"Yes," she whispered against his cheek. "Everyone."

"That's a tough act to follow," he said, his heart hammering.

"You were the one who brought Roberto here."

"Yes. I didn't say anything to you because I wanted to . . . I wasn't sure we could pull it off. I called Florence for his grandfather, who answered but had forgotten all his English. He handed the phone to his son, who knew a bit of English—and then Roberto, whose English is flawless, called me back.

"I said, 'Please, if you could do it, it would give great joy.' And Roberto said, 'My grandfather's life has been spent in giving joy. I will come.'

"I had tickets waiting at the airline counter in Florence, and here, thanks be to God, is Roberto."

"It's the loveliest gift imaginable."

"Miss Sadie is so often on the giving end . . ."

"How long will he be with us?"

"Only a few days. We'll have Andrew step in for a glass of sherry while he's here. They can rattle away in Italian, and we'll do something special for Miss Sadie and Louella. Roberto will occupy my popular guest room. Of course, there's no Puny to give a hand, but we'll manage."

"I'll help you," she said.

He pressed her hand in his. "You always help me."

As the eight-piece orchestra played on, he saw the room revolve around them in a glorious panorama, bathed with afternoon light.

He saw Absalom Greer laughing with Roberto and Miss Sadie.

He saw Andrew Gregory raise a toast to the newlyweds, and Miss Rose standing stiffly with a smiling Uncle Billy, wearing her black suit and a cocktail hat and proper shoes.

He saw Buck Leeper standing awkwardly in the doorway, holding a glass of champagne in his rough hand, and Ron and Wilma Malcolm trying to lure him into the room.

There was Emma wearing a hat, and Harold looking shy, and Esther Bolick sitting down and fanning herself with relief, and Dooley Barlowe walking toward Miss Sadie, who was beaming in his direction.

He saw Winnie Ivey taking something fancy off a passing tray, her cheeks pink with excitement, while J. C. Hogan conferred with Hessie Mayhew next to a potted palm.

And there was Louella, in a handsome dress that brought out the warmth of her coffee-colored skin, dancing with Hal Owen.

The faces of the people in the sun-bathed panorama were suddenly more beautiful to him than heavenly faces on a ceiling could ever be. Let the hosts swarm overhead, shouting hosannas. He wanted to be planted exactly where he was, enveloped in this mist of wisteria.

"Man," said Dooley, as they came toward him off the dance floor, "you were sure dancin' *close.*"

"Not nearly close enough," said Cynthia, looking mischievous.

"Dooley, why don't you dance with Cynthia?" Dooley, who was unable to imagine such a thing, paused blankly. Seizing the moment, Cynthia grabbed Dooley and dragged him at once into the happy maelstrom on the dance floor.

He who hesitates is lost! thought the rector, grinning.

* * *

"Mrs. Walter Harper?"

"The very same!"

"May I kiss the bride?"

"I'll be crushed if you don't."

He kissed her on both cheeks and stood holding her hands, fairly smitten with the light in her violet eyes. "You're a great beauty, Mrs. Harper. But there's even greater beauty inside. I won't say that Hoppy is a lucky man, for I don't believe in luck, but grace. May God bless you both with the deepest happiness, always."

"Thank you. May I kiss my priest and friend?"

"I'll be crushed if you don't."

She kissed him on both cheeks, and they laughed. "I've never been so blessed and happy in all my life. A wonderful husband, a loving and doting aunt . . . and this glorious room that I know was done just for us. How can one bear such happiness?"

"Drink deeply. It's richly deserved."

"I hope you'll soon be doing this yourself, Father."

"This?"

"Getting married, sharing your life."

"I don't know if I could . . ."

She looked at him, smiling but serious. "Don't you remember? Philippians four-thirteen, for Pete's sake!"

A Light in the Window, Ch. 20

The Annual All-Church Feast (Thanksgiving, Lord's Chapel)

THE ANNUAL ALL-CHURCH FEAST, convening this Thanksgiving Day at Lord's Chapel, was drawing its largest crowd in years. Villagers trooped across the churchyard hooting and laughing, as if to a long-awaited family reunion.

It was one of his favorite times of the year, hands down.

People he saw only at the post office or The Local were, on this day, eager to give him the details of their gallbladder operation, inquire how he liked married life, boast of their grandchildren, and debate the virtues of pan dressing over stuffing.

This year, the Presbyterians were kicking in the turkeys, which were, by one account, "three whoppers."

Esther Bolick had made two towering orange marmalade cakes, to the vast relief of all who had heard she'd given up baking and was crocheting afghans.

"Afghans?" said Esther with disgust. "I don't know who started such

a tale as that. I crocheted some pot holders for Christmas, but that's a far cry from *afghans*."

Miss Rose Watson marched into the parish hall and marked her place at a table by plunking her pocketbook in a chair. She then placed a half dozen large Ziploc plastic containers on the table, which announced her intent to do doggie bags again this year.

Ray Cunningham came in with a ham that he had personally smoked with hickory chips, and the mayor, who had renounced cooking years ago, contributed a sack of Winesaps.

Every table in the Lord's Chapel storage closets had been set up, and the Presbyterians had trucked in four dozen extra chairs. The only way to walk through the room, everyone discovered, was sideways.

Cynthia Kavanagh appeared with two pumpkin chiffon pies in a carrier, Dooley Barlowe followed with a tray of yeast rolls still hot from the oven, and the rector brought up the rear with a pan of sausage dressing and a bowl of cranberry relish.

Sophia and Liza arrived with a dish of cinnamon stickies that Liza had baked on her own. Handing them off to her mother, she ran to catch Rebecca Jane Owen, who had grown three new teeth and was toddling headlong toward the back door, which was propped open with a broom handle.

Evie Adams helped her mother, Miss Pattie, up the parish hall steps, while lugging a gallon jar of green beans in the other arm.

Mule and Fancy Skinner, part of the Baptist contingent, came in with a sheet cake from the Sweet Stuff Bakery.

And Dora Pugh, of Pugh's Hardware, brought a pot of stewed apples, picked in August from her own tree. "Get a blast of that," she said, lifting the lid. The aroma of cinnamon and allspice permeated the air like so much incense from a thurible.

In the commotion, George Hollifield's grandchildren raced from table to table, plunking nuts and apples in the center of each, as Wanda Hollifield came behind with orange candles in glass holders.

In his long memory of Mitford's All-Church Feasts, the rector thought he'd never seen such bounty. He thought he'd never seen so many beaming faces, either—or was that merely the flush from the village ovens that had been cranked on 350 since daybreak?

The face he was keeping his eye on, however, was Dooley Barlowe's.

* * *

Following the regimental trooping to the dessert table, someone rattled a spoon against a water glass. No one paid the slightest attention.

Somebody shouted "Quiet, please!" but the plea was lost in the din of voices.

Esther Bolick stepped to the parish hall piano, sat down, and played the opening bars of a ragtime favorite at an intense volume.

A hush settled over the assembly, except for the kitchen crew, which was lamenting a spinach casserole somebody forgot to set out.

"Hymn two-ninety!" announced the rector, as the youth group finished passing out song sheets. "And let me hear those calories *burn!*"

Esther gave a mighty intro, and everyone stood and sang lustily.

> *Come, ye thankful people, come*
> *Raise the song of harvest home*
> *All is safely gathered in*
> *Ere the winter storms begin*
> *God, our Maker, doth provide*
> *For our wants to be supplied*
> *Come to God's own temple, come*
> *Raise the song of harvest home.*

Baptists warbled with Anglicans, Presbyterians harmonized with Methodists, and the Lutherans who had trickled in from Wesley gave a hand with the high notes.

The adults soldiered on through two more hymns, followed by the Youth Choir, who fairly blew out the windows with three numbers in rapid succession. The grand finale was a solo from Dooley Barlowe, whose voice carried all the way to the back of the room and moved several of the women to tears.

"He ain't got th' big head no more'n you or me," said Dora Pugh.

It was some time before anyone could move to help clear the tables.

"Let's just lay down right here," said Mule Skinner, pointing to the floor.

"You 'uns cain't be alayin' down," said Uncle Billy. "You've got baskets to take around, don't you know."

Somebody groaned. "Tell us a joke, Uncle Billy!"

"Well, sir, this feller had a aunt who'd jis' passed on, an' his buddy said, 'Why are you acryin'? You never did like that ol' woman.' And th' feller said, 'That's right, but hit was me as kept her in th' insane asylum. Now she's left me all 'er money an' I have t' prove she was in 'er right mind.'"

Groans and laughter all around. "Hit us again, Uncle Billy!"

"Well, sir, this feller was sent off to Alaska to do 'is work, and he was gone f'r a long time, don't you know, and he got this letter from his wife, and he looked real worried an' all. His buddy said, 'What's th' matter, you got trouble at home?' An' he said, 'Oh, law, looks like we got a freak in th' family. My wife says I won't recognize little Billy when I git home, he's growed another foot.'"

Miss Rose Watson sat silent as a stone, concerned that the Ziploc bags of turkey and dressing would shift under her coat.

Good-byes were said, hugs were given out, and everyone shook the hand of the rector and his new wife, thanking them for a fine Feast. Several inspected Dooley's school blazer and commented that he'd shot up like a weed.

The contingent organized to deliver baskets waited impatiently as the packers worked to fulfill a list of sixteen recipients. These included Miss Sadie and Louella, Homeless Hobbes, and Winnie Ivey, who had shingles.

"You doin' a basket run?" Mule asked the rector.

He nodded. "Over to Miss Sadie's new digs on Lilac Road, then back here to help clean up. What about you?"

"Headed to Coot Hendrick's place. His mama's weak as pond water since th' flu."

"I thought J.C. was coming to the Feast this year."

"He probably boiled off a can of mushroom soup and ate what he didn't scorch."

"It's a miracle he's alive."

"Ain't that th' truth?" Mule agreed.

"There's nothin' wrong with J.C. that a good woman couldn't cure," said Fancy, who was dressed for today's occasion in fuchsia hot pants, spike heels, V-neck sweater, and a belt made of seashells sprayed with gold paint.

"Don't hold your breath on that deal," said Mule.

Sophia came over and hugged the rector around the neck, as Liza clasped his waist and clung for a moment. "We love you, Father," said Sophia. He leaned down and kissed Liza on the forehead.

"Lord have mercy," said Mule, as Liza and Sophia left. "I don't know what these people will do when you retire. I hate t' think about it."

"Then don't," snapped the rector.

He saw the surprised look on his friend's face. He hadn't meant to use that tone of voice.

"Line up and collect your baskets," hollered Esther Cunningham, "and hotfoot it out of here! This is not a cold-cut dinner you're deliverin'."

The delivery squad obediently queued up at the kitchen door.

"If you could knock th' Baptists out of this deal," said Charlie Tucker, "we'd have somethin left to go *in* these baskets. Baptists eat like they're bein' raptured before dark."

"It wasn't the *Baptists* who gobbled up the turkey," said Esther Bolick, appearing to know.

"Well, it sure wasn't the Methodists," retorted Jenna Ivey, taking it personally. "We like fried chicken!"

"It was the dadgum Lutherans!" announced Mule, picking up the basket for Coot Hendrick's mother. "Outlanders from Wesley!"

Everyone howled with laughter, including the Lutherans, who had personally observed the Episcopalians eating enough turkey to sink an oil freighter.

These High, Green Hills, Ch. 3

Father Tim and Cynthia Lost in a Cave

"Uh-oh," said Cynthia, staring at the nearly hidden opening in the side of the hill.

"What do you mean?"

"That hole! I can't go through that hole like some rabbit into a burrow."

"But you love rabbits."

"Rabbits, yes, but not burrows."

He had once seen her crawl on her hands and knees into Miss Rose

Watson's minuscule play hole in the attic of the old Porter place, entirely without a qualm.

"So let's head back," he said. "I'm famished."

"Well . . . but I've never seen a cave. Let's at least have a look."

She climbed the short ascent to the hole, swept aside the weeds and brush, and peered in. "It drops straight down and then flattens out. I can't really see anything."

Personally, he didn't want to see anything. He had no interest in disappearing into a hole in the ground that was hardly bigger around than he was.

His stomach growled. "Remember what happened to Alice in Wonderland. . . ."

"Ummm," she said, sticking her head in the opening. "Ummm."

Which was it, anyway? Did stalactites go up or down? Tite. Tight. Tight to the ceiling! That's what his seventh-grade teacher, Mrs. Jarvis, had said when they studied Mississippi caves, and then actually took a bus trip to a nearby cave. Stalactites hang down, mites stick up! Anita Jarvis. Now, there was a force to reckon with. . . .

"The tites hang down!" he said aloud, looking up as Cynthia's head disappeared into the hole.

He scrambled after her. "Cynthia!"

"Slide in feet first, Timothy. That's the way to do it!"

He did it.

He might have been dropping into a tomb, for all he knew. What if there should be a landslide, a mudslide, any sort of shift in the terrain? The hole would be blocked until kingdom come. He felt his heart pound and his breath constrict.

He slid along the muddy entrance shaft on his backside and landed on his feet behind his wife. Enough light streamed into the mouth of the cave to illumine part of the large chamber in which they stood. It resembled a subway tunnel, long and rather narrow, and he was able to breathe easily again, sensing the space that opened up around them.

Odd, how the air was different. He could tell it at once. He felt the moisture in it, and smelled the earth. Like his grandmother's basement, except better.

"Are you OK?" he asked, noting the absence of an expected echo.

"Wonderful! This is too good for words! A glorious opportunity! I've got a flashlight in here somewhere." She fished in her day pack. "There!"

The beam from the flashlight snaked up the wall. "Good heavens! Look, dearest! It's a whole rank of organ pipes!"

"Limestone. Limestone does this." The vast wall might have been formed of poured marble, richly tinted with rose and blue, and glistening with an omnipresent sheen of moisture. He had never before observed what God was up to in the unseen places. A fine chill ran along his right leg.

The beam of light inched up the wall, shining palely on formations that appeared to be folds of draperies with fringed cornices, overhanging an outcropping of limestone as smooth as alabaster.

"Heavens!" gasped Cynthia. He slipped his forefinger into the band of her jeans as they inched along the chamber wall, looking up.

"Look!" she said. "There's just enough light to see how the ceiling of this thing soars—it's like a cathedral.

"Can you believe we're under the crust of the earth, possibly where no one has ever been before, except Indians? And who knows how old this cave is? It could be millions of years old, maybe billions. . . ."

"Hold the light close to your face for a minute," he said.

"You're interested in seeing another ancient formation, I presume?"

"Your breath is vaporizing on the air."

She turned around and shone the light toward him. "And so is yours! But it doesn't feel cold in here."

"Not cold. But different."

* * *

"What are you doing?"

"We're turning around and going back the way we came."

She sighed. "You're right, of course." They turned and began walking. "I was going to sketch something while you held the light, but I suppose there's not time."

"Darn right. How's the battery in that thing? It looks weak."

"It's just that this place is so huge and so dark, it absorbs the light."

"Let's hope so."

"I guess I'm ready to get out of here, too. I'm starved, not to mention freezing. Are you freezing? Suddenly, it's . . . like a grave in here."

"Kindly rephrase that."

They walked in silence, shining the light along the walls on either side. He had no memory of the little cave in Mississippi looking anything like this; in fact, he remembered being pretty bored with that field trip. The most vivid memory of it was the picture someone took of him with Anita Jarvis, who was nearly as wide as the bus. He had tried to flee the camera, but she grabbed him by the ear and yanked him back, while everyone laughed their heads off. He had wanted to tear the resulting snapshot in a hundred pieces, but was so entranced with having a picture of himself, even with Anita Jarvis, that he couldn't do it.

"I've got an idea," she said. "Why don't we stop and turn the light off? I'd love to see how dark it really is in here."

"Cynthia, Cynthia . . ."

"It will only take a minute. Then we'll go, I promise."

"Well . . ."

Bright, unidentifiable images swam before his eyes, then gradually faded, leaving a velvet and permeating darkness.

He thought he heard her teeth chattering. "Maybe I should turn the light back on."

"Wait," he said, touching her arm. "Our eyes are just starting to get adjusted." They stood together in silence. "I think this place is totally devoid of light," he said at last. "We're in complete and utter darkness. Amazing."

"Scary."

"Don't be scared. I've got you." He put his arm around her shoulders, noting that the musical sounds of water-on-water seemed louder than before.

"I'm glad you're here," she whispered.

"I'll always be here."

"You will? Do you mean that?"

"Of course I mean that. I took a vow on it, for one thing."

Some fragment of a poem came swimming to him, something, he thought, by Wendell Berry: "and find that the dark, too, blooms and sings." What was it about this darkness, the particular, nearly tangible density of it, and the odd sense that he was somehow blending into it?

"Why can't we see light from the mouth of the cave?" Cynthia asked.

"I don't know. We were standing in the light only a minute ago."

"We can't have walked completely away from the light that was coming through the hole." She switched on the flashlight, which glimmered on columns of roseate limestone.

"This isn't the way we came," she said. "We haven't seen these before."

"We must have missed a turn." He puzzled for a moment, rubbing his forehead and feeling disoriented. "You were hauling along there pretty good."

"You get in front and haul, then," she said testily.

"OK, let's retrace our steps and watch where we're going." But they had just retraced their steps. . . .

In less time than it might have taken to recite the Comfortable Words, they'd been thrown off-kilter. He felt for a moment as if his mind had walked out on him.

They had begun to move in the opposite direction when the light faded, glimmered weakly, and failed.

"No," she said, as the darkness overtook them. "Please, no."

These High, Green Hills, Ch. 9

"PRAY, TIMOTHY!"

"I am praying. Keep moving. We're bound to come back to the light from the entrance."

"Are you sure?"

"Positive."

"It's so terribly dark. Don't you have some matches in your shirt pocket? I thought campers always took matches."

"No matches."

"Don't lose me, Timothy."

"I won't lose you. Hang on to my belt; we're doing fine. The wall is leading us."

"The flashlight battery . . . I haven't used that flashlight since I moved next door and the electricity went off. I'm a terrible partner."

"Careful. Slippery here. Feels like . . ."

"Water," she said. "We're stepping in water. It's soaking through my tennis shoes."

He stopped. They hadn't come through water before. His heart pumped like an oil derrick. It wasn't the darkness, exactly, that was disconcerting. It wasn't the sense of being hemmed in by walls of limestone on either side. No, the worst of it was the sudden sense of being turned around, of having no idea at all which way was north, east, south, or west. It was as if the beaters of a mixing machine had been lowered into his brain and turned on high.

"I'm terrified," she said, clinging to his back. Whatever he did, he must not let her sense his own fear.

Something like light flickered at the periphery of his vision.

"Light!" he said. "I saw light."

"Where? Thank God!"

He blinked. Then blinked again. But it wasn't light at all. He realized his nervous system was generating neural impulses that resulted in the strange, luminous flickers.

"Wrong," he said. "Something's going on with our vision. It's still adjusting."

* * *

"I'm thirsty," she said. "Stop and let me take the day pack off. I think I've got a bottle of water."

They stood with their backs to the damp wall, and she found the bottle and shook it. "There's not much left. The flashlight . . . the water. I can't do anything right."

"So, what did I come off with? Nothing. You get extra points."

She unscrewed the cap and reached for his hand and gave him the bottle.

"No," he said. "You first."

"I think you should be first. You're the leader."

"Drink," he said. She took the bottle and drank, and passed it back to him. There wasn't much left, but he drained the bottle and felt revived.

"Why don't I scream for help?"

"Not yet. We can find our way out." Who would hear them if they yelled their heads off?

"I forgot you're one of those men who won't stop at a service station and ask directions."

"There are no service stations anymore," he said unreasonably. "Just places to buy hot dogs and T-shirts and pump your own."

"We should be screaming our heads off. Someone will be looking for us, Timothy. They'll hear us."

He stuffed the empty bottle into her pack. "Save your breath. We've only been in here ten minutes." Had it been ten minutes? Twenty? An hour? He couldn't see his watch. He had never bought a watch with an illuminated dial, thinking it an unnecessary expense. After all, who needed to know what time it was in the dark, except when one was in bed? For that, there was the illuminated face of the clock on his nightstand.

"I hate this," she said, whispering. "It's horrid. We're sopping wet all over."

His unspoken prayers had been scrambled, frantic. He needed to stop, take a deep breath, and state it plainly. He put his arms around her and she instantly recognized the meaning of his touch and bowed her head against his.

"Father, Your children have stumbled into a bit of trouble here, and we're confused. You know the way out. Please show it to us. In Jesus' name."

"Amen!" she said, squeezing his arm.

* * *

They sat with their backs to the wall, and he put his arm around her to warm her, and pulled her to him. He felt the cool slime of mud under them, but he didn't care.

In his life, he had never confronted anything like this. He had never been to war, he had never been in peril, he had never even gone to the woods and lived on berries like Father Roland once boasted of doing. No, he had lived a sheltered life, a life of the soul, of the mind, and what had it gained him in the real circumstances of day-to-day living?

He had spent nearly forty years telling other people how to live in the light, and here he was, lost in a complex maze in the bowels of the earth, in total, devastating darkness.

For no reason he could have explained, he thought of his father calling him into the house that summer night, the night the chain had broken and he had walked his bicycle home from Tommy's house.

"Timothy." The kitchen light was behind his father, throwing him into silhouette at the screen door. He had looked up and been frightened instantly. The silhouette of his father was somehow larger than life, immense.

"Yes, sir?"

"Come in and tell me why."

Come in and tell me why. He would never forget that remark. What did it mean? He knew it had something to do with why he could never do anything right. He had stood there, unable to go in, frozen.

His father had opened the screen door and held it, and he walked inside.

He saw the look on his mother's face. "Don't hurt him, Matthew."

"You're crying," Cynthia whispered, wiping the tears from his cheek. He hadn't known he was weeping until she touched his face. It was as if he stood nearby, watching two people sitting on the floor of the cave, holding each other.

"Dearest . . ." Cynthia whispered, stroking his arm.

The self who stood was humiliated that the priest had broken down and broken apart. The priest who would do this under pressure was a priest who could not get it right.

"I can't get it right," he managed to say, as if repeating some unwritten liturgy.

Unwritten liturgy. All these years, he had spoken the written liturgy, while underneath . . .

"Almighty God, to You all hearts are open, all desires known, and from You no secrets are hid. . . ."

I can't get it right.

"Holy and gracious Father, in Your infinite love You made us for Yourself. . . ."

I can't get it right.

"It's all my fault," she said. "I was the one who insisted we come in here. I led us on a merry chase and brought that no-good flashlight. . . . You mustn't blame yourself."

He didn't want to weep like this, but there was nothing he could do about it; he felt as if he'd broken open like a geode.

"I'm sorry," she said. "Please forgive me."

"He couldn't tolerate anything that wasn't perfect."

"Who, dearest? What . . . ?"

"That's why he was enraged when something broke. It had to be fixed at once—or thrown away. There was a terrible pressure to keep things from breaking, to keep them like new. Mr. Burton's tractor broke down along the road from our house. . . . Mr. Burton pushed it off the road and left it in the field for days. My father never passed that tractor without lambasting the owner's incompetence."

"Ah," she said, quietly.

"I can't retire," he told her. Why had he said that? . . . like a geode.

"Tell me why."

"The way things are, they're running smoothly, most of the bases are covered. I'm trying to get it right, Cynthia. I can't stop now."

"But you have got it right, Timothy."

He didn't want to be placated and mollycoddled. He drew away from her, and she sat in silence.

He was hurting her, he could feel it, but here in this total, mind-numbing darkness, he could not summon what it might take to care. Out there in the light, out there where his ministry was, he could always summon what it took to care.

"Listen to me, dearest, and listen well." He had heard knives in her voice once before, when he'd drawn away from her prior to their marriage. It was knives he heard again, but they were sheathed, and he leaned his head against the cold wall and closed his eyes.

"I lived with Elliott for seventeen years, always trying to get it right. When I tried to kill myself and it didn't work, I remember thinking, I can't even get this right. Elliott was never there for me, not once—he was out making babies with other women, trying in his *own* confused way to get it right. During those long months when I was recovering in a friend's house in the country, God spoke to my heart in a way He hadn't spoken before. No. Erase that. He made me able to listen in a way I couldn't listen before.

"He let me know that trying to get it right is a dangerous thing, Timothy, and He does not like it."

His head pounded where the blood had congealed. "What do you mean?"

"I mean that getting it absolutely right is God's job."

The cold was seeping into him. He was beginning to feel it in his very marrow. He also felt the loss of her living warmth, though she was right beside him. He drew her to him and took her hands and put them inside his shirt and held her. She was shaking.

"Must I remind you that your future belongs to God, and not to you? Please unlock your gate, Timothy. Leave it swinging on the hinges, if you will. This thing about our future must go totally out of our hands. We cannot hold on to it for another moment."

He smiled in the darkness. "Don't preach me a sermon, Mrs. Kavanagh." The weeping had stopped, but the geode lay open. He felt a raw place in himself that seemed infantile, newly hatched.

These High, Green Hills, Ch. 10

SHE HAD FALLEN ASLEEP in his arms, and he sat with his eyes open, staring ahead, not wanting to miss the light when it came.

The feeling of panic had wondrously left him, and in its place had come an odd and surprising peace. Somehow, he wasn't afraid of this place anymore. He could wait.

A line from Roethke surfaced in his mind: *In a dark time, the eye begins to see.*

It was as if he were drifting through space, and every care he had was reduced to nothing. What were his cares, anyway? They were few. So few. Who cared where they put the linen closets in Hope House? He had cared very much out there in the light, just as he had cared about Sadie Baxter hanging up her car keys, and Buck Leeper coming to terms with his Creator, and Dooley Barlowe growing up and having a life that no one could take from him, no matter what.

He had cared that Lord's Chapel was running several thousand dollars behind budget, and that two of his favorite families had gone over to the Presbyterians for no reason he could understand. It was his job to care, but what he was beginning to understand, sitting here in this unspeakable darkness, was that God cared more.

Whether Tim Kavanagh cared wasn't the point, after all, and whether Tim Kavanagh was in control didn't matter in the least. God was fully in control—firmly and finally and awfully—and he knew it for the first time in his heart, instead of in his head.

He felt himself smiling, and wondered at the laughter welling up in him, like a spring seeping into a field where the plow had passed.

But he wouldn't wake her, not for anything, and he pushed the laughter back, and felt its warmth spreading through him like the glowing of a coal.

"Father?" he whispered.

Come in and tell me why. . . .

"I love you," he heard himself saying. "I forgive you. It's all right."

Cynthia murmured in her sleep, and the surge of inexpressible tenderness that stirred in him was unlike anything he'd known before.

He sensed that everything was possible—yet he had no idea what that meant, nor what everything might be.

* * *

Maybe he, too, had fallen asleep and was dreaming.

But he wasn't dreaming.

He heard it again—a kind of woofing or huffing. He sat, frozen, afraid he had imagined it.

Woof, woof!

"It's Barnabas!" he shouted. It was the mighty voice of a Wurlitzer, it was the voice of angels on high, it was his dog!

He heard himself yelling in odd harmony with Cynthia's ear-splitting scream, their voices raised in a single, joyful invective against the primordial dark.

The miner's lamp attached to his collar wildly illuminated the walls as Barnabas licked every exposed part of their bodies, pausing only to bark for the rescue team.

The faces of Larry Johnson and Joe Joe Guthrie finally bobbed toward them under hats with miner's lamps.

"Lord have mercy, are y'all OK?" yelled Joe Joe, tripping over the long rope leash they'd anchored to Barnabas.

"Fine! Wonderful!" shouted the rector.

"I ought to kick your butt," said Larry Johnson, meaning it.

These High, Green Hills, Ch. 11

Sweet Dreams:

The Mitford Books as Sleep Therapy

People often say my books put them to sleep.

Would any author in his right mind covet such an accolade?

And yet I do value this lovely compliment, for it affirms that Mitford isn't scary, isn't stressful, isn't intellectually manipulative, nor is it emotionally off-putting. A reader can open a Mitford novel and soon, I suspect, take a deep breath, as the heart rate slows, the mind stops racing, and . . .

Come to think of it, the book you now hold in your hands is, indeed, very aptly named.

Miss Sadie's Death

SADIE ELEANOR BAXTER died peacefully in her sleep on June 30, in the early hours of the morning.

When the rector of Lord's Chapel received the phone call, he went at once to the hospital room, where he took Miss Sadie's cold hand and knelt and prayed by her bedside.

He then drove to the church, climbed the stairs to the attic, and tolled the death bell twenty times. The mournful notes pealed out on the light summer air, waking the villagers to confusion, alarm, or a certain knowing.

"It's old Sadie Baxter," said Coot Hendrick's mother, sitting up in bed in a stocking cap. Coot, who was feeding a boxful of biddies he had bought to raise for fryers, called from the kitchen, "Lay back down, Mama!"

Mule Skinner turned over and listened, but didn't wake Fancy, who could have slept through the bombing of London. "There went Miss Baxter," he whispered to the darkened room.

J. C. Hogan heard the bells in his sleep and worked them into a dream of someone hammering spikes on a railroad being laid to Tulsa, Oklahoma. *Bong, bong, bong, John Henry was a steel-drivin' man. . . .*

Cynthia Kavanagh got up and prayed for her husband, whose pain she felt as if it were her own, and went to the kitchen and made coffee, and sat at the table in her robe, waiting until a reasonable hour to call Meadowgate Farm and all the others who'd want to know.

Winnie Ivey, awake since four-thirty, stopped in the middle of the kitchen on Lilac Road, where a dim light burned in the hood of the stove, and prayed, thanking God for the life of one who had cared about people and stood for something, and who, as far as she was concerned, would never be forgotten.

Louella Baxter Marshall had not been asleep when she heard the bell toll; she had been praying on and off throughout the night, and weeping and talking aloud to Miss Sadie and the Lord. When the tolling came, she sat up, and, without meaning to, exactly, exclaimed, "Thank you, Jesus! Thank you for takin' her home!"

Lew Boyd heard the bells and woke up and looked at his watch, which he never took off except in the shower, and saw the long line of automobiles snaking up to his gas pumps and buying his candy and cigarettes and canned drinks. Sadie Baxter's funeral would draw a crowd, he could count on it. He sighed and went back to sleep until his watch beeped.

Jenna Ivey, who was up and entering figures in her ledger for Mitford Blossoms, shivered. She would have to hire on help to do the wreaths and sprays for this one. This would be bigger than old Parrish Guthrie's had ever hoped to be, the old so-and-so, and so what if Miss Sadie had never bought so much as a gloxinia from Mitford Blossoms, Sadie Baxter had been a lady and she had loved this town and done more for it than anybody else ever would, God rest her soul in peace.

Esther Bolick punched Gene and woke him up.

"Sadie Baxter's gone," she said.

"How d'you know?"

"The bell's tolling."

"Maybe it's th' president or somebody like that," said Gene, who remembered the hoopla over Roosevelt's passing.

"I don't think so," said his wife. "I saw the president on TV yesterday and he looked fit as a fiddle."

Percy Mosely was leaving his house at the edge of town when he heard the first tolling. He removed his hat and placed it over his heart and was surprised to feel a tear coursing down his cheek for someone he'd hardly ever exchanged five words with in his life, but whose presence above the town, at the crest of the steep fern bank, had been a consolation for as long as he could remember.

* * *

After tolling the bell, the rector went to Lilac Road and sat with Louella and prayed the ancient prayer of commendation: "Acknowledge, we humbly beseech You, a sheep of Your own fold, a lamb of Your own flock. . . . Receive her into the arms of Your mercy, into the blessed rest of everlasting peace, and into the glorious company of the saints. . . ."

Then he did what others after him would do with Sadie Baxter's lifelong friend. He sat and wept with her, sobbing like a child.

These High, Green Hills, Ch. 18

A Posthumous Letter from Miss Sadie

Dear Father,

We have just come home from your lovely wedding ceremony, and I don't know when our hearts have felt so refreshed. The joy of it makes my pen fairly fly over the page.

To see you taking a bride, even after so many years, seemed like the most natural thing in the world. Certainly no one can ever say that you married in haste to repent at leisure!

Long years ago when I loved Willard so dearly and hoped against hope that we might marry, I wrote down something Martin Luther said. He said, there is no more lovely, friendly, and charming relationship, communion, or company than a good marriage.

May God bless you and Cynthia to enjoy a good marriage, and a long and happy life together.

As you know, I have given a lot of money to human institutions, and I would like to give something to a human individual for a change.

I have prayed about this and so has Louella and God has given us the go-ahead.

I am leaving Mama's money to Dooley.

We think he has what it takes to be somebody. You know that Papa was never educated, and look what he became with no help at all. And Willard—look what he made of himself without any help from another soul.

Father, having no help can be a good thing. But having help can be even better—if the character is strong. I believe you are helping Dooley develop the kind of character that will go far in this world, and so the money is his when he reaches the age of twenty-one.

(I am old-fashioned and believe that eighteen is far too young to receive an inheritance.)

I have put one and a quarter million dollars where it will grow, and have made provisions to complete his preparatory education. When he is eighteen, the income from the trust will help send him through college.

I am depending on you never to mention this to him until he is old enough to bear it with dignity. I am also depending on you to stick with him, Father, through thick and thin, just as you've done all along.

When you receive this letter, there are two things you will need to know at once. First, the urn for my ashes is in the attic at Fernbank. When you go up the stairs, turn to the right and go all the way to the back. I have left it there on a little table, it is from czarist Russia, which Papa once visited. Don't scatter me among any rosebushes, Father, I know how you think. Just stick the urn in the ground as far away from Parrish Guthrie as you can, cover it with enough dirt to support a tuft of moss, and add my little marker.

The other thing you need to know at once is that my marker is with Mr. Charles Hartley of Hartley's Monument Company in Holding. It is paid for. You might say it is on hold in Holding, ha ha. I think it is foolish nonsense to choose one's own epitaph, it makes one either overly modest or overly boastful. I leave this task to you, and trust you not to have anything fancy or high-toned engraved thereon, for I am now and always will be just plain Sadie.

I am going to lay down my pen and rest, but will take it up again this evening. It is so good to write this letter, which has been composing in my head for years! It was your wedding today which made me understand that one must get on with one's life, and that always includes the solemn consideration of one's death.

He looked up to see his wife rubbing a chicken with olive oil, and humming quietly to herself. An extraordinary sight, somehow, in view of this even more extraordinary letter.

He noted the renewed strength of Miss Sadie's handwriting as the letter resumed.

We are going to watch TV this evening and pop some corn, so I will make it snappy.

As for Fernbank, I ask you to go through the attic with Olivia and Cynthia and take whatever you like. Take anything that suits you from the house, also. I can't imagine what it might be, but I would like you to select something for Mr. Buck Leeper, who is doing such a lovely job with Hope House. Perhaps something of Papa's would be in order.

Whatever is left, please give it to the needy, or to your Children's Hospital. Do not offer anything for view at a yard sale or let people pick over the remains. I know you will understand.

I leave Fernbank to supply any future requirements of Hope House. Do with my homeplace what you will, but please treat it kindly. If I should pass before Louella, she has a home for life at Hope House, and provision to cover any special needs. I know you will do all in your power to look after her, she is my sister and beloved friend.

It would be grand if I could live to be a hundred, and go Home with a smile on my face. I believe I will! But if not, I have put all the buttons on my affairs, and feel a light spirit for whatever God has in store for me.

May our Lord continue to bless you, Father, you mean the world to yours truly,
Sadie Eleanor Baxter

He looked up and met Cynthia's concerned gaze.

"What is it, dearest?"

"You mustn't speak this to another soul," he said.

"I won't. I promise."

"Sit down," he said. She sat.

"Dooley Barlowe," he told her, "is a millionaire."

* * *

Louella would sing a hymn in her throaty mezzo-soprano, which was as consoling as raisins in warm bread. No, she wouldn't break down, she was wanting to do it! Hadn't she sung with Miss Sadie since they were both little children?

The choir director, who was known for inventiveness, suggested Dooley sing with Louella, but no one thought he would. The rector called the boy, anyway.

"What're we singing?" Dooley asked, already persuaded.

" 'Love Divine, All Loves Excelling.' "

"No problem. What instruments?"

"Organ and trumpets."

"I can't sing over trumpets," said Dooley.

"You don't have to sing when the trumpets are playing."

"When is rehearsal?"

"Tomorrow at three o'clock. I'll see you at Meadowgate around two."

"I'm sorry she died," he said. "It seemed like she'd live a long time."

That, he thought, is the way it always seems with someone we love.

These High, Green Hills, Ch. 18

Miss Sadie's Memorial Service

"THE PEOPLE HAVE gathered, the trumpets have sounded!" he exclaimed. "Sadie Eleanor Baxter is at home and at peace, and I charge us all to be filled with the joy of this simple, yet wondrous fact."

How often had people heard that, for a Christian, death is but the ultimate triumph, a thing to celebrate? The hope was that it cease being a fact merely believed with the head, and become a fact to know with the heart, as he now knew it.

He looked out to the congregation who packed the nave to bursting, and saw that they knew it too. They had caught the spark. A kind of warming fire ran through the place, kindled with excitement and wonder.

When Louella sang, her voice was steady as a rock, mingling sweetly, yet powerfully, with the boy's. Their music flooded the church with a high consolation.

Jesus, Thou art all compassion
Pure, unbounded love Thou art
Visit us with Thy salvation
Enter every trembling heart . . .

Into the silence that followed the music, and true to his Baptist roots, Absalom Greer raised a heartfelt "Amen!"

The rector looked to the pew where Sadie Baxter had sat for the fifteen years he had been in this pulpit, and saw Olivia and Hoppy, Louella and Absalom holding hands. Those left behind. . . .

"We don't know," he said, in closing, "who among us will be the next to go, whether the oldest or the youngest. We pray that he or she will be gently embraced by death, have a peaceful end, and a glorious resurrection in Christ.

"But for now, let us go in peace—to love and serve the Lord."

"Thanks be to God!" said the congregation, meaning it.

The trumpets blew mightily, and the people moved to the church lawn, where Esther Bolick's three-tiered cake sat on a fancy table, where the ECW had stationed jars of icy lemonade, and where, as any passerby could see, a grand celebration was under way.

These High, Green Hills, Ch. 18

Primrose Tea at the Rectory

IF HE AND Cynthia had written a detailed petition on a piece of paper and sent it heavenward, the weather couldn't have been more glorious on the day of the talked-about tea.

Much to everyone's relief, the primroses actually bloomed. However, no sooner had the eager blossoms appeared than Hessie Mayhew bore down on them with a vengeance, in yards and hidden nooks everywhere. She knew precisely the location of every cluster of primroses in the village, not to mention the exact whereabouts of each woods violet, lilac bush, and pussy willow.

"It's Hessie!" warned an innocent bystander on Hessie's early morning run the day of the tea. "Stand back!"

Armed with a collection of baskets that she wore on her arms like so many bracelets, Hessie did not allow help from the Episcopal Church Women, nor any of her own presbyters. She worked alone, she worked fast, and she worked smart.

After going at a trot through neighborhood gardens, huffing up Old Church Lane to a secluded bower of early-blooming shrubs, and combing four miles of country roadside, she showed up at the back door of the rectory at precisely eleven a.m., looking triumphant.

Sodden with morning dew and black dirt, she delivered a vast quantity of flowers, moss, and grapevine into the hands of the rector's house help, Puny Guthrie, then flew home to bathe, dress, and put antibiotic cream on her knees, which were skinned when she leaned over to pick a wild trillium and fell sprawling.

The Episcopal Church Women, who had arrived as one body at ten-thirty, flew into the business of arranging "Hessie's truck," as they called it, while Barnabas snored in the garage and Violet paced in her carrier.

"Are you off?" asked Cynthia, as the rector came at a trot through the hectic kitchen.

"Off and running. I finished polishing the mail slot, tidying the slipcover on the sofa, and trimming the lavender by the front walk. I also beat the sofa pillows for any incipient dust and coughed for a full five minutes."

"Well done!" she said cheerily, giving him a hug.

"I'll be home at one-thirty to help the husbands park cars."

Help the husbands park cars? he thought as he sprinted toward the office. He was a *husband*! After all these months, the thought still occasionally slammed him in the solar plexus and took his breath away.

* * *

Nine elderly guests, including the Kavanaghs' friend Louella, arrived in the van from Hope House and were personally escorted up the steps of the rectory and into the hands of the Altar Guild.

Up and down Wisteria Lane, men with armbands stitched with primroses and a Jerusalem cross directed traffic, which quickly grew snarled. At one point, the rector leaped into a stalled Chevrolet and managed to roll it to the curb. Women came in car pools, husbands dropped off spouses, daughters delivered mothers, and all in all, the narrow street was as congested as a carnival in Rio.

"This is th' biggest thing to hit Mitford since th' blizzard two years ago," said Mule Skinner, who was a Baptist, but offered to help out, anyway.

The rector laughed. "That's one way to look at it." Didn't anybody ever *walk* in this town?

"Look here!"

It was Mack Stroupe in that blasted pickup truck, carting his sign around in their tea traffic. Mack rolled by, chewing on a toothpick and looking straight ahead.

"You comin' to the Primrose Tea?" snapped Mule. "If not, get this vehicle out of here, we're tryin' to conduct a church function!"

Four choir members, consisting of a lyric soprano, a mezzo-soprano, and two altos, arrived in a convertible, looking windblown and holding on to their hats.

"Hats is a big thing this year," observed Uncle Billy Watson, who stood at the curb with Miss Rose and watched the proceedings. Uncle Billy was the only man who showed up at last year's tea, and now considered his presence at the event to be a tradition.

Uncle Billy walked out to the street with the help of his cane and tapped Father Tim on the shoulder. "Hit's like a Chiney puzzle, don't you know. If you 'uns'd move that'n off to th' side and git that'n to th' curb, hit'd be done with."

"No more parking on Wisteria," Ron Malcolm reported to the rector. "We'll direct the rest of the crowd to the church lot and shoot 'em back here in the Hope House van."

A UPS driver, who had clearly made an unwise turn onto Wisteria, sat in his truck in front of the rectory, stunned by the sight of so much traffic on the usually uneventful Holding/Mitford/Wesley run.

"Hit's what you call a standstill," Uncle Billy told J. C. Hogan, who showed up with his Nikon and six rolls of Tri-X.

As traffic started to flow again, the rector saw Mack Stroupe turn on to Wisteria Lane from Church Hill. Clearly, he was circling the block.

"I'd like to whop him upside th' head with a two-by-four," said Mule. He glared at Mack, who was reared back in the seat with both windows down, listening to a country music station. Mack waved to several women, who immediately turned their heads.

Mule snorted. "Th' dumb so-and-so! How would you like to have that peckerwood for mayor?"

The rector wiped his perspiring forehead. "Watch your blood pressure, buddyroe."

"He says he's goin' to campaign straight through spring and summer, right up to election in November. Kind of like bein' tortured by a drippin' faucet."

As the truck passed, Emma Newland stomped over. "I ought to climb in that truck and slap his jaws. What's he doin', anyway, trying to sway church people to his way of thinkin'?"

"Let him be," Father Tim cautioned his secretary and online computer whiz. After all, give Mack enough rope and . . .

* * *

Cynthia was lying in bed, moaning, as he came out of the shower. He went into the bedroom, hastily drying off.

"Why are you moaning?" he asked, alarmed.

"Because it helps relieve exhaustion. I hope the windows are closed so the neighbors can't hear."

"The only neighbor close enough to hear is no longer living in the little yellow house next door. She is, in fact, lying right here, doing the moaning."

She moaned again. "Moaning is good," she told him, her face mashed into the pillow. "You should try it."

"I don't think so," he said.

Warm as a steamed clam from the shower, he put on his pajamas and sat on the side of the bed. "I'm proud of you," he said, rubbing her back. "That was a tea-and-a-half! The best! In fact, words fail. You'll have a time topping that one."

"Don't tell me I'm supposed to *top* it!"

"Yes, well, not to worry. Next year, we can have Omer Cunningham and his pilot buddies do a flyover. That'll give the ladies something to talk about." He'd certainly given all of Mitford something to talk about last May when he flew to Virginia with Omer in his ragwing taildragger. Four hours in Omer's little plane had gained him more credibility than thirty-six years in the pulpit.

"A little farther down," his wife implored. "Ugh. My lower back is killing me from all the standing and baking."

"I got the reviews as your guests left."

"Only tell me the good ones. I don't want to hear about the cheese straws, which were as limp as linguine."

" 'Perfect' was a word they bandied around quite a bit, and the lemon squares, of course, got their usual share of raves. Some wanted me to know how charming they think you are, and others made lavish remarks about your youth and beauty."

He leaned down and kissed her shoulder, inhaling the faintest scent of wisteria. "You are beautiful, Kavanagh."

"Thanks."

"I don't suppose there are any special thanks you'd like to offer the poor rube who helped unsnarl four thousand three hundred and seventy-nine cars, trucks, and vans?"

She rolled over and looked at him, smiling. Then she held her head to one side in that way he couldn't resist, and pulled him to her and kissed him tenderly.

"Now you're talking," he said.

* * *

He sat on the study sofa and took the rubber band off the *Mitford Muse.*

Good grief! There he was on the front page, standing bewildered in front of the UPS truck with his nose looking, as usual, like a turnip or a tulip bulb. Why did J. C. Hogan run this odious picture, when he might have photographed his hardworking, good-looking, and thoroughly deserving wife?

Primrose Tee Draws
Stand-Out Crowd

Clearly, Hessie had not written this story, which on first glance appeared to be about golf, but had given her notes to J.C., who forged ahead without checking his spelling.

Good time had by all . . . same time next year . . . a hundred and thirty guests . . . nine gallons of tea, ten dozen lemon squares, eight dozen raspberry tarts . . . traffic jam . . .

Out to Canaan, Ch. 1

Political Barbecue

"HAVE YOU SEEN Mack's new boards?" asked J.C.

They hadn't.

"They rhyme like those Burma-Shave signs. First one says, *'If Mitford's economy is going to move'* . . . th' second one says, *'we've got to improve.'* Last one says, *'Mack for Mitford, Mack for Mayor.'*"

"Gag me with a forklift," said Mule.

"Esther Cunningham better get off her rear end, because like it or not, Mack Stroupe's eatin' her lunch. She's been lollin' around like this election was some kind of tea party. You're so all-fired thick with the mayor," J.C. said to the rector, "you ought to tell her the facts of life, and the fact is, she's lookin' dead in the water."

"Aha. I thought we agreed not to talk politics."

"Right," said Mule, whose escalating blood pressure had suddenly turned his face beet red.

J.C. looked bored. "So what else is new? Let's see, I was over at the town museum 'til midnight watchin' those turkeys get ready for the festival. Omer Cunningham was draping th' flag on Esther's booth and fell off the ladder and busted his foot."

"Busted his foot?" the rector blurted. "Good Lord! Can he fly?"

"Can he fly? I don't know as he could, with a busted foot."

Mule cackled. "He sure couldn't fly any crazier than when his foot's *not* busted."

"Toast!" said Velma, sliding two orders onto the table.

The rector felt his stomach wrench.

"Biscuits!" said Velma, handing off a plate to J.C.

"May I use your phone?" asked Father Tim.

"You can, if you stay out of Percy's way, you know where it's at."

He went to the red wall phone and dialed, knowing the number by heart. Hadn't he called it two dozen times in the last few days?

No answer.

He hung up and stood by the grill, dazed, his mouth as dry as cotton.

Out to Canaan, Ch. 8

HIS PALMS WERE damp, something he'd never appreciated in clergy. Also, his collar felt tight, even though he'd snapped the Velcro at the loosest point.

When he and Cynthia arrived on the lawn of the town museum at nine thirty-five, they had to elbow their way to the Lord's Chapel booth, which was situated, this year, directly across from the llamas and the petting zoo.

"Excellent location!" said his wife, who was known to rely on animals as a drawing card.

They thumped down their cardboard box filled with the results of last night's bake-a-thon in the rectory kitchen. Three Lord's Chapel volunteers, dressed in aprons that said, *Have you hugged an Episcopalian today?* briskly set about unpacking the contents and displaying them in a case cooled by a generator humming at the rear of the tent.

Though the festival didn't officially open until ten o'clock, the yard of the Porter mansion-cum-town museum was jammed with villagers, tourists, and the contents of three buses from neighboring communities. The rear end of a church van from Tennessee displayed a sign, MITFORD OR BUST.

The Presbyterian brass band was already in full throttle on the museum porch, and the sixth grade of Mitford School was marching around the statue of Willard Porter, builder of the impressive Victorian home, with tambourines, drums, and maracas painted in their school colors.

Why was he surprised to see posters on every pole and tree, promoting Mack Stroupe's free barbecue at his campaign headquarters up the street?

His eyes searched the crowd for the mayor, who said she'd be under the elm tree this year, the one that had miraculously escaped the blight.

"I'll be back," he told Cynthia, who was giving him that concerned look. The way things were going, he'd need more than a domestic retreat, he'd need a set of pallbearers.

* * *

He spotted Esther and her husband, Ray, shaking hands by a booth draped with an American flag and a banner hand-lettered with the mayor's longtime political slogan.

"Mayor! Where's Omer?"

"Where's Omer? I thought you'd know where Omer is."

"What about his foot?"

"Broken in two places."

"Right, but what about . . . can he *fly?*"

She glared at him in a way that made Emma Newland look like a vestal virgin. "That's your business," she said, and turned back to the people she'd been shaking hands with.

He headed to the Lord's Chapel booth, his heart hammering. He was afraid to let his wife see his face, since she could obviously read it like a book—but where else could he go?

Dooley! Of course! A Taste of America!

He hung a hard left in the direction of Avis Packard's tent, cutting through the queue to the cotton candy truck, and ran slam into Omer Cunningham on a crutch.

"Good heavens! *Omer!*" He threw his arms around Esther Cunningham's strapping brother-in-law and could easily have kissed his ring, or even his plaster cast.

Heads turned. People stared. He wished he wasn't wearing his collar.

Omer's big grin displayed teeth the size of keys on a spinet piano. "We're smokin'," he said, giving a thumbs-up to the rector, who, overcome with joyful relief, thumped down on a folding chair at the Baptists' display of tea towels, aprons, and oven mitts.

* * *

He noticed the crowd was starting to thin out, following the aroma of political barbecue.

In his mind, he saw it on the plate, thickly sliced and served with a dollop of hot sauce, nestled beside a mound of coleslaw and a half dozen hot, crisp hush puppies. . . .

He shook himself and ate four raisins that had rolled around in his coat pocket since the last committee meeting on evangelism.

* * *

At eleven forty-five, Ray and Esther Cunningham strode up to the Lord's Chapel booth with all five of their beautiful daughters, who had populated half of Mitford with Sunday school teachers, deacons, police officers, garbage collectors, tax accountants, secretaries, retail clerks, and UPS drivers.

"Well?" said Esther. The rector thought she would have made an excellent Mafia don.

"Coming right up!" he exclaimed, checking his watch and looking pale.

Cynthia eyed him again. Mood swings, she thought. That seemed to be the key! Definitely a domestic retreat, and definitely soon.

And since the entire town seemed so demanding of her husband, definitely not in Mitford.

* * *

Nobody paid much attention to the airplane until it started smoking.

"Look!" somebody yelled. "That plane's on f'ar!"

He was sitting on the rock wall when Omer thumped down beside him. "Right on time!" said the mayor's brother-in-law. "All my flyin' buddies from here t' yonder have jumped on this." The rector thought somebody could have played "Moonlight Sonata" on Omer's ear-to-ear grin.

"OK, that's y'r basic Steerman, got a four-fifty horsepower engine in there. Luke Teeter's flyin' 'er, he's about as good as you can get, now watch this. . . ."

The blue and orange airplane roared straight up into the fathomless blue sky, leaving a plume of smoke in its wake. Then it turned sharply and pitched downward at an angle.

"Wow!" somebody said, forgetting to close his mouth.

The plane did another climb into the blue.

Omer punched him in the ribs with an elbow. "She's got a tank in there pumpin' Corvis oil th'ough 'er exhaust system . . . ain't she a sight?"

"Looks like an *N*!" said a boy whose chocolate popsicle was melting down his arm.

The plane plummeted toward the rooftops again, smoke billowing from its exhaust.

"*M!*" shouted half the festivalgoers, as one.

Esther and Ray and their daughters were joined by assorted grandchildren, great-grandchildren, and in-laws, who formed an impenetrable mass in front of the church booth.

Gene Bolick limped over from the llamas as the perfect *I* appeared above them.

"*M . . . I!*" shouted the crowd.

"Lookit this!" said Omer, propping his crutch against the stone wall. "Man, oh, man!"

The bolt of blue and orange gunned straight up, leaving a vertical trail, then shut off the exhaust, veered right, and thundered across the top of the trail, forming a straight and unwavering line of smoke.

"*M . . . I . . . T!*"

The *M* was fading, the *I* was lingering, the *T* was perfect against the sapphire sky.

The crowd thickened again, racing back from Mack Stroupe's campaign headquarters, which was largely overhung by trees, racing back to the grounds of the town museum where the view was open, unobscured, and breathtaking, where something more than barbecue was going on.

"They won't be goin' back to Mack's place anytime soon," said Omer. "Ol' Mack's crowd has done eat an' run!"

"*F!*" they spelled in unison, and then, ". . . *O . . . R . . . D!*"

Even the tourists were cheering.

J. C. Hogan sank to the ground, rolled over on his back, pointed his Nikon at the sky, and fired off a roll of Tri-X. The *M* and the *I* were fading fast.

Uncle Billy hobbled up and spit into the bushes. "I bet them boys is glad this town ain't called Minneapolis."

"Now, look," said Omer, slapping his knee.

Slowly, but surely, the Steerman's exhaust trail wrote the next word.

T . . . A . . . K . . . E . . . S . . . , the smoke said.

Cheers. Hoots. Whistles.

"Lord, my neck's about give out," said Uncle Billy.

"Mine's about broke," said a bystander.

C . . . A . . . R . . . E . . .

"Mitford takes care of its own!" shouted the villagers. The sixth grade trooped around the statue, beating on tambourines, shaking maracas, and chanting something they'd been taught since first grade.

> *Mitford takes care of its own, its own,*
> *Mitford takes care of its own!*

Over the village rooftops, the plane spelled out the rest of the message.

O . . . F . . . I . . . T . . . S . . . O . . . W . . . N . . .

TAKES soon faded into puffs of smoke that looked like stray summer clouds. *CARE OF* was on its way out, but *ITS OWN* stood proudly in the sky, seeming to linger.

"If that don't beat all!" exclaimed a woman from Tennessee, who had stood in one spot the entire time, holding a sleep-drugged baby on her hip.

Dogs barked and chickens squawked as people clapped and started drifting away.

Just then, a few festivalgoers saw them coming, the sun glinting on their wings.

They roared in from the east, in formation, two by two.

Red and yellow. Green and blue.

"Four little home-built Pitts specials," said Omer, as proudly as if he'd built them himself. "Two of 'em's from Fayetteville, got one out of Roanoke, and the other one's from Albany, New York. Not much power in y'r little ragwings, they're nice and light, about a hundred and eighty horses, and handle like a dream."

He looked at the sky as if it contained the most beautiful sight he had ever seen, and so did the rector.

"I was goin' to head th' formation, but a man can't fly with a busted foot."

The crowd started lying on the grass. They lay down along the rock wall. They climbed up on the statue of Willard Porter, transfixed, and a young father set a toddler on Willard's left knee.

People pulled chairs out of their booths and sat down, looking up. All commerce ceased.

The little yellow Pitts special rolled over and dived straight for the monument.

"Ahhhhhh!" said the crowd.

As the yellow plane straightened out and up, the blue plane nose-dived and rolled over.

"They're like little young 'uns a-playin'," said Uncle Billy, enthralled.

Miss Rose came out and stood on the back stoop in her frayed chenille robe and looked up, tears coursing down her cheeks for her long-dead brother, Captain Willard Porter, who had flown planes and been killed in the war in France and buried over there, with hardly anything sent home but his medals and a gold ring with the initials SEB and a few faded snapshots from his pockets.

The little planes romped and rolled and soared and glided, like so many bright crayons on a palette of blue, then vanished toward the west, the sun on their wings.

Here and there, a festivalgoer tried getting up from the grass or a chair or the wall, but couldn't. They felt mesmerized, intoxicated. "Blowed away!" someone said.

"OK, buddy, here you go," Omer whispered.

They heard a heavy-duty engine throbbing in the distance and knew at once this was serious business, this was what everyone had been waiting for without even knowing it.

The Cunningham daughters hugged their children, kissed their mother and daddy, wept unashamedly, and hooted and hollered like banshees, but not a soul looked their way, for the crowd was intent on not missing a lick, on seeing it all, and taking the whole thing, blow by blow, home to Johnson City and Elizabethton and Wesley and Holding and Aho and Farmer and Price and Todd and Hemingway and Morristown. . . .

"Got y'r high roller comin' in, now," said Omer. The rector could feel the mayor's brother-in-law shaking like a leaf from pure excitement. "You've had y'r basic smoke writin' and stunt flyin,' now here comes y'r banner towin'!"

A red Piper Super Cub blasted over the treetops from the direction of the highway, shaking drifts of clouds from its path, trembling the heavens in its wake, and towing a banner that streamed across the open sky:

ESTHER . . . RIGHT FOR MITFORD, RIGHT FOR MAYOR

The Presbyterian brass band hammered down on their horns until the windows of the Porter mansion rattled and shook.

As the plane passed over, a wave of adrenaline shot through the festival grounds like so much electricity and, almost to a man, the crowd scrambled to its feet and shouted and cheered and whistled and whooped and applauded.

A few also waved and jumped up and down, and nearly all of them remembered what Esther had done, after all, putting the roof on old man Mueller's house, and turning the dilapidated wooden bridge over Mitford Creek into one that was safe and good to look at, and sending Ray in their RV to take old people to the grocery store, and jacking up Sophia's house and helping her kids, and making sure they had decent school buses to haul their own kids around in bad weather, and creating that thing at the hospital where you went and held and loved a new baby if its mama from the Creek was on drugs, and never one time raising taxes, and always being there when they had a problem, and actually listening when they talked, and . . .

. . . and taking care of them.

Some who had planned to vote for Mack Stroupe changed their minds, and came over and shook Esther's hand, and the brass band nearly busted a gut to be heard over the commotion.

Right! That was the ticket. Esther was *right* for Mitford. Mack Stroupe might be for change, but Esther would always be for the things that really counted.

Besides—and they'd tried to put it out of their minds time and time again—hadn't Mack Stroupe been known to beat his wife, who was quiet as a mouse and didn't deserve it, and hadn't he slithered over to that woman in Wesley for years, like a common, low-down snake in the grass?

"Law, do y'all vote in th' *summer?*" wondered a visitor. "We vote sometime in th' fall. I can't remember when, exactly, but I nearly always have to wear a coat to the polls."

Omer looked at the rector. The rector looked at Omer.

They shook hands.

It was done.

Out to Canaan, Ch. 8

Play Ball!

"MAN!" EXCLAIMED DOOLEY.

The stands were full, people were sitting on the grass, and the smell of hot dogs and chili wafted through the humid summer air.

Tommy's dad, who was the plate umpire, looked at the coin he'd just flipped. The Mitford Reds were the home team.

The rector scanned the crowd, just as he always did at Lord's Chapel.

The residents of Hope House were lined up in wheelchairs and seated on the front bleachers, looking expectant.

There was Mack Stroupe, standing with one foot on a bleacher and a cigarette in his mouth, and over to the right, Harley and Lace. He spotted Fancy Skinner and Uncle Billy and Miss Rose and Coot and Omer, and about midway up, Tommy, who had hurt his leg and couldn't play. He noted that quite a few sported a strawberry sucker stuck in their jaw, evidence that the mayor had doled out her customary campaign favors.

From the front row, where she sat with Russell Jacks and Betty Craig, Jessie waved to the field with both hands.

"Ladies and gentlemen," announced town councilman Linder Hayes, "it is my immense privilege to introduce Esther Cunningham, our beloved mayor, who for sixteen years and eight great terms in office has diligently helped Mitford take care of its own! Your Honor, you are hereby officially invited to . . . throw out the first ball."

"Burn it in, Esther!" somebody yelled.

The other umpire ran a ball to the mayor, who stood proudly in the dignitaries' section, cheek by jowl with the county sheriff.

At this, the *Muse* editor bounded from the concession stand to the bleachers and skidded to a stop about a yard from the mayor. He dropped to his knees and pointed the Nikon upward.

"Dadgum it," hissed the mayor, "don't shoot from down there, it gives me three double chins!"

"And behind the plate," boomed Linder Hayes, "our esteemed police chief and vigilant overseer of law and order, Mr. Rodney Underwood!"

Applause. Hoots. Whistles. Rodney adjusted his holster belt and waved to the crowd with a gloved hand.

"Hey, Esther, smoke it in there!"

The mayor threw back her head, circled her arm like a prop on a P-51, and let the ball fly.

"*Stee-rike* one!" said the umpire.

"Oh, *please*," said Cynthia, who was perspiring from infield practice.

"What is it?" whispered the rector.

"I have to use the port-a-john."

"It's your nerves," declared her husband, who appeared to know.

"Take the field!" yelled Buck.

The players sprinted to their positions. Then, the home-plate ump took a deep breath, pointed at the pitcher, and shouted what they'd all been waiting to hear.

"*Play ball!*"

* * *

The Reds' batboy, Poo Barlowe, passed his brother a bat which he had personally inscribed with the name *Dools* and a zigzag flash of lightning. He had rendered this personal I.D. with a red ballpoint pen, bearing down hard and repeatedly until it appeared etched into the wood.

Dooley took a couple of warm-up swings, then stepped into the batter's box. He gripped the bat, positioned his feet, and waited for the pitch.

A high, looping pitch barely missed the strike zone.

"Ball one!"

The second pitch came in chest-high, as Dooley tightened his grip, took a hefty swing, and connected. *Crack!* It was the first ball hitting the bat for the newly formed Mitford Reds; the sound seemed to reverberate into the stands.

"Go, buddy!"

Dooley streaked to first base, his long legs eating the distance, and blew past it to second as the crowd cheered. He slid into second a heartbeat ahead of the ball that socked into Scott Murphy's glove.

"Ride 'em, cowboy!" warbled Miss Pattie, who believed herself to be at a rodeo.

The game was definitely off to a good start.

* * *

"Mama!"

Fancy Skinner waved to her mother, who was shading her eyes and peering into the stands. "I'm up here!"

Fancy was wearing shocking pink tights and a matching tunic, and stood out so vividly from the crowd that her mother recognized her at once and made the climb to the fifth row, carrying a knitting bag with the beginnings of an afghan.

"I declare," said Fancy, "I hardly knew that was you, don't you just love bein' blond, didn't I tell you it would be more fun? I mean, look at you, out at a softball game instead of sittin' home watchin' th' *Wheel* or whatever. And oh, my lord, what're you wearin', I can't believe it, a Dale Jarrett T-shirt, aren't you th' cat's pajamas, you look a hundred years younger!

"Next, you might want to lose some weight, if you don't mind my sayin' so, around forty pounds seems right to me, it would take a strain off your heart. Lord have mercy, would you look at that, he backed th' right fielder clean to th' fence. *Hey, ump, open your eyes, I thought only horses went to sleep standin' up!*

"Oh, shoot, I forgot about your hearin' aid bein' so sensitive, was that me that made it go off? It sounds like a burglar alarm, I thought th' old one was better, here, have some gum, it's sugarless. Look! There he is, there's Mule, Mama, see? Th' one in the grass over yonder, idn't he cute, *Mule, honey, we're up here, look up here, sweetie,* oh mercy, the ball like to knocked his head off. *Pay attention to what you're doin', Mule!*

"Mama, you want a hot dog? I'll get us one at th' end of fifth innin', Velma made th' chili. I didn't say it's chilly, I said Velma—Mama, are you sure that hearin' aid works right, it seems like th' old one did better, and look at what you paid for it, an arm and a leg, you want relish? I can't hardly eat relish, it gives me sour stomach.

"How in th' world you can knit and watch a ball game is beyond me, I have to concentrate. See there, that's th' preacher Mule hangs out with at the Grill, th' one I gave a mask to th' day you got a perm, you remember, I can't tell whether he tries to hit a ball or club it to death. That's his wife on third base, I think she bleaches with a cap, I never heard of a preacher's wife playin' softball, times sure have changed, our preacher's wife leads th' choir and volunteers at th' hospital.

"*Go get 'em, Avis! Hit it outta there!* I wonder why Avis idn't married, I think he likes summer squash better than women, but it's important to really like your work. Lord, he sent that ball to th' moon! Look, Mama, right over yonder, see that man eyeballin' you? So what if he's younger, that's th' goin' thing these days, I told you blondes have more fun. Whoa, did you see that, he winked at you, well, maybe he got somethin' in his eye. *Hey, ump, pitcher's off th' plate, how thick are your glasses?*

"That redheaded kid, that's Dooley, he's sort of th' preacher's boy, he's a real slugger and he can run, too. Was that a spitball, Mama, did it look like a spitball to you? *Spitball! Spitball!* Who is that umpire, anyway, he's blind as a bat and deaf as a tater, oops, I better go down an' get in line, did you say you want relish?"

* * *

Ben Isaac Berman, whose family had brought him to Hope House all the way from Decatur, Illinois, was liking this ball game better than anything he'd done since coming to Mitford in July.

He liked the fresh air, the shouting, the tumult—even the heat was a *makhyeh*—though he didn't like the way his hot dog had landed in his lap, requiring two Hope House attendants to clean it up. What he couldn't figure was how chili had somehow made its way into one of his pants cuffs.

He felt like a *shlimazel* for not having better control of his limbs. But then, there was Miss Pattie sitting right next to him, who couldn't control a thought in her head, God forbid it should happen to him.

He also liked the game because it reminded him of his boyhood, which was as vivid in his recall as if he had lived it last week.

Take that boy at second base, that redhaired kid who could run like the wind. That was the kind of kid he'd been, that was the kind of kid he still was, deep down where nobody else had ever seen or ever would, not even his wife, blessed be her memory. Even he forgot about the kid living inside him, until he came out to a game like this and smelled the mountain air and heard the crack of the bat—that was when he began to feel his own legs churning, flying around to the bases and tearing up the dirt as he slid into home. . . .

* * *

At the bottom of the seventh inning, the score was 10–10.

"It's our bat and we've got three outs," said the rector. "We don't want any extra innings, so let's finish now and go home winners."

His shirt was sticking to him. He felt like he'd been rode hard and put up wet, as Tommy Noles used to say.

He watched as Mule Skinner stepped up to bat.

The ball came in high.

"Ball one!"

Mule swung at the next pitch and cracked it over second base into center field. The rector was amazed at Mule's speed as he sprinted to first. This game would be fodder for the Grill regulars 'til kingdom come.

After Jenna Ivey made the first out of the inning, it was Pauline Barlowe's turn to bat.

She looked confident, he thought. In fact, she'd made a pretty good showing all afternoon, but had a tendency to waffle, to be strong one minute and lose it the next.

She took a couple of pitches and slammed a hit to second base. Dadgum, a double play! But the second baseman kicked the ball, and all runners were safe.

"Time out!" yelled Buck, striding onto the field.

"OK, Pitch," he said to Lew Boyd, "you've been a defensive star all day, I want you to use that bat and get the big hit. Or give me a fly ball to the outfield to advance the runners."

"I'm gonna give you premium unleaded on this 'un."

The first pitch came down the middle.

"Strike one!"

Lew hit the next pitch into right field, where the outfielder nailed it and threw it to third. The runners held.

Two outs.

Dooley hurried into the batter's box and scratched the loose dirt to get a strong foothold.

Buck yelled, "You've got to get on base. Can you do it?"

"I can do it!"

Poobaw Barlowe squeezed his eyes shut and prayed, *Jesus, God, and ever'body* . . .

The rector was holding his breath. Dooley had been on base every time he came to bat today. He saw the determined look on the boy's face as he waited for the pitch.

Realizing her feet were swelling, Fancy Skinner removed her high-heel shoes and put them in her mother's knitting bag.

Coot Hendrick hoped to the good Lord he would not lose the twenty-five dollars he had bet on the Reds. He had borrowed it out of the sugar bowl, leaving only a few packages of NutraSweet and three dimes. He squirmed with anxiety. His mama might be old, but she could still whip his head.

Crack!

Dooley connected on a line shot into the outfield, which was hit so sharply that Father Tim stopped Mule at third.

"Way to go, buddy, way to do it, great job!" he yelled.

Dooley punched his fist into the air and pumped it, as the crowd hooted and cheered.

With two outs and the bases loaded, it was Adele Hogan's turn at bat.

"OK, Adele, let's get 'em, let's go, you can do it!" For tomorrow's services, he would sound like a bullfrog with laryngitis.

"Ball one!"

The second ball came in on the outside.

"Ball two!"

She swung at the next pitch.

"Strike one!"

The stands were going crazy. "Hey, ump," somebody yelled. "Wake up, you're missin' a great game!"

The ball came down the middle.

"Strike two!"

Two balls, two strikes. Adele stooped down, grabbed some dirt, and rubbed it in her hands, then took the bat and gripped it hard. The rector thought he could see white knuckles as she rocked slightly on her feet and watched the pitch.

She caught the ball on the inside of her bat, away from the heavy part, sending it into short left center field.

Nobody called for the ball.

The outfielders all moved at once, collided, and stumbled over each other as the ball fell in. Adele Hogan ran for her life and reached first base as Mule scored.

The game was over.

The crowd was wild.

The score was 11–10.

Ray Cunningham huffed to the field with the mayor's ball and asked Adele to sign it. Unable to restrain himself, he pounded her on the back and gave her a big hug, wondering how in the world J. C. Hogan had ever gotten so lucky.

Ben Isaac Berman pulled himself up on his aluminum walker and waved to the redhaired kid on the field. He squinted into the sun, almost certain that the boy waved back.

The *Muse* editor, who had been sitting under a shade tree, panted to first base and cranked off a roll of Tri-X. All the frames featured his wife, who, as far as he was concerned, looked dynamite even with sweat running down her face. He wondered something that had never occurred to him before; he wondered how he'd ever gotten so lucky, and decided he would tell her that very thing—tonight.

Well, maybe tomorrow.

Soon, anyway.

Out to Canaan, Ch. 14

Father Tim's Deep-sea Fishing Trip

HE WAS AWAKE ten minutes before the alarm went off, and heard at once the light patter of rain through the open window.

"Timothy?"

"Yes?"

"Is it four o'clock?"

"Ten 'til. Go back to sleep."

"You'll have a great time, I just know you will."

"I'm sure of it. And re-member—don't cook din-ner. I'm bringing it home."

"Right, darling. I'm ex-cited. . . ."

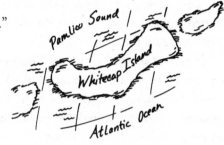

She was no such thing; she was already snoring again. He kissed her shoulder and crept out of bed.

He was accustomed to rising early, but four o'clock was ridiculous, not to mention he couldn't get pumped up for this jaunt no matter how hard he tried.

He'd entertained every fishing yarn anyone cared to tell, trying to mask his blank stare with a look of genuine interest. Ah, well, surely the whole business would pleasantly surprise him—he'd return home with a cooler full of tuna, tanned and vigorous from a day on the wa-ter, whistling a sea chantey.

Chances were—and this was not a perk to be taken lightly—it could even blow a fresh breeze through his preaching, not to mention make him feel more one in spirit with his parish. After all, he'd been on their turf for three months and practically the only thing he'd done that he couldn't have done in Mitford was slap a few mosquitoes and pick sandspurs from his dog's paws.

He dressed hurriedly in the bathroom, brushed his teeth, splashed water on his face, and raced to the kitchen to gulp down a cup of cof-fee he'd set in the refrigerator last night, figuring cold caffeine to be better than no caffeine at all.

He packed the canvas bag with his lunch, having entirely dismissed the notion of fried chicken. Where on earth anybody would find fried chicken at four in the morning was beyond him. He stuffed in plenty of bottled water and a couple of citrus drinks. No time to eat, he'd do that on the boat, he was out of here.

His dog followed him along the hall, thumped down by the front door, and yawned mightily. "Guard the house, old fellow."

Dark as pitch. He turned the lock, shut the door behind him, and patted his jacket pockets for the rolled-up canvas hat and bottle of sunscreen. All there.

He stood on the porch and drew in a deep draft of the cool morning air; it was scented with rain and salt, with something mysteriously beyond his ken. He didn't think he'd ever again take the ocean for granted. He daily sensed the power and presence of it in this new world in which they were living.

All those years ago when he was a young clergyman in a little coastal parish, the water had meant nothing to him; it had hardly entered his thoughts. He might have lived in the Midwest for all the interest he took in the things of the sea, except for the several bushels of shrimp and clams he'd surely consumed during his curacy. His mind, his heart had been elsewhere, in the clouds, perhaps; but now it was different. Though he wasn't one for swimming in the ocean or broiling on the beach, he was making a connection this time, something he couldn't quite articulate and why bother, anyway?

The light rain cooled his head as he trotted down the front steps, opened the gate, and got into the Mustang parked by the street.

Goin' fishin'! he thought as he buckled the seat belt. The way he'd worried about this excursion had made it seem like a trek to Outer Mongolia, but so far, so good. And just think—there were thousands, probably millions of people out there who'd give anything to be in his shoes.

* * *

It was still dark when he found the marina where the charter boats were tied to the dock like horses waiting to be saddled.

He pulled into the nearly full parking lot, took his gear from the trunk and locked up, then stood by the Mustang, peering into the murky light. People were huffing coolers as big as coffins out of vans and cars, muttering, calling to each other, laughing, slamming doors.

More than once, he'd heard charter boats called party boats, and fervently hoped this was not one of those deals.

Raining a little harder now, but nothing serious. He wiped his head with his hat and put it back in his pocket, checking his watch. Five o'clock sharp.

He hefted the cooler and started walking, looking for *Blue Heaven* and trying to get over the feeling he was still asleep and this was a dream.

Someone materialized out of the gray mist, smelling intensely of tobacco and shaving lotion.

"Mornin', Father! Let's go fishin'!"

"Otis? Is that you?"

"Cap'n Willie told me you were on board today. I didn't want you goin' off by yourself and havin' too much fun."

Otis was schlepping a cooler with a fluorescent label that was readable even in the predawn light: BRAGG'S FOR ALL YOUR CEMENT NEEDS.

A bronzed, bearded Captain Willie stood on the deck wearing shorts and a T-shirt, booming out a welcome.

"Father Timothy! Good mornin' to you, we're glad to have you!" He found himself shaking a hand as big as a ham and hard as a rock. "Step over lightly, now, let me take that, there you go, welcome to *Blue Heaven*."

"Good morning, Captain. How's the weather looking?" It seemed the boat was lurching around in the water pretty good, and they hadn't even gone anywhere yet.

"Goin' to fair off and be good fishin'." Captain Willie's genial smile displayed a couple of gold teeth. "Meet my first mate, Pete Brady."

He shook hands with a muscular fellow of about thirty. "Good to see you, Pete."

"Yessir, welcome aboard."

"This your first time?" asked the captain.

"First ever."

"Well, you're fishin' with a pro, here." He pounded Otis on the back. "Go on in th' cabin, set your stuff down, make yourself at home. And Father . . ."

"Yes?"

"Would you favor us with blessin' th' fleet this mornin'?"

"Ah . . . how does that work, exactly?"

"All th' boats'll head out about th' same time, then after the sun rises, you'll come up to th' bridge an' ask th' Lord for safe passage and good fishin'. Th' other boats can hear you over th' radio."

"Consider it done!" he said, feeling a surge of excitement.

"We'll have prayer requests for you, like, the last few days, we've all been prayin' for Cap'n Tucker's daughter, she's got leukemia."

"I'm sorry. I'd feel honored and blessed to do it."

"We thank you. Now go in there and introduce yourselves around, get comfortable."

Father Tim stuck his head in the cabin.

Ernie Fulcher, sitting with a green cooler between his feet, threw up his hand and grinned from ear to ear. "Didn't want you runnin' out th' first time all by your lonesome."

"Right," said Roger, looking shy about butting in. "We didn't think you'd mind a little company."

* * *

Madge Parrott and her friend Sybil Huffman appeared to be dressed for a cruise in the Bahamas. They were clearly proud to announce they were from Rome, Georgia, and this was their first time on a fishing charter. They were out for marlin, would settle for tuna if necessary, but no dolphin, thank you, they'd heard dolphins could sing and had feelings like people.

Both were widows whose husbands had been great fishermen. This trip was about making a connection with the departed, as they'd heard Chuck and Roy talk about deep-sea fishing like it was the best thing since sliced bread. Madge confessed that even though she and Sybil didn't drink beer, they didn't see why they couldn't catch fish like anybody else.

He noted that the group shared a need to explain what they had in their coolers, some even lifting the lids and displaying the contents, and issuing hearty invitations to dip in, at any time, to whatever they'd brought along.

"You run out of drinks, me'n Roger got all you want right here," said Ernie, patting a cooler as big as a Buick. "Got Sun-Drop, Mello Yello, Sprite, just help yourself."

"And there's ham and turkey on rye," said Roger. "I made two extra, just in case, plus fried chicken."

Everybody nodded their thanks, as the engines began to throb and hum. Father Tim was mum about the contents of his own cooler—two banana sandwiches on white bread with low-fat mayo.

"Y'all need any sunscreen," said Madge, "we're loaded with sunscreen. It's right here in my jacket pocket." She indicated a blue jacket folded on the seat, so that one and all might note its whereabouts in an emergency.

"And I've got Bonine," said Sybil, "if anybody feels seasick." She held up her package and rattled the contents.

"Have you ever been seasick?" Madge asked Father Tim.

"Never!" he said. Truth was, he'd never been on the sea but a couple of times, and always in sight of shore, so there was no way he could have been seasick. And for today, he'd done what Ernie and Roger so heartily recommended—he'd stayed sober, gotten a good night's sleep, and didn't eat a greasy breakfast.

"Only twelve percent of people get seasick," Roger said, quoting his most encouraging piece of information on the subject.

Ernie lifted the lid of his cooler. "Oh, an' anybody wants Snickers bars, they're right here on top of th' ice. There's nothin' like a Snickers iced down good'n cold."

Madge and Sybil admitted they'd never heard of icing down a Snickers bar, but thought it would be real tasty, especially on a hot day. Sybil pledged to try one before the trip was over.

Otis announced that anybody who wanted to help themselves to his Kentucky Fried, they knew where it was at. He also had cigars, Johnnie Walker Black, and boiled peanuts, for whoever took a notion.

It was the most instant formation of community Father Tim had ever witnessed. He felt momentarily inspired to stand and lead a hymn.

Captain Willie gunned the engines, and the stern of *Blue Heaven* dug low into the water as they moved away from the dock at what seemed like full speed. Father Tim realized he didn't know how he felt about riding backward, not to mention that the water seemed mighty rough.

Very dadgum blasted rough, he thought as they plowed farther out in an unceasing rain. He looked around the hull of the small cabin, where everyone appeared totally sophisticated about being tossed around like dice in a cup. They were all holding on for dear life to whatever they could grab, and yelling over the roar of eight hundred and fifty horses running wide open.

Otis Bragg was clearly tickled pink to have two women on board who didn't know fishing from frog's legs. He'd already begun a seminar on how to keep your thumb on the fishing line, how to hold the rod, how to hold your mouth, and how to position your feet when reeling in a big one. Father Tim listened as attentively as he could, then finally slumped against the back of the padded bench and peered through the door of the cabin.

Out there, it was rain, churning waters, and diesel smoke. In here, it was earsplitting racket and the worst ride he'd had since Tommy Noles had shoved him down a rocky hillside in a red wagon without a tongue.

* * *

The sun was emerging from the water, staining the silver sea with patches of light and color.

Pete Brady came into the cabin, holding a dripping ballyhoo in one hand. "You'll want to go up to the bridge now, sir. Better put your jacket on."

"Right!" he said. He was glad to leave the cabin; only a moment ago, he'd had the odd sensation of smothering. . . .

He stood, holding on to the table that was bolted to the deck, then made his way to the door, praying he wouldn't pitch into Madge Parrott's lap.

"You tell th' Lord we're wantin' 'em to weigh fifty pounds and up, if He don't mind." Otis chewed his cigar and grinned.

Father Tim clung to the doorjamb. "How do I get to the bridge?" he asked Pete.

The first mate, who appeared to be squeezing the guts from a bait fish, jerked his thumb toward the side of the cabin. "Right up the ladder there."

He peered around and saw the ladder. The rungs were immediately over the water, and went straight up. Three, four, five . . .

"*That* ladder?"

"Yessir, be sure'n hold on tight."

He peered into the black and churning sea, and made a couple of quick steps to a chair that was bolted to the cockpit deck. Pete was bustling around without any difficulty in keeping his footing, but Father Tim had the certain feeling that if he let go of the chair, he'd end up at the Currituck Light.

He turned and lunged for the bottom rung of the ladder, but miscalculated and bounced onto the rail. Too startled to grab hold, he reeled against the cabin wall, finally managing to grip the lower rung. Thanks be to God, Pete was baiting a hook and facing seaward, and his cabin mates were oblivious to his afflictions.

Lord Jesus, I've never done this before. You were plenty good around water, and I'm counting on You to help me accomplish this thing.

He reached to an upper rung and got a firm grip.

The spray was flying, the waves were churning, the sun was rising . . . it was now or never. He swung himself onto the ladder and went up, trying in vain to curl his tennis shoes around the rungs like buns around frankfurters.

He hauled himself to the bridge, grabbed the support rail for the hardtop, and stood for a moment, awed. The view from the bridge literally took his breath away.

How could anyone doubt the living truth of what the psalmist said? *"The heavens declare the glory of God, the skies proclaim the work of his hands!"* He wanted to shout his unabashed praise.

His shirt whipped against his body like a flag; his knees trembled. This boat was flying, no two ways about it, and beneath their feet, the endless, racking, turbulent sea, and a sunrise advancing up the sky like tongues of fire.

Surely this was the habitation of angels, and life in the cabin a thing to be pitied.

He lurched to the helm, where Captain Willie was holding a microphone, and grabbed the back of the helm chair.

"We're glad to have you with us, Father! Greetings to you from th' whole fleet on this beautiful September day!"

His stomach did an odd turn as he opened his mouth to speak, so he closed it again.

The captain winked. "Got a little chop this mornin'."

He nodded.

"A real sharp head sea."

He felt sweat on his brow as the captain spoke into the microphone.

"We're mighty happy to have Father Tim Kavanagh to lead us in prayer this mornin'. He's from over at Whitecap, where Toby Rider has his boat shop. Anybody with a prayer request, let's hear it now."

The VHF blared. "Father, my little boy fell off a ladder on Sunday, he's, ah, in the hospital, looks like he's goin' to be fine, but . . . his name's Danny. We thank you."

"Please pray for Romaine, he had his leg tore up by a tractor fell on 'im. Thank you."

"Just like to ask for . . . forgiveness for somethin' I done, there's no use to go into what, I'd appreciate it."

Several other requests came in as he bent his head and listened intently, gripping the helm chair for all he was worth.

"That it? Anybody else?"

He fished in his pocket for his hat. Though the rain had stopped, he put it on and pulled it down snugly above his ears. Then he took the microphone, surprised that it felt as heavy as a lug wrench.

"We'd like to pray for th' owner of th' marina and his wife, Angie, too," said Captain Willie. "She's got breast cancer. And Cap'n Tucker's daughter, we don't want to forget her, name's Sarah, then there's Toby Rider, lost his daddy and we feel real bad about it. Course we'd like to ask God's mercy for every family back home and every soul on board. . . ."

Captain Willie turned to the helm, grabbed the red knob, and cranked the engines back to idle.

In the sudden quiet, the waves slammed against the hull, dulling the gurgling sound of the exhaust. They seemed to be wallowing now in the choppy sea; they might have been so much laundry tossing in a washing machine.

His heart was hammering as if he'd run a race. But it wasn't his heart, exactly, that bothered him, it was his stomach. It seemed strangely disoriented, as if it had moved to a new location and he couldn't figure out where.

"Our Father, we thank You mightily for the beauty of the sunrise over this vast sea, and for the awe and wonder in all the gifts of Your creation. We ask Your generous blessings upon every captain and mate aboard every vessel in this fleet, and pray that each of us be made able, by Your grace, to know Your guidance, love, and mercy throughout the day. . . ."

The names of the people, and their needs, what were they? His mind seemed desperately blank, as if every shred of thought and reason had been blown away like chaff on the wind.

Lord! Help!

"For Sarah, we ask Your tender mercies, that You would keep her daily in Your healing care, giving wisdom to those attending her, and providing strength and encouragement. . . ."

More than three decades of intercessory prayer experience notwithstanding, he found it miraculous that the names came to him, one by one. He leaned into the prayer with intensity, feeling something of the genuine weight and burden, the urgency, of the needs for which he prayed.

He wiped the sweat from his forehead. "Oh, Lord, who maketh a way in the sea, and a path in the mighty waters, we thank You for hearing our prayers, in the blessed name of Your Son, our Savior, Jesus Christ. Amen."

The captain took the microphone and keyed it, thanking him.

He noted what appeared to be a look of compassion on the captain's face as they shook hands.

"*Blue Heaven, Salty Dog,* come back."

"*Blue Heaven,* go ahead, *Salty Dog.*"

"Just want to say we really appreciate Father Kavanagh's prayers, and sure hope he doesn't succumb to the torments of a rough sea. OK, *Salty Dog* back to eighty."

"*Blue Heaven* standin' by on eighty."

As the captain gunned the engines, Father Tim careened to the rail and leaned over.

The goodwill and fond hope of *Salty Dog* had come too late.

* * *

Twice over the rail should nip this thing in the bud. Already his ribs hurt from the retching; it was probably over now and he could go down the ladder and have something to drink, maybe even a bite to eat—that was the problem, going out on rough seas with an empty stomach. . . .

He was amazed at his agility on the ladder, as if by the earlier practice shot he'd become a seasoned sailor. *No big deal,* he thought, looking down at the waves hammering the boat.

Good grief! He scrambled off the ladder and leaned over the rail, the bile spewing in a flume from his very core, hot, bitter, and fathomless.

* * *

It was his head. He seemed to have lost his head the last time over the rail. He reached up feebly and felt around. No, it was his hat he'd lost. It had slithered off and dropped into the sea, and his scalp was parching like a Georgia peanut.

"Let 'im set there, we ain't findin' any fish," he heard Otis say. He opened his eyes and realized he was sitting in the privileged fighting chair. The fighting chair. What a joke.

"Hat," he said. "Hat."

Nobody heard him, because he found he couldn't speak above a whisper. He had no energy to force audible words through cracked lips.

Fine. He'd just sit here until they dumped him overboard, which he wished they'd do sooner rather than later. He'd never known such suffering in his life, not from mayonnaise that had nearly taken him out at a parish picnic, not from the diabetic coma brought on by Esther Bolick's orange marmalade cake, not from the raging fever he had as a child when he saw his mother as a circus performer who made lions jump through hoops.

"What I don't like about th' Baptists," Otis was saying, "is they won't speak to you at th' liquor store."

Laughing, shuffling around, general merriment—people living their lives as if he weren't there, as if he were invisible, a bump on a log.

* * *

"That's th' way it is, some days," said Pete. "You're either a hero or a zero. Yesterday, we were haulin' 'em in faster than I could bait th' hooks; today, I don't know where they are."

"You got to pump 'em," said Ernie. "Like, say you're reelin' in a fifty-pound tuna, you got to raise the rod up real slow, then drop down quick and *crank*."

Conversations came and went; it was all a kind of hive hum, he thought, as when bees returned from working a stand of sourwoods.

"Now, you take tarpon," said Otis. "I was down in th' Keys where they grow too big to mount on your wall. Tarpon you just jump a few times and then break 'em off before you wear 'em out, you wear 'em out too bad, th' sharks eat 'em."

"I never fished any tarpon," said Ernie.

He opened his eyes and shut them fast. Pete was showing Madge and Sybil how he prepped the bait.

"See, you pop th' eyes out like this . . . then you break up th' backbone . . ."

"Ooooh," said Madge.

"Don't make 'er faint," said Otis.

"I have no intention of fainting, thank you!"

"Then you squeeze their guts out, see. . . ."

"Lord help," said Sybil.

"Thing is, th' more they wiggle in th' water, th' better they catch."

"Clever!" said Madge. "That is *really* clever."

Without realizing how he got there, he was at the rail again, on his knees.

"On his knees at th' rail," said Madge. "That is very Episcopalian."

"Or Luth'ran," said Sybil. "Can't that be Luth'ran?"

He didn't know who it was, maybe Otis or Ernie, but someone held his head while he spewed up his insides and watched the vomitus carried away on the lashing water.

"We been out every day for forty-one days straight," said Pete, who was currently varying the bait, trying anything.

"Sometimes you just pray for a nor'easter so you can get a break, but if th' weather's good, you have to go."

The weather today is not *good,* he tried to say, but couldn't. Why in blazes did we go today if you don't go when the weather's not good? *Answer that!* Plus, *plus . . .* he wished he could discuss this with Roger . . . his math told him that, discounting the crew, he represented more than any twelve blasted percent.

He declined the fighting chair in case anyone got a strike, and sat feebly in an adjacent chair.

"What do you think the winds are right now?" asked Roger.

"Oh, fifteen, sixteen miles an hour. This ain't nothin'. I know somebody was out all night last night in forty-mile winds."

General, respectful silence. Diesel fumes.

"We need to think positive," said Madge. "Smoked loin of tuna! That's how *I'm* thinkin'!"

"Must be lunchtime," said Otis. "Believe I'll have me a little shooter. Want one?"

"Maybe later."

"Thank you, you go on, but I wouldn't mind shuckin' a few peanuts with you."

He was baking, he was broiling, he was frying, he was cooked. Sunscreen. He remembered the sunscreen in his jacket pocket, but he wasn't wearing his jacket. Someone had helped him remove it earlier.

"Look," said Sybil. "Th' poor man needs something."

"What?" said Madge. "Oh, mercy, look at his head, it's red as a poker. Where's his hat?"

"He went to the rail and came back without it."

"Here you go." Otis was patting sunscreen on his head and followed it with a hat.

"Bless you," he managed to whisper.

"What'd he say?"

"He said bless me." He thought Otis sounded touched. "Father, you want some water or Coke? Coke might be good."

"Nossir," said Ernie, "what he needs is ginger ale. Anybody got ginger ale?"

"Fruit juice," said Madge, "that's what I'd give somebody with upset stomach."

"No deal with th' fruit juice," said Pete. "Too much acid."

"How about a piece of ice to just hold in his mouth?"

"I don't know about that. They say when you're real hot you shouldn't swallow somethin' real cold, it can give you a heart attack or maybe a stroke."

"He's moving his lips. What's he saying?"

Otis leaned down and listened. "He's praying," said Otis.

* * *

They had veered east, then south, but weren't finding any fish. Neither was the rest of the fleet. Occasionally a boat would get a couple of strikes, radio the news, and everybody would head in that direction. But so far, *Blue Heaven* had taken only two dolphins, and thrown back a few catches that were too small to gaff.

They were currently idling the boat several miles south of Virginia, and trolling a spreader bar. The chop was as bad as, or worse than, before; they were wallowing like a bear in cornshucks. He thought of looking at his watch, but why bother? The misery was interminable. There was no hope that anyone would turn back to shore for a sick man, much less send a helicopter. He was in this scrape to the bitter end.

He denied to himself that he had to urinate, as doing that would require going through the cabin where this thing first snared and suffocated him. He wouldn't go back in that cabin if they tried to drag him in with a team of mules.

Occasionally, a kind soul visited his chair and stood for a moment in silent commiseration.

"Sorry, Tim."

"You're going to make it, buddy."

Even the captain came down from the bridge and laid a hand on his shoulder. "Hang in there, Father." Their concern was a comfort, he had to admit, though he was hard pressed to get over the humiliation he felt.

At one point, someone assured him he wasn't going to die, which he found altogether lacking in comfort, since he didn't much care either way.

"Did you hear about th' guy got dragged off th' boat reelin' in a marlin?"

"No way."

"It was in th' paper, said th' marlin was four hundred pounds, said it pulled th' guy over th' stern."

"He would've been sucked into th' backwash."

"Wadn't. Somebody went in after 'im, saved 'im. But that's not th' half of it. He got th' marlin."

"Bull. That never happened in this lifetime."

"I'm tellin' you it's th' truth, it was in th' paper."

"I've heard of fish takin' first mates over," said Pete.

"There is no way I want to listen to this mess," said Madge.

He was shocked to find himself kneeling at the rail again, with no power over this thing, none at all. He felt completely out of control, which frightened him utterly; he might have been a piece of bait himself, without will or reason to alter his circumstances.

"Number five," somebody said. "That's th' fifth time."

"Seven. He heaved over th' bridge rail twice."

"You ready to eat? I'm half starved."

"I've been thinkin' about what I made last night. Tuna salad. On French bread! Oh, and there's late tomatoes out of my neighbor's garden. Delicious!" said Madge. "I'll cut 'em up so we can all have a bite."

"Tuna out of a *can?*" asked Otis. "That'd be sacrilegious."

"Are we goin' to just leave 'im out here?" wondered Sybil.

"Father? *Father!*"

Why did people think the sick automatically went deaf?

What? He couldn't say it audibly, so he thought it, which should be sufficient.

"Do you want to go inside?"

"Don't take him inside," said the first mate. "You lose th' horizon when you do that. That's usually what makes people seasick, is losin' th' horizon."

"But he's been sittin' out here since it quit rainin'. I think we should at least put sunscreen on his arms. Look at his arms."

He felt several people pawing over him, and tried to express his gratitude.

"Lookit. He doesn't have socks on. Rub some on his ankles."

"Th' back of his neck," said Ernie. "That's a real tender place, slather some on there."

"He's an *awful* color," said Madge.

He realized he should have been more specific in his will; now it was too late to say that he did not want an open casket.

* * *

He slept, or thought he might be sleeping. Perhaps he'd slipped into a state of unconsciousness, his mind vacant as a hollow gourd. If there was anything he distrusted, it was an empty mind. He forced himself to open his eyes and saw only glare, a shining that moved and heaved and shuddered and danced and tried to force entry to his stomach. In truth, he'd never been especially aware of his stomach. When it was empty, he put something in it; when it was full, he was happy. Now he felt it as a raw and flaccid thing that swung in him like a sheep's bladder with every swell that tossed the boat.

He wanted his wife. Lacking that consolation, he pulled his jacket around him and squeezed his eyes shut and dreamed a dream as vacant as mist.

* * *

Thank God! He might actually be feeling better.

His eyes seemed clear, some strength was returning; but he didn't want to count his chickens, no, indeed. He rubbed Chap Stick on his lips and hunkered down under Otis's hat, wondering about his sugar, which must have dropped straight to the floor of the Gulf Stream. He wished he'd brought his tachometer . . . no, that wasn't it. What was it, anyway? Could he possibly have suffered brain damage from this terrible assault? *Glu*cometer, that's what it was.

Weak . . . terribly weak. He realized he was thinking of Ernie's Snickers bars, iced down cold. A small flicker, a flame of hope rose in his breast. *Thank You, Lord.* . . .

He looked out upon the restless water and saw other boats on the horizon—one there, two there, like family.

"We had the worst nest of yellow jackets in our church wall-l-l!" said Sybil.

"What'd y'all do about it?"

"Swatted 'em with our hymnals and bulletins."

"Why didn't you kill 'em?"

"They only flare up once a year, late April or May, and only on th' side where hardly anybody sits, anyway."

"Yesterday a hero, today a zero," muttered Pete, hauling up bait that looked like a glorified Christmas tree.

Father Tim waved his hand to Ernie, who came over and squatted by the chair.

"What can I do for you, buddy?"

"Snickers," he said, hoarse as a bullfrog.

"Snickers?"

He nodded, feeble but encouraged.

* * *

"We got us one!" yelled Ernie. "Otis! Where's Otis?"

"In th' head. You take it!"

Father Tim had heard of total pandemonium, but he'd never seen it 'til now. Six people erupted into a full horde, and swarmed around him like the armies of Solomon.

"We got a fish here! Yee-hah!"

"Got another one right here. Take it, Madge!"

He looked at the throbbing lines crisscrossed over and around the stern like freeways through L.A.

"That's a keeper!" Pete gaffed something and pulled it in.

"Way to go, Roger!"

He saw the rainbow of color that shimmered on the big fish as it went into the box, where it thrashed like a horse kicking a stall. Pete pulled out the gaff and hosed blood from the deck.

The captain was fishing off the bridge; everybody was fishing. He heaved himself from the chair, out of the fray, and huddled against the cabin.

In the fighting chair, Madge was crouched into the labor of hauling in something big.

Otis had his thumb on her line, helping her raise and lower the rod. "You got to pump 'im, now," he said, clenching his cigar in his teeth.

"Oh, law! This must be an eighteen-wheeler I've got on here!"

"Keep crankin'!"

Captain Willie called over the speaker, "Please tend to the left-hand corner, Pete, tend to the left-hand corner, we got a mess over there."

"A fishin' frenzy," muttered Pete, streaking by in a blur.

Madge cranked the reel, blowing like a prizefighter. "This fish is killin' me. Somebody come and take this bloomin' rod!"

"Don't quit!" yelled Sybil, aiming a point-and-shoot at the action. "Keep goin', Chuck would be proud!"

"That ain't nothin' but solid tuna," said Otis. He helped Madge lift the rod as the fish drew closer to the boat.

Father Tim rubberlegged it to the stern and looked over. The black water of the morning had changed to blue-green, and the fish moved beneath the aqua surface, luminous and quick.

He thought it one of the most beautiful sights he'd ever seen.

"Here it comes!"

He stepped back as Pete darted to the right of the fighting chair, lowered the gaff, and hauled the tuna onto the deck.

"Way to go, Madge!"

"Beautiful! *Beautiful!*"

Whistles, cheers, applause.

"That'll weigh in seventy, seventy-five pounds," Otis said, as Madge staggered out of the chair, grinning into Sybil's camera.

The captain was catching fish, Ernie was catching fish, Roger was catching fish.

"Got a fish on th' line!" yelled Pete. "Who'll take it?"

"I'll take it!" As Father Tim thumped into the fighting chair, hoots of encouragement went up from the entire assembly.

He was back from the dead, he was among the living, he was ready to do this thing.

* * *

"How was it, darling?"

"Terrific!" he said, kissing her. "Wonderful fellowship, great fellowship—fellows in a ship, get it?"

"Got it. And the weather?"

He shrugged. "A little rough, but not too bad."

"What's for supper?" she asked, eyeing the cooler he was lugging.

"Yellowfin tuna and dolphin! Let's fire up the grill," he said, trotting down the hall, "and I'll tell you all about it!" By the time he hit the kitchen, he was whistling.

She hurried after her husband, feeling pleased. He'd come home looking considerably thinner, definitely tanner, and clearly more relaxed. She'd known all along that buying him a chair with Captain Willie was a brilliant idea.

A New Song, Ch. 13

Tourist Season in Whitecap

IN THE VILLAGE, merchants prepared for the wave of tourists that would wash over them only two or three weeks hence. They were eager to see an economy that had slowed to a trickle once again surge like the incoming tide: quite a few prices were discreetly raised and the annual flurry of stocking nearly empty shelves began.

The dress shop reordered Whitecap T-shirts printed variously with images of the lighthouse, the historic one-room schoolhouse moved from the Toe to the village green, and the much-photographed St. John's in the Grove; the grocery store manager decided to dramatically expand his usual volume of hush puppy mix, much favored by tourists renting units featuring a kitchen; and Whitecap Flix, the sixty-two-seat theater rehabbed from a bankrupt auto parts store and open from

May 15 through October 1, voted to open with *Babe,* convinced it was old enough to bill as a classic. To demonstrate their confidence in the coming season, Flix scheduled a half-page ad to hit on May 15, and included a ten-percent-off coupon for people who could prove it was their birthday.

Hearing of the advertising boom coursing through the business community, Mona elected to run a quarter-page menu once a month for three months, something she'd never done before in her entire career. Plus, she was changing her menu, which always thrilled a paltry few and made the rest hopping mad. She figured to put a damper on any complaints by offering a Friday night all-you-can-eat dinner special of fried catfish for $7.95, sure to pacify everybody. Due to space too small to cuss a cat, she had resisted all-you-can-eat deals ever since she opened in this location, since any all-you-can-eat, especially fried, was bad to back up a kitchen. All-you-can-eat was a two-edged sword, according to Ernie—who could not keep his trap shut about her business, no matter what—because while you could draw a crowd with it, in the end you were bound to lose money on it since people around here chowed down like mules. In the end, all-you-can-eat was what some outfits called a loss leader. Mona did not like the word *loss,* it was not in her vocabulary, but she would try the catfish and see how it worked, mainly to draw attention from the fact there was no liver and onions on her new menu, nor would there ever be again in her lifetime, not to mention skillet corn bread that crowded up the oven, cooked cabbage that smelled to high heaven, and pinto beans. Lord knows, she couldn't do everything, this was not New York City, it was White-cap, and though she'd been born and raised here, it was not where she cared to spend the rest of her life, she was investing money in a condo in Florida, even if Ernie had expressed the hope of retiring to Tennessee. Tennessee! The very thought gave her the shivers. All those log cabins, all those grizzlies stumbling around in the dark, plus moonshine out the kazoo . . . no way.

Sometime in April, a sign appeared in the window of Ernie's Books, Bait & Tackle:

> Buy Five Westerns
> Any Title, Get a
> Free Zane Grey
> or Louis L'Amour,
> Take Your Pick

Hardly anyone going in and out of Mona's had ever read Zane Grey, though several had heard of him, and a breakfast regular seemed to remember L'Amour as a prizefighter from Kansas City. Two days after the sign went up, a potato chip rep dropped a hundred and eighty-seven bucks on the special offer and posted Ernie's phone number and address in a chat room devoted to the subject of Old West literature. In the space of eight working days, the book end of the business had blown the bait end in the ditch, and Ernie hired on a couple of high school kids to handle mail orders.

Roanoke Clark was painting one of the big summerhouses, and had hired on a helper who, he was surprised to learn, stayed sober as a judge and worked like a horse. He pondered making this a permanent deal, if only for his partner's nearly new pair of telescoping ladders, not to mention late-model Ford truck, an arrangement that would prevent the necessity of renting Chess Doyle's rattletrap Chevy with a homemade flatbed, for which Chess dunned him a flat forty bucks a week.

In the Toe, Bragg's was busy pumping diesel and dispatching tons of gravel and cement to construction sites as far away as Williamston, not to mention an industrial park in Tyrrell County.

At the north end of the small island shaped like a Christmas stocking, St. John's in the Grove was at last divested of its scaffolding. The heavy equipment had vanished, the piles of scrap lumber and roofing had been hauled away, and the errant flapping of loose tarps was heard no more.

Behind this effort had come a parishwide cleanup. Brooms, rakes, hoes, mattocks, and shovels were toted in, along with fresh nursery stock to replace what had been damaged in the general upheaval.

During the windy, day-long workfest, someone discovered that the coreopsis was beginning to bloom, and Father Tim was heard to say that their little church looked ready to withstand another century with dignity and grace.

A New Song, Ch. 22

Father Tim and Cynthia Exchange Wedding Vows

IN THE NINTH row of the epistle side, next to the stained-glass window of Christ carrying the lost lamb, Hope Winchester blushed to recall her once-ardent crush on Father Tim. She'd taken every precaution to make certain he knew nothing of it, and now it seemed idiotic to have felt that way about someone twice her age.

She remembered the fluttering of her heart when he came into the bookstore, and all her hard work to learn special words that would intrigue him. She would never admit such a thing to another soul, but she believed herself to be the only person in Mitford who could converse on his level. When she'd learned about Cynthia months ago, she had forced herself to stop thinking such nonsense altogether, and was now truly happy that he and his neighbor had found each other. They seemed perfect together.

Still, on occasion, she missed her old habit of looking for him to pass the shop window and wave, or stop in; and she missed pondering what book she might order that would please and surprise him.

It wasn't that she'd ever wanted to marry him, for heaven's sake, or even be in love with him; it was just that he was so very kind and gentle and made her feel special. Plus he was a lot like herself, deep and sensitive, not to mention a lover of the romantic poets she'd adored since junior high. Early on, she had made it a point to read Wordsworth again, weeping over the Lucy poems, so she could quote passages and dig out morsels to attract his imagination.

"Come in out of the *fretful stir*!" she once said as he popped through the door at Happy Endings.

Your author at the age of five, wearing the great fashion of the day:
Shirley Temple curls. The locket was a gift from my great-aunt Hessie,
wife of one of the dearest men I've ever known,
Dr. Clarence Wilson.

*My grandmother Miss Fannie prior to the wedding of her
older sister, Jessie. My grandmother adored her sister, and wept the
livelong night before the photograph was taken. She made this lovely
frock with only scissors, a needle, and thread. I tried to capture
the loving spirit of my remarkable grandmother
in my children's book* Miss Fannie's Hat.
Fannie Belle Bush Cloer, 1893–1993

My beautiful mother, Wanda, who inherited her mother's skill with a needle and thread, once got up from the supper table, removed the cloth, and in nothing flat, made herself a gorgeous sundress. She also enjoys one of Queen Victoria's favorite pastimes of painting on porcelain, and writes poems and songs, lickety–split. Bakes a mean biscuit, too, and can still touch the floor with the palms of her hands.

My mother and father on their honeymoon in Virginia.

My grandmother on her one-hundredth birthday, being dressed by my mother, Wanda. No one who attended Miss Fannie's hilltop celebration will ever forget that wondrous day— it ended with fireworks. Miss Fannie went peacefully Home just three months later.

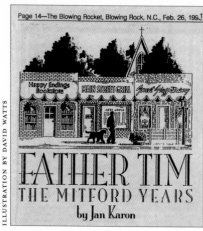

ILLUSTRATION BY DAVID WATTS

FATHER TIM
THE MITFORD YEARS
by Jan Karon

The Mitford series debuted in the early nineties in **The Blowing Rocket**, the village newspaper, which then sold for ten cents. Shades of Charles Dickens.

Father Tim's wife, Cynthia, who taught him a further meaning of the scriptural exhortation "Thou shalt love thy neighbor as thyself."

Uncle Billy liked to say his wife was the rose, and he, "the thorn."

Sweet Uncle Billy. One of my all-time favorite heroes.

Dr. Hoppy Harper. Since I can't really draw, think how handsome this good fellow would be if I could.

The Genghis Khan of church secretaries: Emma Garrett Newland.

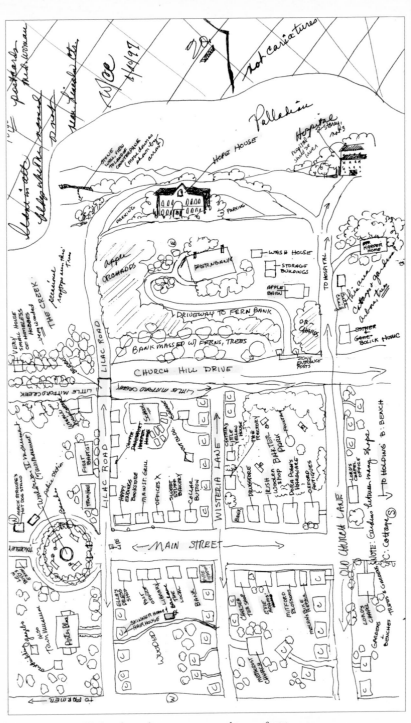

*Had to figure how to get around in my fictitious town,
so I drew this map on a piece of artist's tissue paper.*

I've always been an early riser. Some mornings the mist cloaks the ground in the most magical way, and I'm so grateful my daughter captured that moment for me in this picture.

PHOTOGRAPH BY CANDACE FREELAND

Here's a blessing I count every day. My four-year-old rescue pup, Gracie, is the "heartbeat at my feet."

We had twenty-six lambs this spring, including several sets of triplets and twins.

A companionable bust of Mr. Longfellow, who said, "Build today, then, strong and sure/with a firm and ample base/and ascending and secure/shall tomorrow find its place." Amen to that.

BELOW: With Candace, my daughter and dearest treasure. Many of the photographs in this section were made by Candace, who, like her mother, grandmother, and great-grandmother, is profoundly fond of people.

He had looked up and smiled. "Wordsworth!" he exclaimed, obviously pleased.

How many people would recognize two little words among a poet's thousands? She had felt positively thrilled.

Opening her purse, she examined the contents for the Kleenex she'd stuffed in at the last minute. Though she thought it fatuous to cry at weddings, she deemed it wise to be prepared.

In the fourth row of the epistle side, Gene Bolick wondered what on earth was going on. His watch said five-fifteen. He knew Richard well enough to know he was looking pale after hammering down on the organ all this time with nothing happening.

He glanced again at the bishop's wife, whose head was bowed. Was she praying that the father hadn't chickened out at the last minute? Wouldn't that be a corker if their priest was on a plane bound for the Azores? He didn't know where the Azores were located, but figured it was a distance.

Realizing his fists were clenched and his palms sweaty, he forced his attention to the three-layer orange marmalade cake sitting in the parish hall refrigerator, looking like a million bucks. He hoped to the Lord the temperature was set right and hadn't accidentally been switched to extra cool, which had once frozen two hundred pimiento cheese sandwiches as hard as hockey pucks. He nudged Esther, who appeared to be sleeping under the brim of the hat she wore only to weddings and funerals.

Esther was not sleeping, she was thinking, and ignored the nudge. Didn't she deserve to sit and catch her breath until these people got their act together and got on with it? She was thinking that maybe she'd put in too much sugar, she knew Father Tim didn't like too much sugar, but why, after all these years and hundreds of cakes later, did she still worry and fret over her work as if she'd never baked a cake in her life? The Expert is what some called her, but who could feel like an expert at something as willful and fickle as a cake, cakes having, as she'd always feared, a mind of their own? Use the same ingredients in the same amounts, time after time after time, and were her cakes ever the same? Not as far as she could see.

She'd always depended on Gene to be the judge and he hadn't

failed her yet. Gene would take a taste of the batter and his eyes would wander around the room, as if that little taste had transported him on some round of roving thoughts and idle speculation. After a while, he'd come back to himself. "Best yet!" he might say, or, "Couldn't be better!"

Whatever he said, he would have reasoned it out, thought it through, and she could depend on the answer—which was more than most wives could say of their husbands. Now, you take Father Tim, his wife would be able to depend on him—the only question was, was she deserving of such a prize? She thought she was, she hoped she was; she was crazy about Cynthia, but hadn't her senator husband, or was he a congressman, run around with other women? What did that mean? Cynthia didn't look like a cold fish—the opposite, more like it.

Anyway, didn't their rector have enough sense to come in out of the rain and choose who he wanted to spend the rest of his life with? And in the last few months, hadn't she and everybody else in the parish heard him laugh and joke like never before?

Lord help, it must be virgin's bower that was making her eyes burn and her sinuses drain. Virgin's bower mixed with lilies, the bane of her existence, and nobody with the simple courtesy to remove the pollen from the anthers, which means it would be flying around in here like so much snuff, and her with no Sinu-Tabs in her pocketbook and too late to do anything about it.

Pete Jamison made his way into the nave of Lord's Chapel, where a robed and expectant choir overflowed from the narthex. Embarrassed at being late, he dodged through the throng to the rear wall and stood, reverent and shaken, feeling at once a stranger here and also oddly at home. He realized his breath was coming in shallow gasps, probably because he'd run more than a block from the Collar Button where he'd parked—or was it from the excitement he felt in being here for the first time since his life had been changed forever?

Two rows from the front, on the gospel side, Miss Sadie sat holding hands with Louella, oblivious of the time and enjoying the music. She felt certain that the emotions stirring in her breast were those of any proud mother.

After all, Father Tim wasn't merely her priest, her brother in Christ, and one of the dearest friends of this life, he was also like a son. Who else would run up the hill after a hard rain and empty the soup kettle sitting brimful under the leak in her ceiling? And who else would sit for hours listening to her ramble, while appearing to be genuinely interested? God in His Providence had not seen fit to bless her with children, but He'd given her Olivia Harper and Timothy Kavanagh! And, since she'd helped raise Louella from a baby, she could almost count her pewmate as her child—Lord knows, she wasn't but ten years old when she'd begun diapering and dressing that little dark baby as if it were her own!

Miss Sadie wiped a tear with the handkerchief she had carefully chosen for the occasion, a lace-trimmed square of white Irish linen monogrammed with her mother's initial, and turned and smiled proudly at Louella, who looked a perfect blossom in the lavender dress.

Dooley Barlowe swallowed hard. It would have been fine if everything had started when it was supposed to, but here it was twenty minutes after five and who knew where Cynthia and Father Tim were, like maybe they both got scared and ran off, or had a fight and weren't going through with it. He felt foolish sitting here in the front row, all of them tricked into waiting like a bunch of stupid goats, listening to organ music. He was about to die to go to the toilet, but if he tried now to make it to the parish hall, everybody would know where he was going.

He crossed his legs and squeezed his eyes shut and jiggled his foot and went through the verses again.

Reverend Absalom Greer had purposely followed Sadie Eleanor Baxter into the nave, though he tried to appear as if he had no idea she was anywhere around. He followed her so he could sit behind her and look at her again. Who knows when the Lord might call him Home and this would be his last chance on earth to see her face?

The way it fell out was, he was the first to go into the pew behind her, which meant he had to sit all the way to the end, by the window of Jesus washing the disciples' feet. He thought this location was a blessing from above, seeing as he could look at her in profile instead of at the little gray knot on the back of her head.

Absalom felt such a stirring in his breast that he might have been fourteen years old, going up Hogback to see Annie Hawkins, carrying two shot quails and a mess of turnips in a poke. Annie's mama was dead of pneumonia and her daddy not heard of since the Flood, and as Annie was left to raise a passel of brothers and sisters, he never went up Hogback without victuals; once he'd killed a deer and helped her skin it and jerk the meat.

It had taken him three years to get over big-boned, sassy-mouthed Annie Hawkins, but he'd never gotten over Sadie Baxter. Sadie had filled his dreams, his waking hours, his prayers for many a year; he'd earnestly hoped she would forget Willard Porter and marry him. Finally, the burning hope had fizzled into a kind of faint glow that lay on his heart like embers, making him smile occasionally and nod his head and whisper her name. He'd confessed this lingering and soulful love only to the Almighty and never told another, though sometimes his sister, Lottie, suspicioned how he was feeling and derided him with a cool stare.

Reverend Greer settled stiffly into the creaking pew and nodded to those around him and bowed his head and prayed for his dear brother in the Lord, Tim Kavanagh, as fine a man as God ever gave breath to, amen. When he lifted his head and looked at Sadie's profile and the tender smile on her face, the tears sprang instantly to his eyes and he fetched the handkerchief from his pocket, the handkerchief Lottie had starched and ironed 'til it crackled like paper, and thanked the Lord Jesus that he still had eyes to see and tears to wipe, hallelujah.

Pete Jamison, though six feet three, eased himself up on the balls of his feet so he could see down front to the gospel side. He found the pew where he sat the day he had wandered, alarmed and desperate, into the darkened church. It had been sometime around Thanksgiving and there was snow on the ground; he remembered noticing his incoming tracks as he left the church a different man, one to whom everything seemed fresh and new.

He'd knelt that day and cried out to God, asking a simple question: *Are you up there?* He wasn't trying to get anything from God, he wasn't begging for money or success, though at the time he urgently needed both, he just wanted to know more desperately than he'd ever wanted to know anything in his life, if God was up there—no more ifs, ands, or buts, just *yes or no*. Now he knew the answer more completely than he could ever have hoped or imagined.

He felt tears smart his eyes, and his heart expand. The music was beginning to enter him; he was beginning to hear it over the pounding of his heart, and was glad to feel the joy of this time and place as if it might, in some small way, belong also to him.

Standing outside the church door in the warm September afternoon, Katherine Kavanagh saw the bride and groom literally galloping down the street, and suppressed a shout of relief. She tugged on her skirt for the umpteenth time and tried to relax her tense shoulders so the jacket would fall below her waistline. In the desperate half hour she'd waited for Cynthia to show up, she had decided what to do. The minute she returned home, she was suing the airline, who had gotten away with their criminal behavior long enough.

Though wanting very much to dash across the churchyard and meet Cynthia, she realized this impetuous behavior would cause her skirt to ride up. She stood, therefore, frozen as a mullet as she watched the bride sprinting into the home stretch.

Next to the aisle on the epistle side, Emma Newland nearly jumped out of her seat as the organ cranked up to a mighty roar. The thirty-seven-voice ecumenical choir was at last processing in, sending a blast of energy through the congregation as if someone had fired a cannon.

The congregation shot to its feet, joining the choir in singing hymn number 410 with great abandon and unmitigated relief:

> *Praise my Soul the King of Heaven;*
> *To His feet thy tribute bring;*
> *Ransomed, healed, restored, forgiven,*
> *Evermore His praises sing;*
> *Alleluia, alleluia!*
> *Praise the everlasting King!*

Dooley Barlowe felt something happen to the top of his head. He had opened his mouth with the rest of the congregation and heard

words flow out in a strong and steady voice he scarcely recognized as
his own.

> *Praise Him for His grace and favor;*
> *To His people in distress;*
> *Praise Him still the same as ever,*
> *Slow to chide and swift to bless.*
> *Alleluia, alleluia,*
> *Glorious in His faithfulness.*

Dooley thought Father's Tim's voice carried loud and clear from
where he stood with the bishop and Walter at the rail. The bishop was
decked out in a really weird hat, but looked cool as anything otherwise. As for Father Tim, he'd never seen him in a tuxedo before and
thought he looked . . . *different,* maybe sort of handsome.

The tremor in his stomach subsided; he felt suddenly tall and victorious and forgot about having to go to the toilet.

Hessie Mayhew gazed at Stuart Cullen, whom she found exceedingly good-looking, and thought it was a darned good thing that Episcopal clergy were allowed to marry, otherwise it could cause a rumpus.
She'd never chased after clergy like some women she knew, but she
couldn't dismiss their powerful attraction, either. Anyway, who'd want
to tie the knot with a preacher and end up with a whole churchful of
people pulling you to pieces day and night? *Head this, chair that!* No,
indeed, no clergy for her, thank you very much.

She fluffed her scarf over the odd rash that had appeared on her
neck, dismissing it as one of the several hazards of her calling, and
hoped the bishop was noticing the flowers and that someone would tell
him about Hessie Mayhew, who, even if she was Presbyterian, knew a
thing or two about the right and proper way to beautify a church.

> *Angels, help us to adore Him;*
> *Ye behold Him face to face;*
> *Sun and moon, bow down before Him,*
> *Dwellers in all time and space.*
> *Alleluia, alleluia!*
> *Praise with us the God of grace.*

Jenna Ivey could not carry a tune in a bucket and preferred to look at the stained-glass window for the duration of the processional hymn. The window was of Christ being baptized while John the Baptist stood onshore in his animal skin outfit. It seemed to her that St. John could have presented himself better, seeing it was the Lord Jesus who was getting baptized; like it wasn't as if St. John didn't know He was coming, for Pete's sake. Look at the three wise men, who always appeared nicely groomed, though they'd been riding camels for *two years*.

She was startled by the sound of the trumpet only a few feet away, causing, simultaneously, an outbreak of goose bumps and a wild pounding of her heart.

Then, suddenly, there was the matron of honor charging down the aisle; Jenna didn't have a clue who this woman might be, she was tall as a giraffe. That's the way it was with weddings, they turned out people you'd never seen before in your life and would never see again.

Emma thought the matron of honor blew past like she was going to a fire, canceling any opportunity to study the skimpy cut of Katherine Kavanagh's suit, or to check out the kind of shoes she had on. She did, however, get a whiff of something that wasn't flowers, it was definitely perfume, possibly from Macy's or some such.

Then came Rebecca Jane Owen and Amy Larkin, wearing velvet hair bows the color of green Baxter apples. As far as Emma could tell, they were fairly smothered with flowers; you'd think Hessie Mayhew would scale down for children, but oh, no, Hessie scaled up, these two infants were fairly tottering under the weight of what looked like full bushes of hydrangeas.

Jabbing Harold to do the same, Emma swiveled her head to see the bride trotting behind the small entourage.

Cynthia Coppersmith was flushed as a girl—her eyes shining, her face expectant, her hair curled damply around her face as if she'd just won a game of tag. Emma thought she looked sixteen years old if she was a day, and her suit was exactly the color of a crayon Emma had favored in first grade, aquamarine. She appeared to be moving fast, but that was all right—hadn't she herself run lickety-split to marry Harold Newland, starved to death for affection after ten years of widowhood and thrilled at the prospect of someone to hug her neck every night?

Emma leaned over the arm of the pew so she could see Father Tim as his bride approached the altar. The look on his face made her want to shut her eyes, as if she'd intruded upon something terribly precious and private.

"Dearly beloved, we have come together in the presence of God to witness and bless the joining together of this man and this woman in Holy Matrimony. The bond and covenant of marriage was established by God in creation, and our Lord Jesus Christ adorned this manner of life by His presence and first miracle at a wedding in Cana of Galilee. It signifies to us the mystery of the union between Christ and His Church, and Holy Scripture commends it to be honored among all people.

"The union of husband and wife in heart, body, and mind is intended by God for their mutual joy; for the help and comfort given one another in prosperity and adversity; and, when it is God's will, for the procreation of children and their nurture in the knowledge and love of the Lord. Therefore marriage is not to be entered into unadvisedly or lightly, but reverently, deliberately, and in accordance with the purposes for which it was instituted by God.

"Into this holy union, Cynthia Clary Coppersmith and Timothy Andrew Kavanagh now come to be joined. . . ."

Uncle Billy Watson hoped and prayed his wife would not fall asleep and snore; it was all he could do to keep his own eyes open. Sitting with so many people in a close church on a close afternoon was nearabout more than a man could handle. He kept alert by asking himself a simple question: When it came time, would he have mustard on his ham, or eat it plain?

"Cynthia, will you have this man to be your husband; to live together in the covenant of marriage? Will you love him, comfort him, honor and keep him, in sickness and in health; and, forsaking all others, be faithful to him as long as you both shall live?"

Winnie Ivey clasped her hand over her heart and felt tears burn her cheeks. To think that God would give this joy to people as old as herself and no spring chickens . . .

The bride's vow was heard clearly throughout the nave. "I will!"

"Timothy, will you have this woman to be your wife; to live together in the covenant of marriage? Will you love her, comfort her, honor and keep her, in sickness and in health; and, forsaking all others, be faithful to her as long as you both shall live?"

"I will!"

"Will all of you witnessing these promises do all in your power to uphold these two persons in their marriage?"

"We will!"

At the congregational response, Dooley Barlowe quickly left the front pew by the sacristy door and took his place in front of the altar rail. As he faced the cross and bowed, one knee trembled slightly, but he locked it in place and drew a deep breath.

Don't let me mess up, he prayed, then opened his mouth and began to sing.

> *Oh, perfect Love, all human thought transcending,*
> *Lowly we kneel in prayer before Thy throne,*
> *That theirs may be the love which knows no ending,*
> *Whom Thou forevermore dost join in one.*

It all sounded lovey-dovey, thought Emma, but she knew one thing—it would never work if Cynthia sat around drawing cats while her husband wanted his dinner! Oh, Lord, she was doing it again, and this time without intending to; she was running down a person who didn't have a mean bone in her body. She closed her eyes and asked forgiveness.

She'd held on to her reservations about Cynthia like a tightwad squeezes a dollar, but she felt something in her heart finally giving way as if floodgates were opening, and she knew at last that she honestly approved of the union that would bind her priest's heart for all eternity. Disgusted with herself for having forgotten to bring a proper handkerchief, Emma mopped her eyes with a balled-up napkin from Pizza Hut.

> *Oh, perfect Life, be Thou their full assurance*
> *Of tender charity and steadfast faith,*
> *Of patient hope and quiet, brave endurance,*
> *With childlike trust that fears nor pain nor death.*

Pete Jamison pondered the words "childlike trust that fears nor pain nor death," and knew that's what he'd been given the day he'd cried out to God in this place and God had answered by sending Father Kavanagh. He remembered distinctly what the father had said: "You may be asking the wrong question. What you may want to ask is, Are You down here?"

He'd prayed a prayer that day with the father, a simple thing, and was transformed forever, able now to stand in this place knowing without any doubt at all that, yes, God is down here and faithfully with us. He remembered the prayer as if he'd uttered it only yesterday. *Thank you, God, for loving me, and for sending Your son to die for my sins. I sincerely repent of my sins, and receive Christ as my personal savior. Now, as Your child, I turn my entire life over to You.* He'd never been one to surrender anything, yet that day, he had surrendered everything. When the church was quiet and the celebration over, he'd go down front and kneel in the same place he'd knelt before, and give thanks.

Gene Bolick wondered how a man Father Tim's age would be able to keep up his husbandly duties. As for himself, all he wanted to do at night was hit his recliner after supper and sleep 'til bedtime. Maybe the father knew something he didn't know. . . .

Louella heard people all around her sniffling and blowing their noses, it was a regular free-for-all. And Miss Sadie, she was the worst of the whole kaboodle, bawling into her mama's handkerchief to beat the band. Miss Sadie loved that little redheaded, freckle-face white boy because he reminded her of Willard Porter, who came up hard like Dooley and ended up amounting to something.

Louella thought Miss Cynthia looked beautiful in her dressy suit; and that little bit of shimmering thread in the fabric and those jeweled buttons, now, that was something, that was nice, and look there, she wasn't wearing shoes dyed to match, she was wearing black pumps as smart as you please. Louella knew from reading the magazines Miss Olivia brought to Fernbank that shoes dyed to match were out of style.

It seemed to her that the sniffling was getting worse by the minute, and no wonder—just *listen* to that boy sing! Louella settled back in the pew, personally proud of Dooley, Miss Cynthia, the father, and the whole shooting match.

Finally deciding on mustard, Uncle Billy abandoned the game. He'd better come up with another way to noodle his noggin or he'd drop off in a sleep so deep they'd have to knock him upside the head with a two-by-four. He determined to mentally practice his main joke, and if that didn't work, he was done for.

> *Grant them the joy which brightens earthly sorrow,*
> *Grant them the peace which calms all earthly strife,*
> *And to life's day the glorious unknown morrow*
> *That dawns upon eternal love and life.*
> *Amen.*

Dooley returned to his pew without feeling the floor beneath his feet. He was surprised to find he was trembling, as if he'd been live-wired. But it wasn't fear, anymore, it was . . . something else.

* * *

Father Tim took Cynthia's right hand in his, and carefully spoke the words he had never imagined might be his own.

"In the name of God, I, Timothy, take you, Cynthia, to be my wife, to have and to hold from this day forward, for better for worse, for richer for poorer, in sickness and in health, to love and to cherish, until we are parted by death.

"This is my solemn vow."

They loosed their hands for a moment, a slight movement that caused the candle flames on the altar to tremble. Then she took his right hand in hers.

"In the name of God, I, Cynthia, take you, Timothy, to be my husband, to have and to hold from this day forward, for better for worse, for richer for poorer, in sickness and in health, to love and to cherish, until we are parted by death.

"This is my solemn vow."

As Walter presented the ring to the groom, the bishop raised his right hand. "Bless, O Lord, these rings to be a sign of the vows by which this man and this woman have bound themselves to each other; through Jesus Christ our Lord, Amen."

"Cynthia, I give you this ring as a symbol of my vow, and with all that I am, and all that I have, I honor you, in the name of the Father, and of the Son, and of the Holy Spirit."

She felt the worn gold ring slipping on her finger; it seemed weightless, a band of silk.

Katherine stepped forward then, delivering the heavy gold band with the minuscule engraving upon its inner circle: *Until heaven and then forever.*

"Timothy . . . I give you this ring as a symbol of my vow, and with all that I am, and all that I have, I honor you, in the name of the Father, and of the Son, and of the Holy Spirit."

Hessie Mayhew was convinced the bishop looked right into her eyes as he spoke.

"Now that Cynthia and Timothy have given themselves to each other by solemn vows, with the joining of hands and the giving and receiving of rings, I pronounce that they are husband and wife, in the name of the Father, and of the Son, and of the Holy Spirit.

"Those whom God has joined together . . . let no man put asunder."

Dooley felt the lingering warmth in his face and ears, and heard the pounding of his heart. No, it wasn't fear anymore, it was something else, and he thought he knew what it was.

It was something maybe like . . . happiness.

A Common Life, Ch. 9

A Christmas Eve Party at the Main Street Grill

"Surpri-i-ise!"

"Here we come, ready or not!"

A Mitford crowd always arrived early, and today was no exception.

"Merry Christmas!"

"Surprise! Surprise!"

Pass It On

My grandmother, Miss Fannie, passed on her lovely old spinning wheel to me.

She also passed on her mother's large black comb, her grandfather's homemade wedding band, and boxes of her own stylish hats.

Though precious, all these things are but things. Her most important legacy was the example of her shining faith in God, made known through Jesus Christ.

Her faith was frequently expressed in the stories she told.

For example, when Mama was in her nineties, she woke up one morning completely blind in her left eye. As she was being examined by the eye doctor, who didn't offer any especially good news, she told me she had a sudden and wonderful revelation.

"God can do it!" she blurted to the ophthalmologist.

She believed without any doubt that God could restore sight to her eye—which, of course, He soon did.

She told this seemingly simple story again and again, which encouraged my own faith. Which reminds me of a wise and gentle exhortation from Deuteronomy:

Be very careful never to forget what you have seen the Lord do for you. Do not let these things escape from your mind as long as you live! And be sure to pass them on to your children and grandchildren.

—Deuteronomy 4:9

"We ain't hardly got th' dishes washed," said Percy, drying his hands on his apron.

"Take that apron *off*, it's party time!" Lois Holshouser, who was retired from teaching drama at Wesley High and wanted more fun in her life, untied Percy's apron and flung it over the counter where it landed on a cake box.

"Surprise!" yelled an arriving partygoer.

"It *ain't* a *su'prise*," said Percy, who was tired of hearing that it was.

"How come?" asked Mule. "We told people not to leak it to a livin' soul."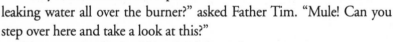

Velma, who had obviously spent the better part of the morning at Fancy Skinner's, peered over her glasses. "Blabbermouth Bradshaw let th' cat out of th' bag."

"Why is this blasted coffeepot leaking water all over the burner?" asked Father Tim. "Mule! Can you step over here and take a look at this?"

"I'm cuttin' cake, buddyroe. Ask Percy."

"Percy's worked this counter for forty years. I'm giving him a break."

"Suit yourself, it's runnin' down on th' floor."

Blast! He flipped the switch to "Off."

Ray Cunningham helped himself to a counter stool. "I hear coffee's on th' house! I'll have a little shooter, and one for your former mayor here."

"Ray, good to see you!" said Father Tim. "Esther, do you know how to work this blasted coffee maker?" Their former mayor could fix anything, including people's lives.

"Let me get back there," said Esther. "I'll handle this."

Mitford's former mayor had the coffeepot up and running and was pouring and serving as if she were campaigning for office. "Percy, you ol' coot, where'm I supposed to get a decent bowl of grits for breakfast?"

"Beats me," said Percy. "An' don't count on gettin' grits in Wesley, they're educated over there at th' college an' don't eat grits."

People were clearly happy to see their former mayor back in the thick of things, especially as their current mayor had been called to a social event at the governor's mansion.

"Congratulations, you dog!" Omer Cunningham, aviator, bon vivant, and in-law of former mayor Esther Cunningham, waded through the crowd, his big teeth gleaming like a piano keyboard. "Where are you an' Velma headed off to?" Omer gave Percy a slap on the back that nearly knocked him into the drink box.

"After gettin' up at four o'clock every mornin' for a hundred years, I'm headed off t' lay down an' sleep 'til Groundhog Day. Velma, she's headed off to th' pet shelter for a dadblame cat."

"Don't get a cat, get a dog!" someone urged.

"Don't get a dog, get a monkey!"

"Don't get nothin'," counseled the fire chief. "Animals strap you down—get somethin' with four legs an' you'll never see th' cherry blossoms, trust me."

Percy eyed the room—the booths and stools had filled up and there was standing room only. Where were these turkeys when business had gone south a couple of times last summer?

"Speech! Speech!" someone hollered from the rear.

"Hold it!" J. C. Hogan blew in the front door, ushering a blast of arctic air into the assembly. "Make way for the press!"

"Oh, law," whispered Minnie Lomax, "it's J. C. Hogan—he wants to be th' bride at every weddin' and th' corpse at every funeral."

A blinding flash went off, then another, and another.

"Stand over there with Velma," ordered the editor. "Velma, look here an' give me a big grin! I know it's hard for you to grin at me, but force yourself, there you go, Betty Grable lives. Okay, let's have a shot of Percy at th' grill. Hey, Mule, move your big rear out of this shot an' let Percy flip somethin' on the grill. . . ."

"His last flip!" said Coot Hendrick.

Lois Holshouser wrinkled her nose. "Who made this cake? Esther Bolick didn't have anything to do with this cake, I can tell you that right now."

"Store-bought," said Winnie Ivey Kendall, who was not having any.

"Whose hat is this?" inquired Avis Packard. "Somebody handed me this hat. Is this your hat?"

"You're supposed to put somethin' in it."

"Like what?"

"Money. For th' cherry blossoms."

"What cherry blossoms?"

Faye Tuttle announced a relative's sad news to Esther Cunningham. "Multiple dystrophy," said Faye, shaking her head.

J.C. mopped his brow with a paper napkin and handed off his Nikon camera to Lew Boyd. "Here you go, buddyroe, you won that big photo contest, crank off a shot of th' Turkey Club with Percy an' Velma. Come on, Mule, come on, Father, get over here. That's it, look right through there and push th' button. . . ."

Flash. Flash.

"Speech! Speech!"

Hand clapping, foot stomping. A spoon ringing against a coffee mug.

"I've made plenty of speeches th' last forty-four years," said Percy, "an' you've done forgot everything I said.

"So I ain't makin' a speech t'day except to say . . ."

In all his years as a regular, Father Tim had never seen Percy Mosely choke up. In case it was catching, he grabbed his handkerchief from his jacket pocket.

". . . except to say . . ."

"What'd he say?" asked someone in the rear.

". . . to say . . ."

"Looks like he can't say it."

It was catching, all right. Father Tim peered around and saw several people wiping their eyes. Velma pushed forward from the crowd. "What he's tryin' to say is, thanks for th' memories."

"Right!" said Percy, blowing his nose.

Applause. Whistles.

"Great speech!" said Coot.

Shepherds Abiding, Ch. 9

The Death of Uncle Billy

"FATHER?"

He glanced at the clock: four a.m.

"Can you come?"

"I'm on my way."

Though he'd been called out in the middle of the night only a dozen or so times in his priesthood, he resolutely adhered to a common practice of fire chiefs—he kept a shirt and pair of pants at the ready, and his shoes and socks by the bed.

He was entering the town limits when he realized he'd just blown past a Mitford police officer.

No need to be surprised, he thought, when he saw the blue light in his rearview mirror.

The officer stooped down to peer in the window. "You were haulin'."

Clearly, Rodney Underwood had begun hiring people twelve years old and under.

"I was, officer. I'm sorry." He adjusted his tab collar, to make sure the officer noticed he was clergy. "It's Uncle Billy." To his surprise, tears suddenly streamed down his cheeks.

"Uncle Billy?"

"One of the most important people in Mitford. He's dying; Dr. Harper called me to come."

"Don't let it happen again."

"Certainly not."

The young turk shook his head, as if greatly mystified.

"I don' know what it is about preachers. All y'all seem t' have a lead foot."

* * *

In his room at Mitford Hospital, Uncle Billy tried to recollect which-away th' lawyer joke started off. Was th' lawyer a-drivin' down th' road when he hit a groundhog, or was he a-walkin' down th' road? An' was it a groundhog or was it a sow pig?

His joke tellin' days was givin' out, that's all they was to it.

He looked at the ceiling which appeared to be thick with lowering clouds, and with something like geese flying south.

Winter must be a-comin'. Seem like winter done come a week or two ago, and here it was a-comin' ag'in, hit was enough t' rattle a man's brains th' way things kep' a-changin'.

He shivered suddenly and pulled the covers to his chin.

Snow clouds, that's what they was! Hit's goin' t' come a big snow or worser yet, a gulley-washin' rain.

Bill Watson! What are you yammering about?

He hadn't opened his trap, as far as he knowed. Out of the corner of his eye, he could see her settin' up in th' bed next t' his 'un, lookin' like a witch on a broom.

Did you say it's going to snow?

He lay as still as a buck in hunting season, and pressed his lips together so no words could escape.

Are you talking to yourself or to me, Bill Watson?

No, dadgummit, I ain't a-talkin' t' you, I ain't said a word t' you! Lord knows, you've fretted me 'til I'm wore to a nubbin. Now, *lay down!*

He squeezed his eyes shut even tighter, in case they popped open and she saw that he was awake.

In a little bit, he'd try an' git his mind back t' th' joke about th' lawyer, maybe he'd stir up a laugh or two if anybody come a-knockin' on th' door, like maybe Preacher Kavanagh.

He breathed easier, then, and opened his eyes and gazed again at the ceiling. The geese had disappeared.

Gone south!

"*Hush my* mouth?" squawked his wife.

He felt a chill go up his spine; he reckoned 'is wife was *a-readin' 'is mind*!

He'd never heered of such a low trick as that!

Lord have mercy, they was no end to it.

He didn't know when he realized he was passing up through a cloud, like a feather floating upward on a mild breeze.

There was light ahead, and the cloud felt like his toaster oven set on low, just nice and warm, as it was a long time ago in his mama's arms.

He kept his eyes squeezed shut so he wouldn't see the ceiling coming at him, then reckoned he must have floated right through it as easy as you please.

The light was getting stronger now. He found it odd that it didn't hurt his eyes one bit; indeed, it felt good, like it was making his worn-out eyes brand-new. . . .

Uncle Billy felt a hand close over his own. It was a touch that seemed familiar somehow. . . .

The Almighty and merciful Lord . . .

Now, he was in the topmost branches of an apple tree, throwing apples down to his little sister, Maisie, and over yonder was his mama, waiting for him. . . .

. . . grant thee pardon and remission of thy sins . . .

It seemed the words came from a very great distance. . . .

He knew only that he was happy, very happy; his heart was about to burst. He tried to utter some word that would express the joy. . . .

". . . and the grace and comfort of the Holy Spirit," said Father Tim. "Amen."

His voice sounded hollow in the empty room.

* * *

The following morning, Mitford learned that two of their own had been taken in the night.

William Benfield Watson had died in his sleep with a smile on his face, and in so doing, had attained the chief aim of every soul who desires a peaceful passing.

Less than an hour later, Gene Bolick died of the causal effects of an inoperable brain tumor. His wife, Esther, worn beyond telling, had left the hospital only a short time earlier at the insistence of the nursing staff.

It was Nurse Herman who stood at Gene's bedside when he spoke his last words.

"Tell Esther . . ."

Nurse Herman leaned down to hear his hoarse whisper.

". . . to pay the power bill."

Nurse Herman didn't know whether to share with Esther these pragmatic sentiments; the bereft widow might have hoped for something more.

Yet her greater concern was that Esther's power might, indeed, be shut off—not a good thing with so many family and friends dropping by.

Thus, with the blessing of Dr. Harper, she recited these last words to Esther, and was vastly relieved when the grieving and exhausted widow thanked her for the reminder.

"Are you sure that's all he said?" Esther mopped her eyes with a wadded-up section of hospital toilet paper.

As ardently as Nurse Herman wanted to report something truly heartwarming, the truth was the truth. "Yes, ma'am, that's all."

Indeed, she had long kept a memorized selection of made-up last words to offer a bereaved family—but only if absolutely, positively necessary.

In this case, *Tell Esther I love her* would have been very nice, though basic.

Tell Esther I appreciate all the years she devoted herself to my happiness would be more flowery, but not completely believable, as Mr. Bolick hadn't been the flowery type.

Tell Esther I'll see her in heaven would be tricky, as it was sometimes impossible to figure who was going to heaven and who was going to the other place.

And then there was her personal favorite: *Tell Esther she was the light of my life.*

She had heard of people saying amazing things as they passed. She would never forget being told in seventh grade what Thomas Edison had said: "It it is very beautiful over there."

That sort of remark was comforting to those left behind; she wished dying patients would say things like that more often.

In any case, she had told Esther the plain truth and, happy to have these odd last words off her chest, reported further that Mr. Bolick had looked peaceful, very peaceful, and had not struggled at the end.

Light from Heaven, Ch. 13

Uncle Billy's Funeral

THE LOSS OF Uncle Billy signaled the end of an era. But an era of what? Something like innocence, he thought, poring over the burial service.

Uncle Billy's rich deposit of memory had included a time when kith and kin went barefoot in summer and, if money was short, even in winter; when pies and cobblers were always made from scratch and berries were picked from the fields; when young boys set forth with a gun or a trap or a fishing pole and toted home a meal, proud as any man to provision the family table; when the late-night whistle of a train still stirred the imagination and haunted the soul. . . .

He sat at the desk in the Meadowgate library and considered the jokes Uncle Billy had diligently rounded up over the years, and told to one and all. Of the legions, he remembered only the census taker and gas stove jokes, the latter worthy, in his personal opinion, of the Clean Joke Hall of Fame, if there was such a thing.

It would certainly be an unusual addition to the 1928 prayer book office for the burial of the dead, but he was following his heart on this one.

He called Miss Rose and asked permission, not an easy task right there. Then he leafed through the Mitford phone book, jotting down numbers.

* * *

What if he carried forth this foolish notion and no one laughed? Would that dishonor the man they'd come to honor?

"Psalm Fifteen," he told the graveside gathering, "says 'the cheerful heart hath a continual feast.' And Proverbs seventeen twenty-two asserts that 'a merry heart doeth good like a medicine.'

"Indeed, one of the translations of that proverb reads 'a cheerful disposition is good for your health; gloom and doom leave you bone-tired.'

"Bill Watson spent his life modeling a better way to live, a healthier way, really, by inviting us to share in a continual feast of laughter. Sadder even than the loss of this old friend, is that most of us never really got it, never quite understood the sweet importance of this simple, yet profound ministry in which he faithfully persevered.

"Indeed, the quality I loved best about our good brother was his faithful perseverance.

"When the tide seemed to turn against loving, he loved anyway. When doing the wrong thing was far easier than doing the right thing, he did the right thing anyway. And when circumstances sought to prevail against laughter, he laughed anyway.

"I'm reminded of how an ardent cook loves us with her cooking or baking, just as Esther Bolick has loved so many with her orange marmalade cakes. In the same way, Uncle Billy loved us with his jokes. And oh, how he *relished* making us laugh, *prayed* to make us laugh! And we did.

"I hope you'll pitch in with me to remember Bill Watson with a few of his favorite jokes. We have wept and we will weep again over the loss of his warm and loyal friendship. But I know he's safe in the arms of our Lord, Jesus Christ, precisely where God promises that each of His children will be after death.

"This wondrous truth is something to joyfully celebrate. And I invite us to celebrate with laughter. May its glad music waft heavenward, expressing our heartfelt gratitude for the unique and tender gift of William . . . Benfield . . . Watson."

He nodded to Old Man Mueller, who, only a few years ago, had regularly sat on the Porter place lawn with Uncle Billy and watched cars circle the monument.

The elderly man stood in his ancient jacket and best trousers and cleared his throat and looked around at the forty other souls gathered under the tent on this unseasonably hot day.

"Feller went to a doctor and told 'im what all was wrong."

He sneezed, and dug a beleaguered handkerchief from his pants pocket.

"So, th' doctor give 'im a whole lot of advice about how t' git well." He proceeded to blow his nose with considerable diligence.

"In a little bit, th' feller started t' leave an' th' doctor says, 'Hold on! You ain't paid me f'r my *ad*vice.' Feller said, 'That's right, b'cause I ain't goin' t' *take* it!'"

Old Man Mueller sat down hard on the metal folding chair, under which his dog, Luther, was sleeping. A gentle breeze moved beneath the tent.

I've stepped in it, now, thought Father Tim. Not a soul laughed—or for that matter, even smiled. He prayed silently as Percy Mosely rose and straightened the collar of his knit shirt.

Percy wished to the dickens he'd worn a jacket and tie, it hadn't even occurred to him until he stood up here to make a fool of himself. But if he was going to be a fool, he wanted to be the best fool he could possibly be—for Uncle Billy's sake. "Put your heart in it!" Father Tim had said.

"A deputy sheriff caught a tourist drivin' too fast, don't you know. Well, sir, he pulled th' tourist over an' said, 'Where're you from?' Th' tourist said, 'Chicago.' 'Don't try pullin' that stuff on me,' said th' deputy. 'Your license plate says lllinoise!'"

Percy swayed slightly on his feet as a wave of sheer terror passed over him. Had he done it? Had he told the joke? His mind was a blank. He sat down.

In the back row, the mayor's secretary giggled, but glanced at the coffin and clapped her hand over her mouth. The Mitford postmaster, whose mother lived in Illinois, chuckled.

The vicar crossed himself.

Solemn as a judge, J. C. Hogan rose to his feet and wiped his perspiring forehead with a handkerchief. He wouldn't do this for just anybody, no way, but he'd do it for Uncle Billy. In his opinion, Uncle Billy was an out-and-out hero to have lived with that old crone for a hundred years.

The editor buttoned the suit jacket he'd just unbuttoned; if he was a drinking man, he'd have had a little shooter before this thing got rolling. And what was he supposed to do, anyway? Talk like Uncle Billy, or talk like himself? He decided to do a combo deal.

"Did you hear the one about the guy who hit his first golf ball and made a hole in one? Well, sir, he th'owed that club down an' stomped off, said, 'Shoot, they ain't nothin' *to* this game, I *quit!*'"

The postmaster laughed out loud. The mayor's secretary cackled like a laying hen. Avis Packard, seated in the corner by the tent pole, let go with what sounded like a guffaw.

The golfers in the crowd had been identified.

Exhausted, J.C. thumped into the metal chair.

The vicar felt a rivulet of sweat running down his back. And where was his own laughter? He had blabbed on and on about the consolations of laughter, and not a peep out of yours truly who'd concocted this notion in the first place.

Mule Skinner stood, nodded to the crowd, took a deep breath, and cleared his throat. This was his favorite Uncle Billy joke, hands down, and he was honored to tell it—if he could remember it. That was the trick. When he practiced it last night on Fancy, he left a gaping hole in the middle which made the punch line go south.

"A ol' man and a ol' woman was settin' on th' porch, don't you know."

Heads nodded. This was one of Uncle Billy's classics.

"Th' ol' woman said, 'You know what I'd like t' have?' Ol' man said, 'What's 'at?'

"She says, 'A big ol' bowl of vaniller ice cream with choc'late sauce an' nuts on top!'"

Uncle Billy, himself, couldn't do it better! thought the vicar.

"He says, 'By jing, I'll jis' go down t' th' store an' git us some.' She says, 'You better write that down or you'll fergit it!' He says, 'I ain't goin' t' fergit it.'

"Went to th' store, come back a good bit later with a paper sack. Hands it over, she looks in there, sees two ham san'wiches."

Several people sat slightly forward on their folding chairs.

"She lifted th' top off one of them san'wiches, says, 'Dadgummit, I told you you'd fergit! I wanted mustard on mine!'"

The whole company roared with laughter, save Miss Rose, who sat stiff and frowning on the front row.

"That was my favorite Uncle Billy joke!" someone exclaimed.

Coot Hendrick stood for a moment, and sat back down. He didn't think he could go through with this. But he didn't want to show disrespect to Uncle Billy's memory.

He stood again, cleared his throat, scratched himself—and went for it.

"A farmer was haulin' manure, don't you know, an' 'is truck broke down in front of a mental institution. One of th' patients, he leaned over th' fence an' said, 'What're you goin' t' do with that manure?'

"Farmer said, 'I'm goin' t' put it on my strawberries.'

"Feller said, 'We might be crazy, but we put whipped cream on ours!'"

Bingo! Laughter all around!

On the front row, Lew Boyd slapped his leg, a type of response the vicar knew Uncle Billy always valued.

Thank you, Lord!

Dr. Hoppy Harper unfolded himself from the metal chair like a carpenter's ruler. He was the tallest one beneath the tent, which inspired a good deal of respect right off the bat.

The town doctor turned to those assembled.

"Uncle Billy told this joke quite a few years ago, when he and Miss Rose came to dinner at Father Tim's rectory. I've never forgotten that evening, for lots of reasons, and especially because another of my favorite patients was then living—Miss Sadie Baxter."

More nodding of heads. A few murmurs. Miss Sadie Baxter!

"Uncle Billy, I hope I don't let you down."

Hoppy shoved his hands into the sport coat he was wearing over his green scrubs.

"A fella wanted to learn to sky dive . . . don't you know. He goes to this school and he takes a few weeks of training, and pretty soon, it comes time to make his jump.

"So he goes up in this little plane and bails out, and down he shoots like a ton of bricks. He gets down a ways . . . don't you know, and starts pulling on his cord, but nothing happens. He's really traveling now, still pulling that cord. Nothing. Switches over to his emergency cord, same thing—nothing happens; he's looking at the tree tops. All of a sudden, here comes this other guy shootin' up from the ground like a rocket. And the guy going down says, 'Hey buddy, d'you know anything about parachutes?' And the one coming up says, 'Afraid not; d'you know anything about gas stoves?' "

Laughter *and* applause. This would be a tough act to follow.

Father Tim waited for the laughter to subside, and stepped forward.

"A census taker was makin' 'is rounds, don't you know."

A burst of laughter.

"I love this one!" Hessie Mayhew whispered to the mayor's secretary.

"Well, sir, he went up to a house an' knocked an' a woman come to th' door. He said, 'How many young 'uns you got, an' what're their names?'

"Woman starts countin' on her fingers, don't you know, says, 'We got Jenny an' Penny, they're ten. We got Hester an' Lester, they're twelve. We got Billie an' Willie, they're fourteen. . . .' "

"Census taker says . . ."

A large knot rose suddenly in his throat. Uncle Billy felt so near, so present that the vicar was jarred profoundly. And what in heaven's name did the census taker *say*? His wits had deserted him; he was sinking like a stone.

Miss Rose stood, clutching a handbag made in 1946 of cork rounds from the caps of soda pop bottles.

"Th' census taker *says*," she proclaimed at the top of her lungs, " 'D'you mean t' tell me you got twins *ever' time?*'

"An' th' woman says, 'Law, no, they was *hundreds* of times we didn't git *nothin'!* ' "

* * *

Cleansed somehow in spirit, and feeling an unexpected sense of renewal, those assembled watched the coffin being lowered into place. It was a graveside procedure scarcely seen nowadays, and one that signaled an indisputable finality.

"Unto Almighty God we commend the soul of our brother, William Benfield Watson, and commit his body to the ground, earth to earth, ashes to ashes, dust to dust; in sure and certain hope of the Resurrection unto eternal life, through our Lord Jesus Christ. . . ."

* * *

He'd always felt daunted by Rose Watson's countenance, for it bore so clearly the mark of her illness. Indeed, it appeared as if some deep and terrible rage had surfaced, and hardened there for all to witness.

She wore a black cocktail hat of uncertain antiquity, and a black suit he remembered from their days at Lord's Chapel. It was made memorable by its padded shoulders from the forties, and a lapel that had been largely eaten away by moths.

Betty Craig gripped Miss Rose's arm, looking spent but encouraged, as people delivered their condolences and departed the graveside.

"Miss Rose . . ."

He took the old woman's cold hands, feeling frozen as a mullet himself. Though he believed he was somehow responsible for her well-being, he hadn't a clue how to proceed.

She threw back her head and mowed him down with her fierce gaze. "I saved your bloomin' neck!" she squawked.

"Yes, you did! By heaven, you did!"

He was suddenly laughing at his own miserable ineptness, and at the same time, weeping for her loss. "And God bless you for it!"

He found himself doing the unthinkable—he was hugging Rose Watson and patting her on the back for a fare-thee-well.

Light from Heaven, Ch. 13

Father Tim Tells Dooley the Big News

HE WAS STANDING at the bookcase when he heard his boy coming along the hall at a clip, probably to pick up the car keys.

Dooley stood before him as if frozen.

"What happened? You're white as a sheet."

"I called him a bad name. A really bad name."

"Who?"

"Blake."

"Why?"

"He argues about everything; I couldn't stand it any longer. I let him have it."

"Unbelievable." This was not good news.

"He's an arrogant, self-righteous . . ."

"That may be. But that's no excuse." He was disappointed in Dooley. Miss Sadie, dadgummit, don't look at me; he knows better.

"But I shouldn't have called him what I did. Actually, I wanted to punch 'im; I had to really hold back. But no matter how blind he is to the truth, I shouldn't have said what I said. Look, I'm sorry. I'll apologize to him, and I apologize to you, too. I know you hate this kind of stuff."

There. The boy had made a mistake and was apologizing to all concerned. Dooley was human, for heaven's sake, what was he waiting for? For his son to be canonized? It was time.

He let his breath out, like the long, slow release of air from a tire gone wrong.

"Let's sit down, son. Take the wing chair."

"That's yours."

"Not really. Right now, it's yours."

"You want me to sit down now or go and do what I have to do with Blake?"

"Do what you have to do with Blake, and get back here fast, I have something important to tell you." He could hardly wait another minute; the waiting was over. But where to start? He'd had this conversation a hundred times in his imagination. . . .

He sat and prayed and stared out the window and scratched his dog behind the ears.

Dooley came back, looking relieved. "He took it pretty well; he knows he's hard to get along with. If he'd just listen. . . ."

"How would you like to have your own practice when you finish school?"

Dooley sat down and glanced at his watch. "Unless somebody leaves me a million bucks. . . ."

Dooley eyed him, grinning.

"Don't look at me, buddyroe. I am definitely not your man on that deal. How would you like to have the Meadowgate practice? Hal's retiring in five years, just one year short of when you get your degree."

"Meadowgate would be, like, a dream. It's perfect, it's everything I could ever want, but it'll take years to make enough money to . . ."

"What if you had the money to buy it?" Why was he asking these questions? Why couldn't he get on with it? He'd held on to his secret for so long, he was having trouble letting it go.

"Well, yes," said Dooley, "but I don't even know what Hal would sell it for. Probably, what do you think, half a million? I've done a little reading on that kind of thing, but . . ." Dooley looked suspicious, even anxious. "Why are we talking about this?"

"Since he's not planning to include the house and land, I'd guess less than half a million. Maybe three or four hundred thousand for the business and five acres. And if you wanted, Hal could be a consultant. But only if you wanted."

"Yeah, and I could fire Blake. Anyway, nice dream." Dooley checked his watch.

"Let me tell you about a dream Miss Sadie had. It was her dream to see one Dooley Barlowe be all he can be, to be all God made him to be. She believed in you."

Dooley's scalp prickled; the vicar's heart pounded.

"She left you what will soon be two million dollars." He had wondered for years how the words would feel in his mouth.

There was a long silence. Dooley appeared to have lost his breath; Father Tim thought the boy might faint.

"Excuse me." Dooley stood and bolted from the library.

"You don't look so good," Father Tim said when Dooley returned. "What happened?"

"I puked."

"Understandable."

Dooley thumped into the wing chair, stupefied.

"What do you think?" asked Father Tim.

"I can't think. There's no way I can think. You aren't kidding me, are you?"

"I wouldn't kid about these numbers."

"It makes me sad that I can't thank her. I mean, why did she do it? I was just a scrawny little kid who cleaned out her attic and hauled her ashes. Why would she *do* it?"

"I can't make it any simpler. She believed in you."

"But why?"

"Maybe because the man she loved had been a boy like you—from the country, trying to make it on his own; smart, very smart, but without any resources whatsoever. It so happens that Willard Porter made it anyway, as you would, also. But she wanted you to have resources."

Tears brimmed in Dooley's eyes. "Man."

"You want to go out in the yard and holler—or anything?"

"I feel . . ." Dooley turned his gaze away.

"You feel?"

"Like I want to bust out cryin'."

"You can do that," he said. "I'll cry with you."

* * *

Cynthia knocked lightly and opened the door. "I can feel it. You know."

Dooley stood. "Yeah. Yes, ma'am."

"And the two of you are bawling about it?"

Father Tim nodded, wiping his eyes.

"You big dopes." She went to Dooley and hugged him and drew his head down and kissed his cheek. "Remember me in my old age."

Dooley cackled.

The air in the room released.

Father Tim put his handkerchief in his pocket.

A new era had begun.

Light from Heaven, Ch. 19

Someone to Say "Bless You"

❧

A friend who distinguishes herself as a fearless cook once sent me a magazine article I've never forgotten.

It was about a couple of gourmands who moved from America to a certain part of southern France "because of the chicken."

"Because of the chicken!" my friend scrawled across the top of the article. "Can you believe it?"

Well, yes. I could, actually.

Their reason for moving thousands of miles to savor that particular version of free-range *poulet* is hardly odder than my reason for leaving a successful career and moving to Blowing Rock, North Carolina.

One of the reasons I moved here is because there's always someone to say "Bless you!" when you sneeze.

Clearly, such nurture finds its zenith in small towns.

There are other simple nurtures at work here, as well. Take, for example, a conversation with two merchant friends.

I had rambled along winding backroads the livelong morning, stopping at a country store for a Cheerwine and two packs of Nabs— a staple lunch menu in these parts.

Around noon, I swung into Blowing Rock and dropped by to see friends who were mountain natives and Main Street store owners.

"Had lunch yet?" I asked.

"Yep, did you?"

"Yep. Two packs of Nabs."

"*Two* packs?"

"Two packs."

"Hon, did you hear that?"

"What's that?"

"She had *two* packs."

"Two packs of what?"

"Nabs."

"Well, I'll say. Two packs. How about that."

"My, my. Two packs."

"Nabs." Long, pondering silence. "I declare!"

This exchange invoked a kind of reverie that felt slightly akin to being wrapped in swaddling clothes.

While some people in our town prefer the reviving heat of a political discussion or a good wrangle over the widening of Highway 321, I prefer conversations which, on the surface, say almost nothing, but are redolent with subterranean meaning. What the above conversation was all about was perfectly clear to me. It was about passing time, and relishing even the smallest of pleasures—as one might savor the minuscule sweetness of a single currant in a scone.

Around here, small pleasures can be gained simply from greeting a neighbor.

"Good morning! How're you?" I ask.

"Oh, well, no rest for th' wicked, and th' righteous don't need none."

Now, that's entertainment.

It doesn't take much for me, as my sister-in-law often says. What she actually says is, "You can make more out of nothing than anybody I know."

WHEN I WAS READY to move out of the fast lane and into a village, I started looking for a house. I didn't, however, have any specific description of the house that would shelter me as I made the transition from writing ads to writing books.

I merely said, "I'm looking for the perfect house."

"What does that mean . . . exactly?" the realtor inquired.

"I don't know. I'll know when I see it."

And, of course, I did know when I saw it, as I am a consummate house person to whom the right house inevitably, speaks.

What a house never tells you when it speaks is how much blood, sweat, and yes, tears it will take to claim it for your own. But who cares? When one has the perfect house, one is willing to settle for less than the perfect truth.

I recently put another house inside this old mountain home. It is a dollhouse, and it occupies the lower shelf of my kitchen spice rack, which was made by my great-uncle Sid before he left for California, where he made a million, lost it, and never returned.

On the wall of this little domicile is a framed cross-stitch that says "Home Sweet Home." Gathered around the fireplace are papa, lately arrived from work at his lumberyard, a baby who has lost a leg, a little boy in a rocking chair, and a mother who is rolling out biscuit dough with a deft hand.

Most of the furniture was made years ago by two nieces, a nephew, and their father. They even thought to take a tiny block of wood, paint it black, and inscribe "Holy Bible" on the cover.

Here, then, is another perfect house. As I roast a chicken, and the fragrances of garlic and homegrown rosemary scent the rooms, I might reach up and move the papa to the table, where he will devour every morsel of an imagined supper, holding the one-legged baby on his lap. Or, I will move the little boy closer to the dough board, where he can watch with amazement as his mother cuts out biscuits with the rim of his favorite drinking cup.

I think of other houses that have spoken to me through the years, though I never claimed them for my own. There was the abandoned house I discovered in the Spanish countryside, with the wind blowing through crumbling walls, and the meadow grass springing up for carpet, and the wide patches of sapphire sky that looked in through a ruined tile roof.

Or the house in East Anglia that, following a group tour of some of England's stateliest homes, revealed its heart to us with such candor that we nearly clapped our hands with delight.

After acres of museum-quality furnishings and paintings, and marathon pelmets of eroding silk, we came to the owner's private quarters, where her telly sat on a rolling aluminum stand. Where her slippers were tossed casually by a slouchy, slipcovered chair. Where her needlepoint-in-progress lay sprawled on a worn ottoman. Where party invitations were tucked carelessly into the frame of a mirror. Where, obviously, someone actually *lived*.

Our tour group stood there, silent with nameless joy. In a memorable moment of shared intimacy, we looked on in wonder at something that reminded us all of home.

BECAUSE I WORK at home, I must keep on very friendly terms with my surroundings.

This means I must love the way the afternoon light illumines the Chinese-red euonymus berries outside my writing window.

It means I must like the way the wall above my desk is dauntingly cluttered with images from magazines, Valentines from loved ones, Scripture from church bulletins, old photos, and the yellowed quote from Horace: "He has half the deed done who has made a beginning."

If I'm at war with the way my room looks, I cannot write a word until it's fixed. I will bolt from my desk like a suddenly wakened sleeper, to straighten a picture that's hanging crooked, or fluff a pillow that sighed and went flat.

For me, working at home and interacting with it is important to my productivity. It does for me what fingering a smooth piece of jade might do for another.

"The problem for writers," says writer Diane Johnson, "is that they practically have to be shut-ins, stay-at-homes . . . consequently, [there is a need] for an ivory tower of their own special variety."

I live in a house that's truly my ivory tower. And if a whole town could possibly be called an ivory tower, then I have found two. For in our village of 1,800 (in the summer, we accelerate to a population of over 4,000), the people are just as warm and quirky, generous and kind as you think small-town folks used to be, but no longer are. Trust me—they still are.

As I write this in the late-autumn stillness of our mountain village, the tourists have gone, the summer people have left, and the russet leaves have fallen. All that remains is what you can make happen on your own during the long months of winter.

There are no more party invitations to tuck into the frame of one's mirror, to rob attention from the novel in progress. It is time to be a shut-in again, and get down to business.

And, when you're looking for a little simple nurturing, you can always go "overtown" and talk about what you had for lunch, or what kind of weather the old-timers are predicting, or who's working on the Community Club auction quilt this year.

You may even find someone who'll say "Bless you"—whether you sneeze or not.

Blowing Rock, 1998

Leaving a career and moving to Blowing Rock was a risk for me. But I agree with Pulitzer-winner Marjorie Rawlings, who moved from New York to remote Cross Creek to write. She said, "It is more important to live the life one wishes to live, and to go down with it if necessary, than to live more profitably but less happily."

—Jan

The Postman's Knock:
The Letters

And none will hear the postman's knock
without a quickening of the heart.

—W. H. Auden, "Night Mail"

You know your author well enough to know that she's not only a romantic, but somewhat on the hopeless side.

So is it any wonder that in *A Light in the Window,* I devoted an entire chapter to love letters?

This is one of my favorite chapters of all the nine books. Mainly because I got to watch two people laying themselves quite bare, even when they thought they were safely "buttoned up."

Oh, the longing in a love letter! Listen to Mr. Jefferson in his plea to Maria Cosway, that gorgeous babe who stole his heart across the pond:

"Write to me often. Write affectionately, and freely, as I do to you. Say many kind things, and say them without reserve. They will be food for my soul."

My goodness. Though I always admired Mr. Jefferson, such carrying-on made him all the more agreeable.

Now hear Duff Cooper, the finest of letter writers, who penned this to his future wife in 1914:

"Don't write too legibly or intelligibly as I have no occupation so pleasant as pondering for hours over your hieroglyphics, and for hours more trying to interpret your . . . sayings. A clearly written simply expressed letter is too like the lightning."

Or perhaps you'd relish knowing what lovely Mary Wordsworth, wife of Father Tim's favorite poet, had to say to her husband in 1810:

"It is not in my power to tell thee how I have been affected by this dearest of all letters—it was so unexpected—so new a thing to see the breathing of thy inmost heart upon paper that I was quite overpowered, & now that I sit down to answer thee in the loneliness & Depth of that love which unites us & which cannot be felt but by ourselves, I am so agitated & my eyes are so bedimmed that I scarcely know how to proceed."

Frankly, I believe that Father Tim and Cynthia might never have married if it hadn't been for their winter parting . . . she in New York, he frozen into Mitford like an ice cube in a tray. The deed was effectively done, I'm convinced, because of the breathing of their inmost hearts upon paper, as Mary Wordsworth called it.

Have you ever dared to breathe your inmost heart upon paper?

I recommend it.

Here's something else I recommend.

Read the letters of Father Tim and Cynthia aloud to a loved one, taking turns.

(My editor, Carolyn Carlson, was courted quite successfully by e-mail. But that's another story.)

THE LETTERS

Dearest Cynthia,

Sometimes, if only for a moment, I forget you're away, and am startled to find your bedroom lamp isn't burning, and all the windows are dark. I must always remind myself that you're coming home soon.

I hope your work is going well and that you're able to do it with a light heart. I've never been to New York, and I'm convinced that my opinion of it is a foolish and rustic one. Surely much humor and warmth exist there, and I'll restrain myself from reminding you to hold on to your purse, be careful where you walk, and pray before you get into a taxicab.

I've mulched your perennial beds, and done some pruning in the hedge. I think we'll both find it easier to pop through.

To the news at hand:

On Saturday, Miss Pattie packed a train case with Snickers bars and a jar of Pond's cold cream and ran away from home. She got as far as the town monument before Rodney found her and brought her home in a police car. It appears that riding in a police car was the greatest event of her recent life, and Rodney has promised to come and take her again. Good fellow, Rodney.

I have at last heard Dooley sing in the school chorus, and must tell you he is absolutely splendid. Cold chills ran down my right leg, which is the surest way I have of knowing when something is dead right. Our youth choir, by the way, will have a stunning program ready for your return at Christmas.

Barnabas pulled the leash from my hand yesterday afternoon, and raced into your yard. He sniffed about eternally, before going up your steps and lying down on the stoop. I can only surmise that he misses you greatly, as does yours truly,

Timothy

Dearest Timothy,

No, scratch that. My dearest neighbor,

I have been riding in taxicabs the livelong day, and have taken your advice. I pray while hailing, as it were, and God has been very gracious to send affable, entertaining, and kindly drivers. One even chased me down the sidewalk to return a scarf I left on the seat. Can you imagine? I look upon this as a true miracle.

O! the shops are brimming with beauteous treasures. I would so love to have you here! I would hold on to your arm for dear life as we looked in the windows and stopped for a warm tea in some lovely hotel with leather banquettes and stuffy waiters. You would overtip to impress me, and I would give you great hugs of gratitude for your coming.

My work is awfully labored just now. Sometimes it has the most wondrous life of its own, it fairly pulls me along—rather like windsurfing! At other times, it drags and mopes, so that I despair of ever writing another word or drawing another picture. I've found that if one keeps pushing along during the mopes, out will flash the most exhilarating thought or idea—a way of doing something that I had never seen before—and then, one is off again, and hold on to your hat!

I am doing the oddest things these days. I brought home a sack of groceries from the deli the other evening and, while thinking of our kisses at the airport, put the carton of ice cream on my bed, and my hat in the freezer.

Worse yet, I'm talking to myself on the street, and that won't do at all! Actually, I'm talking to you, but no one would believe that. "Timothy," I said just the other day when looking in the window at Tiffany's, "I do wish you'd unbutton your caution a bit, and get on an airplane this minute!" How did I know a woman was standing next to me? She looked at me coldly before stomping away. I think it was the part about unbuttoning your caution that did it.

I am thrilled to hear of Dooley's singing, and especially that it ran a fine chill up your leg. As for myself, I know something is right when the top of my head tingles. In any case, I am proud with you, and can barely wait to hear him in chorus when I come home on the 23rd.

A box has been sent to all of you, including my good friend, Barnabas, with a delicious tidbit for Jack, as well. If I were to send you everything that reminds me of you, you should straightaway receive a navy cashmere topcoat, a dove-colored Borsolino hat, a peppered ham and a brace of smoked pheasants, a library table with a hidden drawer, a looking glass with an ivory handle, a 17th-century oil of the 12-year-old Jesus teaching in the temple, a Persian hall runner, a lighted world globe, and a blue bathrobe with your initials on the pocket. There!

Oh, and I haven't forgotten Puny. The truffles are for her, and do keep your mitts off them. They are capable of creating any number of diabetic comas.

Would you please have Mr. Hogan send my Muse *subscription to this address? I suppose I could call him up again, but each time I've tried, there's no answer at his newspaper office. I can't imagine how his news tips come in; he must get them all at the Main Street Grill.*

I will close and go searching for my slippers, which have been missing since yesterday morning. Perhaps I should look in the freezer.

With fondest love to you, and warm hellos to Dooley, Barnabas and Jack . . .

A Light in the Window, Ch. 4

Dearest Timothy,

We've had snow flurries all morning and everyone on the street below is bundled in furs and hats and mufflers, looking like a scene from It's a Wonderful Life.

But, oh, it is not a wonderful life to be in this vast city alone!

Sometimes I think I'd like to fling it all away and go somewhere warm and tropical and wear a sarong! I would like to live in my body for awhile instead of in my head!

I've been working far too hard and find it impossible to turn off my thoughts at night. I lie here for hours thinking of you and Mitford and Main Street and the peace of my dear house—and then, the little army of creatures in the new book starts marching in, single file.

I review the tail of the donkey I did this morning, the snout of the pig I'm doing tomorrow, the heavy-lidded eyes of the chicken, wondering—should a chicken look this sexy??!

This can go on for hours, until I've exhausted all the creatures and go back and start at the beginning with the tail of the donkey that I'm afraid looks too much like the tail of a collie. That's when I get up and go to my reference books and find I'm wrong—it looks exactly like the tail of a jersey cow!

This is the price I pay for calling a halt to the Violet *books. Yet, I should jump out the window if I had to do another* Violet *book! She, by the way, lies curled beside me as I write, dreaming of a harrowing escape from the great, black dog who lives next door in her hometown.*

I'm thrilled at the thought of coming home and spending my second Christmas in Mitford. It is the truest home I've ever known.

I've looked and looked for a letter from you, and if I don't have one soon, I shall ring you up at the Grill and tell you I'm absolutely mad for you, which will make you blush like crazy while all your cronies look on with amusement.

There! That should compel you to write. I'm sure I'll hear by return mail!

With love, Cynthia

Dear Timothy,

Thank you for the note that might have been written to a great-aunt who once invited you to a tea of toast and kippers.

Yours sincerely,
    Cynthia

                                  A Light in the Window, Ch. 5

My Dearest,

You can't know how the living freshness of roses and lavender has rejoiced my heart. The whole apartment is alive with the sweet familiarity of their company, and I'm not so loath now to come home from the deli, or the newsstand, or the café.

Thus, I'm not thanking you for the roses precisely, which are glorious to look at, nor the vast bundle of lavender that appears to have come from the field only moments ago. I thank you instead for their gracious spirit, which soothes and calms and befriends me.

> *"All my soul follows you, love . . . and I live in being yours."*
>
> —Robert Browning to Elizabeth Barrett, 1846

I tried to call your office after the flowers arrived, but the line was busy again and again. And so, I take this other route, this path made familiar by pen and paper, reflection and time.

What a lovely thing it is to begin to love. I shall not dwell on the fear, which seems always to come with it. I shall write only of victory, for that is what is on my heart tonight.

When I met you, Timothy, I had no thought of loving anyone again. Not for anything would I pay the price of loving! I had shut the door, but God had not.

I remember the evening I came to borrow sugar. Though I did nothing more than gobble up your leftover supper, I felt I'd come home. Imagine my bewilderment, sitting there at your kitchen counter, finding myself smitten.

Over your home was a stillness and peace that spoke to me, and in your eyes was something I hadn't seen before in a man. I supposed it to be kindness—and it was. I later believed it to be compassion, and it was that, also.

Yet, I sensed that God had put these qualities there for your flock and your community, to help you do your job for Him. For a long time, I didn't know whether He might have put something there just for me.

Years ago, I went to Guatemala with Elliott. While he was in meetings, I was on the road with a driver and a sketchbook, slamming along over huge potholes, our teeth rattling. We drove in the jungle for miles, seeing nothing but thick, unremitting forest. The light in that part of the world was strange and unfamiliar to me, and I felt a bit frightened, almost panicked.

Suddenly, we drove into a clearing. Before us lay a vast, volcanic lake that literally took my breath away. The surface was calm and blue and serene, and the light that drenched the clearing seemed to pour directly from heaven.

I shall never forget the suddenness and surprise of finding that hidden and remote lake.

I feel that I have come upon a hidden place in you that is vast and deep and has scarcely been visited by anyone before. It is nearly unbearable to consider the joy this hidden place could hold for us, and yet, tonight, I do.

"Love is like measles," Josh Billings said, ". . . the later in life it occurs, the tougher it gets."

May God have mercy on us, my dearest Timothy!

I close with laughter and tears, the very stuff of life, and race to the drawing board with every hope that I can, at last, make the zebra stop looking like a large dog in striped pajamas!

I kiss you.

Love,

Cynthia

Dearest Cynthia,

At the library today, Hessie Mayhew announced that Latin American dance classes will be held at the Community Club, sometime in February. I told her I have my own private Latin dance instructor, which she found to be astonishing.

Then I popped into the children's section and talked to Avette about reading Miss Coppersmith.

"Violet Goes to School *and* Violet Plays the Piano *are my two personal favorites," she said, "although* Violet Goes to France *is hilariously funny. What will it be?"*

"The complete works!" I said.

I must tell you that Hessie Mayhew is no dummy. When she saw my selection, she approved. "The Proust of juvenile authors!" were her exact words.

Now I have innumerable photographs of you, though they are all on the backs of book jackets. I am currently displaying the backside of Violet Goes to the Country *on my desk in the study, where I meet your winsome gaze as I sit and write this letter. I'm afraid the author herself looks exceedingly juvenile, and if that's what writing children's books can do, then I'm willing to have a go at it.*

I shall begin this evening at the top of the pile and plunge straight through to the bottom. Never think that I dismiss lightly the hard work and devotion that go into each small volume. I feel privileged to see behind the scenes, if only a little.

Uncle Billy asks about you and says they'd like to have us over when you come home. You and Dooley can go along for the homemade banana pudding he mentioned as a refreshment, and I'll meet you there later.

He was telling me about the money he keeps hidden between his mattress and box spring. He says Miss Rose usually asks him for ten or fifteen dollars on Monday. On Wednesday, she wants twenty, and every Friday she asks for twenty-five.

When I asked him what she does with all that money, he says he doesn't know; he never gives her any.

I believe that's his newest joke, though he didn't say so.

Your letter spoke of victory, and I hesitate to end on a note that is less than uplifting. Yet I can't ignore your allusion to the hidden lake.

Your analogy was extraordinary to me and made me feel at once that I should surely disappoint you. The lake you discovered in Guatemala was tropical and warm. The lake you say you have found in me suffers a climate entirely of my own making—and there is the rub.

Please pray for me in this, my dearest Cynthia. I am well along in years to have such a terrific case of measles. In truth, I am broken out all over and no help for it.

You are ever in my prayers.

Dooley asks after you, as do Emma and Puny. A candle flame has gone out in this winter village, and we count the days until you are safely home.

Love,
   Timothy

Dearest Timothy,

It was lovely that you called tonight after reading Violet Goes to the Country. *That is my personal favorite, and I'm so happy it made you smile.*

I'm happy, too, that you read it to Barnabas and that he approved. For one as steeped in Wordsworth as he, I'm not surprised that he could appreciate the pastoral setting, though I'm sorry he was upset when you showed him the picture of Violet chasing the sheepdog.

Violet receives a great swarm of attention wherever we go. I put her in the little carrying case with the top undone, and there she rides, licking her paws. The ladies behind the cosmetic counter at Bergdorf's come crowding into the aisles to give her lots of free samples—both salts for her toilette and mascara for her lashes. They like to spray her with French perfume so that I can hardly bear to be in the taxi with her on the way home!

When James was here, he asked me to do Violet Goes to New York.

He took me to such a vastly expensive restaurant and gave such a persuasive argument that I was fairly undone. I did not tell him I would do it, though I did say I'd think about it. The advance would be the largest amount I've ever received. I will appreciate it if you'd pray for me in this. It's confounding to be asked to do something I said I'd never do again!

Thank you for liking my work and finding the fun in it. I look forward to having the letter you wrote tonight before you called— altogether an embarrassment of riches!

Here are those ridiculous pictures taken in a booth on the street. In the spring, you could tack them on a post in your garden to keep the crows away!

I've taken stems of lavender from the vase, dried them a wee bit in the toaster oven, and put them under my pillow. Lavender is said to give one sweet dreams, which is what I wish for you tonight.

You are always in my prayers.

With fondest love from—

    Your neighbor

Dearest Cynthia,

It is Friday evening, and I've just come from a late meeting. This is only to say hello and that I've switched on the lights in your bushes.

The fog is as thick as lentil soup, and they give a cheering glow. As they were not turned on during the

holy days, I hope you won't mind a few hours now, as a send-up of my thoughts of you on this wretched but beautiful winter evening.

God bless you and give you wings for your work. Nay, use them to fly to me here in Mitford. I shall watch for you to glide over the rooftop of your little house and eagerly open my window to let you in.

With loving thoughts,

    Timothy

Timothy, dearest,

Violet has been invited out to dinner this evening by Miss Addison, who lives down the hall.

The invitation was delivered by the lady's footman or something— this is a very swanky place—and was for six o'clock, which is when her elderly cat, Palestrina, likes to dine.

Can you imagine?

I have met Miss Addison several times in the hallway or in the foyer, and she is rather old and quite adorable, wrapped from head to toe in furs.

The footman, or whoever he is, came for Violet on the stroke of six, after I'd brushed her until she shone.

But oh, she is wicked! What did she do five minutes before the bell sounded? I was bringing a flowerpot inside when she dashed to the terrace that is forty stories above the street, leapt onto the railing, and stood looking with absorption at the lights of the Chrysler Building.

She will stay until eight, because they are all watching a video after dinner (surely not 101 Dalmatians?).

I went to dinner the other evening, quite alone, and confess it was a bit pricey. The waiter finally came over and asked, "And how did you find your steak, Madame?"

"Purely by accident," I said. "I moved the potatoes and the peas, and there it was!"

Oh, Timothy, I'm trying so hard to bloom where God planted me. But I am very homesick. I look forward to our talk on Sunday.

Much love to you and to Barnabas. Do tell Dooley hey for me. I should like to see his frank expression and hear his wonderful way of speaking. When I come home, let's all do something together—like—well, you think of something!

I pray for you.

Warmest regards to Emma and my love to Miss Sadie and Louella.

Sunday eve
Dearest Cynthia,

We've just hung up and it seemed so many things went unsaid. Now that I'm sitting down to write, however, I have no idea at all what they were.

I'm delighted that Violet has made a friend, even though her fancy dinner sent her to the litter box throughout the night. Sautéed quail livers with Madeira sauce are notorious in this regard.

As for us, we had our usual Sunday evening banquet. Fried bologna for Dooley with double mustard, and no sermons about a balanced diet, please. This case is beyond me. Unless I'm mistaken, he has not eaten a vegetable in four or five months, and I'm dashed if I know what to do about it. Any ideas?

I forgot to mention that we had a mild, almost balmy day on Saturday.

Miss Rose pulled on galoshes and spent the noon hour directing traffic. After a long confinement, it put the bloom back in her cheeks, Uncle Billy says.

Fancy Skinner has nailed me again about my hair and insists I let her give me a haircut. I hesitate to do this to Joe, who, I'm told, may go with his sister to Tennessee for a week. Possibly I could use his extended absence as an excuse. What do you think?

I've seen Andrew Gregory, who looked smart as all get-out in a cashmere topcoat, and he asked about you. He seems to think that because you're my neighbor, I know all there is to know about you. Yet it occurs to me that I don't even know where you were born.

Well, there you have it. All the urgent things I left unsaid.

Clearly, there's nothing of importance to tell a famous author and illustrator living in New York, whose cat has a more interesting life than most people.

Cynthia, Cynthia—my face grows red when I think of what you said. I hope you will seriously reconsider that outrageous idea, lest I take you up on it.

With something like amazed laughter, and, of course, love,

> *Timothy*

> Nothing new here except my marrying, which to me is a matter of profound wonder.
>
> —Abraham Lincoln

Sunday evening
Timothy!

You rake in a collar! I positively blush like a sophomore when I think of what you said!

You may want to reconsider that outlandish proposal. What if I should take you up on it?

Or was it my idea?

Oh, well, when two hearts beat as one, who knows? And who cares?

I do love you to pieces. You are so funny and wonderful. I knew it the minute I saw that barbecue sauce on your chin, when I came to borrow sugar after just moving in.

Violet has gone down the hall to play with an electronic mouse while Palestrina, who is too old for such nonsense, looks on.

I shall be happy to be home again with people who are ordinary.
Well, almost ordinary.
Much love,
  Cynthia

My dear neighbor, it was your outlandish idea, not mine, and please do
not forget it! I certainly haven't forgotten it. Good grief, I can barely keep
my thoughts on my duties. And there's the rub.

I struggle with what old men with measles fear most: not being able
to think straight, forgetting their Christian names, wandering in a daze
on the street, being late for meetings and early for luncheons, dwelling
everlastingly on some woman who only professes to have measles but in
truth possesses a case so mild that she can go about her duties as cool and
elegant as you please, while the other chap stumbles around trying to locate
his shoes or even the very house where he lives.

Cynthia, Cynthia. Be kind.

yrs,
  Timothy

Dearest Funny Person,

Your wake-up call this morning—how wonderful it was! It was coffee
with brandy, it was eggs Benedict, it was a hot shower and a walk in the
park! Words fail me, but not entirely!

So glad you liked the pictures, though I'm sure you were being kind. I
can be terribly grave in front of a camera, and that fur-lined hood made
me look exactly like an Eskimo woman who has spent the morning
chewing a piece of reindeer hide.

Dearest, I really and truly can't come home. I must work some part of
each day in order to reach the deadline. If I were to pull up stakes at this
point and move home, I should do nothing more than lose time and gain
confusion.

Thus far, I've been given God's speed. Now, if I keep going and nevah,
nevah give up, I shall come to the finish line on schedule.

And so, I have a question that will make your heart fairly leap into
your throat—

Why don't you come to New York?

You could stay here, and while I'm working, you could read or visit the bookshops or pop over to my little café where they've not only adopted me but would take the fondest care of you.

You would have lots of privacy, for this is a very large apartment— and I promise I will not seduce you. Since we've never discussed it, I want to say that I really do believe in doing things the old-fashioned way when it comes to love. I do love you very dearly and want everything to be right and simple and good, and yes, pleasing to God. This is why I'm willing to wait for the kind of intimacy that most people favor having as soon as they've shaken hands.

But enough of what I shall not do, and on to what I shall!

I shall buy fresh bread and fresh fish and vegetables and all the things you love and cook for you right here, and you will save hundreds of dollars on pricey restaurants, which you can give to the children's hospital!

I shall take you to a play with the tickets from my publisher and to the shop with the lighted antique globe, not to mention the Metropolitan Museum and the New York Public Library.

Last but not least, I shall give you as much love and affection and happiness as I am capable of giving. Which, I believe, dearest Timothy, is quite a lot.

There. How can you resist?

Your loving Cynthia

from the office
dearest cynthia,

but i am a rustic, a country bumpkin, a bucolic rube of the worst sort—in a word, a hick.

I can see why you didn't mention this on sunday when we talked— you wanted me to have time to think it over. That indeed is one of the grandest benefits of a letter. it gives one time to reflect, so that one doesn't shout some impulsive, spur-of-the-moment nonsense like yes i'll come to new york and fly in a plane and be stranded in an airport and get lost or maimed, or even killed, not to mention buffeted by throngs on every corner.

Nope. i can't do it. you think i'm kidding, but i am dead serious. I am infamous for my fear of flying—which is chiefly why I hemmed and hawed for twenty years over the trip to Ireland. Large cities are another of my rustic phobias—they literally make me sick—which is the sole reason Kthrn and Wltr and I lodged in the countryside when we went to sligo.

I am willing to take any flailing you dish out—but i cannot come to new york. you're right, the very thought makes my heart leap into my throat. blast, i am sorry,

> *with love,*
> *Timothy*

Dearest Cynthia,

It is Monday evening, and I have read your letter again, feeling like a heel.

Your bright spirit is the light of my life. When I read the gracious things you would do to make me happy, my foolish limitations and fogyisms are humiliating to me.

I can only hope you'll forgive me and know that somehow, in some other way, I shall be forthcoming and good for you.

I, too, hate it that you must be there alone. Emma assures me that men in the publishing field are good-looking, enormously successful, and invariably tall, some of them verging perhaps on nine feet or more.

She went on to suggest that if I don't mind my p's and q's, I will surely lose whatever ground I have gained with you, and you'll be swept away. I would not be surprised if this were true, but I pray it will not be so.

It was consoling to read your brave announcement of what you would not do. No, we have never discussed this, but the time, clearly, was right for you to say it. It is amazing to me that you and I share the same ideal for sexual intimacy, which, needless to say, the world finds exceedingly outdated.

Another consolation is that the world has nothing to do with us in this.

Your openness has widened the door of my own heart, somehow, and I feel a tenderness for you that is nearly overwhelming. I can't think how

I could be worth the care you take with me, the effort you expend, and the ceaseless patience you bring to our friendship.

For this alone, I must love you.

My dearest,

You would be amused if you knew how long I have sat and looked at the two words just above, words that I have never written to anyone in my life. Can it have taken more than six decades for these words to form in my spirit, and then, without warning, to appear on the paper before me, with such naturalness and ease?

Even for this alone, I must love you.

I've come across a letter from Robert Browning to EBB, in which he says:

"I would not exchange the sadness of being away from you for any imaginable delight in which you had no part."

To this sentiment, I say Selah.

I also say goodnight, my dearest love. You are ever in my prayers.

Timothy

Timothy,

I understand. I really do. I could feel the intensity behind your typed note. At one moment, your horror of this place makes me laugh. At another, I wonder what on earth I'm doing here myself!

I feel we should go on as we're going and try to enjoy, somehow, this process of working and waiting. I know there is wisdom in that! But it keeps escaping me, like the flea I picked off Violet this morning.

Can you imagine? Forty stories up, in the dead of winter—and a flea? Certainly, she did not get it at Bergdorf's. Which leaves only one consideration.

Palestrina!

I shudder to think what I should do when her next social invitation arrives in the letter box!

I must get something ready for the pickup service that comes at five, so I'll dash,

with love and understanding,

Cynthia

Dearest Timothy,

When I reached into the letter box yesterday morning, I somehow missed your wonderful letter written on Monday evening. How very odd that I didn't feel it in there yesterday, but odder still that I would have looked in there again this morning, knowing that today's mail had not yet arrived.

I so needed your letter with Mr. Browning's words to Elizabeth and the tender things you spoke to me from your heart. Because, though I honestly do understand your refusal to come, it made me sad that you will not.

I had hoped we could be together here, as free as children from everything familiar. Most of all, I wanted to share what I know of this strangely compelling city and take you 'round and show you off!

But you have called me your dearest. And that is worth any window-shopping at Tiffany's or tea we might have sipped at the Plaza.

More than that—it fills me with happiness that you were able, for your own sake, to speak to me so.

It wasn't easy for me to tell you what I shall not do—it was very hard to know when to say it! So, perhaps you can imagine how comforting it was to learn that we agree in this sacred thing—and to find that you are just as silly and old-fashioned as your neighbor.

When Elliott and I were divorced eleven years ago, the first thing my friends did was "fix me up."

Oh, how I hated being "fixed up!"

Practically the first man I went out with said, "Hello, blah, blah, blah, cute nose, I'm wild about your legs, let's check into a hotel."

I wish I could tell you that I poured scalding coffee in his lap! But all I really did was curl up inside in a tinier knot than I'd curled up in before! I refused to go out with anyone again for nearly three years.

The secret truth, dearest, is that I cannot bear dating. I find it absolutely ghastly. I am so glad we have never ever dated and never ever will! You are just the boy next door, which I find to be the most divine providence since France was handed over to Henry the Fifth.

But please don't think our friend Andrew Gregory was anything less than lovely. He is a prince! Yet, among a variety of other sweet incompatibilities, he is too tall. Yes! When he kissed me on the cheek, he had to practically squat down to do it, which made me laugh out loud every time! Poor Andrew. He deserves far better.

You and I, on the other hand, are the perfect size for each other. As we're very nearly the same height, we're just like a pair of bookends.

I close with sleepy wishes for a riveting sermon at Lord's Chapel on Sunday. Please make a photocopy at Happy Endings and send it to me. I shall be sitting on the gospel side at the little church around the corner.

Love and prayers, Cynthia

P.S. My work is simply pouring through. I am thankful beyond telling. James writes from France that my zebras fairly leap with life. There's not a pair of pajamas in the lot. Pray for me, dearest, I shall be home sooner than we think. Love to Dooley. Here's a bit of a drawing I did of him from memory.

from the office
dear bookend,

i'll have you know i stand 5 feet 9 in my loafers, while you are a mere 5 feet 2. that leaves 7 whole inches waving around in the breeze above your head, and i'll thank you not to forget it.

Dooley laughed at your drawing and must have liked it for he took it to school today. That someone would make a drawing of him was a marvel he did not take lightly. Puny thought it pure genius, and i promised to make her a photocopy when i copy the sermon, which, by the way, was less than riveting, though Miss Rose, to my great surprise, pronounced it stirring.

she refused to wear the sling-back pumps that Uncle billy ordered out of the almanac. She put them on the mantel in the dining room, instead, as a kind of display. She was arrayed in her Christmas finery. Uncle Billy was wearing a new shirt and held himself so stiff and erect i suspect he had left the cardboard in.

Things are back on schedule on the hill and i could hear the hum and buzz of the equipment as i walked in this morning. emma wanted the week off, so i am quite alone here, half-freezing one minute and roasting the next, as the heater has developed a tic and goes on and off at odd moments.

You sounded strong yesterday, so glad Miss Addison invited you for that swell Sunday tea and that you brought home no fleas.

Again, i enjoyed your books more than i can say. i seemed to find all sorts of meaning between the lines.

Love, Timothy

P.S. Dooley says hey

thnx for telling me when you were born, though I forgot, as usual, to ask where. So there'll be no forgetting, i have written your birth date on the wall beside my desk, my first graffiti—except of course for the legend, TOMMY NOLES LOVES PATTY FRANKLIN, that i once chalked on the cafeteria door and which nearly cost my life at the hands of the principal, not to mention Patty Frnkln.

Perhaps you entered the world in maine? or was it massachusetts? You are definitely a Yankee, no doubt about it

Here comes harold

Dearest Timothy,

I've been very sleepless recently. I wish I could call you now, but a ringing phone at such an hour stops the very heart. It would also set Barnabas "to barking" and Dooley "to fussing." So I shall have to be consoled with talking to you in this way.

I've read something wonderful. "Deep in their roots," Roethke said, "all flowers keep the light."

My mind went at once to my tulips, frozen into the black soil of the bed you helped me dig. My imagination burrowed in like a mole and saw, in the center of a frozen bulb, a green place—quick and alive and radiant and indefatigable, the force that survives every winter blast and flies up, in spite of itself, to greet spring.

I am keeping the light, dearest. But sometimes it grows so faint; I'm frightened that I shall lose it entirely.

Why am I not doing the things I should be doing? Going to the library and the bookshops, seeing plays, hearing concerts, looking at great art?

The answer is, there's scarcely anything left of me after bending over the drawing board for hours, and so I send out for Chinese or make the quick walk to the café and am in bed before the late news, only to find I cannot sleep!

I am, however, going faithfully to confirmation class at the little church around the corner, every Thursday evening—and liking it very much.

I pray for us to have long walks together, to dash out into the rain and jump into puddles! Would you jump into puddles with me? I think not, but it's a hope I shall cherish, for it makes me smile to think of it.

Now that I've gotten out of bed, and located the stationery, and rounded up the pen and filled it with ink, and fluffed up the pillows, and adjusted the lamp, and told you I can't sleep, I'm nodding off!

Life is so odd. I can't make heads or tails of it. I'm glad you're a parson and can.

Lovingly yours, C

My dearest C,

Have been pondering our dinner here before you vanished into the sky in that minuscule plane. I can't seem to remember what I fed you, when or how I prepared it, nor even discussing the order with Avis. Though I was sober as a judge, I think I was in a kind of daze—the most I can recall is that we danced, I asked you the question that was so infernally difficult, and you were tender and patient and full of laughter.

This recollection should be more than enough, yet I'm astounded at such a lapse. Something was clearly going on that had little to do with either dinner or dancing and causes me to consider the wisdom of Aiken's poem:

"Music I heard with you was more than music,
And bread I broke with you was more than bread . . ."

So glad you called last night. It was no disturbance at all, quite the contrary. I hope it's some comfort, however small, that you can call me anytime.

Do you hear? Anytime. Please take this to heart.

I've been in parishes where the phone might ring at any hour, from midnight to morning. Mitford, however, is a reserved

> I can neither eat nor sleep for thinking of you my dearest love, I never touch even pudding.
>
> —Horatio Nelson to Lady Emma Hamilton, 1800

parish, and I think the last late-hour call was from Hoppy's wife who was in the agony of dying and wanted prayer—not for herself, but for him.

It occurs to me that I'm not only your neighbor and friend, C, but your parson, as well. All of which seems to make a tight case for your freedom to call me as your heart requires it.

With fondest love to you tonight and prayers for sleeping like an infant,
Timothy

My dear Bookend,

I've had a load of wood carted in and a more splendid fire you've never seen. All this seems to occasion a letter, though I just sent one to you yesterday morning.

A meeting was canceled, thanks be to God. Dooley is spending the night with Tommy, and Barnabas is amused with scratching himself. Wish you were here. It is another night of jollity in our frozen village.

I've just heard from Fr Roland in New Orleans, who complains that my letters to him have dried up like a pond in a drought. Can't imagine why.

Am cooking a pork roast and a pot of navy beans, one more reason I wish you were here. I told Puny I needed to put my hand in again, so she did the shopping with Avis, and I'm handling the rest.

The house is fairly perfumed with a glorious smell, which causes me to remember Mother's kitchen. She always added orange rind to a pork roast and a bit of brandy. Her strong favorite with any roast was angel biscuits, so named for their habit of floating off the plate and hovering above the platter.

I can't help but think how my father never came to the table when called. He would sometimes wait until we were finished or the food had grown cold before sitting down without a word. I remember my mother's disappointment and my own white fury, which often spoiled the meal she had laid.

Later, I could see it was his way of controlling the household, of being the emperor, far above the base need for eating, for loving, for feeling. I remember his refusal of anesthesia when he had an operation on his leg and again a serious abscess on his jaw.

If my mother had not been fashioned of something akin to marzipan, my father's composition of steel would have been my very death.

But why do I waste ink telling you this? It came into the room with the fragrance from the pots and would not let me be.

Sometimes I consider not mailing a letter I've written to you, but you insisted that nothing should be struck through or torn up or unmailed, so there you have it.

Someone has said again that I should work on the book of essays I've long considered. Perhaps when I retire, if I ever do such a thing.

Stuart says I should be making plans for retirement—but his advice made me want to say, oh, stop being a bishop and let me stumble around and fall in a blasted ditch if that's what it takes.

I am homesick for your spirit.

With love,

Timothy

Darling Timothy,

I've dried the lavender and tied it into small bundles that are tucked everywhere. Here are a few sprigs for your pillow. If that seems too twee, as the English say, perhaps you'll find a place for them in your sock drawer.

I've plucked every petal from every faded rose and have two bowls filled with their lingering fragrance. I cannot let them go! I'm enclosing a handful of petals for you to scatter over the last of the snow.

James says the new book must be a different format than the Violet books and even larger than Mouse in the Manger. *"These creatures must have room to breathe!" he says, and I do agree. I'm going to the publishing house tomorrow afternoon and work with the designer. I shall be thrilled to have someone to talk with, though the lovely people who run the café do make the days go faster. I wish you could meet them.*

The weather is still terrible here. A water main froze and broke in the neighborhood, and the streets have been flooded for two days. I've bought fleece-lined boots after weeks of tripping around in the footwear of a Southern schoolgirl!

I got your letter mailed Saturday a.m. You must have given it wings! Thank you for writing about your father. One day, I shall tell you about mine. Alas, there was no steel in him at all. He was constructed entirely of charm, French cigarettes, and storytelling. He was often sad, utterly defenseless, and I loved him madly. He was thrilled that I was a girl, once saying that he didn't know what he would have done with a little person who wanted to kick around a football or go fly-fishing.

Oh, Timothy! I feel wretched. I cannot look at another zebra, another wildebeest, and certainly no more armadillos! I am so very tired.

I want more than anything to scratch through that last remark or start over, for that is what my mother always said. She always said she was tired, and I vowed never to say it, especially to you. But I am tired, and there you have it. I am exhausted in every bone.

I should love to kiss you over and over. Like at the airport. Our kisses made me feel I was flying, long before I got on the little plane. I am weary of having my feet on the ground, dearest. I should like to poke my head in the clouds!

With inexpressible longings,
Your loving bookend

Dearest Bookend,

Hang in there. i have just this moment heard a male cardinal singing. He is sitting on the branch of an icebound bush outside the office window. It is so reviving to hear his song i had to tell you at once. It has gone on and on, as if he can't bear to end it. His mate swoops and dives about the bush, expressing her own glad joy for the sunshine that is with us at last. Let this be a comfort, somehow, and a hope for us. Am off to Wesley with Dooley to buy a parka, as his was ripped on a fence when we delivered Christmas baskets. Know this comes with tenderest love and fervent prayer, and yes, my own longings.

yrs, timothy

A Light in the Window, Ch. 7

My Bookend,

The winter here continues bitter and dark, the work on the book goes poorly, and my heart aches for the consolation of your company. Even so, I am keeping the light . . .

A Light in the Window, Ch. 8

Dearest Timothy,

   Miss Addison had a cocktail party, as she calls it, for four cats in the building. Thank goodness, Violet was not able to go, as she has just had a shot and was not feeling sociable.

According to the superintendent, who came to fix my faucet, Miss Addison's butler or footman or whatever he is put little heaps of catnip on a silver tray and set the tray on the drawing room floor.

   All the cats, it's reported, went absolutely berserk.

   They climbed Miss Addison's silk shantung draperies and gave her Louis XIV sofa a good drubbing with their claws. Then they leapt onto the kitchen counter and gobbled up the smoked salmon intended for the horrified people who owned the cats.

   It's enough to make one wish for a dog.

   Miss Addison said she was told that catnip is a spring tonic and ordered this stuff all the way from a farm in upstate New York. I had entertained the thought of buying some for Violet but have squelched this notion permanently.

   Our streets are full of a general sloshiness that lingers and won't go away, as if a glacier is deicing to the north. I forgot to ask on Sunday if anything has poked its head up in my perennial bed. Would you look? I am so homesick I can hardly bear it. I've worked on this stupid book until my eyes are crossing. You won't recognize me. At the airport, you will peer at me and say, "Cynthia?" Then you'll mutter, "No, no, can't be," and walk on.

   But oh, this book will be good, I think. I really do believe so. Everyone here seems excited about it, and I pray fervently it will be loved by its readers. Do you know that one of my favorite things is seeing a child reading one of my books? They don't even have to like it. It is merely the sight of a small head bowed over the pages that gives me indescribable joy.

   Do you feel the same when your sermons pierce our hearts and convict us of something that must be carried forth or changed in ourselves?

Thank you for sending your typed sermon. I needed to hear all of it. Yes! Intimacy is always about openness, about transparency. Until the Holy Spirit led me into intimacy with Christ, I was as transparent as your iron skillet. It is terribly scary to go around with your very spleen on display, yet, how can He shine through anything that is not made transparent? Well, of course, He could—but well, you understand.

I loved your note confessing that your feelings for me have made you more transparent. Sometimes—well, only once, actually—I've felt a little guilty for falling in love with you. Guilty that I have taken something from you, something very private. I try not to dwell on this.

With much love from
Your bookend

the office

thursday, fog on the heels of sunshine, 56 deg., barnabas snoring, emma making deposit

dear Lord! taken something from me? words cannot express what you have given, do give. that you would love me at all continues to perplex me, i am sorry to say. as we go into Lent ii ponder again and again how the apostles must have felt at losing him, at losing the love that had captured and ennobled and given them something higher than they could have ever known without him. there must have been the deepest despair and disbelief, greater than the ordinary loss of a loved one, until the Holy Spirit arrived on the scene and filled in the blanks. ii have known something of loss, also, in these weeks, these months you have been away, months in which winter has breathed its frost upon our spirits continually. yet i think it is good somehow that we discovered, confessed our feelings for one another and were forced apart to think it through. that at least is true for me, and i am being philosophical about it at the moment. at other moments i could not ask for anything more than to have you here and cook your supper. afterward, we might sit by the fire and look at the new garden catalogs. there, now, I've run you away with the prospect of such dull evenings, while you might be at the club playing cards or doing the tango.

please do not ever think that you have taken anything from me, but know that you have given me something too precious and amazing to contemplate. and never worry that i won't recognize you. ii would know those blue eyes anywhere, crossed or no.

i kiss you. God bless you and keep you. marge and hal pray for you, as does dooley on occasion.

harold cometh
love, timothy

P.S. nothing poking up, will advise

A Light in the Window, Ch. 9

Dear Timothy,

Hanging up on you was a silly and immature thing to do, but I couldn't help it. It just happened. Something came over me.

Your note arrived, telling me about the mix-up, and I've tried to feel remorseful for what I did. Actually, I don't feel one bit remorseful, but I do feel forgiving.

As I thought how you flew to New York to surprise and comfort me, the ice around my heart began to melt and I could not help but love you.

Hasn't our timing, and especially mine, been atrocious? If only I had been here when you arrived, do you think things might have been different? Do you think the ice around your own heart might have melted for eternity?

I've decided I will come home to Mitford at the end of the month and live there always, no matter what the future holds. Nothing can run me away again, not even a neighbor who is kind and loving one moment and distant and indifferent the next.

Somehow, the mention of marriage has strained even the sweet pleasure we found in going steady. It is grieving to think we might throw it all away because we've come to a hard place in the road and cannot cross over it. One would think that two people with brains in their heads could stand in the road and ponder the obstacle and come up with some ingenious way of getting over or round it! I mean, look what Mr. Edison, quite alone, managed to do with the lightbulb!

Perhaps we could be friends, Timothy. But it's time for me to quit suggesting what we might do or be together and let it rest in God's hands.

If you think that sounds spiritually noble, it is not. I simply don't know what else to do.

Cynthia

A Light in the Window, Ch. 13

Dear Cynthia,

It won't be long until lights will burn again in the darkened windows of the little yellow house; bushes will bloom, trees will leaf out, the wrens will build a nest under your eave. So, hurry home, and help these good things to happen.

If you'll let me know when you're arriving, I'd like to fetch you from the airport.

All is well here, only one upset which I'll tell you about. Am investigating schools for Dooley. Thankfully, there are quite a few out there, but must get some tutoring into him before fall. Will likely go on a tour of schools as soon as his classes at Mitford School are over in June.

We will be glad to have you home.

Love, Timothy

A Light in the Window, Ch. 14

My dearest husband,

I regret that I snapped at you this morning. You snapped, I snapped. And for what? As you left, looking hurt, I wanted to run after you and hold you, but I could not move. I stood upstairs on the landing and moped at the window like a schoolgirl, watching as you went along the sidewalk.

I saw you stop for a moment and look around, as if you wanted to turn back. You seemed forlorn, and I was overcome with sorrow for anything I might ever do to give you pain. My darling Timothy, who means all the world to me—forgive me.

It was the slightest thing between us, something that would hardly matter to anyone else, I think. We are both so sensitive, so alike in that region of the heart which fears rejection and resists chastisement.

As I looked down upon you, I received your hurt as my own, and so have had a double measure all these hours.

Hurry home, dearest husband!

Come and kiss me and let us hold one another in that way which God has set aside for us. You are precious to me, more than breath.

Ever thine,

   Cynthia

   (still your bookend?)

P.S. I know it is a pitiable gesture, but I shall roast something savory for your supper and make your favorite oven-browned potatoes.

Truce?

Bookend—

dooley has delivered your letter and is waiting for me to respond. ii have suffered, you have suffered.

Enough!

You are dear to me beyond measure. That God allowed us to have thiis union at all stuns me daily/

"Bright star, would I were steadfast as thou art—"

love, timothy—who, barely two years ago, you may recall, vowed to cherish you always, no matter what

Truce.

ii will gladly wash the dishes and barnabas will dry.

Out to Canaan, Ch. 16

Once Upon a Time

Writing for Children

ॐ

O*nce upon a* time, I realized I also wanted to write for children.

My first book for a young audience was about my grandmother, Miss Fannie. Since families are so widely scattered these days, and grandparents and great-grandparents too seldom known or remembered, I wanted to give young readers an elderly woman who was, in a sense, just like themselves.

"Miss Fannie was ninety-nine years old, and very small. In fact, she had grown to be about the same size as she was as a little girl."

We found that boys and girls alike love *Miss Fannie's Hat,* and "get" the whole notion of sharing, which is what the book is about.

I'm also happy about *Jeremy: The Tale of an Honest Bunny,* which I wrote in longhand in a handmade book, for my daughter, Candace. It is currently published by Puffin Books, an imprint of Viking Children's Books, and is all about a long and circuitous journey with a safe and happy arrival at the place we all long for: Home.

Then there's *The Trellis and the Seed,* a picture book for all ages, which reminds us that God has a plan for each of us, a wisdom that we too often forget as grownups.

I love writing for young readers (after all, I was one, once). But here's an odd thing. I feel that *Violet Comes to Stay,* also published by Viking Children's Books, is one of my own—though I didn't even write it!

Indeed, it is the first in Cynthia Coppersmith's wonderfully written and illustrated series about her white cat, Violet.

Whoa. Cynthia Coppersmith is a fictitious character. How could she write and illustrate a book you can actually hold in your hands?

Long story short, here's how.

I searched for several years to find a writer with a "voice" that would be authentic to Cynthia's. Hurray, we found her! Then we looked for an illustrator who would draw and paint like Cynthia. Hats in the air, we found her!

So what did *I* do?

I meddled in the while affair, to make absolutely, positively certain that you—and Cynthia—would be very pleased, indeed, with *Violet Comes to Stay.*

And what is the story about?

It's about expecting the best, but getting something not quite so rosy . . . until, at the end, we realize that He had a wonderful plan for us, after all.

Which, of course, in life as in fiction, makes for a very happy ending.

Healing the Broken Heart:
The Sermons

Preaching should break a hard heart and heal a broken one.

—John Newton

*J*ohn *Newton knew* a great deal about the hard heart. Before he surrendered his life to Christ, he had one. Indeed, Newton was a profane and merciless slave trader until he became an ardent believer, and later, a priest in the Church of England.

"I once was lost," he wrote in his great hymn "Amazing Grace," "but now I'm found; was blind, but now I see."

Writing Father Tim's sermons is a tough and serious business for me; I make no pretensions to being a preacher. When I come to the sermon in a Mitford book, I come trembling. But I come. After all, my protagonist is a preacher, and he has to preach. Just as in other sorts of books, spies have to spy.

I pray these simple homilies will have some meaning for my readers, and that, in a way I can't know or predict, they will bring healing.

Here's a quote by Abraham Lincoln that Father Tim jotted in his second journal, *A Continual Feast:*

"If I had eight hours to chop down a tree, I'd spend six sharpening my axe." Beside it, he penned: *Best sermon on writing a sermon.*

Now here's one of my own favorite quotes about the great and worthy labor of homiletics.

I preached as never sure to preach again; and as a dying man to dying men.

—Richard Baxter, 1615–19

May it be so.

THE SERMONS

HE STOOD IN the sacristy, vested and waiting with the anxious choir, and the eager procession that extended all the way down the steps to the basement.

There was new music this morning, composed by the organist, something wondrous and not so easy to sing, and choir adrenaline was pumping like an oil derrick. Adding voltage to the electricity bouncing off the walls was the fact that the music required congregational response, always capable of injecting an element of surprise, if not downright dismay.

He peered through the glass panels of the sacristy door into the nave, able to see only the gospel side from this vantage point. He spied quite a few faces he'd never laid eyes on, given that today was Homecoming.

Some of the faithful remnant had been beaten to their pews by the homecomers, so he had to search for Otis and Marlene and the Duncan lineup, on the far right. Down front was Janette with Jonathan on her lap, flanked by Babette and Jason, *thank You, Lord.* And two rows back was Sew Joiner, gazing at the work on the walls and ceiling, and generally looking like he'd hung the moon.

At the sound of the steeple bell, the crucifer burst through the door and into the nave with her procession, the organ played its mighty opening notes, and the choir streamed forth as a rolling clap of thunder.

Carried along by the mighty roar and proclamation of the organ, the choir processed up the aisle with vigor.

> *Sing to the Lord a new song*
> *And His praise from the ends of the earth*
> *Alleluia! Alleluia!*
> *You who go down to the sea, and all that is in it*
> *Alleluia! Alleluia!*

The congregation joined in the first two alleluias as if waking from a long sleep; at the second pair, they hunkered down and cranked into high gear, swept along by the mighty lead of the choir.

> *Let them give glory to the Lord*
> *And declare His praise in the coastlands*
> *Alleluia! Alleluia!*

As the choir passed up the creaking steps to the loft, the organ music soared in the little nave, enlarging it, expanding it, until it might have been o'ercrossed by the fan vaulting of an English cathedral.

Quickly taking their places by the organ, the choir entered again into the fervent acclamations of Isaiah and the psalmist.

> *Sing to Him a new song*
> *Play skillfully with a loud and joyful sound*
> *Alleluia!*
> *For the work of the Lord is right*
> *Alleluia!*
> *And all His work is done in faithfulness!*
> *Alleluia!*

A full minute of organ music concluded the first part of the new work, celebrating God's grace to the people of St. John's, and the joyful first homecoming in three decades. Many of the congregants, marveling at the music that poured forth from the loft, turned around in their pews and looked up in wonderment.

> *Alleluia! Alleluia!*

In the ascending finale, which was sung a cappella, the soprano reached for the moon and, to the priest's great joy and relief, claimed it for the kingdom.

* * *

"When trees and power lines crashed around you, when the very roof gave way above you, when light turned to darkness and water turned to dust, did you call on Him?

"When you called on Him, was He somewhere up there, or was He as near as your very breath?"

He stood in front of the pulpit this morning, looking into the faces of those whom God had given into his hand for this fleeting moment in time.

"What some believers still can't believe is that it is God's passion to be as near to us as our very breath.

"Far more than I want us to have a bigger crowd or a larger parish hall or a more ambitious budget . . . more than anything as your priest, I pray for each and every one of you to sense and know God's presence . . . as near as your breath.

"In short, it has been my prayer since we came here for you to have a personal, one-on-one, day-to-day relationship with Christ.

"I'm talking about something that goes beyond every Sunday service ever created or ever to be created, something you can depend on for the rest of your life, and then forever. I'm talking about the times you cry out in the storm that prevails against you, times when your heart and your flesh fail and you see no way out and no way in, when any prayer you utter to a God you may view as distant and disinterested seems to vanish into thin air.

"There are legions who believe in the existence of a cold and distant God, and on the occasions when they cry out to Him in utter despair and hear nothing in reply, must get up and stumble on, alone.

"Then there are those who know Him personally, who have found that when they cry out, there He is, as near as their breath—one-on-one, heart-to-heart, savior, Lord, partner, friend.

"Some have been in church all their lives and have never known this mighty, marvelous, and yet simple personal relationship. Others believe that while such a relationship may be possible, it's not for them— why would God want to bother with them, except from a very great distance? In reality, it is no bother to God at all. He wants this relationship far, far more than you and I want it, and I pray that you will ponder that marvelous truth.

"But who among us could ever deserve to have such a wondrous and altogether unimaginable thing as a close, personal, day-to-day relationship with Almighty God, creator of the universe?

"It seems unthinkable, and so . . . we are afraid to think it.

"For this fragile time in history, this tender and fleeting moment of our lives, I am your priest; God has called me to lead this flock. As I look out this morning, my heart has a wish list for you. For healed marriages, good jobs, the well-being and safety of your children; for Eleanor, knees that work; for Toby, ears that hear; for Jessie, good news from her son; for Phillip, good news from his doctor. On and on, there are fervent desires upon my heart for you. But chief among the hopes, the prayers, the petitions is this: *Lord . . . let my people know.* Let them know that the unthinkable is not only real, but available and possible and can be entered into, now, today—though we are, indeed, completely undeserving.

"It can be entered into today, with only a simple prayer that some think not sophisticated enough to bring them into the presence of God, not fancy enough to turn His face to theirs, not long enough, not high enough, not deep enough. . . .

"Yet, this simple prayer makes it possible for you to know Him not only as Savior and Lord, but as a friend. 'No longer do I call you servants,' He said to His followers in the Gospel of John, 'but friends.'

"In the storms of your life, do you long for the consolation of His nearness and His friendship? You can't imagine how He longs for the consolation of yours. It is unimaginable, isn't it, that He would want to be near us—frail as we are, weak as we are, and hopeless as we so often feel. God wants to be *with us.* That, in fact, is His name: Immanuel, God with us. And why is that so hard to imagine, when indeed, He made us for Himself? Please hear that this morning. The One who made us . . . made us for Himself.

"We're reminded in the Book of Revelation that He created all things—for His pleasure. Many of us believe that He created all things, but we forget the very best part—that He created us . . . *for His pleasure.*

"There are some of you who want to be done with seeking Him once a week, and crave, instead, to be with Him day after day, telling him everything, letting it all hang out, just thankful to have such a blessing in your life as a friend who will never, under any circumstances, leave you, and never remove His love from you. Amazing? Yes, it is. It is amazing.

"God knows who is longing to utter that simple prayer this morning. It is a matter between you and Him, and it is a prayer which will usher you into His presence, into life everlasting, and into the intimacy of a friendship in which He is as near . . . as your breath.

"Here's the way this wondrous prayer works—as you ask Him into your heart, He receives you into His. The heart of God! What a place to be, to reside for all eternity.

"As we bow our heads to pray under this new roof and inside these new walls, I ask that He graciously bless each and every one of us today . . . with new hearts."

He bowed his head and clasped his hands together and heard the beating of the blood in his temples. Ella Bridgewater, sitting next to the aisle with her walker handy, looked on approvingly. Captain Larkin, seated to her right, bowed his head in his hands.

"Sense, feel God's presence among us this morning . . ."

He waited.

". . . as those of you who are moved to do so, silently repeat this simple prayer:

"Thank You, God, for loving me . . .

". . . and for sending Your Son to die for my sins.

"I sincerely repent of my sins . . .

". . . and receive Jesus Christ as my personal savior.

"Now, as Your child . . .

". . . I turn my entire life over to You.

"Amen."

He raised his head, but didn't hurry on. Such a prayer was mighty, and, as in music, a rest stop was needed.

The recitation of the Nicene Creed was next in the order of service, and he opened his mouth to say so, but closed it again.

He looked to the epistle side and saw Mamie and Noah; Mamie

was smiling and nodding her head. Behind them were Junior Bryson and Misty Summers; he thought Junior's grin was appreciably wider than his tie.

"If you prayed that prayer and would join me at the altar, please come." He hadn't known he would say this; he had utterly surprised himself.

Some would be too shy to come, but that was God's business; he hoped he wouldn't forget and leave out the Creed altogether.

"If you'd like to renew your baptism vows in your heart, please come. If you'd like to express thanksgiving for all that God has fulfilled in your life, please come. If you'd like to make a new beginning, to surrender your life utterly into His care, please come."

Though this part of the service was entirely unplanned, he thought it might be a good time for a little music. His choir, however, was stricken as dumb as wash on a line.

From the epistle side, four people rose and left their pews and walked down the aisle.

On the gospel side, five parishioners and a homecomer stood from the various pews and, excusing themselves, stepped over the feet of several who were furiously embarrassed and looking for the door.

Father Tim opened a vial of oil, knelt for a moment on the sanctuary side of the rail, and prayed silently. One by one, the congregants dropped humbly to their knees, at least two looking stern but determined, others appearing glad of the opportunity to do this reckless thing, to surrender their hearts in an act of wild and holy abandon and begin again.

He dipped his right thumb in the oil and touched the forehead of the first at the rail, making the sign of the cross and saying, "I anoint you, Phillip, in the name of the Father, and of the Son, and of the Holy Spirit. . . ."

In the choir loft, the organist rose from the bench, and walked stiffly down the stairs and along the center aisle with the aid of a cane.

Madeleine Duncan scrambled to her knees in the pew and whispered in her mother's ear, "Look, Mommy, it's a little tiny man with a big head."

Observing the penitent who now approached the altar, Leonard

Lamb didn't realize he was staring with his mouth open, nor that tears suddenly sprang to his eyes.

Marion Fieldwalker poked Sam in the ribs. "Who's that?"

"Good gracious alive!" Sam whispered, as if to himself.

As Father Tim touched the forehead of the man kneeling before him, it seemed that an electric shock was born from the convergence of their flesh; it arced and flashed along his arm like a bolt.

"I anoint you, Morris, in the name of the Father, and of the Son, and of the Holy Spirit, and beseech the mercy of our Lord Jesus Christ to seal forever what is genuine in your heart. May God be with you always, my brother."

A New Song, Ch. 22

HÉLÈNE PRINGLE STEPPED from the bright, warm sunlight into the cool, sweet shadow of the narthex.

Before she quite recovered from the small shock to her senses, someone thrust a copy of the pew bulletin into her hand and gave her a surprised, albeit warm, greeting, which, to her regret, she returned in French.

She was trembling slightly, with both fear of the unknown and a deep, childlike excitement.

The service would be different from the services her grandmother had forced her, for a brief period, to attend in that great, cold church built of stone. She'd hardly ever understood anything the priest had said, for the echo made his voice sound tremulous and metallic, as if it were coming from the walls and not from a man. The acoustics, however, had done wondrous things for the voices of the choir; she remembered the goose bumps she felt as a nine-year-old; they prickled along her spine and made her hair feel as if it were standing.

She was afraid she wouldn't know what to say or do in this morning's service, though someone had declared that Episcopal and Catholic liturgies weren't so vastly different, in the end. Of course, the whole Episcopal thing had come about in the first place because of Henry the Eighth, who'd been a vain and vulgar man, to say the least. She wondered that anyone would admit to being part of something he'd established. But she sensed the moment she awoke this morning that she had to be here, and so she had arisen and dressed, asking the unseen Being on the other side of the drapery to help her select attire that wouldn't stand out or offend.

She suspected there would be a lot of kneeling and jostling about, which led her to choose the very back row, on the side by the stained-glass window of the Sermon on the Mount, where she tried to shrink herself as small as she possibly could, so no one would notice she was there.

How lovely is thy dwelling place,
O Lord of hosts, to me!
My thirsty soul desires and longs
Within thy courts to be;
My very heart and flesh cry out,
O living God, for thee.

Beside thine altars, gracious Lord,
The swallows find a nest;
How happy they who dwell with thee
And praise thee without rest,
And happy they whose hearts are set
Upon the pilgrim's quest.

They who go through the desert vale
Will find it filled with springs,
And they shall climb from height to height
Till Zion's temple rings
With praise to thee, in glory throned
Lord God, great King of kings.

One day within thy courts excels
A thousand spent away;
How happy they who keep thy laws
Nor from thy precepts stray,
For thou shalt surely bless all those
Who live the words they pray.

Hope Winchester entered the church as the pipe organ began the prelude, and looked around anxiously for a place to sit. There was only one person in the rear pew on the left.

Thinking the rear pew a good choice, she slid in quickly, noting that Hélène Pringle occupied the other end. She nodded to Miss Pringle, who had bought note cards at Happy Endings just last week.

She consulted her pew bulletin, turned in the prayer book to page 355, and hugged the open book to her chest. She'd been inside Lord's Chapel only twice before, and was feeling utterly naked, as if she were raw and exposed altogether. She hoped she wouldn't make a fool of herself, and especially hoped that George wasn't sitting where he could see her in case she did. She only knew that it was important to be here this morning, though she wasn't sure why.

Perhaps, she thought, it was because she'd given up being a noun, and was being transformed into a verb.

* * *

"In the name of the Father, and of the Son, and of the Holy Spirit, amen," he said, crossing himself.

"I wrestled with this morning's message as Jacob wrestled with the angel, until at last I said to God, 'I will not let You go until You bless me.'

"I had prayed and labored over a sermon, the title of which is listed in your bulletin and which no longer has anything to do with what I have to say to you this morning, nor does it delve the meaning of to-day's Propers.

"What I'd hoped to say was something we all need to know and ponder in our lives, but the message would not come together, it would not profess the deeper truth I felt God wanted me to convey.

"And the reason it would not is simple:

"I was writing the wrong sermon.

"Then . . . at the final hour, when hope was dim and my heart bruised with the sense of failure, God blessed me with a completely different message—a sermon expressly for this service, this day, this people."

Father Tim smiled. "The trouble is, he gave me only four words.

"I was reminded, then, of Winston Churchill, how he was called to deliver the convocation address at his old school—where, by the way, he had not done well, his headmaster had predicted nothing but failure for Churchill. He was called to give the address and he stood to the podium and there was an enormous swell of excitement among the pupils and faculty that here was a great man of history, a great man of letters and discourse, about to tell them how to go forward in their lives.

"Mr. Churchill leaned over the podium, looked his audience in the eye, and here, according to legend, is what he said; this is the entire text of his address that day:

"'Young men, nevah, nevah, nevah give up.'

"Then he sat down. That was his message. Seven words. In truth, if he had said more, those seven words might not have had the power to penetrate so deeply, nor counsel so wisely.

"Last night, alone in my study, God gave me four words that Saint Paul wrote in his second letter to the church at Thessalonica. Four words that can help us enter into obedience, trust, and closer communion with God Himself, made known through Jesus Christ.

"Here are the four words. I pray you will inscribe them on your heart."

Hope Winchester sat forward in the pew.

"In everything . . . give thanks."

Father Tim paused and looked at those gathered before him. At Emma Newland . . . Gene Bolick . . . Dooley Barlowe . . . Pauline Leeper . . . Hope Winchester . . . Hélène Pringle. Around the nave his eyes gazed, drawing them close.

"In *everything,* give thanks. That's all. That's this morning's message.

"If you believe as I do that Scripture is the inspired Word of God, then we see this not as a random thought or an oddly clever idea of His servant Paul, but as a loving command issued through the great apostle.

"Generally, Christians understand that giving thanks is good and right.

"Though we don't do it often enough, it's easy to have a grateful heart for food and shelter, love and hope, health and peace. But what about the hard stuff, the stuff that darkens your world and wounds you to the quick? Just what is this *everything* business?

"It's the hook. It's the key. *Everything* is the word on which this whole powerful command stands and has its being.

"Please don't misunderstand; the word *thanks* is crucial. But a deeper spiritual truth, I believe, lies in giving thanks in . . . everything.

"In loss of all kinds. In illness. In depression. In grief. In failure. And, of course, in health and peace, success and happiness. In everything.

"There'll be times when you wonder how you can possibly thank Him for something that turns your life upside down; certainly there will be such times for me. Let us, then, at times like these, give thanks *on faith alone* . . . obedient, trusting, hoping, believing.

"Perhaps you remember the young boy who was kidnapped and beaten and thrown into prison, yet rose up as Joseph the King, ruler of nations, able to say to his brothers, with a spirit of forgiveness, 'You thought evil against me, but God meant it for good, that many lives might be spared.' Better still, remember our Lord and Savior Jesus Christ, who suffered agonies we can't begin to imagine, fulfilling God's will that you and I might have everlasting life.

"Some of us have been in trying circumstances these last months. Unsettling. Unremitting. Even, we sometimes think, unbearable. Dear God, we pray, stop this! Fix that! Bless us—and step on it!

"I admit to you that although I often thank God for my blessings, even the smallest, I haven't thanked Him for my afflictions.

"I know the fifth chapter of First Thessalonians pretty well, yet it just hadn't occurred to me to actually take Him up on this notion. I've been too busy begging Him to lead me out of the valley and onto the mountaintop. After all, I have work to do, I have things to accomplish . . . alas, I am the White Rabbit everlastingly running down the hole like the rest of the common horde.

"I want to tell you that I started thanking Him last night—this morning at two o'clock, to be precise—for something that grieves me deeply. And I'm committed to continue thanking Him in this hard thing, no matter how desperate it might become, and I'm going to begin looking for the good in it. Whether God caused it or permitted it, we can rest assured—there is great good in it.

"Why have I decided to take these four words as a personal commission? Here's the entire eighteenth verse:

"'In everything, give thanks . . . for this is the will of God Jesus concerning you.'

"His will concerning you. His will concerning me.

"This thing which I've taken as a commission intrigues me. I want to see where it goes, where it leads. I pray you'll be called to do the same. And please, tell me where it leads you. Let me hear what happens when you respond to what I believe is a powerful and challenging, though deceptively simple, command of God.

"Let's look once more at the four words God is saying to us . . . by looking at what our obedience to them will say to God.

"Our obedience will say, 'Father, I don't know why You're causing, or allowing, this hard thing to happen, but I'm going to give thanks in it because You ask me to. I'm going to trust You to have a purpose for it that I can't know and may never know. Bottom line, You're God—and that's good enough for me.'

"What if you had to allow one of your teenagers to experience a hard thing, and she said, 'Mom, I don't really understand why you're letting this happen, but you're my mom and I trust you and that's good enough for me'?"

He looked around the congregation. "Ah, well," he said, "probably not the best example."

Laughter.

"But you get the idea.

"There are, of course, many more words in the first letter to the Thessalonians. Here are just a few:

"'Pray without ceasing.'

"'Abstain from all appearance of evil.'

"'Quench not the Spirit.'

"These words, too, contain holy counsel and absolute truth.

"But the words which God chose for this day, this service, this pastor, and this people, were just four. Yes, do the other things I command you to do, He says, but mark these."

He gazed upon his former flock with great tenderness.

"Mark these."

Hélène Pringle realized she had been holding her breath for what seemed like a very long time.

"When we go out into this golden morning and meet in our beautiful churchyard, let those who will, follow yet another loving command from Paul's letter. 'Greet the brethren with a holy kiss!'

"Amen."

Miss Pringle exhaled; and then, with the congregation, gave the response.

"Amen!"

In This Mountain, Ch. 19

HE HAD WELCOMED the newcomers for a fare-thee-well, put forth a bit of church history, invited one and all to stay for their dinner on the grounds, and moved briskly onward.

In all his years as a priest, he had experienced few Sundays so richly promising, and so dauntingly filled, as today would be.

"Your pew bulletins were printed on Friday, well before I received some thrilling news, news that affects our entire parish—news that, indeed, causes the angels in heaven to rejoice.

"Add to that yet another evidence of God's favor to Holy Trinity, and I daresay your bulletin will be somewhat hard to follow."

He removed his glasses and looked out to his congregation; he felt a smile having its way with his face. "In short, he prepared for the best!"

Several of the congregation peered at their pew mates, wondering.

"In the fifth chapter of the book of James, we're exhorted to confess our sins, one to another. In the third chapter of the book of Matthew, we read, 'Then went out to him,' meaning John the Baptist, 'Jerusalem and all Judea, and all the region round about Jordan, and were baptized of him . . . confessing their sins.'

"I've always esteemed the idea of confession, and in my calling, one sees a good bit of it. But this notion of confessing our sins *one to another* is quite a different matter. Indeed, it involves something more than priest and supplicant; it means confessing to the community, within the fellowship of saints.

"When I left Holy Trinity on Friday, I was going home. But God pointed my truck in the opposite direction.

"I drove to see someone I've learned to love, as I've learned to love so many of you since coming to Wilson's Ridge.

"We had talked and visited several times, and I could see that his distance from God had made things uphill both ways. But I always hesitated to ask him one simple question.

"I didn't hesitate this time. I asked him if he would pray a simple prayer with me that would change everything."

His eyes roved the packed pews, to those seated in folding chairs that lined the aisle. There was Jubal. And all the Millwrights. And Robert and Dovey and Donny, and Ruby Luster holding Sissie on her lap . . .

"Now, the thought of having everything changed in our lives is frightening. Even when the things that need changing are hard or brutal, some of us cling to them, anyway, because they're familiar. Indeed, our brother had clung . . . and it wasn't working.

"In our hymn this morning, we sang, 'They who go through the desert vale, or any parched and arid valley, will find it filled with springs.' When we choose to walk through the valley with Him, He will be our living water. He will not only sustain us, but give us the grace to move, as that beautiful hymn says, from height to height.

"In a moment, we will have a joyous baptizing, our first since Holy Trinity opened its doors again after forty years. As part of the service for Holy Baptism, our brother has asked if he might make his confession to all of us here today.

"Before I call him forward, I'd like to recite the simple prayer he prayed, similar to one I prayed myself . . . long after I left seminary.

"It's a prayer you, also, may choose to pray in the silence of your heart. And when you walk again through the parched valley, as you've so often done alone, He will be there to walk through it with you. And that's just the beginning of all that lies in store for those who believe on Him."

He bowed his head, as did most of the congregation.

"Thank You, God, for loving me. And for sending Your son to die for my sins. I sincerely repent of my sins, and receive Jesus Christ as my personal savior. Now, as Your child, I turn my entire life over to You.

"Amen.

"Robert Cleveland Prichard, will you come forward?"

Robert moved along the crowded aisle, trembling; his knees were water and his veins ice.

He stood by the pulpit and opened his mouth, but instead of words, tears came. For two days, that had been his worst fear. He turned away for a moment, then faced the people again.

"I'd like t' confess t' you . . . ," he said.

The very air in the nave was stilled. Robert raised his right hand.

". . . b'fore God . . . that I didn't do it."

Father Tim looked out to Miss Martha and Miss Mary, both of whom had forgotten to close their mouths. He saw Lace, riveted by what was taking place; and there was Agnes, pale as a moonflower. . . .

"I cain't go into th' details of all th' stuff about m' granpaw, 'cause they's little young 'uns in here. But Friday e'enin' I done a thing with Father Tim that I guess I've wanted t' do, but didn't know how t' do. I give it all over t' Jesus Christ, like I should've done when m' buddy talked t' me about 'im in prison.

"All I can say is, it's good. It's good." Robert nodded, as if to himself "I thank y'."

He gazed peaceably into the eyes of those seated in the nave.

Agnes Merton stood, and together with Dooley Kavanagh, presented the century-old tin basin to Father Tim, who poured creek water into it from a tin pitcher.

There was the sound of a log shifting in the firebox; something like a deep, collective sigh stirred among the pews.

> *My faith looks up to thee,*
> *Thou Lamb of Calvary,*
> *Savior divine!*
> *Now hear me while I pray,*
> *Take all my guilt away;*
> *O let me from this day*
> *Be wholly thine.*
>
> *May thy rich grace impart*
> *Strength to my fainting heart,*
> *My zeal inspire;*
> *As thou has died for me,*
> *O may my love to thee*
> *Pure, warm and changeless be*
> *A living fire . . .*

At the time of announcements, and with no suggestion of what to come, Father Tim introduced Lloyd Goodnight and Clarence Merton.

The two men took their places by the pulpit.

Lloyd cleared his throat, blushed, and adjusted his shirt collar. He'd completely forgotten to check his fly, but it was too late, now.

"What it'll be is two stalls, one f'r ladies, one f'r men, four b' six each, with wash basins an' all."

He pulled a note from his pocket, studied it a moment, and once again addressed the congregation.

"Me an' Clarence will be y'r builders. We'll run a pipeline to th' spring, like th' ol' schoolhouse done. We'll have a tin roof an' a concrete slab, an' real good ventilation.

"We thank you."

The congregation stood as one, and applauded.

* * *

Rooter had pretty much felt his hair drying out by the end of the first hymn. He didn't know which way it might be shooting up since Granny chopped it off with a razor. But he couldn't think about that, he'd just gotten the signal from Father Tim and he had a job to do.

He stood as close to the vicar as he could, for protection—though he wasn't sure from what—and made the sign he'd learned this week from Clarence.

"Watch Rooter," said the vicar. Rooter made the sign, which involved three separate movements, three times. He was careful to do it slowly.

"Now it's our turn." Some got it right off the bat, others struggled.

"What are we saying here, Rooter?"

"God . . . loves . . . us!" shouted Rooter.

He hadn't meant to shout. His face felt hot as a poker.

"Amen!" said someone in the back row.

"I'm asking you to give that sign to someone today," said Father Tim. "And do it like you mean it, because He means it. Indeed, I would ask you to allow yourself . . . to really believe, from a deep place in your soul, that . . ."

His eyes searched the faces as he and Rooter signed.

. loves . . . us.

:o Sparkle and the choir. Clarence took up the cross.

> *Blest be the tie that binds*
> *Our hearts in Christian love;*
> *The fellowship of kindred minds*
> *Is like to that above.*
>
> *Before our Father's throne*
> *We pour our ardent prayers;*
> *Our fears, our hopes, our aims are one,*
> *Our comforts and our cares.*
>
> *We share each other's woes,*
> *Our mutual burdens bear;*
> *And often for each other flows*
> *The sympathizing tear . . .*

The rain began at dusk.

It quickly gathered force, and soon came down in sheets, filling dry creek beds and scattering cattle to the shelter of trees and run-in sheds.

In the downpour, anyone driving past Green Valley Baptist probably wouldn't have noticed the bold black letters of the sign by the road.

LOVE IS AN ACT OF ENDLESS FORGIVENESS

Light from Heaven, Ch. 20

MISS MARTHA HAD supervised the greening of the church this afternoon. The sharp, pungent odor of pine and cedar filled the nave; sticks of hardwood burned bright in the firebox.

"In the name of the Father . . ."

He crossed himself ". . . and of the Son, and of the Holy Spirit. Amen.

"I wrote a sermon this week, but discovered something as I reflected upon it.

"It told us more than we need to know."

Someone chuckled. He could have some fun with that, but time was of the essence; a big snow was predicted for tonight.

"Well, Lord, I said, please give me what we do need to know. And He did.

"As many of you are aware, this pulpit was built and beautifully hand carved by one of our own—Clarence Merton. The church was not open when he did it; in fact, there was no earthly assurance that it would ever be open again.

"Yet Clarence chose to make this pulpit, anyway.

"Why would he do that? He did it to the glory of God."

"And then, a vandal broke in, and he took out his knife and began to do his own carving, right on this magnificent pulpit."

Someone gasped.

"For those of you who haven't seen that particular carving, it's right here." He leaned to his left and made a gesture toward the oak side-panel.

"I consider it to constitute the most profound sermon that could be preached from this or any other pulpit.

"'JC,' it reads, 'loves CM.'

"When Agnes and Clarence saw what had been done, they might have wept. But what did they do? They gave thanks.

"They might have felt it a sacrilege. But what did they do? They considered it a word from God.

"JC, Jesus Christ . . . loves CM, Clarence Merton."

A relieved murmur sounded among the congregants.

"The thrilling thing about this inscription is that it's filled with truth, not just for Clarence Merton, but for every one of us on this hallowed eve of His birth.

"In everything God has told us in His Word, He makes one thing very clear:

"He loves us.

"Not merely as a faceless world population, but one by one.

"J.C., Jesus Christ, loves you, Miss Martha. He loves you, Miss Mary. He loves you, Jubal.

"And you and you and you—individually, and by name. 'My sheep hear my voice,' He says, 'and I call them by name.'

"On this eve of His birth, some of you may still be asking the age-old question, Why was I born?

"In the book of Revelation, we're told that He made all things—that would include us!—for Himself Why would He do that? For His pleasure, Scripture says.

"There's your answer. You were made by Him . . . and for Him, for His good pleasure.

"Selah! Think upon that.

"And why was *He* born?

"He came that we might have life. New life, in Him. What does this gift of new life in Him mean? In the weeks to come, we'll talk about what it means, and how it has the power to refine and strengthen and transform us, and deliver us out of darkness into light.

"Right now, Clarence has a gift for every one in this room. And a wonderful gift it is." He nodded to his crucifer. "Would you come forward, Clarence?"

Clarence came forward, carrying a large, flat, polished board.

He held it aloft for all to see.

"Oak," said the vicar. "White oak, the queen of the forest.

"This is a place for us to carve our own inscription, like the one on the pulpit. The board will be here every Sunday until Easter, and whoever wishes to do it will get help from Clarence, if needed. You don't even have to bring your own knife, we have one. When that's done, we'll hang the board on the wall over there, where years later, others can see it, and be reminded that He loves them, too."

He gazed a moment at the faces before him, at those whom God had given into his hand. *Shine, Preacher! In thy place . . .*

"For God so loved the world," he said, "that He gave His only begotten Son, that whosoever . . ."

Many of the congregants joined their voices with his as they spoke the verse from the Gospel of John.

". . . believeth in Him should not perish, but have everlasting life.

"For this hour," he said, "that's all we need to know."

Light from Heaven, Ch. 21

How Mitford Got Out There

❧

Once upon a time, the manuscript of the first Mitford novel was slowly (very slowly) making its rounds to publishers.

The agent who represented me then, and whose name I can no longer remember, managed to get eleven responses from editors during the year and a half she handled it.

"Not for our list."

"Not for our list."

"Too preachy."

"Not for our list."

You get the idea.

(As an aside, I must tell you that I've since met several of those editors, all of whom devoutly wish they'd bought *At Home in Mitford.* Smile.)

I decided to sell the darned thing myself, and shipped it off to a publishing firm in the UK, who'd done a picture book I liked.

"Not for our list," they said. "But maybe for the list of our sister company in the U.S."

The U.S. side liked it, bought it, and published it. But they failed to distribute or promote it. (New authors, take note.)

Foiled again.

Then one day, a dear friend named Mary Richardson introduced my first book to one of America's favorite booksellers, Nancy Olsen of Quail Ridge Books in Raleigh, North Carolina, and Nancy put me in touch with a *real* agent.

Liz Darhansoff is the genuine coin in the literary-agent realm. She's tough. She's quick. She's hardworking. And—she likes writers from the South.

In true Valkyrie fashion, Liz began at once making calls on behalf of the greatly misunderstood Mitford.

She had tea one afternoon with a young associate editor at Viking Penguin. The editor's name was Carolyn Carlson.

Carolyn, one of four daughters of a Lutheran minister, "got" Mitford immediately. She had grown up there and gone to church there and knew all the people in this fictional small town in the mountains of North Carolina. Bingo! Something her mother would like to read. Something, in truth, Carolyn liked reading herself.

It just so happens that Carolyn had been sending her mother books from the company's free shelf. Though her mother, Marjorie, is an ardent reader, Marjorie didn't seem especially thrilled with Carolyn's selections.

"Carolyn dear," she said, "don't you ever publish any *nice* books?"

That's sort of how it all happened.

And why you now have nice books with no cussin', no murder, and no mayhem, to share with your children, your parents, and your friends.

How revolutionary!

To Mary Richardson, Nancy Olsen, Liz Darhansoff, Carolyn Carlson, and Carolyn's mother, Marjorie:

Thank you.

A Cheerful Heart:
Uncle Billy's Jokes

"A cheerful
heart

doeth good like
a medicine."

. . . the cheerful heart has a continual feast.

—Proverbs 15:15, New International Version

For years, Uncle Billy Watson was one of my favorite—and most esteemed—Mitford characters.

Though he lived with the schizophrenic and exceedingly difficult Rose Watson for more than five decades, he maintained a cheerful spirit and positive outlook that made people glad to see him coming.

He was also a man of honor.

When Father Tim asked Uncle Billy how he'd managed to live with Miss Rose all these years, the old man replied:

"Well, Preacher, I took a vow."

His truest mission, however, was to be a bearer of jokes. In truth, the chief delight of his long life was to make people laugh, and you'll find dozens of Uncle Billy jokes throughout the Mitford novels. Just as Esther Bolick was the Cake Queen, Uncle Billy was the unchallenged Joke King.

In the final Mitford novel, *Light from Heaven,* I knew that someone had to be called up higher. And it wasn't going to be Father Tim. I really didn't want to let Uncle Billy go any more than I wished to part with Miss Sadie, whom I had loved as if she were flesh and blood.

But Uncle Billy did go—on the same night Esther Bolick's husband, Gene, died from the effects of an inoperable brain tumor.

The town was sad about this double loss. And though it was un-spoken, the loss of Uncle Billy was felt more keenly. The old man had been a fixture in Mitford for longer than most people could remember. They'd laughed at, and repeated, most of his jokes, and not a few had favorites they could pull out at church parties or ball games or Rotary meetings.

At Uncle Billy's funeral, which Father Tim preached, something most unusual happened.

Soon afterward, this phenomenon spread through Mitford like a brush fire. Here's a scene.

He scooted to Dora Pugh's hardware, jingling the bell above the door.

"I been lookin' for you in th' obituaries!" said Dora.

"Don't look there yet!"

"Have you heard about Coot Hendrick's new job?"

"Coot's *working*?" As far as he knew, Coot hadn't struck a lick at a snake in at least two decades.

"Has a hundred and seventy people under him."

"What?"

"Weed-eats th' town graveyard."

He laughed. "Ah, Dora, you're a sly one.'

"I hear Bill Sprouse up at First Baptist cut his chin pretty bad while shavin', said he had his mind on his sermon."

"I'll be darned. Sorry to hear it."

"They say he should've kep' his mind on his chin and cut 'is sermon."

"You got me twice in a row!"

Next, he zooms by Lew Boyd's Exxon for a fill-up.

"You hear th' one about th' police pullin' th' woman f'r speedin'?" asked Lew.

"Haven't heard it." It was an epidemic!

"She come flyin' by 'im with 'er husband in th' car, police caught up to 'er, said, 'I'm writin' you a ticket, did you know you're doin' ninety-two?' She said, 'Sure I know it, it says so on that sign yonder.'

"He says, 'That's a highway sign, for gosh sake. Husband's settin' there white as a sheet,' *po*lice says, 'What's th' matter with him?'

"She says, 'We just come off of 116.'"

No doubt about it, Uncle Billy left a legacy. And though he's gone to Glory, as Absalom Greer would have said, his spirit lives on in Mitford. In the last chapters of *Light from Heaven,* even the curmudgeonly J. C. Hogan and the no-nonsense Avis Packard are telling jokes.

I loved Uncle Billy, and shall miss his cheerful heart.

Requiescat in pace.

UNCLE BILLY'S JOKES

"So ROSE SAID t' me, she said, 'Bill Watson, I'm goin' t' give you a piece of my mind,' and I said, 'Just a small helpin', please.'" He grinned broadly at the rector.

"Yessir, I told Rose what you said about givin' th' house to th' town, an' them givin' her a nice, modern place all fixed up in th' back, and she said th' only way she'd do it was if the statue was like Sherman or Grant or one of them, don't you know. That's when I said he ought t' be settin' down, and she like to th'owed a fit."

Uncle Billy chuckled. "Preacher, I took Rose f'r better or worse, but I declare, she's much worse than I took 'er for!"

At Home in Mitford, Ch. 22

"UNCLE BILLY! How are you?"

"No rest f'r th' wicked, and th' righteous don't need none!" he said, cackling. "Jis' thought I'd call up to chew th' fat, and tell you things is goin' good up here at th' mansion."

"I'm always glad to hear that," said the rector, tucking the receiver under his chin and signing the letter he'd just typed.

"I don't know what you think about preacher jokes. . . ."

"What have you got? I could use a good laugh."

"Well, sir, this preacher didn't want to tell 'is wife he was speakin' to th' Rotary on th' evils of adultery. She was mighty prim, don't you know, so he told her he was goin' to talk about *boating.*

"Well sir, a little later, 'is wife run into a Rotarian who said her husband had give a mighty fine speech.

"'That's amazin',' she said, 'since he only done it twice. Th' first time he th'owed up and th' second time 'is hat blowed off.'"

A Light in the Window, Ch. 4

WHEN THE OLD man called the office, he felt instantly encouraged.

"Uncle Billy, how are you?"

"Pretty good, considerin' I done fell off a twelve-foot ladder."

"Good Lord! Is anything broken? Why, it's a miracle you survived!"

"Well, sir, t' tell th' truth, I only fell off th' bottom rung."

"Aha."

Uncle Billy sounded disappointed. "That's m' new joke, don't you know."

"I was supposed to laugh?"

"That's th' general thinkin' behind a joke."

A Light in the Window, Ch. 13

"HOW YOU 'UNS comin'?" Uncle Billy stuck his head in the hatch door and peered into the gloom.

"We need a joke!" said the rector. They had packed seventy-two boxes, all told, not a few of which were breakables that had already been broken.

"How about if I stand right here t' tell it," said Uncle Billy. "Arthur won't let me come down steps, don't you know." Activity subsided as the old man reared back to deliver his contribution to moving day.

"Did you 'uns hear about th' feller lookin' for a good church?"

"No!" chorused his audience.

"Well sir, he searched around and found a little fellowship where th' preacher and th' congregation were readin' out loud. They were sayin', 'We have left undone those things which we ought to have done, and we have done those things which we ought not to have done.'

"Th' feller dropped into th' pew with a big sigh of relief. 'Hallelujah,' he said to hisself, 'I've found my crowd at last.'"

The rector laughed heartily. "It's about time you worked our bunch into your repertoire."

"Hit us again, Uncle Billy," said Mule.

"This feller, he went t' th' doctor and told 'im what all was wrong, so th' doctor give 'im a big load of advice about how to git well. Th' feller started to leave, don't you know, when th' doctor said, 'Hold up. You ain't paid me for my advice.' 'That's right,' th' feller said, 'because I ain't goin' t' take it.'"

"I'll print that one," said J.C., scribbling in his pocket notebook.

A Light in the Window, Ch. 16

"YOU REMEMBER THAT dictionary I found in th' Dumpster?" Uncle Billy asked him when they met on the street.

"I do."

"I cain't hardly enjoy readin' it n' more."

"Is that right?"

"Yessir, it's one thing here and another thing there—they're always changin' th' subject, don't you know."

The rector rolled his eyes and chuckled.

"That's m' new joke, but it's not m' main joke. I'm workin' out m' main joke for spring. By th' almanac, spring comes official on June twenty-one."

"Well, then, you've got a little time," he said. "Let me treat you to a cheeseburger."

Uncle Billy grinned, his gold tooth gleaming. "I'd be beholden to you, Preacher. An' I wouldn't mind a bit if you'd tip in some fries."

He put his arm around the old man's shoulders as they walked toward the Grill. He'd be et for a tater if he didn't love Bill Watson like blood kin.

These High, Green Hills, Ch. 8

WHEN HE LEFT the bakery, he looked up the street and saw Uncle Billy sitting in a dinette chair on the grounds of the town museum, watching traffic flow around the monument.

He walked up and joined him. "Uncle Billy! I'm half starved for a joke."

"I cain't git a new joke t' save m' life," said the old man, looking forlorn.

"If you can't get a joke, nobody can."

"My jokes ain't workin' too good. I cain't git Rose t' laugh f'r nothin'."

"Aha."

"See, I test m' jokes on Rose, that's how I know what t' tell an' what t' leave off."

"Try one on me and see what happens."

"Well, sir, two ladies was talkin' about what they'd wear to th' Legion Hall dance, don't you know, an' one said, 'We're supposed t' wear somethin' t' match our husband's hair, so I'll wear black, what'll you wear?' an' th' other one sorta turned pale, don't you know, an' said, 'I don't reckon I'll go.'"

"Aha," said Father Tim.

"See, th' feller married t' that woman that won't be goin' was *bald,* don't you know."

The rector grinned.

"It don't work too good, does it?" said Uncle Billy. "How about this 'un? Little Sonny's mama hollered at 'im, said, 'Sonny, did you fall down with y'r new pants on?' An' Sonny said, 'Yes 'um, they won't time t' take 'em off.'"

The rector laughed heartily. "Not bad. Not half bad!"

"See, if I can hear a laugh or two, it gits me goin'."

"About like preaching, if you ask me."

Out to Canaan, Ch. 6

"WELL, SIR, A feller died who had lived a mighty sinful life, don't you know. Th' minute he got down t' hell, he commenced t' bossin' around th' imps an' all, a-sayin' do this, do that, and jump to it. Well, sir, he got so dominatin' that th' little devils reported 'im to th' head devil who called th' feller in, said, 'How come you act like you own this place?'

"Feller said, 'I do own it, my wife give it to me when I was livin'.'"

Out to Canaan, Ch. 19

UNCLE BILLY STOOD as straight as he was able, holding on to his cane and looking soberly at the little throng, who gave forth a murmur of coughing and throat-clearing.

"Wellsir!" he exclaimed, by way of introduction. "A farmer was haulin' manure, don't you know, an' 'is truck broke down in front of a mental institution. One of th' patients, he leaned over th' fence, said, 'What're you goin' t' do with y'r manure?'

"Farmer said, 'I'm goin' t' put it on m' strawberries.'

"Feller said, 'We might be crazy, but we put whipped cream on our'n.'"

Uncle Billy grinned at the cackle of laughter he heard.

"Keep goin'!" someone said.

"Wellsir, this old feller an' 'is wife was settin' on th' porch, an' she said, 'Guess what I'd like t' have?'

"He said, 'What's that?'

"She said, 'A great big bowl of vaniller ice cream with choc'late sauce and nuts on top!'

"He says, 'Boys howdy, that'd be good. I'll go down to th' store and git us some.'

"Wife said, 'Now, that's vaniller ice cream with choc'late sauce and nuts. Better write it down.'

"He said, 'Don't need t' write it down, I can remember.'

"Little while later, he come back. Had two ham san'wiches. Give one t' her. She looked at that san'wich, lifted th' top off, said, 'You mulehead, I told you t' write it down, I wanted mustard on mine!'"

Loving the sound of laughter in the cavernous room, Uncle Billy nodded to the left, then to the right.

"One more," he said, trembling a little from the excitement of the evening.

"Hit it!" crowed the mayor, hoping to remember the punch line to the vanilla ice-cream story.

"Wellsir, this census taker, he went to a house an' knocked, don't you know. A woman come out, 'e said, 'How many children you got, an' what're their ages?'

"She said, 'Let's see, there's th' twins Sally and Billy, they're eighteen. And th' twins Seth an' Beth, they're sixteen. And th' twins Penny an' Jenny, they're fourteen—'

"Feller said, 'Hold on! Did you git twins ever' time?'"

"Woman said, 'Law, no, they was hundreds of times we didn't git nothin'.'"

The old man heard the sound of applause overtaking the laughter, and leaned forward slightly, cupping his hand to his left ear to better take it in. The applause was giving him courage, somehow, to keep on in life, to get out of bed in the mornings and see what was what.

A New Song, Ch. 2

UNCLE BILLY STRAIGHTENED his tie and coughed, then got down to business.

"Wellsir! They was two fellers a-workin' on th' sawmill, don't you know, an' th' first 'un got too close to th' saw an' cut 'is ear off. Well, it fell in th' sawdust pit an' he was down there a-tryin' t' find it, don't you know. Th' other feller said, 'What're you a-doin' down there?' First 'un said, 'I cut m' ear off an' I'm a-lookin' f'r it!'"

"Th' other feller jumped in th' pit, said, 'I'll he'p you!' Got down on 'is hands an' knees, went to lookin' aroun', hollered, 'Here it is, I done found it!'"

"First feller, he took it an' give it th' once-over, don't you know, said, 'Keep a-lookin', mine had a pencil behind it!'"

In This Mountain, Ch. 9

"LET ME SAY that last 'un back t' make sure I learned it right."

"Take your time," said the trucker, who had just ordered apple pie à la mode. "This is a easy run, nothin' perishable like last week when I was haulin' cantaloupes to Pennsylvania."

Uncle Billy cleared his throat. "Woman went to th' new doc, don't you know, he was s' young he was hardly a-shavin'. Wellsir, she was in there a couple of minutes when all at once't she busted out a-hollerin' an' run down th' hall."

Uncle Billy paused.

"You got it," said the trucker. "Keep goin'."

"Wellsir, a doc that was a good bit older took off after 'er, said, 'What's th' problem?' an' she told 'im. Th' ol' doc went back to th' young doc, said, 'What's th' dadjing matter with you? Miz Perry is sixty-five a-goin' on sixty-six with four growed chil'ren and seven grans—an' you told 'er she was a-goin' t' have a *young 'un?*"

"New doc grinned, don't you know, said, 'Cured 'er hiccups, didn't it?'"

Uncle Billy knew when a joke hadn't gone over, and this one hadn't gone over—not even with the person he'd gotten it from in the first place.

The trucker gazed thoughtfully at his reflection in the chrome napkin dispenser. "Seem like it was funny when I heard it th' first time, but now it might be what you call . . ." He shrugged.

"Flat," said Uncle Billy, feeling the same way himself.

"I'd advise you to axe it," said the trucker, digging into his apple pie. "Start off with your two guys on a bench, slide in with your cab-driver joke, and land you a one-two punch with th' ol' maids."

Uncle Billy wished he had some kind of guarantee this particular lineup would work.

In This Mountain, Ch. 13

"A PREACHER DIED, don't you know, an' was a-waitin' in line at th' Pearly Gates. Ahead of 'im is a feller in blue jeans, a leather jacket, an' a tattoo on 'is arm. Saint Pete says to th' feller with th' tattoo, says, 'Who are you, so I'll know whether t' let you in th' Kingdom of Heaven?'

"Feller says, 'I'm Tom Such an' Such, I drove a taxicab in New York City.'

"Saint Pete looks at th' list, says, 'Take this silk robe an' gold staff an' enter th' Kingdom of Heaven!' Then he hollers, 'Next!'

"Th' preacher steps up, sticks out 'is chest, says, 'I'm th' Rev'rend Jimmy Lee Tapscott, pastor of First Baptist Church f'r forty-three years.'

"Saint Pete looks at 'is list, don't you know, says, 'Take this flour-sack robe an' hick'ry stick an' enter th' Kingdom of Heaven.'

"Preacher says, 'Wait a dadjing minute! That man was a taxicab driver an' he gits a silk robe an' a gold staff?'

"Saint Pete says, 'When you preached, people slept. When he drove, people prayed.'"

Father Tim threw back his head and hooted with laughter. Then he clapped his hands and slapped his leg a few times, still laughing. Uncle Billy had never seen such carrying on. Why didn't the preacher save something back for the last joke?

"Hold on!" he said. "I got another'n t' go."

"Right," said Father Tim. "That was a keeper."

"You can use that'n in church, won't cost you a red cent."

Uncle Billy felt his heart pumping, which was, in his opinion, a good sign. He straightened up a moment and rested his back, then leaned again on his cane as if hunkering into a strong wind. This was the big one and he wanted it to go as slick as grease.

"Wellsir, three ol' sisters was a-livin' together, don't you know. Th' least 'un was eighty-two, th' middle 'un was ninety-some, an' th' oldest 'un was way on up in age. One day th' oldest 'un run a tub of water. She put one foot in th' water, started a-thinkin', hollered downstairs to 'er sisters, said, 'Am I a-gittin' *in* th' tub or *out* of th' tub?'

"Th' middle sister, she started up th' stairs t' he'p out, don't you know, then thought a minute. Yelled to 'er baby sister, said, 'Was I a-goin' *up* th' stairs or a-comin' *down*?'

"Th' baby sister, she was settin' in th' kitchen havin' a cup of coffee, said, 'Guess I'll have t' go up yonder an' he'p out . . . boys, I hope I never git that forgetful, knock on wood!'

"Went t' knockin' on th' table, don't you know, then jumped up an' hollered, 'I'll be there soon as I see who's at th' door!'"

Uncle Billy couldn't help but grin at the preacher, who was not only laughing, but wiping his eyes into the bargain. The old man took it to be his proudest moment. He'd had laughs before; he reckoned anybody could get a laugh now and again if he worked hard enough, but crying . . . that was another deal, it was what every joke teller hoped for. His heart was hammering and his knees were weak. He sat down, hard, in the preacher's leather chair and heard something he hadn't heard in a good while—

It was the sound of his own self laughing.

In This Mountain, Ch. 14

A Useful Tool: The Seasons

I find weather one of the most useful tools ever made available to an author, not to mention poets, whose work absolutely thrives on it. The Mitford novels are full of weather, and would be intolerably weak tea without it.

First of all, the books are set in western North Carolina, which is characterized by its sometimes violent, often lovely, always unpredictable weather patterns.

Thus, in the nine novels of the series, Mitford endures the effects of a hurricane that blows inland by several hundred miles; gully-washing downpours; hail; ice; a Hundred Years snow; minor drought; and, of course, wind.

If there's one thing you can count on in these mountains, it is high wind. It keens around the house, sounding like the sound track for a horror film. It blows your garden bench down the hill, and sends your hanging baskets crashing onto the neighbor's porch. It sets rocking chairs in the street, uproots trees, upends the doghouse, and whips your pillowcases off the line and delivers them into the next county.

For my money, you can have the milder forms of mountain weather such as the occasional twelve inches of snow. For sheer turbulence and general aggravation, give me a windstorm—but only in fiction, please.

Perhaps you recall the blizzard that arrived in Mitford during Chapter Five of *A Light in the Window*. The day after Father Tim and Dooley trimmed the Christmas tree, the snow began, looking innocent enough.

As he turned the corner toward the office, he saw that Mitford was fast becoming one of those miniature villages in a glass globe, which, when shaken and set on its base, literally teemed with falling flakes.

Soon, the snow picks up, the wind roars in, and the power goes out, casting the village into darkness.

The houses of Mitford were frozen like so many ice cubes in a tray. . . . The high winds did not cease. . . . Cars that been abandoned on the street appeared to be the humps of a vast white caterpillar, inching up the hill toward Fernbank.

Before it's over, he and Dooley are breaking up the old chairs stored in the garage and burning them in the rectory fireplace—not only for warmth, but to roast their supper of hot dogs, which they threaded onto coat hangers.

I remember going to the Outer Banks of North Carolina to do research for *A New Song,* set on the fictional island of Whitecap. While we were driving back to the mountains, a monumental rain came upon us. It was so instant, so hard, and so furious that afterward, I couldn't get it out of my mind. So I put its facsimile in the novel.

(We won't talk about chapter 13 of that same book, in which weather also played a huge role. I get seasick just thinking about it.)

To put a fine point on the whole thing, what Mark Twain said about New England weather applies equally to weather in the Mitford books:

"The weather is always doing something . . . always attending strictly to business; always getting up new designs and trying them on people to see how they will go . . . I have counted one hundred and thirty-six different kinds of weather inside of twenty-four hours."

When a story cries out for edge and atmosphere, some authors favor blue language, murder, or mayhem. As for me, I'll take a strong dose of weather, any day.

Autumn drew on in Mitford, and one after another, the golden days were illumined with changing light. New wildflowers appeared in the hedges and fields. Whole acres were massed with goldenrod and fleabane. Wild phlox, long escaped from neat gardens, perfumed every roadside. And here and there, milkweed put forth its fat pods, laden with a filament as fine as silk. There were those who were ecstatic with the crisp new days of autumn and the occasional scent of wood smoke on the air. And there were those who were loath to let summer go, saying it had been "the sweetest summer out of heaven," or "the best in many years."

But no one could hold on to summer once the stately row of Lilac Road maples began to turn scarlet and gold. The row began its march across the front of the old Porter place, skipped over Main Street and the war monument to the town hall, paraded in front of First Baptist, lined up along the rear of Winnie Ivey's small cottage, and ended in a vibrant blaze of color at Little Mitford Creek. When this show began, even the summer diehards, who were by then few enough in number to be counted on the fingers of one hand, gave up and welcomed the great spectacle of a mountain autumn.

At Home in Mitford, Ch. 8

The weather was turning colder, the flame of autumn had torched the red maples along Lilac Road, and now and again he caught the scent of wood smoke. It was his favorite perfume, right up there with horse manure and new-mown hay.

A Light in the Window, Ch. 2

The houses of Mitford were frozen like so many ice cubes in a tray. Lights shone from windows onto the drifting snow, as leaden skies made even the daylight seem one long dusk. Everywhere, spirals of chimney smoke were violently snatched by the wind and blown through the streets, so that the stinging drafts of arctic air contained a reassuring myrrh of wood smoke.

The high winds did not cease. In some places, snowdrifts covered doors and windows so completely that people had to be dug out by more fortunate neighbors. Cars that had been abandoned on the street appeared to be the humps of a vast white caterpillar, inching up the hill toward Fernbank.

Percy Mosely lived too far from town to make it to the Grill and open up, but Mule Skinner, who lived only a block away, managed to open the doors at seven on Tuesday morning, brew the coffee extra-strong, and fry every piece of bacon on hand. J. C. Hogan, who was waiting out the storm in his upstairs newspaper office, came down at once. The weary town crew, unable to start the frozen diesel engines of their snowplows, were the only other customers.

Unlike most snows, this one did not bring the children to Baxter Park. The sleds stayed in garages, the biscuit pans shut away in cupboards. This was a different snow, an ominous snow.

A Light in the Window, Ch. 5

SPRINGTIME WAS ON its way, no doubt about it.

Hessie Mayhew's gardening column made its annual appearance in the *Muse,* under a photograph of the author taken thirty years ago. The first column of the season always disclosed Lady Spring's current whereabouts.

It seemed she was tarrying on a bed of moss and violets down the mountain, where the temperature was a full ten degrees warmer.

Do not look for her, Hessie cautioned, *for she never arrives until we've given up hope. Once you've sunk into despair over yet another snowfall in April or a hard freeze after planting your beans, she will suddenly appear in a glorious display of Miss Baxter's apple blossoms—not to mention lilacs along south Main Street and wild hyacinths on the creek bank near Winnie Ivey's dear cottage.*

Lest anyone forget what a wild hyacinth looked like, Hessie had done a drawing from memory that J.C. reproduced with startling clarity.

A Light in the Window, Ch. 13

AUTUMN HAD COME to the mountains, at last.

Here, it set red maples on fire; there, it turned oaks russet and yellow. Fat persimmons became the color of melted gold, waiting for frost to turn their bitter flesh to honey. Sassafras, dogwoods, poplars, redbud—all were torched by autumn's brazen fire, displaying their colorful tapestry along every ridge and hogback, in every cove and gorge.

The line of maples that marched by First Baptist to Winnie Ivey's cottage on Little Mitford Creek was fully ablaze by the eleventh of October.

"The best ever!" said several villagers, who ran with their cameras to document the show.

The local newspaper editor, J. C. Hogan, shot an extravagant total of six rolls of film. For the first time since the nation's bicentennial, readers saw a four-color photograph on the front page of the *Mitford Muse*.

Everywhere, the pace was quickened by the dazzling light that now slanted from the direction of Gabriel Mountain, and the sounds of football practice in the schoolyard.

Avis Packard put a banner over the green awning of The Local: *Fresh Valley Hams Now, Collards Coming.*

Dora Pugh laid on a new window at the hardware store featuring leaf rakes, bicycle pumps, live rabbits, and iron skillets. "What's th' theme of your window?" someone asked. "Life," replied Dora.

The library introduced its fall reading program and invited the author of the *Violet* books to talk about where she got her ideas. "I have no idea where I get my ideas," she told Avette Harris, the librarian. "They just come." "Well, then," said Avette, "do you have any ideas for another topic?"

The village churches agreed to have this year's All-Church Thanksgiving Feast with the Episcopalians, and to get their youth choirs together for a Christmas performance at First Presbyterian.

At Lord's Chapel, the arrangements on the altar became gourds and pumpkins, accented by branches of the fiery red maple. At this time of year, the rector himself liked doing the floral offerings. He admitted it was a favorite season, and his preaching, someone remarked, grew as electrified as the sharp, clean air.

These High, Green Hills, Ch. 1

HE LOVED THE soft shine of the streetlamps in their first hour of winter dark. And now, Christmas lights added to the glow. Up and down

Main Street the tiny lights burned, looping around every streetlamp with its necklace of fresh balsam and holly. If he never left Mitford at all, it would suit him. He had been happier here than in any parish of his career. To tell the truth, there wasn't even a close second, except, perhaps, for the little mission of fifty souls where he had served at the age of twenty-seven. They had taken him under their wing and loved him, but refused to protect him from sorrow and hardship. Indeed, there had been plenty of both, and that little Arkansas handful had made a man and a priest of him, all at once.

He looked up to see clouds racing across the moon, as Barnabus lifted his leg on a fire hydrant.

A line came to him, written by a fellow named Burns, who put out the newspaper in a neighboring village.

Big cities never sleep, but little towns do.

These High, Green Hills, Ch. 5

Lady Spring's Grand Surprise
—by Mitford Muse *reporter Hessie Mayhew*

Lady Spring has surprised us yet again.

Arriving in our lofty Citadel prematurely this year, she caught us looking to the mending of our winter mittens. As early as mid-April, the first bloom of the lilac peeked out, whilst in years past, not one of us had caught its virtuous scent until May. Last April at this time, you may recall, we were shivering in our coats as white icing lay upon the bosom of our Village as upon a wedding cake.

In any case, Lady Spring has left her calling card in our expectant Garden—this little Niche where, upon the margin of a rushing streamlet, the woods violet first revealed its innocent face on yesterday morn.

Those with an eye for fashion will wonder what fanciful attire our Lady is wearing this year. I have as yet glimpsed her only briefly, and cannot be certain of every detail, but she appears to have arrayed herself in lacy ferns from her maiden Breast to her unshod feet, and crowned her fickle head with trumpet vines and moss.

At any moment, she will make her couch upon the banks of Miss Sadie Baxter's hillside orchard, so that every rude Cottage and stately pile might have a view of Heaven come down to earth.

Gentle Reader, may fragrant breezes fan thy brow this Spring, and whether you meet our Lady upon the wild summit or in the sylvan glade, please remember:

Do not plant until May 15.

He dropped the newspaper beside his wing chair, laughing.

Hessie Mayhew had been reading Wordsworth, again, while combing the village environs with looking-glass and flower press.

Rude cottages and stately piles, wild summits and sylvan glades! Only in the *Mitford Muse,* he thought, unashamedly proud of a newspaper whose most alarming headline in recent months had been "Man Convicted of Wreckless Driving."

These High, Green Hills, Ch. 7

IF SPRING HAD blown in like a zephyr, its mood soon changed. Gentle rains became wind-lashed torrents, washing seeds from furrows and carving deep gullies in driveways and lawns. Power blinked off and surged on again, those with computers kept them unplugged, and TVs went down before the lightning like so many ducks in a shooting gallery. Sudden, startling downpours of hail unleashed themselves on the village, leaving holes the size of dimes in the burgeoning hosta, and flattening whole groves of trillium and Solomon's seal. Seedlings kneeled over in the mud, and Winnie Ivey's hens and chicks scattered for high ground.

Mitford was driven indoors for three days running, to watch the mildew make its annual invasion of basements, bathrooms, and closets.

It was Tuesday morning before the village awoke to a dazzling sunrise, clear skies, and balmy temperatures. The foul weather, however, lingered on in his secretary.

"If I ever read another word about Hessie Mayhew's Lady Spring, I'll *puke*," Emma said.

These High, Green Hills, Ch. 9

FIELDS OF BROOM sedge turned overnight into lakes of gold, and the scented vines of Lady's Mantle crept into hedges everywhere, as the sun moved and the light changed, and the brisk, clean days grew shorter.

"You always say this is the best fall we've had," Dora Pugh scolded a customer at the hardware. "How can every year be the best?"

Avis Packard put up a banner, Percy Mosely at last took his down, and the Collar Button was having its annual fall sale. The latter encouraged the rector to make a few purchases for Dooley Barlowe, now back at school, which included three pairs of khakis, four pairs of socks, and a couple of handkerchiefs that Dooley would never use for their intended purpose.

These High, Green Hills, Ch. 21

AN EARLY OCTOBER hurricane gathered its forces in the Caribbean, roared north along the eastern seaboard, and veered inland off Cape Hatteras. In a few short hours, it reached the mountains at the western end of the state, where it pounded Mitford with alarming force.

Rain lashed Lord's Chapel in gusting sheets, rattled the latched shutters of the bell tower, blew the tarps off lumber stacked on the construction site, and crashed a wheelbarrow into a rose bed.

The tin roof of Omer Cunningham's shed, formerly a hangar for his antique ragwing, was hurled toward Luther Green's pasture, where the sight of it, gleaming and rattling and banging through the air, made the cows bawl with trepidation.

Coot Hendrick's flock of three Rhode Island Reds took cover on the back porch after nearly drowning in a pothole in the yard, and Lew Boyd, who was pumping a tank of premium unleaded into an out-of-town Mustang, reported that his hat was whipped off his head and flung into a boxwood at the town monument nearly a block away.

Phone lines went out; a mudslide slalomed down a deforested ridge near Farmer, burying a Dodge van; and a metal Coca-Cola sign from Hattie Cloer's market on the highway landed in Hessie Mayhew's porch swing.

At the edge of the village, Old Man Mueller sat in his kitchen, trying to repair the mantel clock his wife asked him to fix several years before her death. He happened to glance out the window in time to see his ancient barn collapse to the ground. He noted that it swayed slightly before it fell, and when it fell, it went fast.

"Hot ding!" he muttered aloud, glad to be spared the aggravation of taking it down himself. "Now," he said to the furious roar outside, "if you'd stack th' boards, I'd be much obliged."

* * *

The villagers emerged into the sunshine that followed, dazzled by the spectacular beauty of the storm's aftermath, which seemed in direct proportion to its violence.

The mountain ridges appeared etched in glass, set against clear, perfectly blue skies from horizon to horizon.

At Fernbank, a bumper crop of crisp, tart cooking apples lay on the orchard floor, ready to be gathered into local sacks. The storm had done the picking, and not a single ladder would be needed for the job.

"You see," said Jenna Ivey, "there's always two sides to everything!" Jenna had closed Mitford Blossoms to run up to Fernbank and gather apples, having promised to bake pies for the Bane just three days hence.

"But," said another apple gatherer, "the autumn color won't be worth two cents. The storm took all the leaves!"

"Whatever," sighed Jenna, who thought some people were mighty hard to please.

Out to Canaan, Ch. 18

"THE LAST TIME we had snow at Christmas, we burned the furniture, remember that?" he asked, as Dooley turned onto Main Street. It was, in fact, the blizzard the media had called the Storm of the Century.

Dooley cackled. "We were bustin' up that ol' chair and throwin' it in th' fireplace, and fryin' baloney . . ."

"Those were the good old days," sighed the rector, who certainly hadn't thought so at the time.

Dashing through the snow . . .

He was losing track of time, happy out here in this strange and magical land where hardly a soul marred the snow with footprints, where Dooley sang along with the radio, and Harley looked as wide-eyed as a child. . . .

And there was Fernbank, ablaze with lights through the leafless winter trees, crowning the hill with some marvelous presence he'd never seen before. He wanted suddenly to see it up close, feel its warmth, discover whether it was real, after all, or a fanciful dream come to please him at Christmas.

* * *

They eased down the Fernbank drive and saw the town lying at the foot of the steep hill like a make-believe village under a tree. There was the huge fir at Town Hall with its ropes of colored lights, and the glittering ribbon of Main Street, and the shining houses.

An English writer, coincidentally named Mitford, had said it so well, he could recite it like a schoolboy.

She had called her village "a world of our own, close-packed and insulated like . . . bees in a hive or sheep in a fold or nuns in a convent or sailors in a ship, where we know everyone, and are authorized to hope that everyone feels an interest in us."

Go tell it on the mountain, over the hills and everywhere . . .

After a stop by Tommy's and then by Hattie Cloer's, they headed home.

"Harley, want to have a cup of tea with us before tonight's service?"

"No, sir, Rev'rend, I'm tryin' t' fool with a batch of fudge brownies to bring upstairs tomorrow."

Temptation on every side, and no hope for it.

"Say, Dad, want to watch a video before church? Tommy loaned me his VCR. It's a baseball movie, you'll like it."

If there were a tax on joy on this night of nights, he'd be dead broke.

"Consider it done!" he said.

He sat clutching the pint of cream in a bag, feeling they'd gone forth and captured some valuable trophy or prize, as they rode slowly between the ranks of angels on high and turned onto their trackless street.

Out to Canaan, Ch. 21

THE RAIN THAT began so violently at two-thirty stopped at three o'clock, then returned around three-thirty to pummel the car with renewed energy, as lightning cracked around them with a vengeance.

Sitting on the shoulder since the last downpour began, they briefly considered trying to get back on the highway and drive to a service station, a bridge, anything, but visibility was zero.

Pouring sweat in the tropical humidity of the car, they found the air-conditioning was no relief. Its extreme efficiency made them feel frozen as cods in their wet clothing.

If only they were driving the Buick, he thought. The feeble air-conditioning his wife had so freely lambasted would be exactly right for their circumstances. In fact, his Buick would be the perfect security against a storm that threatened to rip a frivolous rag from over their heads and fling it into some outlying tobacco field.

The temperature in the car was easily ninety degrees. He remembered paying ten pounds for an hour's worth of this very misery in an English hotel sauna, without, of course, the disagreeable odor of steaming dog and cat fur.

"When life gives you lemons . . . ," he muttered darkly.

". . . make lemonade," said his wife, stroking her drenched cat.

"Four o'clock," he said, pulling onto the highway. "We've lost nearly two hours. That means we'll get into Whitecap around dark."

"Ah, well, dearest, not to worry. This can't go on forever."

He hoped such weather would at least put a crimp in the ridiculous notion of wearing grass skirts at tomorrow night's cookout.

* * *

The aftermath of the storm was not a pretty sight. Apparently, they'd missed the worst of it.

Here and there, billboards were blown down, a metal sign lying in the middle of the highway advertised night crawlers and boiled peanuts, and most crops stood partially immersed.

"Our baptism into a new life," he said, looking at the dazzling light breaking over the fields.

* * *

When they reached the bridge to Whitecap, the wind and rain had stopped; there was an innocent peace in the air.

A sign stood at the entrance to the bridge, which had been closed off with a heavy chain and a soldierly row of orange cones.

BRIDGE OUT
FERRY 2 Blocks
and left $10
No Ferry
After 10 p.m.

"Good heavens," said his wife, "isn't it after ten o'clock?"

"Five 'til," he said, backing up. He made the turn and hammered down on the accelerator.

"That's *one* block . . . ," she said.

Going this fast on wet pavement didn't exactly demonstrate the wisdom of the ages. "This is two," he counted.

"Now turn left here. I'm praying they'll be open."

He turned left. Nothing but yawning darkness. Then, a dim light a few yards ahead, swinging.

They inched along, not knowing what lay in their path. A sign propped against a sawhorse revealed itself in the glare of the headlights.

Ferry to Whitecap
Have Your $ Ready

A lantern bobbed from the corner of what appeared to be a small building perched at the edge of the water.

He'd read somewhere about blowing your horn for a ferry, and gave it a long blast.

"Lord, is this a joke?" his wife inquired aloud of her Maker.

A light went on in the building and a man came out, wearing a cap, an undershirt, and buttoning his pants.

Father Tim eased the window down a few inches.

"Done closed."

"Two minutes," said Father Tim, pointing to his watch. "Two whole minutes before ten. You've got to take us across." He nearly said, *I'm clergy,* but stopped himself.

"You live across?"

"We're moving to Whitecap."

"Don't know as you'd want to go across tonight," said the man, still buttoning. "'Lectricity's off. Black as a witch's liver."

Father Tim turned to Cynthia. "What do you think?"

"Where would we stay over here?"

"Have t' turn back fourteen miles."

Cynthia looked at her husband. "We're going across!"

"Twenty dollars," said the man, unsmiling.

"Done," said Whitecap's new priest.

A New Song, Ch. 4

Lady Spring Coy
Flirtation Fails to Amuse
—*by* HESSIE MAYHEW

For three days in mid-February, Lady Spring cajoled our wintry spirits with zephyrs so balmy that we found ourselves utterly deceived. How quickly we forget, year to year, the heart-wrenching extent to which this frivolous and unrepentant lady betrays us.

Our power lines felled by ice storms in March! Our rooftops laden with snow in April! Our lilacs lashed by bitter winds on May Day! One shudders to think what June may bring, the dear June that once gave us roses and clematis!

On the southerly slopes of the mountain, where the Japonica has long since shed its crimson petals, we, hapless stepchildren that we are, must find delight in adorning our homes with sprigs of withered berries!

However much the heart may yearn toward Lady Spring's vernal passage, hearken, I implore you, to the one bit of counsel that, come what may in this earthly life, will never, ever betray you:

Do not plant until May 15.

Hessie Mayhew's annual spring angst. . . .

He sighed and dropped the newspaper to the floor.

Once he'd clipped along through the *Mitford Muse* in twenty, thirty minutes, max. Looking at his watch, he was dismayed to learn he'd just spent an hour and a half with the darned thing, as absorbed as if it were the *Chicago Tribune*.

In This Mountain, Ch. 2

THE STORM REACHED Mitford shortly after dark. He'd taken Barnabas to the backyard as the rain began—fat, pelting drops that smarted when they hit his shirt. At ten o'clock, a full-bore electrical storm was up and running, dousing power in the village and waking him from a deep sleep.

A dazzling flash of platinum lit the room. He turned on his side and listened to the pounding of rain on the roof, and the great flume of water flushing through the downspouts.

He hadn't taken his medication for depression; he would leave it off for a few days and see what happened. It was humiliating to be taking such a thing. The only consolation was that millions of others were in the same boat; depression was common, run-of-the-mill stuff. But he'd never aspired to being run-of-the-mill; he was certain that in a few days, his energy would increase—his spirits would be stronger, his outlook brighter, and this whole miserable experience would be over.

He was clinging to the Rock, trusting it to cleft for him.

In This Mountain, Ch. 10

THE RAIN BEGAN punctually at five o'clock, though few were awake to hear it. It was a gentle rain, rather like a summer shower that had escaped the grip of time or season and wandered into Mitford several months late.

By six o'clock, when much of the population of 1,074 was leaving for work in Wesley or Holding or across the Tennessee line, the drops had grown large and heavy, as if weighted with mercury, and those running to their cars or trucks without umbrellas could feel the distinct smack of each drop.

Dashing to a truck outfitted with painter's ladders, someone on Lilac Road shouted "*Yee*haw!," an act that precipitated a spree of barking among the neighborhood dogs.

Here and there, as seemingly random as the appearance of stars at twilight, lamps came on in houses throughout the village, and radio and television voices prophesied that the front passing over the East Coast would be firmly lodged there for two days.

More than a few were fortunate to lie in bed and listen to the rain drumming on the roof, relieved to have no reason to get up until they were plenty good and ready.

Others thanked God for the time that remained to lie in a warm, safe place unmolested by worldly cares, while some began at once to fret about what the day might bring.

Shepherds Abiding, Ch. 1

WHEN THE CONGREGANTS poured out into the night through the red doors, the snow was swirling down in large, feathery flakes, anointing collars and hats, scarves and mittens. Two people put their heads back and stuck out their tongues and felt the soft, quick dissolve of the flakes.

"Merry Christmas, Father!"

"Merry Christmas, Esther, Gene! God bless you! And there's Hessie, merry Christmas to you, Hessie!"

"Why Tom Bradshaw! Merry Christmas! What brings you back to the sticks?"

Laughter. Vaporizing breath. The incense of snuffed candles wafting on the air . . .

"Merry Christmas, Cynthia!"

"Merry Christmas, Hope, how lovely you look! And Scott, dear— merry Christmas!"

Shepherds Abiding, Ch. 9

THE FIRST FLAKE landed on a blackberry bush in the creek bottom of Meadowgate Farm.

In the frozen hour before dawn, others found their mark on the mossy roof of the smokehouse; in a grove of laurel by the northwest pasture; on the handle of a hoe left propped against the garden fence.

Close by the pond in the sheep paddock, a buck, a doe, and two fawns stood motionless as an owl pushed off from the upper branches of a pine tree and sailed, silent and intent, to the ridge of the barn roof.

The owl hooted once, then twice.

As if summoned by its velveteen cry, the platinum moon broke suddenly from the clouds above the pond, transforming the water's surface into a gleaming lake of molten pearl.

Then, clouds sailed again over the face of the moon, and in the bitter darkness, snowflakes fell thick and fast, swirling as in a shaken globe.

It was twelve minutes after six o'clock when a gray light rose above the brow of Hogback Mountain, exposing an imprint of tractor tires that linked Meadowgate's hay barn to the cow pasture and sheep paddock. The imprints of work boots and dog paws were also traceable along the driveway to the barn, and back to the door of the farmhouse, where smoke puffed from the chimney and lamplight shone behind the kitchen windows.

From the tulip poplar at the northeast corner to the steel stake at the southwest, all hundred and thirty acres of Meadowgate Farm lay under a powdery blanket of March snow.

Light from Heaven, Ch. 1

ON FRIDAY EVENING at Holy Trinity, sheets of rain lashed the windows, rattling the panes in their fragile mullions. On the lower branches of the rhododendron behind the stone wall, a male cardinal bent his crested head beneath his wing and waited out the storm with his mate.

Down the road and around the bend, 129 squirrel tails nailed to the logs of Jubal Adderholt's cabin whipped wildly in the blowing rain; smoke pouring from the chimney was snatched by the wind and driven hard toward the east where Donny Luster's double-wide was stationed.

Inside the trailer, images of a revolving sapphire necklace broke into colored blocks on the television screen; moments later, the screen went black. In the darkened front room, an unfiltered Camel burned down in the ashtray as Donny Luster sat looking out the window, seeing nothing. In their bedroom, Dovey and Sissie Gleason slept as close as spoons in a drawer, oblivious to the shuddering of the trailer on its pad of concrete blocks.

Two miles to the northwest, in the well-stocked yard of the McKinney sisters, the old watering trough filled up, overflowed, and ran into a ditch worn by years of overspill. On the porch, the orange and white cat hunkered under an ancient washing machine covered with a flapping tarp.

A half mile to the west, Robert Prichard's TV antenna was torn off the roof and flung into a stand of rotting rabbit hutches. It was briefly trapped among the hutches, then hurled down the slope behind the two-room house. It landed near a pile of stones dug from the black soil over a century ago by someone wanting a corn patch, and came to rest by a maverick narcissus in full bloom.

Scornful of calendar dates or seasonal punctuality, spring was announcing its approach on the blue mountain ridges above the green river valley.

Light from Heaven, Ch. 11

FUN FOR THE WHOLE FAMILY

Mitford Trivia

❧

Trivia Questions

1. Barnabas appears to be controlled by what?
2. Meadowgate Farm's bay mare is known as _____ Owen.
3. Father Tim prefers _____ on his turnip greens.
4. What color are Cynthia's eyes?
5. What is Sadie Baxter's middle name?
6. Miss Sadie drove a 1958 _____.
7. Buckwheat, Bowser, Baudelaire, Bodacious, and Bonemeal live at _____.
8. In the little village of less than a _____.
9. China Mae's nickname for Miss Sadie was _____ _____.
10. Violet was invited to dine with Miss Addison and her elderly cat, _____.
11. Bishop Stuart Cullen's old flame was _____ Hathaway.
12. Whose wedding reception was held in the Fernbank ballroom?
13. What is Mule's last name?
14. Stone wall overlooks the _____ of Counterpane, according to Fr. Tim.
15. What does Omer Cunningham call his plane?
16. *The Muse* headline, "Man Convicted of _____ Driving."
17. Emma Newland's brown poodle is named _____.
18. According to *The Muse,* Fr. Tim and Cynthia were lost _____ hours in the cave.
19. What is the name of Fernbank's restaurant?

20. What flour company awarded Winnie Ivey a cruise?
21. How much money did Miss Sadie put "where it will grow" for Dooley?
22. Whom did Winnie Ivey marry?
23. Hope Winchester's ginger-colored cat is named _____.
24. Who was Coot Hendrick's bearded ancestor?
25. Father Tim reads these letters on or around his birthday every year.
26. Barbizon, the cat, belongs to _____.
27. Ella _____ says the Lord calls her Ella Jean.
28. Who claims to be the illegitimate daughter of Josiah Baxter?
29. The engraved plaque on Morris Love's house reads *Nouvelle* _____ , *1947*.
30. Hessie Mayhew's warning: DO NOT PLANT UNTIL _____ 15!
31. Lace's dog's name, "Guber," is short for _____.
32. Uncle Billy loves to peel a _____ _____ apple from the tree in his backyard.
33. What line of text do *Mitford Snowmen, Esther's Gift,* and *Shepherds Abiding* have in common?
34. Absalom Greer called the small churches scattered through the coves his _____.
35. What is a vicar?
36. Holy Trinity had stood empty for _____ years.
37. Holy Trinity was nicknamed _____ because of its seating capacity of a mere _____ souls.
38. Jubal Adderholt called a groundhog a _____.
39. What were Edith Mallory's first three words after her accident? _____ _____ _____.
40. Where in Miss Sadie's Plymouth did she hide the stack of bills?
41. For the live Nativity scene, what was used for the infant?

Mitford Crossword Puzzle

35. Louella's mother, China ___
36. Esther Bolick's cake (2 wds.)
38. Wkly. delivery to Russell Jacks
41. Capt. Willie's boat, _____ *Heaven*
42. Red maples along ____ Road
45. "____ no corrupt communication . . ." (Eph. 5:29)
46. Fr. Tim's "Tom Sawyer"
47. Love thy _____
50. Louella's husband, _____Marshall
52. ". . . world without ____. Amen."
53. Loretta Burgess's vehicle
54. Fr. Tim's cousin
55. ___ rest for the wicked. . . .
56. The ____ and Blessing event
57. Fr. Tim and Cynthia
59. Company _____
63. It was moved through the hedge
64. Primrose ___
65. ____ Skinner
66. Jan Karon was born here

DOWN

2. One of the guys
3. "Take no thought ___ the morrow"
4. Mitford malady
5. Mitford's newspaper, *The _____*
6. Out to_____
7. "Philippians 4:13, for ____ sake"
8. The prayer that never _____

11. The man in the _____
13. Bishop Stuart _____
14. Barnabas, big as a _____
15. Father Timothy _____
16. Puny calls it "Old Faithful"
17. No Clue
18. Fr. Tim's favorite poet
20. ____Ivey, Sweet Stuff Bakery
21. Lord's _____
24. Burns incense
25. "Eat Here Once, and You'll Be _____ "
28. ____of Godlight
29. It's found between layers
31. Mitford pet, Perry ____
32. Avis Packard's The _____
34. Hattie Cloer's dog
35. Hal & ____ Owen
37. Ernie's Books, Bait & Tackle cat
39. _____ *Goes to the Beach*
40. _____ Roulade
43. "___ a dazzler!" Hessie says of June in Mitford
44. Familiar exclamation
45. Fernbank's restaurant
48. Edith Mallory's driver, ____Coffey
49. Oxford Antiques, Andrew____
51. Barnabas, "___ of consolation" (Acts 4)
54. College town (15 mi. from Mitford)
57. The Collar _____
58. Thy will be _____
60. ____ Like a Stone (Mitford chapter)
61. ____ House
62. Fr. Tim's birth month

Trivia Answers

1. Scripture (*At Home in Mitford,* Ch. 1)
2. Goosedown (*At Home in Mitford,* Ch. 8)
3. Butter (*At Home in Mitford,* Ch. 19)
4. Like sapphires, with a nearly violet hue (*A Light in the Window,* Ch. 1)
5. Eleanor (*A Light in the Window,* Ch. 18)
6. Plymouth (*At Home in Mitford,* Ch. 2)
7. Meadowgate Farm (*At Home in Mitford,* Ch. 2)
8. Thousand (*At Home in Mitford,* Ch. 4)
9. Little Toad (*At Home in Mitford,* Ch. 19)
10. Palestrina (*A Light in the Window,* Ch. 7)
11. Susan (*A Light in the Window,* Ch. 5)
12. Olivia Davenport and Dr. Walter Harper (*A Light in the Window,* Ch. 20)
13. Skinner (*At Home in Mitford,* Ch. 2)
14. Land (*These High, Green Hills,* Ch. 2)
15. Ragwing taildragger (*These High, Green Hills,* Ch. 7)
16. Wreckless (*These High, Green Hills,* Ch. 7)
17. Snickers (*These High, Green Hills,* Ch. 8)
18. Fourteen (*These High, Green Hills,* Ch. 11)
19. Lucera (*Out to Canaan,* Ch. 19)
20. Golden Band (*Out to Canaan,* Ch. 16)
21. One and a quarter million dollars (*Out to Canaan,* Ch. 17)
22. Thomas Kendall from Topeka, Kansas (*Out to Canaan,* Ch. 19)
23. Margaret Ann (*A New Song,* Ch. 1)
24. Hezekiah (*A New Song,* Ch. 2)
25. St. Paul's letters to Timothy (*A New Song,* Ch. 2)
26. Hélène Pringle (*A New Song,* Ch. 3)
27. Bridgewater (*A New Song,* Ch. 8)
28. Hélène Pringle (*A New Song,* Ch. 16)
29. *Chanson* (*A New Song,* Ch. 14)
30. May (*In This Mountain,* Ch. 2)
31. Gubernatorial (*In This Mountain,* Ch. 18)
32. Rusty Coat (*Shepherds Abiding,* Ch. 3)
33. Each book closes with this line: "After all, it was Christmas."

34. Little handfuls (*Light from Heaven,* Ch. 2)
35. "A vicar is the priest of a church that isn't a parish church." (*Light from Heaven,* Ch. 3)
36. Forty (*Light from Heaven,* Ch. 3)
37. Little Trinity . . . 40 (*Light from Heaven,* Ch. 3)
38. Whistle pig (*Light from Heaven,* Ch. 7)
39. God . . . is . . . good (*Light from Heaven,* Ch. 19)
40. Dome light (*Light from Heaven,* Ch. 19)
41. A loaf of bread (wrapped in Lace's blouse) (*Light from Heaven,* Ch. 21)

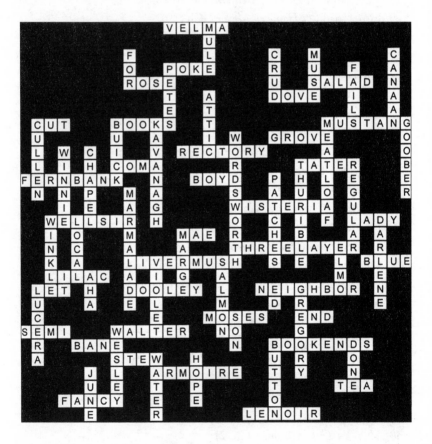

Crossword Puzzle Answers

Reading Aloud

The Gift of Gifts

Entire books have been written about reading aloud. One of the best-known is Jim Trelease's *The Read-Aloud Handbook.*

According to these books, reading aloud can foster (and nurture) all sorts of wonderful benefits for the reader as well as the listener. It can, for example, increase vocabulary, sharpen grammatical skills ("Grammar is more caught than taught," says bestselling author Trelease), cultivate curiosity and learning, extend one's attention span . . .

You get the idea.

To all the above, I say as the Baptists often say, Amen and *amen!*

Now here's how I condense the knowledge contained in these books into one simple wisdom:

When you read aloud with a true heart, to children or adults, friends or spouse, it isn't just words that pour out. Love pours out.

It has long been my belief that reading aloud to one another is The Gift of Gifts in this mortal world. It wraps us closer. It gives wings to the imagination. It fosters conversation and the sharing of ideas. It makes us feel loved and secure. It heightens, and sweetens, the sense of family or friendship. I could go on and on.

Over and again, I've heard from entire families who enjoy reading the Mitford series together. Often, a mother and father take turns reading to the children. And if the children are of reading age, they pitch in also.

I was once sent a photograph of a young ranch family reading a Mitford book. The photo was taken on a bitter winter day when the power had gone out and the father got to spend a whole afternoon snuggled close to the woodstove with his family, reading aloud from *These High, Green Hills.*

Indeed, family read-alouds had a great heyday in the time of Mr. Dickens. When one of his fiction installments was released, fathers thronged to join the queue and surrender their coin. At home in the evening, these Victorian dads would sit and read through the new installment, making certain there was nothing too dire or traumatic for young ears. That done, and supper eaten, in would troop the whole darned family to listen, enraptured, as Father read the latest episode of what was always, always a fine and captivating story by the gifted Charles Dickens.

But reading aloud isn't just for families. Consider the couples.

Often, the passenger reads to the driver as they wend their way somewhere in the car. Or, they listen to the Mitford audio tapes or CDs, read aloud by your author, or by the gifted actor John McDonough, who, say his legion of fans, *is* Father Tim. And many tell me they read my books together in bed. Indeed, not a few have said, "Your books are so wonderful, they put us to sleep at night." I love this!

I also love the story about the man who flatly *refused* to read my books, aloud or otherwise.

I was doing a book signing when a woman came through the line. "My husband, Harold, won't read your books," she said, plenty aggravated, "because there's no sex in your books!"

I peered at Harold, who stood nearby, looking sheepish.

"Harold, honey," I said, "there's plenty of sex in my books. You just don't know where to find it!"

Take, for example, this line from a short scene written about Father Tim and Cynthia, and found, as I recall, in *Out to Canaan:*

She turned to him, smiling in the dark.

That is, indeed, my finest hour when it comes to sex scenes.

There are also legions who report they're reading the Mitford series aloud to residents of nursing homes, or to an elderly or ill relative or friend; and quite a few have read the series to the blind. What a sacrificial gift, to read aloud to someone—and a whole *series,* for heaven's sake!

This may be a bit irregular, but I confess I sometimes read aloud in the evening. To *myself*! (So, sue me.) The perfect evening, however, would be this:

Sitting with a loved one by the fire, thumbing through Wordsworth or Longfellow, or relishing a good yarn by A. B. Guthrie, Jr., who really *got* the westward movement.

There are several scenes in the series in which Father Tim and Cynthia read aloud to one another. Forthwith, an episode from *Light from Heaven:*

They had prayed their Lenten prayer, eaten their modest supper, and made the pie—which would doubtless improve by an overnight repose in the refrigerator.

Now, they drew close by the fire, to the sound of a lashing March wind; she with *Mrs. Miniver* and he with *The Choice of Books,* a late nineteenth-century volume he'd found in the Owens' bedroom. He was vastly relieved that she'd made no more mention of his hair, what was left of it.

"Listen to this, Timothy."

Cynthia adjusted her glasses, squinting at the fine print. "'It's as important to marry the right life as it is the right person.'"

"Aha! Never thought of it that way."

"I considered that very thing when I married you."

"Whether I was the right person?"

"Whether it would be the right life," she said.

"And?"

"And it is. It's perfect for me."

His wife, who preferred to read dead authors, put her head down again.

"How dead, exactly, must they be?" he once asked.

"Not *very* dead; I usually draw the line at the thirties and forties, before the mayhem began setting in like a worm. So . . . moderately dead, I would say."

He tossed a small log onto the waning fire; it hissed and spit from the light powder of snow that had blown into the wood box by the door. A shutter on the pantry window made a rattling sound that was oddly consoling.

"And here's something else," she said.

"'This was the cream of marriage, this nightly turning out of the day's pocketful of memories, this deft, habitual sharing of two pairs of eyes, two pairs of ears. It gave you, in a sense, almost a double life: though never, on the other hand, quite a single one.'"

He nodded slowly, feeling a surge of happiness.

"Yes," he said, meaning it. *"Yes!"*

Over the years, I've heard from literally hundreds of readers who espouse the joys of reading aloud, and I urge you from my heart to discover these joys for yourself.

Here's a little something to get you started.

Make four copies of the following script, taken from the many scenes set in the rear booth of the Main Street Grill. Round up three people who're fun to be with. Look over your scripts. Now. Gather 'round the fire, or the kitchen table, and start reading.

Tip: Be serious about developing your character; really try to nail his personality. The fair sex can read these male roles, too, for what it's really all about is *interpretation*—and, of course, fun.

For more about reading aloud, go to a search engine and simply type in "reading aloud." You'll find great material to help you be your most captivating and entertaining self when you read aloud.

There is no robber worse than a bad book.
—Italian proverb

*The worst thing about new books is that they keep us
from reading the old ones.*
—Joseph Joubert

*Richer than I you can never be, I had a mother
who read to me.*
—Strickland Gillilan

A real book is not one that we read but one that reads us.
—W. H. Auden

Setting: MAIN STREET GRILL

PERCY

I got to do somethin' to rake in b'iness.
(*beat*)
Maybe I ought t'mess around with th' menu. Come up with a special I could run th' same day ever' week.

MULE

Gizzards!

PERCY

What about gizzards?

MULE

I've told you for years . . . gizzards is th' answer to linin' your pockets.

PERCY
(*irritated*)
Don't talk to me about gizzards, dadgummit! They're in th' same category as what goes over th' fence last. You'll never see *me* sellin' gizzards.

MULE

To make it in th' restaurant business you got to set your personal choices aside. Gizzards are a big draw.

J.C.
(*earnestly*)
He's right. You can sell gizzards in this town.
(*thumps the table, emphatic*)
This is a gizzard kind of town.

MULE

All you got to do is put out a sign and see what happens.

PERCY
(*beat*)

What kind of sign?

MULE

Just a plain, ordinary sign. Write it up yourself an' put it in th' window.
(*beat*)

No big deal.

PERCY

When me an' Velma retire at th' end of th' year, I want to go out in th' black. Maybe send 'er to Washington to see the cherry blossoms. She's never seen th' cherry blossoms.

MULE

That's what gizzards are about.

PERCY
(*perplexed*)

What d'you mean?

MULE

Gizzards'll get some cash flow in this place.

PERCY

Seem like chicken livers would draw a better crowd.

J.C.

Livers tie up too much capital. Too much cost involved with livers. You want to go where the investment's low and the profit's high.

MULE

You been readin' th' *Wall Street Journal* again.

PERCY

What would I put on th' sign?

MULE

Here's what I'd put . . .
            (*makes a sweeping gesture*)
. . . GIZZARDS TODAY.

PERCY
(*incredulous*)

That's it? "Gizzards Today?"

MULE

That says it all right there. Like you say, run your gizzard special
once a week . . . maybe on . . .

J.C.

Tuesday! Tuesday would be good for gizzards. You wouldn't
want to start out on Monday with gizzards . . . that'd be
too early in the week. And Wednesday . . . you'd want something . . .

MULE
(*brightly*)

. . . more upbeat!

FATHER TIM

Right!

J.C.

Wednesday could be lasagna day. I'd pay good money for some
lasagna in this town.
            (*Silence. Mule BELCHES. They give him a look . . . .*)

MULE

'Scuse me.

PERCY

Do y'all eat gizzards?

J.C.

Not in *this* lifetime.

MULE

No way.

FATHER TIM

I pass. I ate a gizzard in first grade. That was enough for me.

PERCY

I don't get it. You're some of my best reg'lars. Why should I go sellin' somethin' y'all won't eat?

J.C.

We're a different demographic.

PERCY

Oh. So how many gizzards would go in a servin', do you think?

J.C.

How many chicken tenders d'you put in a serving?

PERCY

Six. Which is one too many for th' price.

J.C.

OK. As gizzards are way less meat than tenders, I'd offer fifteen.
(*beat*)
Sixteen, minimum. Be sure you batter 'em good, fry 'em crisp, an' serve with a side of dippin' sauce.

PERCY

Fifteen gizzards. Two bucks.

(*brightens*)

What d'you think?

FATHER TIM

I think Velma's going to D.C.

In This Mountain, Ch. 3

Oops!

Bloopers in Mitford and How They Got There

Why was the box that Fr. Tim found in Miss Sadie's attic postmarked? In A New Song, *Hélène said it had been shipped by boat from France.*

The shippers, you recall, went to the Paris apartment of Hélène Pringle's mother and packed many items which Mr. Baxter wished to be shipped to America. The bronze angel was put into a box already on the premises, which had been previously used—and postmarked—for another purpose. The entire shipment had then been packed into a container and sent to America.

Is Absalom Greer's sister a widow or a spinster? You've referred to her as both Lottie Miller and Lottie Greer.

You have me here. To my great chagrin, I wrote it both ways, don't you know. But of course Miss Lottie has to be one or the other, doesn't she? So let's say she was briefly married to a Mr. Miller, who vanished, after which she took on the lifelong care of her brother, Absalom Greer, and later resumed the use of her maiden name. Indeed, Absalom was Lottie's greatest devotion, reminding us of Dorothy Wordsworth's devotion to William, her brother.

In At Home in Mitford, *you briefly mentioned Annie Owen, daughter of Hal and Marge Owen. We never met her or heard of her again until the final novel. Why?*

Frankly, I forgot all about Annie until *Light from Heaven,* in which we learn that after college, Annie joined foreign services and thus was conveniently absent from the story line for several years.

* * *

I daresay there are other bloopers and mis-thinks in a series of novels that range over a period of ten years and involve hundreds of characters.

Oh, for a concordance of names and places and special words (liver-mush, buddyroe, etc.), not to mention a list of who smokes Camels (or was it Chesterfields?) and drinks vodka (or was it gin?), and who has amber eyes and who has brown, and where was Buck Leeper from and is Harley's surname spelled with a *C* or an *S,* and how old are the Barlowe kids, and in which book will I find Cynthia's middle name? Ugh.

There are dozens, and sometimes hundreds, of details to be re-called about each character, which is why rosemary (for remembrance) is my all-time favorite kitchen herb!

Cast of
Characters

The Very Thing

❧

Long before Mitford was conceived, Jane Austen wrote this in a letter to her niece, Anna:

"You are now collecting your people delightfully, getting them exactly into such a spot as is the delight of my life; three or four families in a country village is the very thing to work on."

I chanced upon this pertinent counsel when writing the second novel, *A Light in the Window*. It was of enormous encouragement as I wrote further into a series that would have no voguish noir, no pop sentiment, no murder, no mayhem, and no cussin'.

Indeed, I was thrilled to have such estimable permission to write of ordinary people living ordinary lives in a country village.

By the way, one of Jane Austen's many distinguished biographers, Carol Shields, disputes the wisdom of calling her "Miss Austen." I shall have to do it, nonetheless.

"Collecting your people" is how Miss Austen put it. But, truth be told, my people collected *me*. One after another, characters appeared, quite full-blown, and demanded that I *do* something with them.

Almost immediately after Father Tim "left the coffee-scented warmth of the Main Street Grill" on page one of *At Home in Mitford*, the second character showed up.

Had I expected a dog the size of a sofa to pop into the story? Actually, I had no idea what to expect, for I'd never written a novel and didn't have the hang of how things are supposed to proceed.

Momentum, if one dares use that word for a Mitford book, built quickly. Close on the heels of Barnabas, a third character presented herself.

Pretty grouchy, that Emma, and not my cup of tea in real life (though I can be pretty grouchy, myself, at times). But there she was, as ready-made as if she were flesh and blood, and there she remained for all nine novels. She was even wearing a familiar scent, My Sin, which I thought was rather amusing for a church secretary.

I knew, soon on, that my main character was a bachelor with many characteristics that make for a comfortable single life. He read widely (always a boon for someone living alone). He cooked (had to, of course). He enjoyed gardening, and music, and was affable enough to be invited 'round to someone's house on occasion.

Thus, I didn't try to hook him up with an eager and companionable parishioner; I felt he had enough substance to be interesting, himself. So imagine my surprise when Cynthia Coppersmith moved in next door.

"No surprise in the author, no surprise in the reader," said, let's see, Sandburg, I think. Or was it Frost?

But if I wasn't consciously structuring the characters and designing the circumstances, what, then, was going on?

There's a sense in which I "came upon" these characters in the midst of living out their lives, and they allowed me, if you will, to tag along.

Indeed, I wished to be as much observer as creator, I even wanted the work to have a documentary quality, to capture the living-out of a simple, decent, and quite ordinary life. A simple, decent, ordinary life! Compared to what I'd been finding in bookstores and on the shelves of my town library, this was radical stuff.

If one is to move forward with such loosely defined parameters, one must, of course, give one's characters the very precious—and equally dangerous—gift of free will, which God gives all of us.

I read that Iris Murdoch wrote lengthy outlines of each of her novels. Forty pages, I believe her husband said. Not too surprising. Many authors make extensive outlines. What amazes me is that Ms. Murdoch is said to have stuck to them.

I found as I worked at the beginning of the series that I loved dialogue. And no wonder. I had grown up listening to my grandmother's endless stories—about an enthralling childhood in which she was the only pupil in her one-room schoolhouse to own a pair of shoes. About the five suitors who vied for her hand in marriage, and the riveting analysis of their personal characteristics. About the dresses of lawn and marquisette and silk faille (arcane and wonderful-sounding), which she sewed by hand, and the hats she ornamented with grosgrain ribbons and the wings of birds. Her voice was a music that played throughout my girlhood and has continued throughout my life. To put it in the vernacular, I got my ear from Mama.

Characters started stacking up like planes over Atlanta.

And they were all talkers.

I remember realizing that there was very little plot in what I was writing and believed I should remedy this miserable deprivation at once.

But the characters kept talking. And talking. And I kept listening, and liking it.

And so I learned to say that my novels are not plot-driven but character-driven, which redeems me a little, I hope.

Though I'm not sure I realized it, I had chosen a main character through whose eyes we—you and I—would be privy to everything that goes on in a small town. As another author may write of many characters viewing one circumstance, I was compelled to write of one character viewing many circumstances. Who could be counted upon to process deeply human behavior in a way that makes a difference and inspires the reader (and the author, while we're at it)? And who would be more trusted than a truly decent priest, who is confessor, shepherd, and friend?

Thus, it is Father Tim's sympathetic—and genuinely authentic—kindness that draws the characters out and opens them up, so that we can gaze into their lives without, well, *prying*.

I'm reminded of how I love to glance into other people's homes as I pass on a nighttime street during Christmastide. A glittering tree, the way the curtains are drawn back, the frame on a painting—it's merely a glimpse, but it connects me to utter strangers in a way that is moving and real.

Perhaps, then, what I seek to do with my own "three or four families in a country village" is connect you to a group of characters in a way that is moving and real.

By the time we got to the seventh novel, *In This Mountain,* and Father Tim was struggling desperately with the thing that ails too many of us today, some of you felt so connected to this man that you went to my Web site and gave him a good tongue-lashing for not taking his medication!

On a much earlier occasion, a woman came up to me at a reading and declared (I recall that she had her hands on her hips), "If you don't let Father Tim marry Cynthia, I'm goin' to quit foolin' with you!"

And I shall never forget a speaking event in the barn at Fearrington Inn. As I greeted each of three hundred guests, I noticed a man standing quietly to himself, observing. He was tall, and rugged, and attractive into the bargain. Everyone had gone when he came up to me, and I shook the hand of a man whose palm gave evidence that he works out of doors.

There was a lovely quietude about him as he said only this:

"Miss Karon, I want to thank you. I was Buck Leeper."

When you open a Mitford novel, I hope you'll feel that it's all quite familiar, somehow. Comfortable, even. And instead of keeping your shoulders hunched up about your ears, as a stressful world teaches us to do, you might take a deep breath and relax, and maybe even laugh out loud in this quirky, fictional place that seems, oddly enough, like home.

Indeed, that is the very thing that would please your author most. The very thing.

Where Did They All Come from, Anyway?

❧

There are more than seven hundred characters who appear—or are mentioned—in the Mitford series, including many four-legged pets and a canary named Louise.

The following Cast of Characters will, however, have its limitations. Chiefly, I will describe those characters who have true meaning to the story line, and only rarely those characters whom we never, or almost never, meet. For example, though Parrish Guthrie is dead as a doornail and merely referred to in the series, he was a parishioner of some importance and will therefore live on in Mitford history.

I'd give absolutely anything if I didn't have to do this list (which I find onerous in the extreme), but I can understand why so many of you have requested it. The Mitford series is like an immense Russian novel in which hordes of characters, often with funny names, must be met, sorted out, and in the reader's mind, assigned their proper places. Worse yet, some of these characters have the same surname, *though they aren't even related*. And several share the same Christian name, just as in real life.

Why so many characters, anyhow?

Just as I'm smitten with people of various sorts, I love characters of various sorts, and nearly any character at all has been allowed to walk into my stories, demand their moment, and by some mystery which I shall never, ever understand, completely alter and rearrange the scheme of things if they feel so inclined. I'm telling you, Gentle Reader, characters will take over a book as if they owned it.

You'll recall Buck Leeper.

Buck Leeper sauntered into *A Light in the Window* wearing a hard hat and muddy boots, smoking like a depot stove and cussing like the proverbial sailor. What on earth would I do with him—hit Delete? Or wait and see what he had in mind? I chose to do the latter.

But—and here's the rub:

How can books with no cussin' feature a character whose language is obscene?

I didn't want this broken, driven man coming off like a pantywaist. I wanted him to be bold and authentic. Indeed, he was so authentic to your author that I found myself, on two occasions, praying for him!

(I said to myself, Child, you are working *way* too hard!)

In any case, instead of revealing his language, I revealed his anguish. And readers got it.

While we're at it, who expected Lace Turner to jump from a tree and land at the feet of Absalom Greer? Or who knew, when Father Tim was given the daunting challenge of reviving a remote mountain church, that Agnes Merton would be sent to him, as surely as the angel was sent to Daniel?

Over the years, people have asked again and again:

Where do you get your characters?

As you can see, my characters get me.

They walk into the story, blasé as anything, and I have to deal with them.

In *A New Song,* I had no idea who lived behind the wall; I knew only that someone did, and he was in trouble. Then, once I met Morris Love, I had no idea what to do with him. Long periods of head-scratching, praying, sleepless nights, bafflement. Then, the ardently sought *Aha!*

Or, take George Gaynor, the so-called Man in the Attic. I was totally surprised to find someone living surreptitiously in Lord's Chapel— it was when Father Tim smelled chicken soup in the empty church that I realized something was definitely up.

Thank goodness, God knows all this stuff, and is gracious enough to let me in on how it all works, though I must tell you He hardly ever gives me the big picture. I get only a little insight at a time—in the same way the beam of a flashlight, on a very dark night, gives just enough illumination for one step at a time.

By the way, thanks for walking with me all these years. In a way, we stepped into the light of the beam together, again and again and again. May it ever be so.

Author's Note: You'll find in these casts of characters that I include a character's name in the first book in which that character appears—but not in every subsequent book. Otherwise the lists would be so long and this book so heavy that it would require a crane to place it at your bedside.

I've done my best to include every character who might add anything of significance to the story lines. However—I may have missed a few. If so, I hope you'll pencil them into the list. And if I've included some who, in your opinion, have no significance whatsoever, I ask your forgiveness in advance.

Cast of Characters
(*in order of appearance*)

AT HOME IN MITFORD

Father Timothy Andrew Kavanagh: Known to nearly everyone as Father Tim, he turns sixty as the series opens, and seventy before the series ends. Thus we glimpse just ten years in the life of an ordinary man, and find it filled, rather equally, with the mundane and the miraculous.

Born an only child in Holly Springs, Mississippi, to a warm-spirited Baptist mother and a coldly indifferent Episcopalian father, he was interested in things of the soul from an early age. Enjoys Wordsworth, Oswald Chambers, C. S. Lewis, G. K. Chesterton, George McDonald, and the two books of Timothy, which he feels were written as directly to him as to St. Paul's beloved sidekick.

To put a fine point on it, Timothy Kavanagh is the real thing, the genuine article. And yes, there are clergy like him. But only a few. Only a very few.

Emma Garrett: Father Tim's part-time secretary is the quintessential "bane and blessing." Impertinent, holier-than-thou, thick-skinned— but also big-hearted, thoughtful, and intensely loyal. Approach her boss intending harm, and she will scratch your eyes out, plain and simple. Widowed, and soft on the postman.

Harold Newland: Speaking of the postman . . . Harold is a good sort who looks forward to wearing his summer postal service uniform of shorts and knee socks. A bit of a farmer in his off-hours.

Bishop Stuart Cullen: Father Tim's buddy in seminary, now old friend and confidante. Though dogged by schedules and overwork, all important missives are penned "by his own hand," an example set by St. Paul.

Martha Cullen: The over-stretched bishop's good wife, who monitors his physical and emotional stamina, urging him to bed when he persists in muddling through diocesan matters by the light of midnight oil.

Peggy Cramer: Ah! Peggy Cramer. We never meet her in the Mitford Series, we only sense her presence, something like the drift of an alluring but unidentifiable fragrance on the breeze. Long story short, Father Tim was engaged to her while in seminary. Not a good idea.

Percy Mosely: Grumpy, hot-headed, exhausted—the usual scenario with someone in the restaurant business. Proprietor of the Main Street Grill, which he inherited from his father, who inherited it from his father, and so on back into unrecorded history. Serves a mean bowl of buttered grits.

Velma Mosely: Percy's wife. Takes no prisoners. Waits the several tables and booths at the Grill.

Hessie Mayhew: Such a good egg, Hessie! Robs the town's peony bushes, strips the hedgerows, and rogues her neighbor's hydrangeas— all to make glorious wedding bouquets for marrying members of the community. A widow and a Presbyterian, though not necessarily in that order.

Miss Rose Watson: A favorite Mitfordian. Indeed, she inspires the way I dress to go to the post office. Wears her long-deceased brother's military jackets, combat boots, with cocktail hats adorned by mashed flowers. Schizophrenic. Fierce. Married to one of the dearest fellows in fiction or in truth.

Uncle Billy Watson: Little did I know he would become a truly beloved friend to your author. For the ten plus years I wrote this series, he and I scattered to the four winds trying to find clean jokes to make you laugh. As someone who not only put up with, but loved, Miss Rose, he is to be counted noble among men.

Esther Cunningham: The best mayor Mitford ever had, or possibly ever will have. Her motto: *Mitford Takes Care of Its Own.* Who sees to it that the Watsons have oil in their tank for winter? Who goes to the hospital to rock the "crack babies" that occasionally turn up? Who robbed her own family room to furnish the town office? Go, Esther!

Winnie Ivey: A hard-working, good-hearted woman, who gave Mitford a crossroads for the whole town in her beloved Sweet Stuff Bakery.

Miss Sadie Baxter: I am ill-equipped to treat such a noteworthy character in only a few words. Suffice it to say that the elderly mistress of Fernbank was a type of hub on which the wheel of Mitford turned more sweetly. Rich, but wisely stingy, she invested well, earned much, and gave freely. Her life will greatly affect many lives in Mitford, now and in the future.

Hal Owen: Veterinarian who owns Meadowgate Farm (and an animal clinic), fifteen or twenty minutes from Mitford. Longtime friend of Father Tim, and active in the life of Lord's Chapel.

Marge Owen: Hal's wife and Father Tim's first friend in Mitford. A grand cook and ardent gardener.

Walter Kavanagh: Father Tim's first cousin, and, as far as is known, his only living blood relative. An attorney in New Jersey.

Katherine Kavanagh: Walter's fun-loving wife, who has a ministry to the elderly. A great sport. Calls Father Tim by the affectionate nickname, Teds.

Louella Baxter Marshall: Bosomy. Like a down pillow. But tough. Miss Sadie likes to say she "raised" Louella, who, over the years, has been housekeeper, confidante, friend, and sister in Christ. Bakes a mean biscuit.

Dr. Walter Harper: Known to all as "Hoppy." Harvard man. Looks a dash like Walter Pidgeon. Overworked. Beloved.

Harry Nelson: Lord's Chapel parishioner. A pain. Just ask Emma.

Charlie Garrett: Emma's deceased husband.

Mule Skinner: The kind of fellow who orders a cheeseburger without cheese, a BLT without lettuce. Hangs out at the Grill; makes Velma Mosely crazy. A town realtor, and old pal of the rector.

Willard Porter: Brother to Rose Watson. Was in love with Miss Sadie Baxter and, regrettably, died in France in combat. He built what is commonly called "the old Porter place," a Victorian mansion on the town green, now the home of his Miss Rose and Uncle Billy.

Susan Parnell Phillips: A realtor from the big city, who tried to wheedle the Porter place from the Watsons. Just doing what a girl sometimes has to do.

Rachel Livingstone Baxter: Miss Sadie's long-deceased mother, and former mistress of Fernbank.

Fancy Skinner: Mitford hairdresser. Mule's wife. Talks a mile a minute. If you see her coming, duck.

Hattie Cloer: Has a little grocery store on the bypass, and a Chihuahua named Darlene. As Hattie is a notorious hypochondriac, one shops at Cloer's Market only in desperation.

Clyde Cloer: Hattie's long-suffering husband.

Avis Packard: Proprietor of Mitford's Main Street grocery store, The Local. "One thing Father Tim liked about Avis Packard was the way he got excited about his vegetables." A veritable poet in describing his comestibles; a bachelor known to be "married to his work."

Luther Lovell: Luther and his boys raise fryers and baking hens down in the valley, exclusively for The Local.

Dora Pugh: Runs the hardware store. Enjoys dressing the display windows in accordance with the seasons.

Uncle Haywood: But for the prompting of Miss Sadie's long-deceased uncle, Miss Sadie and her mother would never have gone to Paris, where they met a bright young chap from Mitford, of all places. The plot thickens.

China Mae: China Mae washed, ironed, and cooked for Miss Sadie's mother at Fernbank. One day, the young Miss Sadie came home from school and found a little brown baby lying in China Mae's bed. It was Louella. Miss Sadie liked to help bathe and dress Louella, and pull her around in her wagon. They were sisters from the beginning.

Joe Hadleigh: If it hadn't been for Joe Hadleigh willing his little house in Mitford to his niece, Father Tim would never have met the children's book author and illustrator who moved into it, right next door to the rectory. So, let's hear it for Uncle Joe.

Father Jeffrey Roland: Rector of a New Orleans parish, an ardent letter writer, and old friend of the rector. Doesn't hesitate to ask for money for a good cause, which, of course, is a good thing.

J. C. Hogan: Editor of the *Mitford Muse*. Until late in the series, he refused to upgrade his software with SpellCheck, resulting in this now-famous headline: MAN CONVICTED OF WRECKLESS DRIVING.

Pearly McGee: Resident of the Assisted Living annex at Mitford Hospital. At her death, left $1,400 in a Pearly McGee Happiness Fund, which the rector prayerfully dispensed on her behalf.

Andrew Gregory: The owner of Oxford Antiques on South Main Street, Andrew is tall, trim, and handsome. Indeed, Father Tim usually feels short, fat, and homely in his company. But not to worry . . .

Russell Jacks: The sexton at Lord's Chapel for many years, and the grandfather of Dooley Barlowe.

Dooley Barlowe: We meet the freckled, red-haired Dooley at the age of eleven. Abandoned by his parents to a grandfather unable to care for him, he ends up on Father Tim's doorstep—a circumstance which will change many lives, forever.

Puny Bradshaw: Though this earnest young housekeeper was thrust upon the unwilling rector by a vestry concerned for his health, Father Tim comes to love her as his own. Most of my readers yearn for their own Puny Bradshaw. Indeed, she is the cream of the cream.

Ray Cunningham: I'm wild about this fellow. Retired, and married to Mitford's Type-A mayor, Esther, he spends his time serving her as she labors to serve the community. He might call up and say, "How about me runnin' up there with a jar of lemonade, Sweet Pea?" Or, "Hurry home after your meetin', Doll Face, we're havin' ribs an' cole slaw."

Joe Ivey: Father Tim's longtime barber and a former security guard at Graceland. Keeps a little peach brandy on hand for special customers.

Rodney Underwood: Mitford's overzealous Chief of Police.

Luther: Miss Sadie's handyman.

Roberta Simpson: A wealthy summer resident of Mitford, whom parishioners tried to foist on their bachelor priest. "Better hook this one," somebody advised. "You could afford to give up preachin'."

Becky Nelson: A petite and charming widow who thought Wordsworth was a Dallas department store. The subject of still another valiant, but failed, effort by Lord's Chapel matchmakers.

Dottie Newland: Mother of Harold Newland, the postman.

Reba Cooley: A recent widow whom Father Tim meets on a house call with Hal Owen, to deliver a calf.

Ron Malcolm: Parishioner, retired contractor; heads a committee to oversee the building of Hope House.

Jeb Reynolds: A parishioner involved with the Hope House project.

Harold Johnson: An early schoolmate of Father Tim's, whose knowledge of farm life the rector had found enviable.

Raymond Lereaux: An early schoolmate who "showed horses and won blue ribbons that he brought to school for Show and Tell."

Jessica Raney: When disease wiped out Father Tim's entire herd of rabbits as a boy, she sent a card expressing sympathy. "He put it in his sock drawer, where it stayed for a very long time."

Olivia Davenport: Smart and attractive, wise in the Scriptures. Moves to Mitford to face certain death, and finds new life instead.

Cynthia Coppersmith: Blonde, beautiful, spirited; an award-winning writer and illustrator of children's books about her white, green-eyed cat, Violet. Moves into the little yellow house next door to the rectory, which teaches Father Tim the wisdom, and then some, of Matthew 22:39. "Great legs," observes Mule Skinner. All in all, a prize catch for our affable rector, who thinks so himself.

Evie Adams: Poor Evie. Can't leave her mother alone a minute, or who knows what will happen?

Miss Pattie: Known to have put the wet laundry in the oven. Said to take a bath with a hat on. Once gave away her daughter, Evie's, favorite garden sculpture—to a tourist, more's the pity.

Buster Austin: Dooley's archenemy.

Myra Hayes: Mitford School's no-nonsense principal.

Jenna Ivey: Owner of the local florist shop, Mitford Blossoms. I have incorrectly spelled her name "Jenna" in some of the books—which counts as yet another "Oops" for your author.

Marlene: A new resident in Mitford, who find the bachelor supply disappointing, if not downright depressing.

Lew Boyd: Owner of Lew Boyd's Exxon, still often referred to as "th' Esso station." Widowed. Proud of his canned pickles.

Rebecca Jane Owen: Daughter born to Marge and Hal Owen.

Esther Bolick: Married to Gene. Creator of the now-legendary recipe for Orange Marmalade Cake. If she never does another thing for society, she once mused, that recipe would be enough. (See recipe on page 100.)

Hilda Lassiter: A parishioner who, when the Orange Marmalade Cake went missing from the church kitchen, "like to cried when they couldn't find it."

Marge Houck: A parishioner whose "pineapple upside down" didn't have enough distinction, apparently, to be stolen in the caper cited above.

Samuel K. ("Homeless") Hobbes: A wounded veteran of the advertising business who moves back to Little Mitford Creek, and resumes speaking in his native vernacular. Reads widely; friend and confidante of the rector.

Parkinson Hamrick, Lydia Newton: Two parishioners whose ashes are contained in urns in the hall closet of Lord's Chapel.

Parrish Guthrie: An old so-and-so if ever there was one. Miss Sadie left strict directions to place her ashes at a great distance from Mr. Guthrie's. What did the old galoot *do,* anyway? The Mitford books never tell us, but here's the scoop. He helped himself to funds from the church treasury, though he was as rich as Croesus by anybody's post-Depression standards. His beleaguered wife, Netta, left Mitford and never returned, which the Lord's Chapel choir considered a woeful loss given Netta's glorious soprano. Legend has it that her beloved dog, Wolfie, found his way back to Mitford where he was taken in by Percy Mosely's daddy. Some say Wolfie lived at the

Grill, and slept under the table of the rear booth, long occupied in later years by Father Tim, Mule Skinner, and J. C. Hogan.

Nurse Herman: Head of the nursing staff at Mitford Hospital; Hoppy Harper's right arm. Solves a major mystery in *Light From Heaven.*

Pauline Barlowe: Dooley's mother. Pauline's long and ravaging years of alcoholism scattered Dooley and his siblings, Pooh, Jessie, Sammy, and Kenny, to the four winds. One of the themes of the Mitford series is based upon a verse from Joel 2:25: "I will restore unto you the days the locusts have eaten. . . ."

Ida Jacks: Russell Jacks's deceased wife.

Dr. Leo Baldwin: A distinguished surgeon at Mass General, who plays a major role in the lives of both Olivia Davenport and Hoppy Harper.

Absalom Greer: An old-fashioned revival preacher of a most singular sort. Self-educated, obedient to God, an esteemed friend of the rector. One of my sworn favorites among the Mitford characters.

Coot Hendrick: An old coot, what can I say?

Bailey Coffey: As above.

Dr. Wilson: Hoppy Harper's new hire, but who wants their appendix removed by the new hire? Mitford doesn't like change, but all's well that ends well.

Pete Jamison: Part of a later much-talked-about "two-for-one deal." As Father Tim led a stranger, Pete Jamison, in a prayer that surrendered Pete's life to Christ, someone was listening.

Joe Joe Guthrie: One of the nearly two dozen grandchildren of Esther and Ray Cunningham. An officer for the MPD.

Lottie Miller/Greer: Absalom's widowed/divorced sister. This confusion of surname and marital history is explained in an essay entitled "Oops," on p. 443.

Mrs. Kershaw: Olivia Davenport's devoted housekeeper.

George Gaynor: I think it was Sandburg who said, "No surprise in the author, no surprise in the reader." I hope you were as surprised as I was when George Gaynor made his appearance at Lord's Chapel.

Uncle Chester: Father Tim's long-deceased uncle on his mother's side, who was fond of saying, "Circumstances alter cases."

Betty Craig: Good-hearted Betty! A local nurse who cares for patients in her home, and will step up to the plate for Father Tim on several occasions in the series.

Omer Cunningham: Mayor Cunningham's brother-in-law. Aviator. Hail-fellow-well-met. Gets the rector out of a jam more than once in the Mitford chronicles.

Marcie Guthrie: One of four beautiful, well-built Cunningham daughters. Joe Joe's mama, and grandmother of seven; employed at the Oxford Antique Shop.

Uncle Gus: Actually, a great-uncle of Father Tim on the maternal side, who said, in describing the rector's mother and father: "A high-falutin', half-frozen Episcopalian and a hidebound, Bible-totin' Baptist!"

Tommy: Dooley's first friend in Mitford.

Tommy Noles: Father Tim's boyhood friend, often mentioned in the series.

Miss Lureen Thompson: Miss Lureen was the mistress of Boxwood, a fine, early home that stood where Mitford's First Baptist Church stands today. Her parents died in a fall from an overhanging rock where they were picnicking. Miss Lureen's chauffeur, **Soot Tobin,** was Louella Baxter Marshall's father.

Mr. Kingsley: All we know of him is that he tutored the young Miss Sadie, and had "the worst bad breath in the world."

Amos Medford: Grazed his cows on the village green, where the Porter place stands today.

Miss Lydia, Miss Caroline: Suffice it to say they were, and are, vitally important in the lives of two of Mitford's loveliest souls.

Kenny Barlowe: Dooley's oldest brother and best friend.

Jessie Barlowe: Dooley's baby sister.

Henry (variously **Poobaw, Pooh,** and **Poo) Barlowe:** Dooley's youngest brother.

Sammy Barlowe: Dooley's next-to-oldest brother.

Jenny: A pretty—and persevering—young neighbor of Father Tim's.

Elizabeth Mooney: When she was twelve, Father Tim took her to see a movie, *Flying Tigers,* while her parents waited in a nearby café, drinking coffee.

Nurse Kennedy: Another of the indispensable nurses at Mitford Hospital, and Joe Joe Guthrie's first cousin.

Elliott: Cynthia Coppersmith's former husband. A senator and a "womanizer," but not necessarily in that order.

David: Elliott's nephew, with whom Cynthia got to be "the fastest of friends and comrades."

Kenny McGuire: A friend of Dooley's who lives on a farm near Meadowgate.

Gene Bolick: Husband of the famed originator of the Orange Marmalade Cake.

Father Douglas, Father Lewis, Father Randall: Possible contenders for fill-ins when Father Tim spends his enforced sabbatical in Ireland.

Mitford Pets

While our pets are just like people to us, I chose, nonetheless, to give them a separate category. So, bear with me here.

Buckwheat, Bowser, Baudelaire, Bodacious, and **Bonemeal** are dogs of various breeds who live at Meadowgate Farm. **Goosedown Owen** is a Meadowgate horse who tosses Dooley in the pig slop. **Flopsy** and **Mopsy** are of the genus *Sylvilagus,* as is **Jack.**

Barnabas and **Violet,** of course, are two very prominent stars in the series. As you may already know, **Barnabas** is a mixed-breed dog as big as a Buick (predominantly Bouvier in appearance) who adopted Father Tim early on, and has been the rector's boon companion ever since. Named for the good sort who accompanied St.

Paul on his first missionary journey, Barnabas's rambunctious behavior is controlled only by the loud proclamation of Scripture.

While Barnabas is known by everyone locally, **Violet** has an international profile. Indeed, her mistress, Cynthia Coppersmith, has written and illustrated a veritable carload of award-winning books about Violet who, in the books at least, does everything from play the piano to have kittens, go to school, and travel through France.

A LIGHT IN THE WINDOW

Edith Mallory: Resides at Clear Day; everlastingly attempts to seduce the rector.

Pat Mallory: Edith's husband who died while Father Tim was in Sligo.

Father Appel: Emma reminds Father Tim that Father Appel got married when he was *sixty-five,* for heaven's sake, right after his Social Security kicked in.

Buck Leeper: Job Superintendent at Hope House.

Fane Leeper: Buck's father, so called because a preacher once said he was the most profane man he'd ever met.

Leonard Bostic: Attends a town council meeting with the mayor.

Linder Hayes: Mitford attorney who complains to the town meeting about Miss Rose directing traffic around the monument.

Ernestine Ivory: She feels Miss Rose does "a real good job" of directing traffic.

Ed Coffey: Edith Mallory's driver, who's seen around town in a black Lincoln "the size of a condominium."

Josiah Baxter: Miss Sadie Baxter's deceased father.

Magdolen: Edith Mallory's cook who is famous for her spoonbread.

Tad Sherrill: Tad attends Edith's dinner party with Ron Malcolm.

Winona Presley: Attends Edith's dinner party/committee meeting.

Ed Malcolm: Ron Malcolm's son who comes from Colorado to work on the Hope House project.

Avette Harris: Mitford's local library head.

Bishop Slade: Once said that Father Tim was "Kind like his mother! Patient like his mother! Easygoing like his mother!"

Helen Boatwright: Works with Cynthia's publishing company in New York.

Erin Donovan: Hosted a tea in Ireland, where Father Tim met several distant relatives.

Meg Patrick: Father Tim's Irish cousin?

Miss Pruitt: Presbyterian Sunday School supervisor.

Aunt Lily: Father Tim's aunt; one of her progeny was killed in a train accident, the other vanished.

Aunt Martha: Father Tim's aunt, who married a man thirty years her senior.

Aunt Peg: Father Tim's spinster aunt, who, immediately after college, had her linens monogrammed with her own initials, declaring she would never marry.

Amy Larkin: Young daughter of Margaret Ann Larkin.

Susan Hathaway: Bishop Cullen's old flame.

Peehead Wilson: At Christmas, Dooley drew Buster's name at school, but swapped it with Peehead Wilson for Jenny's name.

James McNeely: Cynthia's editor and friend.

Miss Addison: Lives down the hall from Cynthia during Cynthia's winter sojourn in New York.

Patty Franklin: TOMMY NOLES LOVES PATTY FRANKLIN. Chalking this inscription on the cafeteria door was an act that nearly cost Timothy Kavanagh his life at the hands of the school principal—not to mention Patty Franklin.

Miz Cranford: Mule Skinner said Miz Cranford went to visit her daughter and asked Coot Hendrick to "watch" her house. Coot thought she asked him to "wash" it. Well, he did. Said he borrowed every ladder he could get his hands on.

Mack Stroupe: Proprietor of the hot dog stand next to Lew Boyd's gas station.

Miss Pearson: Keeps the secret that Dooley Barlowe was going to sing a solo with the full force of the Mitford School Mixed Chorus behind him.

Barney Adams: Evie Adams's deceased husband. The consequent yard sale of his clothing and personal items is where Mule Skinner bought a salmon-colored sport coat.

John Brewster: Director, Wesley Children's Hospital.

Gillian Murphy: Nine-year-old patient at the Children's Hospital.

Nurse Moody: Nurse who put ribbons in Gillian Murphy's hair.

Great-grandfather Michael, Glynis Flanagan, Lorna, Fergus, Sybil, Tyrone, Cormac, Lisbeth, Letty Noonan, Matthew, Stephen, Little Betty, Katie Crain, Gillian Elmurray, Reagan, Brian, Kevin, Eric, Inis, Deidre Connors, Allie, Meg, Nolle, Anthony, Stephen, Mary, Arthur, Allen, Asey, Abigail, and **Daphne** . . . a few of the names mentioned by Meg Patrick as Kavanagh relatives.

Riley Kavanagh: Father Tim's Irish cousin in Massachusetts.

Emil Kettner: Owns the construction company doing the five-million-dollar Hope House project.

Nurses Phillips, and **Jennings:** Mitford Hospital staff.

Dr. Hadleigh: Neurosurgeon at Wesley Hospital.

Michelangelo Francesca: Artist from Italy who paints the ballroom ceiling at Fernbank.

Leonardo Francesca: Michelangelo's son, also an artist.

Louise Appleshaw: Her name enters the conversation when Father Tim and Cynthia discuss a tutor for Dooley.

Roberto: Leonardo Francesca's grandson.

Pastor Trollinger: Local Methodist minister.

Dr. Browning: Local Presbyterian minister.

Mitford Pets

Palestrina: Miss Addison's feline who entertained Violet at dinner on several occasions.

Barkless: Homeless Hobbes's little brown-and-white spotted dog; mute.

THESE HIGH, GREEN HILLS

Angie Burton: Seven years old; suffered from a ruptured appendix and septic shock, and later died.

Sophia Burton: Angie Burton's mother.

Liza Burton: Angie Burton's sister.

Charlie Tucker: "If you could knock th' Baptists out of this deal," said Charlie Tucker at the All-Church Thanksgiving Feast, "we'd have somethin' left to go *in* these baskets. Baptists eat like they're bein' raptured before dark."

Abner Hickman: Announces a showy sunset at the rock wall, and the cleanup crew at Lord's Chapel piles into vans to witness it.

Lacey Turner: A young girl from the Creek community, later to be called "Lace."

Adele Lynwood: A new addition to Mitford's Police Department.

Lida Willis: The stern, young personnel director at Hope House.

Bill Sprouse: The new preacher at First Baptist.

Rachel Sprouse: Bill Sprouse's wife.

Bailey Coffey: One of the regulars at Lew Boyd's Esso.

Harvey Upton: Dooley and Harvey crashed into each other while sledding.

Dr. Richard Fleming: Headmaster at Dooley's prep school.

Lank Pitts: Lank Pitts drove a pickup load of rotted manure into town and parked it in front of Dora Pugh's hardware, where he sold it by the pound in garbage bags.

Larry Johnson: Lord's Chapel Youth Group leader.

Father Hanes: Installed a fireplace in the study of the rectory long before Father Tim moved in.

Bo Derbin: A Youth Group member with a surging, but nonetheless repressed, attraction to Lila Shuford.

Lila Shuford, Lee Lookabill, Luke Burnett, Clarence Austin, and **Henry Morgan:** Members of the Youth Group.

Phyllis Pringle: Was in Cynthia's girls' club when they all learned to do something boys did. Phyllis learned to shoot marbles, Alice Jacobs took up the slingshot, and Cynthia learned to whistle.

Anita Jarvis: Father Tim's seventh grade teacher.

Justine Ivory: As a boy, Father Tim wanted to hold her hand while standing by the blind trout pool, but didn't have the guts.

Russell Lowell: Cynthia fell in love with him in fifth grade.

Matthew Kavanagh: Father Tim's father, an attorney in Holly Springs.

Miss Phillips: Cynthia's fourth grade teacher.

Kaitlin and **Kirsten** (**Sissy** and **Sassy**): Puny's twin girls.

Widder Fox: To avoid her drunken father, Lacey Turner ran to the widow's house.

Dave: Computer technician.

Vince Barnhardt: Vince and his wife, Susan, give Dooley a ride home from school.

Joseph Barnhardt: The Barnhardts' son.

Cate Turner: Lacey Turner's father.

Slap Jones: Drives Homeless to town to pick up what the grocery store throws out; also ferries him around to dumpsters.

Scott Murphy: New chaplain at Hope House.

Granma and **Granpa Murphy:** Scott Murphy's grandparents, who were killed in an automobile accident.

Granma and **Granpa Lewis:** Scott Murphy's maternal grandparents. Granpa Lewis was killed in the accident, also. Granma Lewis was left in a coma.

Nurse Gilbert: Mitford Hospital nurse.

Dr. Cornell Wyatt: Flies to Mitford with his burn nurse to assess Pauline Barlowe's injuries.

Lewis Cromwell: An attorney with Miss Sadie's Wesley law firm, Cromwell, Cromwell and Lessing.

Charles Hartley: Owner of Hartley's Monument Company in Holding.

Doug Wyeth: A social worker in Wesley.

Lester Marshall: Pauline Barlowe lived with him.

Harley Welch: Lives in a trailer in the Creek community; a caring, albeit unofficial guardian of Lacey Turner.

Granny Sykes: Granny and Lacey are the only ones who use the steep trail to Harley Welch's house.

Mitford Pets

Sparky: Bill Sprouse's dog; looks like a tumbleweed on a leash.

Snickers: Emma's brown poodle.

Alexander: A cat belonging to Miss Phillips, one of Cynthia's early school teachers, who named him Alexander the Great.

Luke and **Lizzie:** Scott Murphy's two Jack Russells.

OUT TO CANAAN

Minnie Lomax: Manager, Irish Woolen Shop.

Georgia Moore: Attended the Primrose Tea at the rectory. According to Cynthia, "She opened every cabinet door in the kitchen. She said she was looking for a water glass, when I know for a fact she was seeing if the dishes were stacked to her liking."

Dot Hamby: Proprietor of The Shoe Barn.

Helen Huffman: Owner of Happy Endings Bookstore.

Junior Watson: A notorious race driver for whom Harley Welch had been Crew Chief.

Lucy Stroupe: Mack Stroupe's wife, more's the pity.

Rhody Davis: Pauline Barlowe's mother's second cousin; absconded with the young Jessie Barlowe.

Lila Turner: Lace Turner's mother.

Father Henry Townsend: Rector at Lord's Chapel prior to Father Tim.

Blake Eddistoe: Hal Owen's vet assistant at Meadowgate.

Mike Jones: Rector of a mountain church, who's said to look forward to a retirement of "cruising and fishing in the Caribbean."

Buddy Benfield: Gave a closing prayer at Lord's Chapel.

Ruth Wallace, Beth Lawrence, Helen Nelson, and **Marge Beatty:** On Fancy Skinner's appointment book for everything from acrylic nails to a perm.

Ingrid Swenson: With Miami Development Group; interested in developing Fernbank.

Mona Gragg: Former Lord's Chapel Sunday School teacher.

Johnny: Winnie Ivey's deceased husband.

Old Man Mueller: An elderly Mitford resident; Esther Cunningham was responsible for the new roof on his house; has a dog named Luther.

Henry Watts: Donated $15 to Mack Stroupe's campaign.

Marie Sanders: Donated an armoire to The Bane and Blessing sale.

Ben Isaac Berman: An elegant old gentleman whose family brought him all the way from Decatur, Illinois, to Hope House, because of its outstanding reputation for nursing care and its beautiful surroundings.

Sandra Harris: Attends the Fernbank meeting; can't wait to step outside for a smoke.

Clarence Daly: Troops into the meeting with a tray of cups and a pot of coffee.

Marsha Hunt: In charge of Lord's Chapel preschoolers, including Puny's twins.

Erlene Douglas: President of Episcopal Church Women.

Father Douglas: Cynthia hopes he'll take the service for Father Tim one Sunday, so her exhausted husband can get some rest.

Luther Green: "The tin roof of Omer Cunningham's shed, formerly a hangar for his antique ragwing, was hurled toward Luther Green's pasture, where the sight of it, gleaming and rattling and banging through the air, made the cows bawl with trepidation."

Vanita Bentley: A *Muse* reporter and Bane and Blessing volunteer who helps gouge the Orange Marmalade Cake recipe out of its reluctant originator.

Marge Crowder: "You wouldn't use a *tablespoon* of baking powder in a *cake!*"

Anna Nocelli Gregory: Andrew Gregory's third cousin, and beautiful new Italian wife, into the bargain.

Antonio Nocelli: Anna Nocelli Gregory's brother.

Dewey Morgan: An old acquaintance of Father Tim's who worked at the state capitol.

Thomas Kendall: A pastry chef from Topeka, Kansas; Winnie Ivey discovered him on a cruise ship, and brought him home to Mitford.

The Perkinses: Big Esther-for-Mayor fans, working to bring in the vote.

Mitford Pets

Baxter: A cheerful dachshund at Hope House.

Hector, Barney, Muffin and **Lucky:** Cats that can be "rented" for up to two hours a day at Hope House.

Barney: A small pig in a petting zoo at the Political Barbecue.

Taco: Louella "rents" Taco every week; he obliges her by sitting in her lap for two hours, or until her leg goes to sleep.

Harry: A beagle at Hope House.

A NEW SONG

Marjorie Lamb: An ECW member involved in readying Dove Cottage for the new rector and his wife.

Leonard Lamb: Marjorie's husband.

Sam Fieldwalker: Husband of Marion Fieldwalker, and one of the workers who spruced up Dove Cottage.

Father Morgan: Prior rector of St. John's in the Grove.

Marion Fieldwalker: Librarian and long-time vestry member of St. John's in the Grove; greets Father Tim and Cynthia with a glorious breakfast in their new home.

Bishop Harvey: Bishop of Father Tim's new diocese.

Jimmy Duncan: Dooley went home from college with Jimmy. Jimmy drives a Wrangler, his mom drives a Range Rover, and his dad has a BMW 850, according to Dooley in a letter to Father Tim and Cynthia.

Hezikiah Hendrick: Coot Hendrick's bearded ancestor, and founder of the town of Mitford.

Mary Jane Hendrick: Hezikiah's English bride, whose maiden name was Mitford.

Father Bellwether: Father Tim moved into a rectory in Alabama vacated by Father Bellwether, who left behind "a 1956 Ford on blocks, several leaf bags filled with old shirts and sweaters, a set of mangled golf clubs, three room-size rugs chewed by dogs, an assortment of cooking gear, several doors without knobs, a vast collection of paperback mysteries, and other litter that couldn't be completely identified."

Miss McNolty: One of Father Tim's teachers.

Lee Adderholt: One of the boys who smeared dog poop just inside the double doors of the schoolhouse, in an incident that earned the young Tim Kavanagh the nickname "Slick."

Mr. Lewis: The principal in whose office Father Tim ended up after beating the stuffing out of Tommy Noles.

Redmon Love: Owned the house next door to Dove Cottage.

Otis Bragg: A parishioner who bought Dove Cottage and had it completely rehabbed. Otis and his wife, Marlene, offered it to the parish for the new interim priest.

Ernie Fulcher: Proprietor of Ernie's Books, Bait & Tackle, the only bookstore on Whitecap. "It's mostly used paperbacks of Louis L'Amour," says Marion Fieldwalker.

Mona Fulcher: Ernie's wife, who runs Mona's Cafe across the hall from Ernie.

Marshall Duncan: Sam Fieldwalker's junior warden.

Penny Duncan: Marshall Duncan's wife.

Roanoke Clark: A house painter whom Father Tim meets at the bait and tackle shop. Father Tim thinks his weathered face resembles "an apple that had lain too long in the sun."

Junior Bryson: Another crony at the bait and tackle shop. Father Tim pitches in to help Junior find a wife.

Redmon Love: The gravesite of the Redmon Love family is guarded by an iron fence and a tall, elaborately formed angel clothed in lichen.

Jean Ballenger: Parishioner at St. John's in the Grove.

Avery Plummer: "Ran off" with another woman's husband.

Jeffrey Tolson: Former choir director and, according to Marlene Bragg in a letter to Father Tim, "a scoundrel."

Marlene Bragg: Blonde, tan, married to Otis Bragg.

Jonathan Tolson: The toddler belonging to Jeffrey and Janette Tolson.

Barbara Harvey: Bishop Harvey's wife.

Reverend Stanley Harmon: Local Baptist minister.

Janette Tolson: Estranged wife of Jeffrey Tolson.

Louise Parker: In a bit of news from Mitford, Esther Bolick tells Father Tim that Louise went to Wesley with Reverend Sprouse, to pick out her casket.

Father Hayden: The interim at Lord's Chapel.

Roger Templeton: A crony at the bait and tackle shop, always accompanied by his blind dog, Lucas. Roanoke says "Roger's his seein' eye human."

Babette Tolson: Janette and Jeffrey Tolson's daughter.

Jason Tolson: A son of Janette and Jeffrey Tolson.

Morris Love: Lives across the street from Dove Cottage, behind a wall and locked gate.

Father Tracey: Who, with his good wife, adopted fourteen children.

Father Moultrie: This fellow collected twenty-one children of various ages and backgrounds and had managed, so it was said, "to keep the whole lot in good order, though the addition he built to his suburban home had literally fallen down one night after a communal pillow fight."

Ella Jean Bridgewater: Organist at St. John's in the Grove.

Minor: A young explorer with Admiral Byrd, who spent his last years as a maker of hot-air balloons. At the age of forty-seven, Ella Jean Bridgewater confessed to having fallen "head over heels" for Minor.

Ray Porter: Bondsman whom Father Tim uses to release Dooley from jail.

Agnes: Secretary to Otis Bragg.

Ava Goodnight: Answered Junior Bryson's personal ad.

Father Jack Ferguson: Asked to supply at St. John's while Father Tim and Cynthia make a trip to Mitford.

Earlene Ferguson: Father Jack Ferguson's wife.

Father Talbot: The new priest at Lord's Chapel, to be installed on All Saints' Day.

Ed Sikes: Pauline Barlowe gave her young son, Kenny, to this man, in exchange for a gallon of whisky.

Drew Merritt: Son of Matthew Kavanagh's law colleague. Father Tim's father chose this boy over Tommy Noles to go along on a family vacation.

Cap'n Larkin: Was a longtime member at St. John's; now living with his twin brother on Dorchester Island.

Captain Willie: Captain of the deep-sea fishing boat, *Blue Heaven.*

Pete Brady: Captain Willie's first mate.

Madge Parrott: A widow whose late husband spoke of deep-sea fishing "like it was the best thing since sliced bread."

Sybil Huffman: Traveling with Madge, and also a widow. Both are from Rome, Georgia.

Bishop Quayle: An old bishop who counseled with Father Tim many years ago.

Caroline: Dooley's girlfriend from Miss Hemingway's school in Virginia.

Father Grace: Served St. John's until he was eighty-seven.

Father Harry: Was seventy-one when his life as an interim began.

Beulah Mae Hendrick: ninety-two-year-old mother of Mitford Mayoral candidate, Coot Hendrick.

Bill Deal: County Sheriff who serves papers on Father Tim.

Hélène Pringle: Rents the rectory in Mitford.

Francoise: Hélène Pringle's mother.

Louis d' Anjou: Hélène Pringle's attorney.

Mamie: Morris Love's housekeeper.

Misty Summers: A waitress at Mona's.

Betty: Ava Goodnight's upbeat sister.

Brother: Cap'n Larkin's identical twin brother.

Dora: Cap'n Larkin's deceased wife.

Loretta Burgess: Truck driver.

Ray Gaskill: Lives in a house close to St. John's.

Albert Gragg: Informs Father Tim that Miss Ella had fallen and broken her hip.

Stanley Harmon: Neighbor of Father Tim and Cynthia.

Mildred Harmon: Stanley's wife.

Sewell Joiner: Otis sends him to make repairs to Dove Cottage, after the storm.

Orville Hood: He keeps St. John's oil tank filled.

Maude Proffitt: Her ceiling caved in during the storm, barely missing the chair in which she was sitting.

Sue Blankenship: Parishioner at St. John's.

Ann Hartsell: A nurse and a St. John's parishioner.

Edith Johnson: An ECW "bigwig."

Martha Talbot: Father Tim and Cynthia move into her million-dollar home while Dove Cottage is being repaired.

Noah: Husband of Mamie, Morris Love's housekeeper.

Big Daddy Johnson: Used to take Mamie and Noah across in a little fishing boat, then came the ferry and afterward, the bridge.

Tante Brigitte: Hélène Pringle's grandfather's sister.

William Perry: Hélène Pringle's father left a codicil to his final will and testament in the keeping of his solicitor, William Perry of Philadelphia.

Albert Pringle: Hélène Pringle's stepfather.

Madeleine Duncan: During a church service at St. John's, she whispers in her mother's ear, "Look, Mommy, it's a little tiny man with a big head."

Mitford Pets

Margaret: Hope Winchester's ginger-colored cat, also known as Margaret Ann.
Barbizon: Hélène Pringle's cat.
Jeff: Tommy Noles's dog.
Bitsy: The Fieldwalker's dog.
Lucas: Roger Templeton's blind dog.
Elmo: Elmo, th' Book Cat, belonging to Ernie Fulcher.
Mick: A stray dog that Father Tim took up with one summer in Pass Christian, Mississippi.
Louise: Ella Jean Bridgewater's canary.
Paul and **Silas:** Mildred and Stanley Harmon's dogs.

A COMMON LIFE

Mike Stovall: The Presbyterian choirmaster who offered to throw in sixteen voices for the wedding ceremony, which, including the voices at Lord's Chapel, would jack the total to thirty-seven. "A real tabernacle deal!" enthused the choirmaster. "We'll even throw in a trumpet!"
Richard: Lord's Chapel organist and choirmaster.
Bobby Prestwood: An old suitor of Esther Cunningham's. He tried everything to get in her good graces, including making a fool of himself in Sunday School when he stood up one morning and told what he was thankful for. "I'm thankful for my Chevy V-8, my mama and daddy, and Esther Lovell!"
Moses Marshall: Louella's deceased husband. "She closed her eyes to rest them and held the picture against her heart, and saw her husband-to-be walking into the kitchen of the Atlanta boardinghouse. She was fifteen years old, with her hair in cornrows and the sense that

something wonderful was about to happen. Moses Marshall flashed a smile that nearly knocked her winding. She had never seen anybody who looked like this when she was growing up in Mitford. The only people of color in Mitford were old and stooped over."

Miss Sally Lou: She was so little and dried up, some said she was a hundred, but Louella knew she was only eighty-two, "and still the boss cook of three meals a day at the boardinghouse."

Lot Stringman: A seller of produce in Holly Springs, Father Tim's hometown. "'Let me pick them peaches out for you, Miz Kavanagh,' Mr. Stringman would say. 'No, thank you, Mr. Stringman,' his mother would say, 'I like the doing of it myself.'"

Annie Hawkins: The young Absalom Greer's sweetheart. "He felt such a stirring in his breast that he might have been fourteen years old, going up Hogback to see Annie Hawkins, carrying two shot quail and a mess of turnips in a poke. Annie's mama was dead of pneumonia and her daddy not heard of since the flood, and as Annie was left to raise a passel of brothers and sisters, he never went up Hogback without victuals."

Henry Oldman: He meets the newlyweds at the airport in the Cullen camp car, a 1981 turquoise Chevy Impala that made the rector's Buick look mint condition.

Miz Oldman: Henry's wife, who outfits the Kavanaghs with rations for their honeymoon in the lodge on a lake in Maine.

IN THIS MOUNTAIN

Sophie Hawthorne: One of Hélène Pringle's music students.

Miss Helman: Sassy's teacher, who asks the class to paint "somebody you like a lot, and *not* your mama or daddy." Sassy painted Father Tim (he thought his nose looked like a turnip).

Ada Rupert: Father Tim and the twins run into her at the bakery, where Father Tim is reminded of her "notoriously sharp tongue."

Hamp Floyd: Mitford's earnest fire chief.

Shorty Justice: Dooley remembers that his father, Clyde Barlowe, had a best friend, a drinking buddy named Shorty.

Clyde Barlowe: Dooley's long-vanished father.

The Right Reverend Paul Jared Sotheby: He once counseled Father Tim, saying: "Timothy, stop this nonsense of preparing for the worst and spend your time preparing for the best!"

Maude Boatwright: Her gravestone inscription at St. John's reads: "Demure at last," an epitaph Father Tim finds amusing

Cedric Hart, Esq. (from Mitford, England): He writes to say that it was a "thumping good idea to have your Mitford and ours become sister villages."

Judy Hart: Cedric Hart's wife.

Cate Turner: Lace Turner's alcoholic, often-violent father.

Caldecott Turner: An old high-school sweetheart of Emma Newland. She searches the Internet for him while searching for Cate.

Hope Winchester: Manager, Happy Endings Bookstore.

Tate Smith: Works at the drugstore in Mitford.

Alicia: School friend of Lace Turner who invites Lace to visit Alicia's aunt in Martha's Vineyard.

Richard and **Trudy:** They share a mountain ministry with the irrepressible Father Harry.

Joyce Havner: Cleans house at Meadowgate every Monday and Friday.

Lewis: Bush hogs at Meadowgate.

Sam Rayner: Does the milking at Meadowgate.

Bo Davis: Handles the odd jobs at Meadowgate.

Miss Wright: Father Tim's Sunday School teacher when, at the age of twelve, he recited the whole of the sixteenth Psalm.

Abner: A neighboring boy of Father Harry who comes to Father Harry's door looking for work.

Yancey: One of Father Tim's grandfathers; died at the age of seventy.

Dorene Little: "She is our favorite Arthur," says Dorene Little in a *Mitford Muse* article, FAMED LOCAL ARTHUR TO RECEIVE AWARD.

Pink Shuford: A pool shooter; Father Tim and Hélène run into him while looking for Sammy.

Skin Head Bug Eye Snaggle Tooth Austin (Bug): Shoots pool with Pink Shuford.

Mary Talbot: Wife of Lord's Chapel rector, Father Henry Talbot.

Marcello: Roberto's close friend who made Cynthia's art box from olive wood. Inside the box are seven of Roberto's grandfather Leonardo's pastelli.

Lon Burtie: A Vietnam vet who lives in a rehabbed gas station; often gives Sammy a ride to town.

Minnie Louder: Hessie Mayhew delivers flowers to Minnie, who has just undergone a kidney operation and turned eighty-four, all in the same day.

Neese Simmons: His family grows Silver Queen corn in the valley, and delivers it to The Local. It's always a big day in Mitford when the first corn comes in.

Vada Simmons: Neese's wife.

Reba Sanders: A girlfriend of Dooley's, and a skilled motorcycle mechanic.

Miniver Tarleton: Legendary, eightysomething author/illustrator/role model, according to Cynthia.

Earlene: Lew Boyd's sweetheart.

Juanita Boyd: Lew Boyd's wife, who died six years ago.

Jonathan Ferguson: His signature appears on a check from a bank in Miami, as a donation to the Wesley Children's Hospital—to be cashed only if Father Tim agrees to conduct a service in the mountain village of Kinloch.

Jaybird Johnson: Clyde Barlowe gives this alias to Buck Leeper and Father Tim when they go looking for Sammy.

Mary Fisher: "The roads to Kinloch were winding—it would be more than an hour and a half in each direction. He rang Mary Fisher twice but got an answering machine with a digital recording that declined to take a message."

Emeline Poovey: Percy says Coot Hendrick once pursued Emeline, who was from "over at Blackberry."

Sauce Harris: Emeline married this legendary bootlegger who robbed The Local when Avis's daddy owned it.

Miss Tomlinson: Waves to Hope Winchester and mouths "Are . . . you . . . all right?" when she sees Hope sitting in the bookstore window, dazed.

Tran van Hoi: A farmer in Vietnam, who was kind to Lon Burtie.

Reverend Millie Tipton: Pastors the local Methodist Chapel.

Maisie: Uncle Billy's little sister, whom he often mentions in the series.

Beverly Hobgood: Bishop Cullen's secretary.

Jeanine Stroup: An employee at Mitford Hospital who calls Father Tim to say that Bill Watson's asking for the preacher.

Richard Crandon: Writes a letter to the *Mitford Muse* editor and signs it "Richard Crandon, POLITICALLY CORRECT AND PROUD OF IT!!"

Johnson Cutliffe: Attorney for Coot Hendrick.

Mrs. Marshall Hendrick: Coot Hendrick's elderly mother.

Mildred: "For more information on getting Mrs. Hendrick to sing for your club or group, call 555-6240 at the town office and ask for Mildred."

Andrew and Margaret Hart: The Mitford (UK) Sister Village Coordinating Committee plans to send this couple to Mitford.

Louise: Hope Winchester's sister.

Bill Adkins: One of the neighbors gathered on Edie Adams's front lawn, observing the fire on the ridge.

Gary Barnes: Owns a paper over the mountain that's gone from black-and-white to full color.

Buster Boyd: Chief Floyd gets the call about the fire from Buster Boyd.

Mitford Pets

Buddy: Bill Sprouse's new dog.

Willie: The Fieldwalkers dog. (*It* adopted *them*.)

Guber: Lace Turner's Labrador (short for gubernatorial).

SHEPHERDS ABIDING

Fred Addison: Works at Oxford Antique Shop.

Reverend Simon: A fervent Bible scholar and Father Tim's mother's much-loved Baptist preacher.

Miss Grayson: First grade teacher at Mitford School.

Emily Townsend: Third grade Mitford school student.

Lois Holshouser: Retired drama teacher at Wesley High.

Bob Hartley: Is giving his boy, Harry, a Roto-Tiller.

Faye Tuttle: Announces a relative's sad news to Esther Cunningham. "Multiple dystrophy," says Faye.

Peggy: A young woman of color who worked for the Kavanaghs in Holly Springs; helps Mrs. Kavanagh with cooking, washing, and ironing; lives in a small cabin down the lane.

Rufe: A handyman who worked part-time for the Kavanaghs.

Mamy Phillips: Lives in a small house next to Lord's Chapel with her cat, Popeye.

Nurse Austin: Nurse at Hope House.

Mitford Pets

Popeye: A cat belonging to Mamy Phillips.

Luther: Old Man Mueller's dog; known to have precisely 241 freckles on his belly.

LIGHT FROM HEAVEN

Willie Mullis: Full-timer at Meadowgate who lives on the farm and looks after the livestock.

Joyce Havner: Longtime housekeeper at Meadowgate.

Thomas and **Timothy:** Twin boys belonging to Puny and Joe Guthrie; nicknamed Tommy and Timmy.

Tracy: Trustee handling Dooley's trust account.

Buster: Local locksmith.

Agnes Merton: Mother of Clarence Merton; former deaconess at Holy Trinity Church and school.

Clarence Merton: Deaf, and an accomplished woodworker; he and his mother cared for Holy Trinity and its grounds for more than thirty years.

Jessie Bennett: Young deaconess who accompanied Agnes Merton from Maine.

Moses McKinney: Built the trestle table in the old schoolhouse where Agnes and Clarence now live.

Little Bertie: Jessie Bennett's niece.

Granny Meaders: Neighbor who took Rooter in when his parents abandoned him as a baby.

Rooter: Bright, headstrong, talkative; Granny Meaders considers him a grandson.

Robert Pritchard: In prison for eleven years for allegedly killing his grandfather; owns an automobile repair shop in Lambert.

Lloyd Goodnight: Came to Holy Trinity as an infant and was baptized in Wilson's Creek; later acted as crucifer.

Jubal Adderholt: Hasn't been off the ridge in fourteen years. Stubborn, irascible, and an ardent squirrel hunter.

Ruthie Adderholt: Jubal's former wife, who once baked him a blueberry pie and left a note saying, "I'm gone and don't look for me."

Quint Severs: Local mechanic who worked on Agnes's Buick.

Martha and **Mary McKinney:** Sisters who were cradle Episcopalians, but switched to the Methodists after Holy Trinity closed.

Johnny Chiltosky: Mary McKinney's deceased part-Cherokee husband of forty-two years.

Portman Henshaw: Bank clerk in Holding. Martha McKinney rode with him each day to Granite Springs, where she was a teacher.

Miss Hettie Henshaw: Portman's wife. Martha McKinney had to write Miss Hettie a formal note every January, asking permission to ride down the mountain with her husband.

Thomas Henshaw: Portman's eldest son, who takes Miss Martha and Miss Mary food shopping once a week.

Donny Luster: Agnes refers to him as "a most remarkable young man." Sings, plays guitar and mandolin, preaches, raises cattle, and mows hay for a livelihood.

Sissie Gleason: Five-year-old daughter of Dovey Gleason, Donny's sister.

Dovey Gleason: Mother of Sissie Gleason; sister to Donny.

Mamaw Ruby Luster: Donny's and Dovey's mother, imprisoned for killing her husband.

Pansy Flower: One of the famed Flower Girls who clean and cook in the valley. The family consists of Iris, Lily, Rose, Arbutus, Delphinium, Violet, Daisy, Jack in the Pulpit, and Sweet William.

Sparkle Foster: A hairdresser in the valley.

Wayne Foster: Sparkle's husband.

Grace Monroe: Provided a home to Agnes during and after Agnes's pregnancy with Clarence.

George Monk: Clarence met him in a woodworking class. Mr. Monk was ninety-four and owned a tool chest from Sheffield, England, which had come down in his family of woodworkers. When Clarence was eleven, George Monk died and left the chest to Clarence, whom he called "gifted."

Fred Lynch: Lives in a school bus; accuses Robert Pritchard of killing his grandfather, Cleve Pritchard.

Judd and **Cindy Baker:** From California; bought the old Greer Store.

Cleve Pritchard: Robert Pritchard's grandfather.

Leanna Millwright: mother of seven; attends Holy Trinity.

Rankin Cooper: A lapsed Baptist, but a "God-fearing Christian" who would consider visiting Holy Trinity if he could talk his Methodist wife into going with him.

Hank Triplett: Owns the store at the bridge.

Buster: Works with Lloyd at Meadowgate.

Bud Wyzer: Proprietor of Bud's Billiards in Wesley.

Dunn Crawford: A pool hustler, nicknamed Hook.

Sally Triplett: Hank Triplett's fourteen-year-old daughter.

Edna Swanson: A Methodist neighbor of Miss Martha and Miss Mary.

Roy Dale and **Gladys:** A young brother and sister who occasionally attend Holy Trinity.

John Owen: Hal and Marge's son who died in his teens of severe encephalitis.

Marsha Ford: Donates to Holy Trinity the piano that her husband, Frank, played.

Officers Justice and **Daly:** Answered the Meadowgate call regarding a missing boy.

Mamie Millwright: One of the seven Millwright children.

Junior Bentley: Married to Arbutus, one of the famed Flower Girls.

They live in a brick house with two screened porches, across from Red Pig Barbecue.

Morris Millwright: Leanna's husband and father of seven.

Paul Taggart: Is from Lambert; his grandparents attended Holy Trinity.

Mitford Pets

Luther: A recent mixed-breed addition to the Meadowgate pack.

Malachi: A dog of mild demeanor who belongs to the preacher at Green Valley Baptist Church.

Waste Not, Want Not:

The Father Tim Novels

As I pen this, I'm in the early chapters of *Home to Holly Springs,* the first of three books in my upcoming series, The Father Tim Novels.

Why continue to write about Father Tim if, indeed, we've left Mitford behind?

Because I like him. Because I trust him. And because he can be a dash of fun when he puts his mind to it.

Besides, if one has struck what one believes to be a good and authentic character, why waste him? Why not heed the old Yankee proverb?

There is also another consideration. This fellow's been clinging to Mitford like moss to a log for years on end. Afraid of flying, you know. Well, who isn't, when you get down to it? But he's older and wiser, now, and also well-loved by his irrepressible wife. (Being well-loved is, of course, a very freeing thing.)

Long story short, I wanted to see what he'd get up to in different surroundings.

Thus, he's returning to his Mississippi birthplace, Holly Springs, for the first time in nearly four decades. A trip that, to say the least, will be life-changing.

Then, he and Cynthia are off to Ireland to meet Father Tim's first cousin, Walter, and his wife, Katherine, and poke around Kavanagh graveyards and explore the family castle, now in great ruin. This book will be called *Party of Four.*

Afterward, perhaps, I'll send them off to England in *A Family Face.*

By the end of the series, I shall most likely be, as my grandmother put it, "a pile of wrinkles up in the attic." Nonetheless, I hope to then write a book about the building of a mid-eighteenth-century house in the Virginia countryside, and the extraordinary woman who got the job done. This will take two years to research, and perhaps four years to write, and with God's favor, should be released in 2017. (Hope you'll stick around.)

Following that great hurrah, I'd love to have a deep draft of what Father Tim experienced in the Afterword of *Light from Heaven.*

Father Tim lay on his back in the far corner of the sheep paddock, looking into the shining cumulus cloud that swelled above him. . . .

A bee thrummed in the clover; he drowsed, but did not sleep. . . .

Since childhood, he had avoided lying in the grass, knowing only too well that spiders and beetles and worms lived there. Instead, he had discomfited himself in hardback chairs—and look what he had missed!

He closed his eyes, and laid a hand on his dog, who drowsed beside him. "Dogs are our link to paradise," Milan Kundera had said "To sit with a dog on a hillside on a glorious afternoon is to be back in Eden, where doing nothing was not boring, it was peace."

Where doing nothing was not boring, it was peace. Yes!

I should like to plumb the depths of doing nothing, and discover its particular (and for me, elusive) mystery.

Perhaps I shall choose to do nothing in an Italian villa overlooking the sea, with a gardener busy at the lavender hedge and a cook making fresh pasta in the kitchen. My loved ones will be there, I fondly hope, and we shall eat and laugh and walk in the garden and play Scrabble and read aloud to one another—the Psalms and Wordsworth and Cowper and Herrick and the lovely George Herbert—trying not to waste a minute of the beautiful life that remains, and saying with Michelangelo who, at the age of eighty-seven, penned this:

Ancora imparo (I am still learning).

The Almost Complete, Only Somewhat Partially Abridged Scoop on the Mitford Years Series and Your Author, Jan Karon

J AN KARON HAS written nine novels in the Mitford Years series, and several gift books, all published by Viking Penguin:

At Home in Mitford
A Light in the Window
These High, Green Hills
Out to Canaan
A New Song
A Common Life: The Wedding Story
In This Mountain
Shepherds Abiding
Light from Heaven
Patches of Godlight: Father Tim's Favorite Quotes
A Continual Feast: Words of Comfort and Celebration Collected by
    Father Tim
The Mitford Snowmen
Esther's Gift
Jan Karon's Mitford Cookbook & Kitchen Reader

The first novel, *At Home in Mitford,* was nominated for an ABBY by the American Booksellers Association for three consecutive years. Thirty-six Logos bookstores, nationwide, gave Mitford novels their Best Fiction of the Year award for four consecutive years.

The novels consistently appear on the *New York Times, Wall Street Journal, USA Today,* and other best-seller lists.

:king stuffer" Christmas stories, *The Mitford Snowmen*
Gift, were also *New York Times* best sellers.

ord books have been translated into German, Czech, Ital-
, French, Polish, Norwegian, and numerous other lan-
guages.

Penguin Audiobooks offers all titles, abridged and unabridged, on
audiocassette and CD; Jan Karon read the early novels in an abridged
format. The unabridged versions are available from Penguin Audiobooks and Random House, and are read by the gifted New York stage
actor John McDonough.

Viking Penguin offers these free resources:

1. Study guides to each novel, to aid book clubs, literary leagues, and
   for personal reading pleasure. These are available separately, or in the
   back of the trade paperback edition of *At Home in Mitford* and online (see below).
2. A Web site for author news, book release dates, and reader interac-
   tion at www.mitfordbooks.com.

Jan Karon is also the author of a children's picture book, *Miss Fannie's
Hat,* which was inspired by her grandmother. It is available in paperback from Puffin Books, an imprint of Penguin Group.

Her second children's book, *Jeremy: The Tale of An Honest Bunny,* is
published by Viking Children's Books, and was written for her daughter,
Candace Freeland.

Her illustrated book of encouragement, *The Trellis and the Seed,* is
published in hardcover by Viking Children's Books and was a # 1 *New
York Times* best seller. It is recommended for all ages.

Jan's newest children's book, *Violet Comes to Stay,* will be a favorite
of every Mitford fan who's always wanted to read a book by Cynthia
Coppersmith. Art is by Caldecott Medalist Emily Arnold McCully.

* * *

Jan Karon lives and writes on a farm in central Virginia.

Her favorite authors include Wordsworth, Longfellow, Jon Hassler
(*A Green Journey* and *Dear James*), James Herriot, Louis L'Amour (espe-

cially the Sackett chronicles and *Last of the Breed*), A. B. Guthrie, Jr., Conrad Richter, Wendell Berry . . .

Jan likes to recommend *Catherwood,* a novel by North Carolinian Marly Youmans; *Down the Common: A Year in the Life of a Medieval Woman,* the first novel of an eightysomething English writer, Ann Baer; *Jim the Boy,* a novel by Tony Earley; *The Long Walk,* by Slavomir Rawicz, a true chronicle of survival against impossible odds; Knut Hamsun's *Growth of the Soul;* Khaled Hosseini's *The Kite Runner;* and Irène Némirovsky's *Suite Française.*

Her favorite movies include *Babe, Song of the South* (unavailable in the U.S.; must be bootlegged from the UK), and *The Straight Story.* (She admits she doesn't see many movies.)

Her favorite Christmas hymns are "In the Bleak Midwinter," by the poet Christina Rossetti, and "Once in Royal David's City."

Her favorite things to do are to complete a manuscript; direct a family skit; laugh with loved ones; walk with her dog, Agatha Grace; and make her signature dinner: lamb chops (*not* from her own flock, she hastens to avow), roast potatoes, a salad with slices of fresh, sweet orange and spring scallions, followed by Ben & Jerry's vanilla ice cream with toasted almonds and Cointreau.

Someday, she hopes to make a perfect lemon soufflé, work intricate needlepoint patterns, and dance the tango. She has given up completely on learning to fly an airplane.

She confesses she will never have "work" done (too scary), or learn to use a microwave (too tech).

Her most longed-for privilege? Time to take a deep breath and enjoy God's boundless provisions, possibly in an Italian villa overlooking the sea or even in her own backyard.

NEW *from* VIKING . . .

JAN KARON'S
HOME TO
HOLLY SPRINGS
A FATHER TIM NOVEL

After nine bestselling Mitford novels, Jan Karon opens a new chapter in the life of Father Tim as she enchants us with the story of the newly retired priest's spur-of-the-moment adventure. For the first time in decades, Father Tim returns to his birthplace, Holly Springs, Mississippi, in response to a mysterious, unsigned note saying simply: *"Come home."* Little does he know how much these two words will change his life.

The first in Jan Karon's new series of novels, *Home to Holly Springs* offers a rich story of long-buried secrets, forgiveness, and the wonder of discovering new people, places, and depth of feeling.

VIKING